FOR THE
TERM OF HIS
NATURAL LIFE

FOR THE TERM OF HIS NATURAL LIFE

A specially condensed illustrated edition of
Marcus Clarke's classic Australian novel

MARCUS CLARKE

Angus & Robertson Publishers

ANGUS & ROBERTSON PUBLISHERS
London • Sydney • Melbourne

This condensed paperback edition first published by Angus &
Robertson Publishers, Australia, 1983

First published in the United Kingdon by Angus &
Robertson (UK) Ltd in 1985

Copyright © text Angus & Robertson Publishers 1982

Copyright © illustrations Angus & Robertson Publishers 1982

ISBN 0 207 14748 5

Typeset in 10 pt Goudy Old Style Roman
Printed in Great Britain by Richard Clay (The Chaucer Press) Ltd,
Bungay, Suffolk

CONTENTS

BOOK THREE
Port Arthur — 1838

BOOK FOUR
Norfolk Island — 1846

On the evening of the 3rd of May, 1827, the garden of a large red-brick bow-windowed mansion called North-End House, which stands on the eastern

PROLOGUE

height of Hampstead Heath, was the scene of a domestic tragedy. Three persons were the actors. One was an old man with white hair and wrinkled face, who stood erect in the attitude of one surprised into sudden passion, and held uplifted the heavy ebony cane upon which he was ordinarily accustomed to lean. He was confronted by a man of two-and-twenty, tall and athletic of figure, dressed in rough seafaring clothes, who held in his arms a lady of middle age. The face of the young man wore an expression of horror, and the slight frame of the woman was convulsed with sobs.

These three people were Sir Richard Devine, his wife, and his only son Richard, who had returned from abroad that morning.

"So, madam," said Sir Richard, in high-strung accents, "you have been for twenty years a living lie! For twenty years you have cheated and mocked me. For twenty years—in company with a scoundrel whose name is a byword for all that is profligate and base—you have laughed at me for a credulous and hood-winked fool; and now, because I dared to raise my hand to that reckless boy, you confess your shame, and glory in the confession!"

"Mother, dear mother!" cried the young man, in a paroxysm of grief, "say that you did not mean those words; you said them but in anger!"

Lady Devine shuddered, creeping close, as though to hide in the broad bosom of her son.

The old man continued: "I married you, Ellinor Wade, for your beauty; you married me for my fortune. I was a plebeian, a ship's carpenter; you were well born, your father was a man of fashion, a gambler, the friend of rakes and prodigals. I was rich. I had been knighted. I was in favour at Court. He wanted money, and he sold you. I paid the price he asked, but there was nothing of your cousin, my lord Bellasis and Wotton—your *lover*—in the bond."

"Spare me, sir, spare me!" said Lady Ellinor faintly.

"Spare you! Ay, you have spared me, have you not? Lookye," he cried, in sudden fury, "to-morrow your father, your sisters, all the world, shall know the story you have told me!"

"By heaven, sir, you will not do this!" burst out the young man.

"Silence, *bastard*!" cried Sir Richard. "Ay, bite your lips, the word is of your precious mother's making!"

Lady Devine fell on her knees at her husband's feet.

"Do not do this, Richard. I have been faithful to you for two-and-twenty years. I have borne all the slights and insults you have heaped upon me. The shameful secret of my early love broke from me when, in your rage, you threatened my son. Let me go away; kill me; but do not shame me."

Sir Richard, who had turned to walk away, stopped suddenly, and his great white eyebrows came together in his red face with a savage scowl.

"You would preserve your good name then. You would conceal this disgrace from the world. You shall have your wish—upon one condition."

"What is it, sir?" she asked, rising, but trembling with terror.

The old man looked at her and then said slowly,—

"That this impostor shall abandon for ever the name he has usurped; keep himself from my sight, and never set foot again in house of mine!"

"You would not part me from my only son!" cried the wretched woman.

"Take him with you to his father then!"

Richard Devine gently loosed the arms that again clung around his neck, kissed the pale face, and turned towards the old man.

"I owe you no duty," he said. "You have always hated and reviled me. Now when I learn for the first time whose son I really am, I rejoice to think that I have less to thank you for than I once believed. I accept the terms you offer. I will go. Nay, mother, think of your good name."

Sir Richard Devine laughed again. "I am glad to see you are so well disposed. Listen now. To-night I send for Quaid to alter my will. My sister's son, Maurice Frere, shall be my heir in your stead. I give you nothing. You leave this house in an hour. You change your name; you never by word or deed make claim on me or mine. No matter what strait or poverty you plead—if even your life should hang upon the issue—the instant I hear that there exists on earth one who calls himself Richard Devine, that instant shall your mother's shame become a public scandal. You know me. I keep my word. I return in an hour, madam; let me find him gone."

He strode down the garden with the vigour that anger lends, and took the road to London.

"Richard!" cried the poor mother. "Forgive me, my son! I have ruined you."

Richard Devine tossed his black hair from his brow in a sudden passion of love and grief.

"Mother, dear mother, do not weep," he said. "I am not worthy of your tears. Forgive! It is I—impetuous and ungrateful during all your years of sorrow—who most need forgiveness. I can earn a name—a name that I need not blush to bear nor you to hear. I am strong. I can work. The world is wide. Farewell! my own mother!"

"Not yet, not yet! Ah! see he has taken the Belsize road. Oh, Richard! pray heaven they may not meet. A terror of I know not what coming evil overpowers me. I tremble for the future. Oh, Richard! forgive me!"

"Hush, dearest! Come, let me lead you in. I will write. I will send you news of me once at least, ere I depart."

Sir Richard Devine, knight, shipbuilder, naval contractor, and millionaire, was the son of a Harwich boat carpenter. Early left an orphan with a sister to support, he soon reduced his sole aim in life to the accumulation of money. In the Harwich boat-shed, nearly fifty years before, he had contracted—in defiance of prophesied failure—to build the *Hastings* sloop of war for His Majesty King George the Third's Lords of the Admiralty. This contract was the thin end of that wedge which eventually split the mighty oak block of Government patronage into three-deckers, and ships of the line; which did good service under Pellew, Parker, Nelson, Hood; which exfoliated and ramified into huge dockyards at Plymouth, Portsmouth, and Sheerness, and bore, as its buds and flowers, countless barrels of measly pork and maggoty biscuit.

The sole aim of the hard-headed son of Dick Devine was to make money. He had cringed and crawled, licked the dust off great men's shoes, and danced attendance in great men's ante-chambers. Nothing was too low, nothing too high for him. A shrewd man of business, a thorough master of his trade, troubled with no scruples of honour or of delicacy, he made money rapidly, and saved it when made. In 1805, he married his sister to a wealthy Bristol merchant, one Anthony Frere, and married himself to Ellinor Wade, the eldest daughter of Colonel Wotton Wade, a boon companion of the Regent, and uncle by marriage of a remarkable scamp and dandy, Lord Bellasis. At that time, what with lucky speculations and the legitimate profit on his Government contracts, he had accumulated a princely fortune. But parsimony and avarice were not to be shaken off, and the only show he made of his wealth was purchasing, on his knighthood, the rambling house at Hampstead, and ostensibly retiring from active business.

His retirement was not a happy one. He was a stern father and a severe master. His servants hated, and his wife feared him. His only son Richard appeared to inherit his father's strong will and imperious manner. Under a just rule he might have been guided to good; but left to his own devices outside, and galled by the iron yoke of parental discipline at home, he became reckless and prodigal. The mother—poor, timid Ellinor, who had been rudely torn from the love of her youth, her cousin, Lord Bellasis—tried to restrain him, but the headstrong boy, though owning for his mother that strong love which is often a part of such violent natures, proved intractable, and after three years of parental feud, he went off to the Continent, to pursue there the same reckless life which in London had offended Sir Richard. Sir Richard, upon this, sent for Maurice Frere, his sister's son—the abolition of the slave trade had ruined the Bristol House of

Frere—and bought for him a commission in a marching regiment, hinting darkly of special favours to come. His open preference for his nephew had galled to the quick his sensitive wife.

Between the houses of *parvenu* Devine and long-descended Wotton Wade there had long been little love. Sir Richard felt that the Colonel despised him for a city-knight, and had heard that over claret and cards Lord Bellasis and his friends had often lamented the hard fortune which gave the beauty, Ellinor, to so sordid a bridegroom.' Armigell Esmé Wade, Viscount Bellasis and Wotton, was a product of his time. Of good family (his ancestor, Armigell, was reputed to have landed in America before Gilbert or Raleigh), he had inherited his manor of Bellasis, or Belsize, from one Sir Esmé Wade, ambassador from Queen Elizabeth to the King of Spain. No sooner had he become master of his fortune than he took to dice, drink, and debauchery with all the extravagance of the last century. He was foremost in every riot, most notorious of all the notorious "bloods" of the day.

At thirty years of age, having lost together with his estates all chance of winning the one woman who might have saved him—his cousin Ellinor—he became that most unhappy of all beings, a well-born blackleg. When he was told by Colonel Wade that the rich shipbuilder, Sir Richard Devine, had proposed an alliance with fair-haired gentle Ellinor, he swore, with fierce knitting of his black brows, that no law of man nor Heaven should further restrain him in his selfish prodigality. "You have sold your daughter and ruined me," he said, "look to the consequences." Colonel Wade sneered at his fiery kinsman: "You will find Sir Richard's house a pleasant one to visit, Armigell; and he should be worth an income to so experienced a gambler as yourself." Lord Bellasis did visit at Sir Richard's house during the first year of his cousin's marriage; but upon the birth of the son who is the hero of this history, he affected a quarrel with the city-knight, and cursing him to the Prince and Poins for a miserly curmudgeon, who neither diced nor drank like a gentleman, departed, more desperately at war with fortune than ever, for his old haunts. The year 1827 found him a hardened, hopeless old man of sixty, battered in health and ruined in pocket; but who, by dint of stays, hair-dye, and courage, yet faced the world with undaunted front.

On the evening of the 3rd of May, 1827, Lord Bellasis had been attending a pigeon match at Hornsey Wood, and having resisted the importunities of his companion, Mr. Lionel Crofton (a young gentleman-rake, whose position in the sporting world was not the most secure), who wanted him to go on into town, he had avowed his intention of striking across Hampstead to Belsize. "I have an appointment at the Fir Trees on the Heath," he said.

"With a woman?" asked Mr. Crofton.

"Not at all; with a parson."

"A parson!"

"You stare! Well, he is only just ordained. I met him last year at Bath on his vacation from Cambridge, and he was good enough to lose some money to me."

"And now waits to pay it out of his first curacy. I wish your lordship joy with all my soul."

"Thanks, my dear sir," said Lord Bellasis, dryly. "To-morrow you can settle with me for the sitting of last week. Hark! the clock is striking nine. Let us set out."

At half-past nine Richard Devine quitted his mother's house to begin the new life he had chosen and so, drawn together by that strange fate of circumstance which creates events, the father and son approached each other.

As the young man gained the middle of the path which led to the Heath, he met Sir Richard returning from the village. It was no part of his plan to seek an interview with the man whom his mother had so deeply wronged, but seeing him thus alone returning to a desolated home, the prodigal was tempted to utter some words of farewell and regret. To his astonishment, however, Sir Richard passed swiftly on, with eyes unconscious of surroundings, staring straight into the distance. Half-terrified at this strange appearance, Richard hurried onward, and at a turn of the path stumbled upon something which horribly accounted for the curious action of the old man. A body lay in the heather; beside it was a riding whip stained with blood, and an open pocket-book. Richard took up the book and read, in gold letters on the cover, "Lord Bellasis".

The unhappy young man knelt down beside the body and raised it. The skull had been fractured by a blow, but it seemed that life yet lingered. Overcome with horror—for he could not doubt but that his mother's worst fears had been realised—Richard knelt there holding his murdered father in his arms, waiting until the murderer, whose name he bore, should have placed himself beyond pursuit. It seemed an hour to his excited fancy before he saw a light pass along the front of the house he had quitted, and knew that Sir Richard had safely reached his chamber. With some bewildered intention of summoning aid, he left the body and made towards the town. As he stepped out on the path he heard voices, and presently some dozen men burst out upon him and flung him to the ground.

At first the young man did not comprehend his own danger. His mind, bent upon one hideous explanation of the crime, did not see another obvious one which had already occurred to the mind of the landlord of the Three Spaniards.

"God defend me!" cried Mr. Mogford, scanning the features of the murdered man, "it is Lord Bellasis!—oh, you bloody villain! Jem, bring him along here, p'r'aps his lordship can recognise him!"

"It was not I!" cried Richard Devine. "For God's sake, my lord, say—" then he stopped abruptly and remained staring at the dying man, in sudden and ghastly fear.

In the terrible instant when his eyes met those of Lord Bellasis, Richard Devine realised to the full his personal peril. An hour ago escape would have been easy. He would have had but to cry, "I am the son of Sir Richard Devine. Come with me to yonder house, and I will prove to you that I have but just quitted it." That course of action was impossible now. Knowing Sir Richard as he did, and believing, moreover, that in his raging passion the old man had murdered the destroyer of his honour, the son of Lord Bellasis and Lady Devine saw himself in a position which would compel him either to sacrifice himself, or to purchase safety at the price of his mother's dishonour and the death of the man whom his mother had deceived. If the outcast son were brought a prisoner to North-End House, Sir Richard—now doubly oppressed of fate—would be certain to deny him; and he would be compelled, in self-defence, to reveal a story which would at once bring his mother to open infamy, and send to the gallows the man who had been for twenty years deceived. He knelt, stupefied, unable to speak or move.

"Come," cried Mogford again; "say, my lord, is this the villain?"

Lord Bellasis rallied his failing senses, his glazing eyes stared into his son's face with horrible eagerness; he shook his head, raised a feeble arm as though to point elsewhere, and fell back dead.

"If you didn't murder him, you robbed him," growled Mogford, "and you shall sleep at Bow-street to-night. Tom, run on to meet the patrol, and tell him to leave word at the Gate-house that I've a passenger for the coach!—bring him on, Jack!—What's your name, eh?"

He repeated the rough question twice before his prisoner answered, but at length Richard Devine raised a pale face and said, "Dawes—Rufus Dawes."

That night Rufus Dawes, charged with murder and robbery, lay awake in prison, waiting for the fortune of the morrow.

Two other men waited as eagerly. One, Mr. Lionel Crofton; the other, the horseman who had appointment with the murdered Lord Bellasis under the shadow of the fir trees on Hampstead Heath. As for Sir Richard Devine, he waited for no one, for upon reaching his room he had fallen senseless in a fit of apoplexy.

BOOK ONE
The Sea - 1827

In the breathless stillness of a tropical afternoon, the shadow of the *Malabar* lay solitary on the surface of the glittering sea.

THE PRISON SHIP

The sun—who rose every morning a blazing ball, to move slowly through the unbearable blue, until he sank fiery red in the ocean—had just got low enough to peep beneath the poop-deck awning and awaken a young man, in an undress military uniform, who was dozing on a coil of rope.

"Hang it!" said he, rising and stretching. "I must have been asleep." Holding by a stay, he turned about and looked down into the waist of the ship.

Save for the man at the wheel and the guard at the quarter-railing, he was alone on the deck. A few birds flew round about the vessel, and a lazy albatross rose with a dabbling sound to leeward. The seams of the well-scrubbed decks were sticky with melted pitch, and the brass plate of the compass-case sparkled in the sun. There was no breeze, and as the clumsy ship rolled on the heaving sea, her idle sails flapped against her masts. On the forecastle, some half-dozen soldiers were playing at cards, smoking, or watching the fishing-lines hanging over the catheads.

So far the appearance of the vessel differed in nowise from that of an ordinary transport. But in the waist a curious sight presented itself. It was as though one had built a cattle-pen there. At the foot of the foremast, and at the quarter-deck, a strong barricade, loop-holed and furnished with doors for ingress and egress, ran across the deck from bulwark to bulwark. Outside this cattle-pen an armed sentry stood on guard; inside, standing, sitting, or walking monotonously, within range of the shining barrels in the arm chest on the poop, were some sixty men and boys, dressed in uniform grey. The men and boys were prisoners of the Crown, and the cattle-pen was their exercise ground. Their prison was down the main hatchway, on the 'tween decks, and the barricade, continued down, made its side walls.

It was the fag end of the two hours' exercise graciously permitted each afternoon by His Majesty King George the Fourth to prisoners of the Crown, and the prisoners of the Crown were enjoying themselves. It was not, perhaps, so pleasant as under the awning on the poop-deck, but that sacred shade was only for such great men as the captain and his officers, Surgeon Pine, Lieutenant Maurice Frere, and, most important personages of all, Captain Vickers and his wife.

That the convict leaning against the bulwarks would like to have been able to get rid of his enemy the sun for a moment, was probable enough. His companions were laughing and talking, with blasphemous and obscene merriment; but he, with cap pulled over his brows, and hands thrust into the pockets of his coarse grey garments, held aloof from their dismal joviality.

The sun poured his hottest rays on his head yet the man stood there, motionless and morose, staring at the sleepy sea. He had stood thus, in one place or another, ever since the groaning vessel had escaped from the rollers of the Bay of Biscay, and the miserable hundred and eighty creatures among whom he was classed had been freed from their irons, and allowed to sniff fresh air twice a day.

The coarse-featured ruffians grouped about the deck cast many a leer of contempt at the solitary figure, but their remarks were confined to gestures only. There are degrees in crime, and Rufus Dawes, the convicted felon, who had but escaped the gallows to toil for all his life in irons, was a man of mark. He had been tried for the robbery and murder of Lord Bellasis. The friendless vagabond's lame story of finding on the heath a dying man would not have availed him, but for the curious fact sworn to by the landlord of the Spaniards' Inn, that the murdered nobleman had shaken his head when asked if the prisoner was his assassin. The vagabond was acquitted of the murder, but condemned to death for the robbery, and London, who took some interest in the trial, considered him fortunate when his sentence was commuted to transportation for life.

It was customary on board these floating prisons to keep each man's crime a secret from his fellows, so that he could lead a new life in his adopted home, without being taunted with his former misdeed. But the expedient was only a nominal one, and few out of the doomed hundred and eighty were ignorant of the offence which their companions had committed. Moreover, a deed so bloodthirsty and a respite so unexpected, had invested the name of Rufus Dawes with a grim distinction, which his superior mental abilities, no less than this haughty temper and powerful frame, combined to support. A young man of two-and-twenty owning to no friends, and existing among them but by the fact of his criminality, he was respected and admired. The vilest of all the vile horde penned between decks, if they laughed at his "fine airs" behind his back, cringed and submitted when they met him face to face—for in a convict ship the greatest villain is the greatest hero.

The young man on the poop caught sight of the tall figure leaning against the bulwarks.

"Here you!" he called out with an oath, "get out of the gangway!"

Rufus Dawes was not in the gangway—was, in fact, a good two feet from it, but at the sound of Lieutenant Frere's voice he started, and went obediently towards the hatchway.

"Touch your hat, you dog!" cried Frere, coming to the quarter-railing. "Touch your damned hat! Do you hear?"

Rufus Dawes touched his cap, saluting in half military fashion.

"I'll make some of you fellows smart, if you don't have a care," went on the angry Frere. "Insolent blackguards!"

And then the noise of the sentry, on the quarter-deck below him, grounding arms, turned the current of his thoughts. A thin, tall, soldier-like man, with a cold blue eye, and prim features, came out of the cuddy below, handing out a fair-haired, mincing lady, of middle age. Captain Vickers of Mr. Frere's regiment, ordered for service in Van Diemen's Land, was bringing his lady on deck.

Mrs. Vickers was forty-two (she owned to thirty-three), and had been a garrison-*belle* for eleven weary years before she married prim John Vickers. The marriage was not a happy one. Vickers found his wife extravagant, vain and snappish, and she found him harsh, disenchanted and commonplace. A daughter, born two years after their marriage, was the only link that bound them. Vickers idolised little Sylvia, and when the recommendation of a long sea-voyage for his failing health induced him to exchange into the —th, he insisted upon bringing the child with him, despite Mrs. Vickers's objections on the score of educational difficulties. He could educate her himself, if need be, he said; and she should not stay at home.

So Mrs. Vickers, after a struggle, gave up the point and her dreams of Bath together, and followed her husband with the best grace she could muster.

When fairly out to sea she seemed reconciled to her fate, and employed the intervals between scolding her daughter and her maid, in fascinating the boorish young Lieutenant, Maurice Frere.

Admiration was all Julia Vickers lived for: and even in a convict ship, she must flirt, or perish of mental inanition. There was no harm in the creature. She was simply a vain, middle-aged woman, and Frere took her attentions for what they were worth. Moreover, her good feeling towards him was useful for reasons which will shortly appear.

Running down the ladder, cap in hand, he offered her his assistance.

"Thank you, Mr. Frere. These horrid ladders. John, the camp-stool. Sylvia! Sylvia! John, have you my smelling salts? Still a calm, I suppose? These dreadful calms!"

This semi-fashionable slip-slop, within twenty yards of the wild beasts' den on the other side of the barricade, sounded strange; but Mr. Frere thought nothing of it. Familiarity destroys terror, and the incurable flirt fluttered her muslins, and played off her second-rate graces, under the noses of the grinning convicts, with as much complacency as if she had been in a Chatham ball-room.

Vickers, with a bow to Frere, saw his wife up the ladder, and then turned for his daughter.

She was a delicate-looking child of six years old, with blue eyes and bright hair. Though indulged by her father, and spoiled by her mother, the natural sweetness of her disposition saved her from being disagreeable, and the effects of her education as yet only showed themselves in a thousand imperious prettinesses, which made her the darling of the ship. Little Miss Sylvia was privileged to go anywhere and do anything, and even convictism shut its foul mouth in her presence. Now she ran hither and thither, asked questions, laughed, sang, gambolled, even ran down to the quarter-deck and pulled the coat-tails of the sentry on duty. At last, tired of running about, she took a little striped leather ball from the bosom of her frock, and calling to her father, threw it up to him as he stood on the poop. He returned it, and, shouting with laughter, the child kept up the game.

The convicts—whose slice of fresh air was nearly eaten—turned with eagerness to watch this new source of amusement. Innocent laughter and childish prattle were strange to them. It was as though, out of the sultry heat, a cool breeze had suddenly arisen.

In the midst of this mirth, the officer of the watch, glancing round the horizon, paused abruptly, and looked out intently to the westward.

Frere, who found Mrs. Vickers's conversation a little tiresome, noticed the action.

"What is it, Mr. Best?"

"I don't know exactly. It looks to me like a cloud of smoke."

And, taking the glass, he swept the horizon.

"Let me see," said Frere; and he looked also.

On the extreme horizon, just to the left of the sinking sun, there seemed to rest a tiny black cloud. But the gold and crimson splashed all about the sky rendered a clear view almost impossible.

"I can't quite make it out," says Frere, handing back the telescope. "We can see as soon as the sun goes down a little."

Then Mrs. Vickers must, of course, look also, and applied herself to the instrument with much girlish giggling, finally declaring that "positively she could see nothing but sky, and believed that wicked Mr. Frere was doing it on purpose."

At last the sun went down with a jerk, as though it had slipped through a slit in the sea, and the black spot, swallowed up in the gathering haze, was seen no more. As the sun sank, the relief guard came up the after hatchway, and the relieved guard prepared to superintend the descent of the convicts. At this moment Sylvia's ball hopped over the barricade, and rolled to the feet of Rufus Dawes, who was still leaning, lost in thought, against the side.

The bright spot of colour rolling across the white deck caught his eye; stooping mechanically, he picked up the ball, and stepped forward to return it. The door of the barricade was open, and the sentry did not notice the prisoner pass through it. In another instant he was on the sacred quarter-deck.

Her cheeks aglow, her eyes sparkling, Sylvia had turned to leap after her plaything, but even as she turned, from under the shadow of the cuddy glided a rounded white arm; and a shapely hand caught the child by the sash and drew her back. The next moment the young man in grey had placed the toy in her hand.

Maurice Frere, descending the poop ladder, had not witnessed this little incident; on reaching the deck, he saw only the convict uniform.

"Thank you," said a voice, as Rufus Dawes stooped before the pouting Sylvia.

The convict raised his eyes and saw a young girl of eighteen or nineteen years of age, tall and well developed, standing in the doorway. She had black hair, white skin and large dark eyes, and as she smiled at him, her scarlet lips showed her white even teeth.

He knew her at once. She was Sarah Purfoy, Mrs. Vickers's maid, but he never had been so close to her before; and it seemed to him that he was in the presence of some strange tropical flower, which exhaled a heavy, intoxicating perfume.

For an instant the two looked at each other, and then Rufus Dawes was seized from behind by his collar, and flung upon the deck.

Leaping to his feet, his first impulse was to rush upon his assailant, but he saw the ready bayonet of the sentry gleam, and he checked himself with an effort, for his assailant was Mr. Maurice Frere.

"What the devil do you do here?" asked that gentleman with an oath. "You lazy skulking hound, if I catch you putting your foot on the quarter-deck again, I'll give you a week in irons!"

Rufus Dawes opened his mouth to justify himself, but allowed the words to die on his lips. What was the use?

"Go down below, and remember what I've told you," cried Frere; and comprehending at once what had occurred, he made a mental minute of the name of the defaulting sentry.

The convict turned on his heel without a word, and went back through the oak door into his den.

Frere leant forward and took the girl's shapely hand with an easy gesture, but she drew it away, with a flash of her black eyes.

"You coward!" she said.

The stolid soldier close beside them heard it, and his eye twinkled. Frere bit his thick lips with mortification, as he followed the girl into the cuddy. Sarah Purfoy, however, glided into her mistress's cabin with a scornful laugh, and shut the door behind her.

Convictism having been safely got under hatches, and put to bed in its government allowance of sixteen inches of space per man, cut a little short

SARAH PURFOY

by exigencies of shipboard, the cuddy was wont to pass some not unpleasant evenings. Mrs. Vickers, who was poetical, often sang to her guitar. Captain Blunt was a jovial, coarse fellow, Surgeon Pine had a mania for story-telling, while Frere was always hearty. The table was well served, and the sultry evenings passed away with a rapidity of which the wild beasts 'tween decks had no conception.

On this particular evening, however, the cuddy was dull. Dinner fell flat, and conversation languished.

"No signs of a breeze, Mr. Best?" asked Blunt, as the first officer came in and took his seat.

"None, sir."

"These awful calms," says Mrs. Vickers. "A week, is it not, Captain Blunt?"

"Thirteen days, mum," growled Blunt.

"I remember, off the Coromandel Coast," put in cheerful Pine, "when we had the plague in the *Rattlesnake*—"

"Captain Vickers, another glass of wine?" cries Blunt, hastening to cut the anecdote short.

"Thank you, no more. I have the headache."

"Headache—um—don't wonder at it, going down among those fellows. It is infamous the way they crowd these ships. Here we have over two hundred souls on board, and not boat room for half of 'em."

"Two hundred souls! Surely not," says Vickers. "By the King's Regulations—"

"One hundred and eighty convicts, fifty soldiers, thirty in ship's crew, all told, and—how many?—one, two, three—seven in the cuddy. How many do you make that?"

"We *are* just a little crowded this time," says Best.

"It is very wrong," says Vickers, pompously. "Very wrong. By the King's Regulations—"

But the subject of the King's Regulations was even more distasteful to the cuddy than Pine's interminable anecdotes, and Mrs. Vickers hastened to change the subject.

"Are you not tired of this dreadful life, Mr. Frere?"

"Well, it is not exactly the life I had hoped to lead," said Frere, rubbing a freckled hand over his stubborn red hair; "but I must make the best of it."

"Yes, indeed," said the lady, in that subdued manner with which one comments upon a well-known accident, "it must have been a great shock to you to be so suddenly deprived of so large a fortune."

"Not only that, but to find that the black sheep who got it all, sailed for India within a week of my uncle's death! Lady Devine got a letter from him on the day of the funeral to say that he had taken his passage in the *Hydaspes* for Calcutta, and never meant to come back again!"

"Sir Richard Devine left no other children?"

"No, only this mysterious Dick, whom I never saw, but who must have hated me."

"Dear, dear! These family quarrels are dreadful things. Poor Lady Devine to lose in one day a husband and a son!"

"And the next morning to hear of the murder of her cousin! You know that we are connected with the Bellasis family. My aunt's father married a sister of the second Lord Bellasis."

"Indeed. A horrible murder! So you think that the dreadful man you pointed out the other day did it?"

"The jury seemed to think not," said Mr. Frere, with a laugh; "but I don't know anybody else who could have a motive for it. However, I'll go on deck and have a smoke."

"I wonder what induced that old hunks of a shipbuilder to try to cut off his only son in favour of a cub of that sort," said Surgeon Pine to Captain Vickers as the broad back of Mr. Maurice Frere disappeared up the companion.

"Some boyish follies abroad, I believe; self-made men are always impatient of extravagance. But it is hard upon Frere. He's not a bad sort of fellow, and when a young man finds that an accident deprives him of a quarter of a million of money and leaves him without a sixpence beyond his commission in a marching regiment under orders for a convict settlement, he has some reason to rail against fate."

"How was it that the son came in for the money after all, then?"

"Why it seems that when old Devine returned from sending for his lawyer to alter his will, he got a fit of apoplexy, the result of his rage, I suppose, and when they opened his room door in the morning they found him dead."

"And the son's away on the sea somewhere," said Mr. Vickers, "and knows nothing of his good fortune. It is quite a romance."

"I am glad that Frere did not get the money," said Pine. "I have seldom seen a face I liked less, even among my yellow jackets yonder."

"Oh dear, Dr. Pine! How can you?" interjected Mrs. Vickers.

" 'Pon my soul, ma'am, some of them have mixed in good society, I can tell you. There's pickpockets and swindlers down below who have lived in the best company."

"Dreadful wretches!" cried Mrs. Vickers, shaking out her skirts. "John, I will go on deck."

At the signal, the party rose.

"Ecod, Pine," says Captain Blunt, as the two were left alone together, "you and I are always putting our foot into it!"

"Women are always in the way aboard ship," returned Pine.

"Ah! doctor, you don't mean that, I know," said a rich soft voice at his elbow.

It was Sarah Purfoy emerging from her cabin.

"Here is the wench!" cries Blunt. "We were talking of your eyes, my dear."

"Well, they'll bear talking about, captain, won't they?" asked she, turning them full upon him.

"By the Lord, they will!" says Blunt, smacking his hand on the table. "They're the finest eyes I've seen in my life, and they've got the reddest lips under 'm that—"

"Let me pass, Captain Blunt, if you please. Thank you, doctor."

And before the admiring commander could prevent her, she modestly swept out of the cuddy.

"She's a fine piece of goods, eh?" asked Blunt, watching her. "A spice o' the devil in her, too."

Old Pine took a huge pinch of snuff.

"Devil! I tell you, Blunt, I'd rather trust my life with the worst of those ruffians 'tween decks, than in *her* keeping, if I'd done her an injury."

Blunt laughed.

"I don't believe she'd think much of sticking a man, either!" he said rising. "But I must go on deck, doctor."

Pine followed him slowly. "I don't pretend to know much about women," he said to himself, "but that girl's got a story of her own, or I'm much mistaken. What brings her on board this ship as lady's maid is more than I can fathom. She's after no good, I'll swear."

At that moment his arm was touched by a soldier who had come up the hatchway.

"What is it?"

The man drew himself up and saluted.

"If you plase, doctor, one of the prisoners is taken sick, and as the dinner's over, and he's pretty bad, I ventured to disturb your honour."

"You ass!" says Pine—who had a good heart under his rough shell—"why didn't you tell me before?"

In the meantime the woman who was the object of the grim old fellow's suspicions was walking up and down the deserted poop, in close *tête-à-tête* with no less a person than Captain Blunt himself.

"You weren't put out, my wench," he asked, "at what I said to you below?"

She affected surprise.

"What do you mean?"

"Why, at my—at what I—at my rudeness, there! For I was a bit rude, I admit."

"I? O dear, no. You were not rude. But you *would* have been—if I had let you."

"How do you know?"

"I saw it in your face. Do you think a woman can't see in a man's face when he's going to insult her?"

"Insult you, hey! Upon my word!"

"Yes, insult me. You're old enough to be my father, Captain Blunt, but you've no right to kiss me, unless I ask you."

"Haw, haw!" laughed Blunt. "I like that. Ask me! Egad, I wish you would, you black-eyed minx!"

"So would other people, I have no doubt."

"That soldier officer for instance. Hey, Miss Modesty? I've seen him looking at you as though he'd like to try."

The girl flashed at him with a quick side glance.

"You mean Lieutenant Frere, I suppose. Are you jealous of him?"

"Jealous! Why, damme, the lad was only breeched the other day. Jealous!"

"I think you are—though you've no need. He is a stupid booby."

"So he is. You are right there, by the Lord."

Sarah Purfoy laughed a low, full-toned laugh, whose sound made Blunt's pulse take a jump forward.

"Captain Blunt," said she, "how old are you?"

"Forty-two, if you must know."

"Oh! And you are going to fall in love with a girl of nineteen."

"Who is that?"

"Myself!" she said, giving him her hand and smiling at him with her rich red lips.

Blunt felt the breath of this strange woman warm on his cheek and the small hand he held burnt like fire.

"I believe you are right," he cried, "I *am* half in love with you already."

She gazed at him contemptuously and withdrew her hand.

"Then don't get to the other half or you'll regret it."

"Shall I?" asked Blunt. "That's my affair. Come, you little vixen, give me that kiss you said I was going to ask you for below," and he caught her in his arms.

In an instant she had twisted herself free.

"You dare!" she cried. "Kiss me by force! Pooh! you make love like a schoolboy. If you can *make* me like you, I'll kiss you as often as you will. If you can't, keep your distance, please."

Blunt did not know whether to laugh or be angry at this rebuff. He was conscious that he was in rather a ridiculous position, and so decided to laugh.

"You're a spit-fire, too. What must I do to make you like me?"

She made him a curtsey.

"That is your affair," she said; and as the head of Mr. Frere appeared above the companion, Blunt walked aft, feeling considerably bewildered, and yet not displeased.

"She's a fine girl, by jingo," he said, cocking his cap, "and I'm hanged if she ain't sweet upon me."

Maurice Frere's greeting was short enough.

"Well, Sarah," he said,—"have you got out of your temper?" She frowned.

"What did you strike the man for? He did you no harm."

"What business had he to come aft? One must keep these wretches down, my girl."

"Or they will be too much for you, eh? Do you think one man could capture a ship, Mr. Maurice?"

"No, but one hundred might."

"Nonsense! What could they do against the soldiers? There are fifty soldiers."

"So there are, but——"

"But what?"

"Never mind. It's against the rules, and I won't have it."

" 'Not according to the King's Regulations,' as Captain Vickers would say."

Frere laughed at her imitation of his pompous captain.

"You are a strange girl; I can't make you out. Come," and he took her hand, "tell me what you are really? You were not a lady's-maid all your life."

She pulled her shawl closer round her and shivered.

"People are not born ladies'-maids, I suppose?"

"Well, who are you, then? Have you no friends? What have you been?"

She looked up into the young man's face and, creeping closer to him, whispered,—

"Do you love me, Maurice?"

He raised one of the little hands that rested on the taffrail, and, under cover of the darkness, kissed it.

"You know I do," he said. "You may be a lady's-maid or what you like, but you are the loveliest woman I ever met."

"Then, if you love me, what does it matter?"

"If *you* loved me, you would tell me," said he quickly.

"But I have nothing to tell, and I don't love you—yet."

He let her hand fall with an impatient gesture; and at that moment Blunt—who could restrain himself no longer—came up.

"Fine night, Mr. Frere!"

"Yes, fine enough."

"No signs of a breeze yet, though."

"No, not yet."

Just then, from out of the violet haze that hung over the horizon, a strange glow of light broke.

"Hallo!" cries Frere, "did you see that?"

Blunt rubbed his eyes.

"I saw it," he said, "distinctly. A flash of light. There must be thunder in the air."

At that instant a thin streak of light shot up and then sank again.

There was no mistaking it this time, and a simultaneous exclamation burst from all on deck. From out of the gloom rose a column of flame that lighted up the night for an instant, and then sank, leaving a dull red spark upon the water.

"It's a ship on fire!" cried Frere.

THE MONOTONY BREAKS

The tiny spark still burned, and immediately over it there grew out of the darkness a crimson spot, that hung like a lurid star in the air. The soldiers and sailors on the forecastle had seen it also, and in a moment the whole vessel was astir. Mrs. Vickers, with little Sylvia clinging to her dress, came up to share the new sensation; and at the sight of her mistress, the modest maid withdrew discreetly from Frere's side.

"Captain, you'll lower a boat, eh? We may save some of the poor devils," cries Frere, his heartiness reviving at the prospect of excitement.

"Boat!" said Blunt, "why, she's twelve miles off and more, and there's not a breath o' wind!"

"But we can't let 'em roast like chestnuts!" cried the other.

"They've got their own boats," says Blunt, whose coolness was in strong contrast to the young officer's impetuosity; "and if the fire gains, they'll take to 'em you may depend. In the meantime, we'll show 'em that there's some one near 'em." And as he spoke, a blue light flared hissing into the night.

"There, they'll see that, I expect!" he said, as the flame rose, extinguishing the stars for a moment.

"Mr. Best—lower and man the quarter-boats! Mr. Frere—you can go in one, if you like, and take a volunteer or two from those grey jackets of yours amidships. I shall want as many hands as I can spare to man the long-boat and cutter, in case we want 'em. Steady there, lads! Easy!" and as the first eight men who could reach the deck parted to the larboard and starboard quarter-boats, Frere ran down on the main-deck.

Mrs. Vickers, of course, was in the way, and gave a genteel scream as Blunt rudely pushed past her with a scarce-muttered apology; but her maid was standing erect and motionless, by the quarter-railing, and as the captain paused for a moment to look round him, he saw her dark eyes fixed on him admiringly. He was, as he said, forty-two, burly and grey-haired, but he blushed like a girl under her approving gaze.

Meanwhile Maurice Frere had passed the sentry and leapt down into the 'tween decks. At his nod, the prison door was thrown open. The air was hot, and that strange, horrible odour peculiar to closely-packed human bodies filled the place.

He ran his eye down the double tier of bunks which lined the side of the ship, and stopped at the one opposite him.

There seemed to have been some disturbance there lately, for instead of the six pair of feet which should have protruded therefrom, the gleam of the bull's-eye showed but four.

"What's the matter here, sentry?" he asked.

"Prisoner ill, sir. Doctor sent him to hospital."

"But there should be two."

The other came from behind the break of the berths. It was Rufus Dawes. He held by the side as he came, and saluted.

"I felt sick, sir, and was trying to get the scuttle open."

Maurice Frere stamped his foot indignantly.

"Sick! I'll give you something to sweat the sickness out of you. Stand on one side here!"

Rufus Dawes, wondering, obeyed. He seemed heavy and dejected, as he rubbed his hand across his forehead.

"Which of you fellows can handle an oar?" Frere went on. "There, curse you, I don't want fifty! Three'll do. Come on now, make haste!"

The heavy door clashed again, and in another instant the four "volunteers" were on deck. The crimson glow was turning yellow now, and spreading over the sky.

"Two in each boat!" cries Blunt. "I'll burn a blue light every hour for you, Mr. Best; and take care they don't swamp you. Lower away, lads!"

As the second prisoner took the oar of Frere's boat, he uttered a groan and fell forward, recovering himself instantly. Sarah Purfoy, leaning over the side, saw the occurrence.

"What is the matter with that man?" she said. "Is he ill?"

Pine was next to her, and looked out instantly. "It's that big fellow in No. 10," he cried. "Here, Frere!"

But Frere heard him not. He was intent on the beacon that gleamed ever brighter in the distance. "Give way, my lads!" he shouted. And amid a cheer from the ship, the two boats shot out of the bright circle of the blue light, and disappeared into the darkness.

Sarah Purfoy looked at Pine for an explanation, but he turned abruptly away. For a moment the girl paused, as if in doubt; and then, ere his retreating figure turned to retrace its steps, she cast a quick glance around, and slipping down the ladder, made her way to the 'tween decks.

The iron-studded oak barricade that, loop-holed for musketry, and perforated with a plated trap-door for sterner needs, separated soldiers from prisoners, was close to her left hand, and the sentry at its padlocked door looked at her inquiringly. She laid her little hand on his big rough one—a sentry is but mortal—and opened her brown eyes at him.

"The hospital," she said. "The doctor sent me;" and before he could answer, her white figure vanished down the hatch, and passed round the bulkhead, behind which lay the sick man.

Though not so hot as in the prison, the atmosphere of the lower deck was close and unhealthy, and the girl turned strangely sick and giddy. She drew

THE HOSPITAL

herself up, however, and held out her hand to the young soldier who came rapidly out of the shadows to meet her.

"Well, miss," he said, "I am here, yer see, waiting for yer."

"You are a good boy, Miles; but don't you think I'm worth waiting for?"

Miles grinned from ear to ear.

"Indeed you be," said Miles, grinning from ear to ear.

The girl produced a small object from the pocket of her dress. If Mrs. Vickers had seen it she would probably have been angry, for it was nothing less than the captain's brandy-flask.

"Drink," said she. "It's the same as they have upstairs."

The fellow needed no pressing. He took off half the contents of the bottle at a gulp, and then stood staring at her.

"That's prime!"

"Is it? I dare say it is. Brandy is all you men understand."

Miles—still sucking in his breath—came a pace closer.

"I understand something else, miss, I can tell yer."

The tone of the sentence seemed to remind her of her errand in that place, and she laughed merrily, placing her hand on the speaker's arm. The boy— one of those ill-reared country louts who leave the plough-tail for the musket and a shilling a day—reddened to the roots of his closely cropped hair.

"There, that's quite close enough. You're only a common soldier, Miles, and you mustn't make love to me."

"Not make love to yer!" says Miles. "What did yer tell me to meet yer here for then?"

She laughed again.

"What a practical animal you are! Suppose I had something to say to you?"

Miles devoured her with his eyes.

"It's hard to marry a soldier," he said, with a recruit's proud intonation of the word; "but yer might do worse, miss, and I'll work for yer like a slave, I will."

She looked at him with pleasure. Though her time was precious, she could not resist listening to praises of herself.

"I know you're above me, Miss Sarah. You're a lady, but I love yer, I do, and you drives me wild with yer tricks."

"Do I?"

"Do yer? Yes, yer do. What did yer come an' make up to me for, and then go sweetheartin' with them others?"

"What others?"

"Why, the cuddy folk—the skipper, and the parson, and that —— Frere. I see yer walkin' the deck wi' un o' nights. Dom'um, I'd like to put a bullet through his red head."

"Hush! Miles dear—they'll hear you."

Encouraged by the epithet, Miles put his arm round her slim waist, just as Blunt had done, but she did not resent it so abruptly.

"Hush!" she whispered, with admirably-acted surprise—"I heard a noise!"

"There is no one!" cried he.

"Isn't there? My mistake, then. Now tell me, Miles, who is in the hospital?"

"I dunno."

"Well, I want to go in."

Miles scratched his head, and grinned.

"Against the doctor's orders. He told me special to let no one in but himself."

"Nonsense."

"It ain't nonsense. There was a convict brought in to-night, and nobody's to go near him. Don't ask me, miss. It's against orders, and——"

She turned away. "Oh, very well. If this is all the thanks I get for wasting my time down here, I shall go on deck again. Mr. Frere will let me go in, I dare say, if I ask him."

Miles swore under his breath.

"Dom Mr. Frere! Go in if yer like," he said; "I won't stop yer, but remember what I'm doin' of."

She turned and came quickly back. "That's a good lad. I knew you would not refuse me." Smiling at the poor lout, she passed into the cabin.

There was no lantern, and from the partially-blocked stern windows came only a dim, vaporous light. The sick man's heavy breathing seemed to fill the air. Raising her arm, conspicuous by its white sleeve in the gloom, Sarah Purfoy beckoned Miles.

"The lantern," she whispered—"bring me the lantern!"

As he brought it to her, the man in the bunk sat up and twisted himself towards the light. "Sarah!" he cried, in shrill tones. "Sarah!"

The convict was a young man of about four-and-twenty. His hands—clutched convulsively now on the blanket—were small and well-shaped, and the unshaven chin bristled with promise of a strong beard. His wild black eyes glared with the fire of delirium, and as he gasped for breath, the sweat stood in beads on his sallow forehead.

Miles, drawing back with an oath, did not wonder at the terror which had seized Mrs. Vickers's maid. With open mouth and agonised face, she stood in the centre of the cabin, lantern in hand, like one turned to stone, gazing at the man on the bed.

"Ecod, he be a sight!" says Miles, at length. "Come away, miss—he's raving, I tell yer."

She dropped the lantern, and rushed to the bed.

"You fool; he's choking! Water! Give me water!"

And wreathing her arms around the man's head, she pulled it down on her bosom, rocking it there.

Awed into obedience, Miles dipped a pannikin into a puncheon and gave it her; and, without thanking him, she placed it to the prisoner's lips. He drank greedily, and closed his eyes with a grateful sigh.

Just then the quick ears of Miles heard the jingle of arms.

"Here's the doctor coming, miss!" he cried. "I hear the sentry saluting. Come away! Quick!"

She seized the lantern and extinguished it.

"Say it went out," she said in a fierce whisper.

She bent over the convict as if to arrange his pillow, and then glided out of the cabin, just as Pine descended the hatchway.

"Hallo!" cried he, stumbling, "where's the light?"

"Here, sir," says Miles, fumbling with the lantern. "It's all right, sir. It went out, sir."

"Went out! What did you let it go out for, you blockhead!" growled the unsuspecting Pine. "Just like you boobies!"

As he groped his way in the darkness, Sarah Purfoy slipped past him unnoticed, and gained the upper deck.

THE BARRACOON

In the prison of the 'tween decks reigned a darkness pregnant with murmurs. The sentry at the entrance to the hatchway was supposed to "prevent the prisoners from making a noise," but he put a very liberal interpretation upon the clause, and so long as the prisoners refrained from shouting, yelling, and fighting—eccentricities in which they sometimes indulged—he did not disturb them.

To one coming in from the upper air, the place would have seemed in pitchy darkness; but the convict eye, accustomed to the sinister twilight, was enabled to discern surrounding objects with tolerable distinctness. The prison was about fifty feet long and fifty feet wide, and ran the full height of the 'tween decks, viz., about five feet ten inches high. The barricade was loop-holed here and there, and the planks were in some places wide enough to admit a musket barrel. On the aft side, next the soldiers' berths, was a trap-door, like the stoke-hole of a furnace. At first sight, this appeared to be contrived for the purpose of ventilation, but a second glance dispelled this conclusion. The opening was just large enough to admit the muzzle of a small howitzer, secured on the deck below. In case of a mutiny, the soldiers could sweep the prison from end to end with grape shot. Such fresh air as there was filtered through the loop holes, and came, in somewhat larger quantity, through a wind-sail passed into the prison from the hatchway. But the wind-sail being at one end only of the place, the air it brought was pretty well absorbed by the twenty or thirty lucky fellows near it, and the other hundred and fifty did not come so well off. The scuttles were open, certainly, but as the row of bunks had been built against them, the air *they* brought was the peculiar property of such men as occupied the berths into which they penetrated. The berths were twenty-eight in number, each containing six men, and ran in a double tier round the sides of the prison. Each berth was presumed to be five feet six inches square, but the necessities of stowage had deprived them of six inches, and even under that pressure twelve men were compelled to sleep on the deck. Pine did not exaggerate when he spoke of the custom of overcrowding convict ships; and as he was entitled to half a guinea for every man he delivered alive at Hobart Town, he had some reason to complain.

It is impossible to convey, in words, any idea of the hideous phantasmagoria of shifting limbs and faces which moved through the evil-smelling twilight of this terrible prison-house. Callot might have drawn it, Dante might have suggested it, but a minute attempt to describe its horrors would but disgust.

Stalwart burglars and highway robbers slept side by side with wizened pickpockets, forgers and body-snatchers. The man of education learned strange secrets of house-breakers' craft, and the fraudulent clerk and the flash "cracksman" interchanged experiences. The smuggler's stories of lucky ventures were capped by the footpad's reminiscences of foggy nights and stolen watches. The fast shopboy, whose love of fine company and high living had brought him to this pass, had shaken off the first shame that was on him, and listened eagerly to the narratives of successful vice that fell so glibly from the lips of his older companions. The old fellows laughed with all the glee of past experience, and listening youth longed for the time when it might do likewise. Society was the common foe, and magistrates, jailers, and parsons were the natural prey of all noteworthy mankind. Each new comer was one more recruit to the ranks of ruffianism, and not a man penned in that reeking den of infamy but became a sworn hater of law, order, and "free-men."

The conversation ran upon the sudden departure of the four. What could they want with them at that hour?

"I tell you there's something up on deck," says one. "Don't you hear all that rumbling and rolling?"

"What did they lower boats for? I heard the dip o' the oars."

"Don't know, mate. P'r'aps a burial job," hazarded another. "Or maybe the skipper agone fishin'."

"The skipper don't go fishin', yer fool. What would he do fishin'—special in the middle o' the night."

"That 'ud be like old Dovery, eh?" says a fifth, alluding to an old grey-headed fellow, who—a returned convict—was again under sentence for body snatching.

"Ay," put in a young man, who had the reputation of being the smartest "crow"[1] in London—"'fishers of men,' as the parson says." A laugh followed this speech.

Just then a miserable little cockney pickpocket, feeling his way to the door, fell into the party.

A volley of oaths and kicks received him.

"I beg your pardon, gen'l'men," cries the miserable wretch, "but I wan h'air."

"Go to the barber's and buy a wig then!" says the Crow.

"Vater!" cried the cockney. "Give us vater, for mercy's sake. I haven't moist'ned my chaffer this blessed day."

"What have yer done with yer half gallon, eh?" asked the Crow, derisively.

"Some one stole it," said the sufferer.

[1]Crow—The "look-out man" of a burglars' gang.

"He's been an' blued it," squealed some one. "Been an' blued it to buy a Sunday veskit with! Oh, ain't he a vicked young man?"

All this time the miserable little cockney—a tailor by trade—had been grovelling at the feet of the Crow and his companions.

"Let me h'up, gents," he implored. "I feel as if I should die—I do."

"Let the gentleman up," says a humorist. "Don't yer see his kerridge is avaitin' to take him to the Hopera?"

The conversation had got a little loud, and, from the the topmost bunk on the near side, a bullet head protruded.

"Ain't a cove to get no sleep?" cried a gruff voice. "My blood, if I have to turn out, I'll knock your empty heads together."

It seemed that the speaker was a man of mark, for the noise ceased instantly; and, in the lull which ensued, a shrill scream broke from the wretched tailor.

"Wot's the matter?" roared the silencer of the riot, jumping from his berth, and scattering the Crow and his companions right and left. "Let him be, can't yer?"

"H'air!" cried the poor devil—"h'air; I'm fainting!"

Just then there came a groan from a man in the opposite bunk.

"Well I'm blessed!" said the giant, glaring round him. "Here's a pretty go! All the blessed chickens ha' got the croup!"

The groaning of the man in the bunk redoubled.

"Pass the word to the sentry," says some one more humane than the rest.

"Ah," says the humorist, "pass him out; it'll be one the less."

"Sentry, here's a man sick."

But the sentry had been well informed of the artfulness of convict stratagems; and, moreover, Captain Vickers had carefully apprised him *"that by the King's Regulations, he was forbidden to reply to any question or communication addressed to him by a convict, but, in the event of being addressed, was to call the non-commissioned officer on duty."* Now, though he was within easy hailing distance of the guard on the quarter-deck, he felt disinclined to disturb those gentlemen merely for the sake of a sick convict, and knowing that, in a few minutes, the third relief would come on duty, he decided to wait until then.

In the meantime the tailor began to moan dismally.

"Here!" called out his supporter in dismay. "Don't come the drops 'ere. Pass him down, some of yer," and the wretch was hustled down the line to the doorway.

"Vater!" he whispered, beating feebly with his hand on the thick oak. "Get us a drink, mister, for Gord's sake!"

But the prudent sentry answered never a word until the ship's bell warned him of the approach of the relief guard; and then honest old Pine, coming to inquire after his charge, received the intelligence that there was another prisoner sick. He had the door unlocked and the tailor was outside in an instant. One look at the flushed, anxious face was enough.

"Who's that moaning in there?" he asked.

It was the man who had tried to call for the sentry an hour back, and Pine had him out also; convictism beginning to wonder a little.

"Take 'em both aft to the hospital," he said; "and, Jenkins, if there are any more men taken sick, pass the word for me at once. I shall be on deck."

As Pine went up the hatchway, he met Blunt.

"We've got the fever aboard!"

"Good God! Do you mean it, Pine?"

Pine shook his grizzled head.

"It's this cursed calm that's done it; though I expected it all along, with the ship crammed as she is. A hundred and eighty men penned into a place fifty feet long, with the air like an oven—what could you expect?"

"It isn't my fault," Blunt cried. "If the Government will overload these ships, I can't help it."

"The Government! Ah! The Government! The Government don't sleep, sixty men a-side, in a cabin only six feet high. The Government don't get typhus fever in the tropics, does it?"

"No—but——"

"But what does the Government care, then?"

Blunt wiped his hot forehead.

"Who was the first down?"

"No. 97 berth; ten on the lower tier. John Rex he calls himself."

"Are you sure it's the fever?"

"As sure as I can be. Head like a fire-ball, and tongue like a strip of leather. I've got him moved into the hospital. Hospital! I've seen dog-kennels I liked better."

He nodded towards the volume of lurid smoke that rolled up out of the glow. "And suppose there is a shipload of those poor devils?"

"We'll have to run for the Cape, with the first breeze, if they *do* come, that is all I can see for it," says Blunt gloomily, and he turned away to watch the burning vessel.

In the meantime the two boats made straight for the red column that rose like a gigantic torch over the silent sea.

THE FATE OF THE "HYDASPES"

As Blunt had said, the burning ship lay a good twelve miles from the *Malabar*, and the pull was a long and a weary one. Once fairly away from the protecting sides of the vessel that had borne them thus far on their dismal journey, the adventurers seemed to have come into a new atmosphere. The immensity of the ocean revealed itself for the first time. On board the prison ship, surrounded with all the memories if not with the comforts of the shore they had quitted, they had not realised how far they were from that civilisation which had given them birth. The well-lighted, well-furnished cuddy, the homely mirth of the forecastle, the setting of sentries and the changing of guards, even the gloom and terror of the closely-locked prison, combined to make the voyagers feel secure against the unknown dangers of the sea. But now—with one ship growing smaller behind them, and the other lying a burning wreck in the black distance ahead of them—they began to feel their own littleness. The *Malabar* lay on the water like a glow-worm on a floating leaf, and the glare of the signal-fire made no more impression on the darkness than a candle would have made in a coal-pit.

The water over which the boats glided was black and smooth, rising into huge foamless billows, the more terrible because they were silent. When the sea hisses, it speaks, and speech breaks the spell of terror; when it is inert, heaving noiselessly, it is dumb, and seems to brood over mischief. As the blades struck the dark water, it flashed fire, and the tracks of the boats resembled two sea-snakes writhing with silent undulations through a lake of quicksilver.

It had been a sort of race hitherto, and the rowers, with set teeth and compressed lips, had pulled stroke for stroke. At last the foremost boat came to a sudden pause. Best gave a cheery shout and passed her, steering straight towards the broad track of crimson ahead.

"What is it?" he cried.

But he heard only a smothered curse from Frere. It was, in fact, nothing of consequence—only a prisoner "giving in."

"Curse it!" says Frere. "Dawes! Of course, Dawes. I never expected anything better from such a skulking hound. Come, this sort of nonsense won't do with me. It isn't as nice as lolling about the hatchways, I dare say, but you'll have to go on, my fine fellow."

"He seems sick, sir," said compassionate bow.

"Sick! Not he. Shamming. Come, put your backs into it!"

But, for all Mr. Frere's urging, he could not recover the way he had lost, and Best was the first to run in under the black cloud that hung over the crimsoned water.

At his signal the second boat came alongside.

"Keep wide," he said. "If there are many fellows yet aboard, they'll swamp us." Raising his voice as the exhausted crew lay on their oars, he hailed the burning ship.

She was a huge, clumsily-built vessel, with great breadth of beam and a lofty poop-deck. Strangely enough, though they had so lately seen the fire, she was already a wreck, and appeared to be completely deserted. The fire roared like a cataract, and huge volumes of flame-flecked smoke poured up out of the hold, and rolled away in a low-lying black cloud over the sea.

As Frere's boat pulled slowly round her stern, he hailed the deck again and again.

Still there was no answer, and though the blood-red flood of light illuminated every rope and spar, his straining eyes could see no living soul aboard. As they came nearer, they could distinguish the gilded letters of her name.

"What is it, men?" cried Frere above the roar of the flames. "Can you see?"

"The *Hydaspes!*"

Frere gasped.

The *Hydaspes!* The ship in which his cousin Richard Devine had sailed! The *Hydaspes* which—something he had heard during the speculations as to this missing cousin flashed across him.

"Back water, men! Round with her! Pull for your lives!"

Best's boat glided alongside.

"Can you see her name?"

Frere, white with terror, shouted a reply.

"The *Hydaspes!* I know her. She is bound for Calcutta, and she has five tons of powder aboard!"

There was no need for more words. The single sentence explained the whole mystery of her desertion. The crew had taken to the boats on the first alarm, and had left their death-fraught vessel to her fate. They were miles off by this time, and unluckily for themselves, perhaps, had steered away from the side where rescue lay.

The boats tore through the water. The flames had even now reached the poop; in a few minutes it would be too late. With straining arms and labouring chests, the rowers tugged at the oars, their eyes fixed on the lurid mass they were leaving.

Another moment, and all would be over. Ah! it had come at last.

A dull rumbling sound; the burning ship parted asunder; a pillar of fire rose up out of the ocean; there was a terrific crash, as though sea and sky were coming together; and then a mighty mountain of water rose, advanced, caught, and passed them, and they were alone—deafened, stunned, and breathless.

The splashing of falling fragments awoke them from their stupor, and then the blue light of the *Malabar* struck out a bright pathway across the sea, and they knew that they were safe.

On board the *Malabar* two men paced the deck, waiting for dawn.

It came at last, and as the sky lightened, the man at the masthead hailed the deck. The boats were in sight, and as they came towards the ship, a crowd of spectators hanging over the bulwarks cheered and waved their hats.

"Not a soul!" cried Blunt. "No one but themselves!"

The boats drew alongside, and shortly Frere was upon deck.

"Well, Mr. Frere?"

"No use," cried Frere, shivering. "We only just had time to get away."

"Didn't you see any one?"

"Not a soul. They must have taken to the boats."

"Then they can't be far off," cried Blunt, sweeping the horizon with his glass. "They must have pulled all the way, for there hasn't been enough wind to fill a hollow tooth with."

"Perhaps they pulled in the wrong direction," said Frere. "They had a good four hours' start of us, you know."

"You had better go and turn in, Frere," said Pine gruffly. "It's no use whistling for a wind *here* all day."

Frere laughed. "I think I will—I'm dog tired, and as sleepy as an owl."

Pine took a couple of turns up and down the deck, and then catching Blunt's eye, stopped in front of Vickers.

"Captain Vickers, it's just as well if we don't find these poor devils. We have quite enough on our hands as it is."

"What do you mean, Mr. Pine?" says Vickers. "You would not surely leave the unhappy men to their fate."

"Perhaps," returned the other, "they would not thank us for taking them aboard."

"I don't understand you."

"The fever has broken out."

Vickers raised his brows. He had no experience of such things, and he apprehended no danger to himself.

"It is a great misfortune; but, of course, you will take such steps——"

"It is only in the prison, *as yet*," says Pine, with a grim emphasis on the word; "but there is no saying how long it may stop there."

"Well, sir, all authority in the matter is in your hands. Any suggestions you make, I will, of course, do my best to carry out."

"And you had better keep your wife and the little girl as much on deck as possible."

Vickers turned pale at the mention of his child. "Good heaven! do you think there is any danger?"

"There is, of course, danger to all of us; but with care we may escape it. There's that maid, too. She has a trick of roaming about the ship I don't like. Infection is easily spread, and children always sicken sooner than grown-up people."

Blunt put in a word for the defence of the absent woman. "The wench is right enough, Pine," said he. "What's the matter with her?"

"Yes, *she's* all right, I've no doubt. You can see her vitality in her face—as many lives as a cat. But she'd *bring* infection quicker than anybody."

"I'll—I'll go at once," cried poor Vickers, turning round.

The woman of whom they were speaking met him at the ladder. Her face was pale, and dark circles round her eyes gave evidence of a sleepless night. She opened her red lips to speak.

"I came for Dr. Pine, sir."

Vickers, with the quick intelligence of affection, guessed her errand. "Some one is ill?"

"Miss Sylvia, sir. It is nothing to signify, I think. A little feverish and hot, and my mistress——"

Vickers was down the ladder in an instant.

Pine caught the girl's arm. "Where have you been?"

Two great flakes of red came out in her white cheeks, and she shot an indignant glance at Blunt.

"Come, Pine, let the wench alone!"

"Were you with the child last night?" he demanded.

"No; I have not been in the cabin since dinner yesterday. Mrs. Vickers only called me in just now. Let go my arm, sir, you hurt me."

Pine loosed his hold. "I beg your pardon," he said gruffly. "I did not mean to hurt you. But the fever has broken out in the prison, and I think the child has caught it. You must be careful where you go."

And then, with an anxious face, he went in pursuit of Vickers.

Sarah Purfoy stood motionless for an instant, her lips parted, her eyes glittering.

"Ship fever! I have heard of it! Men have died like rotten sheep in crowded vessels like this."

"Tush! Not they. Don't be frightened; Miss Sylvia won't die, nor you neither." He took her hand. "It may knock off a few dozen prisoners or so, that's all."

She drew her hand away, and then, remembering herself, gave it him again.

"What is the matter?"

"Nothing—a pain. I did not sleep last night."

"There, there; you are upset. Go and lie down."

She was staring away past him over the sea, intently, as if in thought. Then she brought her fine straight brows together for a moment and raised them, with the action of a thinker who has decided on his course of conduct.

"I have the toothache," said she, putting her hand to her face.

"Take some laudanum," says Blunt. "Old Pine'll give you some."

To his astonishment she burst into tears.

"There—there! Don't cry, my dear. What are you crying about?"

She dashed away the bright drops, and raised her face with a rainy smile of trusting affection.

"Nothing! I am lonely. So far from home; and—and Dr. Pine hurt my arm. Look!"

She bared that shapely member as she spoke, and sure enough there were three red marks on the white and shining flesh.

"The ruffian!" cried Blunt, "it's too bad." After a hasty look round him, the infatuated fellow kissed the bruise. "I'll get the laudanum for you," he said. "You shan't ask that bear for it. Come to my cabin."

Blunt's cabin was in the starboard side of the ship, just under the poop awning, and possessed three windows—one looking out over the side, and two upon deck. The corresponding cabin on the other side was occupied by Mr. Frere. He closed the door, and took down a small medicine chest.

"Here," said he. "I've carried this little box for years, but it ain't often I want to use it, thank God. Now, then, put some o' this into your mouth, and hold it there."

"Good gracious, Captain Blunt, you'll poison me! Give me the bottle; I'll help myself."

The door was shut, and as she put the bottle in her pocket, the amorous captain caught her in his arms.

"What do you say? Come, I think I deserve a kiss for that."

Her tears were all dry long ago, and had only given increased colour to her face. This agreeable woman never wept long enough to make herself distasteful. She raised her dark eyes to his for a moment, with a saucy smile. "By-and-by," said she, and escaping gained her cabin. It was next to that of her mistress, and she could hear the sick child feebly moaning. Her eyes filled with tears—real ones this time.

"Poor little thing," she said; "I hope she won't die."

And then she threw herself on her bed, and buried her hot head in the pillow. The intelligence of the fever seemed to have terrified her. Had the news disarranged some well-concocted plan of hers? Had the sudden and unexpected presence of disease cast an obstacle in her path?

"She die! and through me? How did I know that he had the fever? Perhaps I have taken it myself—I feel ill." She turned over on the bed, as if in pain. "Perhaps *he* might die! The fever spreads quickly, and if so, all this plotting will have been useless. It must be done at once. It will never do to break down *now*." Taking the phial from her pocket, she held it up to see how much it contained. It was three parts full. "Enough for both," she said, between her set teeth. The action of holding up the bottle reminded her of amorous Blunt, and she smiled. "A strange way to show affection for a man," she said to herself, "and yet *he* doesn't care, and I suppose I shouldn't by this time. I'll go through with it, and, if the worst comes to the worst, I can fall back on Maurice." She loosened the cork of the phial, so that it would come out with as little noise as possible, and then placed it carefully in her bosom. "I will get a little sleep if I can," she said. "They have got the note, and it shall be done to-night."

The felon Rufus Dawes had stretched himself in his bunk and tried to sleep.
But though he was tired and sore and his head felt like lead, he could not

TYPHUS
FEVER

but keep broad awake. The long pull through the
pure air, if it had tired him, had revived him and
he felt stronger; but for all that, the fatal sickness that was
on him maintained its hold; his pulse beat thickly, and his
brain throbbed with unnatural heat. Before his eyes was still the burning
Hydaspes—that vessel, whose destruction had destroyed for ever all trace of
the unhappy Richard Devine.

As yet there had been no alarm of fever. The "Old Hands"—who had
been through the passage before—suspected, but said nothing, save among
themselves. It was likely that the weak and sickly would go first, and that
there would be more room for those remaining. The "Old Hands" were
satisfied.

Three of these old hands were conversing together just behind the
partition of Dawes's bunk. Of these, the giant—who had the previous night
asserted his authority in the prison—seemed to be the chief. His name was
Gabbett. He was a returned convict, now on his way to undergo a second
sentence for burglary. The other two were a man named Sanders, known as
"the Moocher," and Jemmy Vetch the "Crow". They were talking in
whispers, but Rufus Dawes, lying with his head close to the partition, was
enabled to catch much of what they said.

At first the conversation turned on the catastrophe of the burning ship
and the likelihood of saving the crew. From this it grew to anecdote of wreck
and adventure, and at last Gabbett said something which made the listener
start into sudden broad wakefulness.

It was the mention of his own name coupled with that of the woman he
had met on the quarter-deck.

"I saw her speaking to Dawes yesterday," said the giant, with an oath.
"We don't want no more than we've got. I ain't going to risk my neck for
Rex's woman's fancies."

"It was something about the kid," says the Crow. "I don't believe she ever
saw him before. Besides, she's nuts on Jack, and ain't likely to pick up with
another man."

"If I thort she was agoin' to throw us over, I'd cut her throat as soon as
look at her!" snorts Gabbett, savagely. "Now, if we're for bizness, let's come
to bizness."

"What are we to do?" asked the Moocher. "Jack's on the sick-list, and
the gal won't stir a'thout him."

"Ay," returned Gabbett, "that's it."

"My dear friends," said the Crow,—"my keyind and keristian friends, it is to be regretted that when natur' gave you such tremendously thick skulls, she didn't put something inside of 'em. I say that now's the time. Jack's in the 'orspital; what of that? That don't make it no better for him, does it? Not a bit of it; and if he drops his knife and fork, why then, it's my opinion that the gal won't stir a peg: It's on *his* account, not ours, that she's been manoovering, ain't it?"

"Well!" says Mr. Gabbett, with the air of one who was but partly convinced, "I s'pose it is."

"All the more reason of getting it off quick. Another thing, when the boys know there's fever aboard, you'll see the rumpus there'll be. They'll be ready enough to join us then. Once get the snapper chest, and we're right as ninepenn'orth o' hapence."

This conversation had an intense interest for Rufus Dawes. By reason of his surroundings ignorant of the death of his father and his own fortune, he had hitherto—in his agony—held aloof from the scoundrels who surrounded him. He now saw his error. He knew that the name he had once possessed was blotted out, that any shred of his old life which had clung to him hitherto, was shrivelled into the fire that consumed the *Hydaspes*. The secret of his birth would be now for ever safe; for Richard Devine was dead—lost at sea with the crew of the ill-fated vessel in which, deluded by a skilfully-sent letter from the prison, his mother believed him to have sailed. Richard Devine was dead, and Rufus Dawes, his *alter ego*, alone should live. Rufus Dawes, the convicted felon, should live to claim his freedom, and work out his vengeance; or, rendered powerful by the terrible experience of the prison-sheds, should seize both, in defiance of gaol or gaoler.

With his head swimming, and his brain on fire, he eagerly listened for more.

"But we can't stir without the girl," Gabbett said. "She's got to stall off the sentry and give us the orfice."

The Crow's sallow features lighted up with a cunning smile.

"Dear old caper merchant! Hear him talk!" said he. "As if he had the wisdom of Solomon! Look here!"

And he produced a dirty scrap of paper, over which his companions eagerly bent their heads.

"Where did yer get that?"

"Yesterday afternoon Sarah was standing on the poop throwing bits o' toke to the gulls, and I saw her a-looking at me very hard. At last she came down as near the barricade as she dared, and by-and-by a pretty big lump fell close to my foot. Watching a favourable opportunity, I pouched it. Inside was this bit o' rag-bag."

"Ah!" said Mr. Gabbett, "read it out, Jemmy."

The writing, though feminine in character, was bold and distinct. Sarah had evidently been mindful of the education of her friends.

All is right. Watch me when I come up to-morrow evening at three bells. If I drop my handkerchief, get to work at the time agreed on. The sentry will be safe.

Rufus Dawes, though a terrible lassitude almost paralysed his limbs, eagerly drank in the whispered sentence. There was a conspiracy to seize the ship. Sarah Purfoy was in league with the convicts—was herself the wife or mistress of one of them. She had come on board armed with a plot for his release, and this plot was about to be put in execution. He had heard of the atrocities perpetrated by successful mutineers. He knew the characters of the three ruffians who, separated from him by but two inches of planking, jested and laughed over their plans of freedom and vengeance, and he could not but know how *they* would proceed to wreak their vengeance on their gaolers.

With such a powerful ally outside as the mock maid-servant, the chance of success was enormously increased. There were one hundred and eighty convicts and but fifty soldiers. If the first rush proved successful—and the precautions taken by Sarah Purfoy rendered success possible—the vessel was theirs. Rufus Dawes thought of the little bright-haired child who had run so confidingly to meet him, and shuddered.

"There!" sneered the Crow, "what do you think of that? Does the girl look like nosing us now?"

"No," says the giant, stretching his great arms with a grin of delight, "that's right, that is. That's more like bizness."

"England!" said Vetch, with a strangely mock-heroic air. "You'd like to go home again, wouldn't you, old man?"

Gabbett turned on him fiercely, his face savage.

"*You!*" he said—"You think the chain's fine sport, don't yer? But I've been there, my young children, and I *knows what it means.*"

There was silence for a minute. The giant was plunged in gloomy abstraction, and Vetch and Moocher interchanged a significant glance. Gabbett had been ten years at the penal settlement of Macquarie Harbour, and he had memories that he did not confide to his companions. When he indulged in one of these fits of recollection, his friends found it best to leave him to himself.

Rufus Dawes did not understand the sudden silence. With all his senses stretched to the utmost to listen, the cessation of the whispered colloquy affected him strangely. Old artillery men have said that, after being at work for days in the trenches, a sudden pause in the firing will cause them intense pain. Something of this feeling was experienced by Rufus Dawes. The blood rushed into his eyes and ears. He made a violent, vain effort to retain his consciousness, but with a faint cry, fell back, striking his head against the edge of the bunk.

The noise roused the burglar in an instant. There was some one in the berth!

"It's Dawes!" said the Moocher. "We had forgotten him!"

Gabbett uttered a furious oath, and flinging himself on to the prostrate figure, dragged it to the floor. The sudden vertigo saved Rufus Dawes's life. The robber was preparing to deliver a blow that should for ever silence the listener, when Vetch caught his arm. "He's been asleep," he cried. "Don't hit him! See, he's not awake yet."

A crowd gathered round. The giant relaxed his grip, but the convict gave only a deep groan. Gabbett took another look at the purpling face and the bedewed forehead, and then sprang erect, rubbing at his hand, as though he would rub off something sticking there.

"He's got the fever!" he roared, with a terror-stricken grimace.

"The what?" asked twenty voices.

"The Fever, ye fools!" cried Gabbett. "I've seen it before to-day. The Typhus is aboard, and he's the fourth man down!"

It was late in the afternoon when Sarah Purfoy awoke from her uneasy slumber. She had been dreaming of the deed she was about to do, and was

A DANGEROUS CRISIS

flushed and feverish, but, mindful of the consequences which hung upon the success or failure of the enterprise, she rallied herself, bathed her face, and ascended, with as calm an air as she could assume, to the poop-deck.

Nothing was changed since yesterday. The ship rolled and creaked on the swell of the dreamy sea, the prison-cage was crowded with the same cheerless figures, and even Mr. Maurice Frere was lounging on the same coil of rope as the day before.

Yet the eye of an acute observer would have detected some difference beneath this outward varnish of similarity. The man at the wheel looked round the horizon more eagerly, and spat into the swirling water with a more dejected air than before. The soldiers and sailors on the forecastle gloomily stared at each other. Vickers was in the cuddy writing; Blunt was in his cabin; and Pine, with two carpenters at work under his direction, was improvising increased hospital accommodation. The noise of mallet and hammer echoed in the soldiers' berth ominously; the workmen might have been making coffins. The prison was strangely silent, with the lowering silence which precedes a thunderstorm; and the convicts on deck sat moodily patient, as if waiting for something.

Three men—two prisoners and a soldier—had succumbed since Rufus Dawes had been removed to the hospital; and though as yet there had been no symptom of panic, the face of each man wore an expectant look, as though he wondered whose turn would come next. The *Malabar* seemed to be enveloped in an electric cloud, whose sullen gloom a chance spark might flash into a blaze.

The woman who held in her hands the two ends of the chain that would produce this spark, leant against the poop-railing and looked down into the barricade. The prisoners were in knots of four and five, and to one group in particular her glance was directed.

Three men watched her every motion.

"There she is," growled Mr. Gabbett. "Flash as ever, and looking this way, too."

"I don't see no wipe," said the practical Moocher.

"Patience is a virtue, most noble knuckler!" says the Crow. "Give the young woman time."

"Blowed if I'm going to wait no longer," says the giant, licking his coarse lips. "We've been bluffed off day after day, and kep' dancin' round the

Dandy's wench like a parcel o' dogs. The fever's aboard, and we've got all ready. What's the use o' waitin'? I'm for bizness at once!"

"There, look at that," he added, with an oath, as Maurice Frere appeared by her side, and the two turned away up the deck together.

"It's all right, you confounded muddlehead!" cried the Crow. "How can she give us the office with that cove at her elbow?"

Since their conversation the previous evening, Maurice Frere had made up his mind to be fooled no longer. The girl was evidently playing with him, and he would show her that he was not to be trifled with.

"Well, Sarah! How well you are looking to-day! Positively lovely!"

"You have told me that so often," says she, with a pout. "Have you nothing else to say?"

"Except that I love you."

"That is no news. I know you do."

"Curse it, Sarah, what is the use of playing fast and loose with a fellow this way?"

"I didn't ask you to fall in love with me, did I? If you don't please me, it is not your fault, perhaps."

"What do you mean?"

"You soldiers have so many things to think of—your guards and sentries, and visits and things. You have no time to spare for a poor woman like me."

"Spare!" cries Frere, in amazement. "Why, damme, you won't let a fellow spare! I'd spare fast enough, if that was all."

A modest flush rose in her cheeks. "There are so many eyes upon me, I cannot stir without being seen," she said in a half-whisper.

Frere, smiling with delight at her change of manner, came close to her, and whispered in her ear. She affected to start, and took the opportunity of exchanging a signal with the Crow.

"I will come at eight o'clock," said she, with modestly averted face.

"They relieve guard at eight," he said.

She tossed her head. "Very well, then, attend to your guard; I don't care."

"But, Sarah, consider——"

"As if a woman in love *ever* considers!" said she, turning upon him a burning glance.

——She loved him then! What a fool he would be to refuse. Surely the guard could relieve itself for once without his supervision.

"Very well, at eight then, dearest."

"Hush!" said she. "Here comes that stupid captain."

As Frere left her, she turned, and, with her eyes fixed on the convict barricade, dropped her handkerchief over the poop-railing. It fell at the feet of the amorous captain, and with a quick upward glance, that worthy fellow picked it up and brought it to her.

"Oh, *thank* you, Captain Blunt," said she, and her eyes spoke more than her tongue.

"Did you take the laudanum?" whispered Blunt.

"Some of it," said she. "I will bring you back the bottle to-night."

Blunt walked aft, humming cheerily, and saluted Frere with a slap on the back. The two men laughed, each at his own thoughts.

Sarah Purfoy, casting her eyes toward the barricade, observed that the Crow, having taken off his prison cap, held it at arm's length with one hand, while he wiped his brow with the other. Her signal had been observed.

During all this, Rufus Dawes, removed to the hospital, was lying flat on his back, staring at the deck above him, trying to think of something he wanted to say.

He remembered being torn out of his bunk by fierce hands, remembered that, while lying on his blankets, he had overheard a conversation of vital importance to himself and to the ship, but of the purport of that conversation he had not the least idea. He only knew that a terrible danger menaced him; that could he but force his brain to reason connectedly, he could give such information as would avert that danger, and save the ship. But, lying with hot head, parched lips, and enfeebled body, he was as one possessed—he could move nor hand nor foot.

The place where he lay was but dimly lighted, and he could but just distinguish the outlines of three other berths, apparently similar to his own. The only sounds that broke the silence were the gurgling of water below him, and the *Tap tap, Tap tap*, of Pine's hammers at work upon the new partition. By-and-by the noise of these hammers ceased, and then the sick man could hear gasps and mutterings—the signs that his companions yet lived.

All at once a voice called out, "Of course his bills are worth four hundred pounds; but, my good sir, four hundred pounds to a man in my position is not worth the getting. Why, I've *given* four hundred pounds for a freak of my girl Sarah! Is it right, eh, Jezebel? She's a good girl, though, as girls go. Mrs. Lionel Crofton, of the Crofts, Sevenoaks, Kent—Sevenoaks, Kent—Seven——"

A gleam of light broke in on the darkness which wrapped Rufus Dawes's tortured brain. The man was John Rex, his berth mate. With an effort he spoke.

"Rex!"

"Yes, yes. I'm coming; don't be in a hurry. The sentry's safe, and the howitzer is but five paces from the door. A rush upon deck, lads, and she's ours! That is, mine. Mine and my wife's, Mrs. Lionel Crofton, of Seven Crofts, no oaks—Sarah Purfoy, lady's-maid and nurse—ha! ha!"

Sarah Purfoy! Now Rufus Dawes remembered each detail of the conversation he had so strangely overheard, and how imperative it was that he should, without delay, reveal the plot that threatened the ship.

He attempted to rise, but found that his fever-thralled limbs refused to obey the impulse of his will. He made an effort to speak, but his tongue clove to the roof of his mouth. He could not raise a finger nor utter a sound. The boards over his head waved like a shaken sheet, and as the cabin whirled round, he closed his eyes with a terrible sigh of despair, and resigned himself to his fate. At that instant the door opened. It was six o'clock and Pine had come to have a last look at his patients before dinner.

With Pine was honest Vickers, who, though agonised for the safety of his child, would not abate a jot of his duty, and had sternly come to visit the sick men, aware as he was that such a visit would necessitate his isolation from the cabin where his child lay.

"Here they are," said Pine. "This fellow"—going to the side of Rex—"is the worst. If he had not a constitution like a horse, I don't think he could live out the night."

"Good-night, my lord, good-night," muttered Rex. "Hark! The clock is striking nine; five, six, seven, eight!"

"A dangerous fellow," says Pine. "That is, he *was*. This is the place, you see—a regular rat-hole; but what can one do?"

"Come, let us get on deck," said Vickers, shuddering.

Rufus Dawes felt the sweat break out on his forehead. They were going away. He *must* warn them. With a violent effort he thrust out his hand from the blankets.

"Hallo! what's this?" cried Pine. "Lie down, my man. Eh!—water, is it? There, steady with it now;" and he lifted a pannikin to the blackened, froth-fringed lips. The cool draught moistened his parched gullet, and the convict made a last effort to speak.

"Sarah Purfoy—to-night—the prison—MUTINY!"

The last word, almost shrieked out, recalled the wandering senses of John Rex.

"Hush!" he cried. "Is that you, Jemmy? Sarah's right. Wait till she gives the word."

"He's raving," said Vickers.

Pine caught the convict by the shoulder. "What do you say, my man? A mutiny of the prisoners!"

With his mouth agape and his hands clenched, Rufus Dawes made a last effort to nod assent, but his head fell upon his breast; the next moment, the flickering light, the gloomy prison, the eager face of the doctor, and the astonished face of Vickers, vanished from before his straining eyes.

The two discoverers of this awkward secret held a council of war. Vickers was for at once calling the guard, and announcing to the prisoners that the

WOMAN'S WEAPONS

plot had been discovered; but Pine overruled this decision.

"You don't know these fellows as well as I do," said he. "In the first place there may be no mutiny at all. The whole thing is, perhaps, some absurdity of that fellow Dawes—and should we once put the notion of attacking us into the prisoners' heads, there is no telling what they might do."

"But the man seemed certain," said the other. "He mentioned my wife's maid, too!"

"Suppose he did?—and begad, I daresay he's right,—I never liked the look of the girl. To tell them that we have found them out this time won't prevent 'em trying it again. We don't know what their scheme is either. If it *is* a mutiny, half the ship's company may be in it. No, Captain Vickers, allow me to settle our course of action. You are aware that——"

"——That, by the King's Regulations, you are invested with full powers," interrupted Vickers. "Of course, I merely suggested—and I know nothing about the girl, except that she brought a good character from her last mistress—a Mrs. Crofton I think the name was. We were glad to get *anybody* to make a voyage like this."

"Look here," says Pine. "Let us double the sentries, and quietly get the men under arms. Let Miss Sarah do what she pleases, and *when* the mutiny breaks out, we will nip it in the bud; clap all the villains we get in irons, and hand them over to the authorities in Hobart Town."

"But surely, Mr. Pine, have you considered the probable loss of life? Prevention, you know——"

Pine turned round upon him with a grim expression. "Have *you* considered the safety of the ship, Captain Vickers? You know, or have heard of, the sort of things that take place in these mutinies. Have you thought of the fate of your own wife and child?"

Vickers shuddered.

"Be easy, sir," says old Pine; "I am acting for the best. You don't know what convicts are, or rather what the law has made 'em—*yet*——"

"Poor wretches!" says Vickers. "Kindness might do much for them. After all, they are our fellow-creatures."

"Yes," returned the other, "they are. But if you use that argument to them when they have taken the vessel, it won't avail you much. Let me manage, sir; and for God's sake, say nothing to anybody. Our lives may hang upon a word."

Vickers promised, and kept his promise so far as to chat cheerily with Blunt and Frere at dinner, only writing a brief note to his wife to tell her that, whatever she heard, she was not to stir from her cabin until he came to her.

According to the usual custom on board convict ships, the guards relieved each other every two hours, and at six p.m. the poop guard was removed to the quarter-deck, and the arms which, in the day-time, were disposed on the top of the arm-chest, were placed in an arm-rack constructed on the quarter-deck for that purpose. Trusting nothing to Frere—who, indeed, by Pine's advice, was, as we have seen, kept in ignorance of the whole matter—Vickers ordered all the men, save those who had been on guard during the day, to be under arms in the barrack, forbade communication with the upper deck, and placed as sentry at the barrack door his own servant, an old soldier, on whose fidelity he could thoroughly rely. He then doubled the guards, took the keys of the prison himself from the non-commissioned officer whose duty it was to keep them, and saw that the howitzer on the lower deck was loaded with grape. It was a quarter to seven when Pine and he took their station at the main hatchway, determined to watch until morning.

At about this time, any curious person looking through the window of Captain Blunt's cabin would have seen an unusual sight. That gallant commander was sitting on the bed-place, with a glass of rum and water in his hand, and the handsome maid of Mrs. Vickers seated on a stool by his side. At first glance it was perceptible that the captain was very drunk. He had drunk a larger quantity of wine than usual at dinner, in sheer delight at the approaching assignation, and now he was winking and blinking like an owl in the sunshine.

"Cuc-come, Sarah," he hiccuped. "You needn't be so—hic—proud, you know. I'm a plain s'lor, Srr'h. Ph'n'as Bub—blunt, commander of the Mal-Mal-Malabar. Giv'sh—kiss, Sarah."

Sarah got up and went to the door.

"Wotsh this? Goin'! Sarah, don't go." Hiccuping with love and rum, Blunt approached to take the kiss he coveted.

The ship's bell struck seven. Now or never was the time. Sarah Purfoy surrendered herself to his embrace, drew from her pocket the laudanum bottle, and passing her hand over his shoulder, poured half its contents into the glass.

"Think I'm—hic—drunk, do yer? Nun-not I, my wench."

"You will be if you drink much more. Come, finish that and be quiet, or I'll go away."

But she threw a provocation into her glance which belied her words, and which penetrated even the sodden intellect of poor Blunt. He stared at her with a fatuous smile of drunken admiration, hiccuped with much solemnity thrice and swallowed the contents of the glass at a gulp. The effect was almost instantaneous. He dropped the tumbler, lurched towards the woman at the door and then fell into his bunk, snoring like a grampus.

Some time later, Sarah Purfoy tapped at Frere's door. With a strong effort she dispelled the dizziness that almost overpowered her, and held herself erect. It would never do to break down now.

The door opened, and Maurice Frere drew her into the cabin. "So you have come?" he said.

"You see I have. But if I should be seen!"

"Seen? Nonsense! Who is to see you?"

"Captain Vickers, Doctor Pine, anybody."

"Not they. They've gone off down to Pine's cabin since dinner. They're all right."

Gone off to Pine's cabin! What was the cause of such an unusual proceeding? Surely they did not suspect? "What do they want there?" she asked.

"Who knows? I don't. Confound 'em," he added irritably, "what does it matter to us? We don't want them, do we, Sarah?"

She seemed to be listening for something, and did not reply. Her nervous system was wound up to the highest pitch of excitement. The success of the plot depended on the next five minutes.

"Look at me, can't you? What eyes you have! What hair!"

At that instant the report of a musket-shot broke the silence. The mutiny had begun!

The sound awoke the soldier to a sense of duty. He sprang to his feet, and disengaging the arms that clung about his neck, made for the door. The moment for which the convict's accomplice had waited, approached. She hung upon him with all her weight. Her long hair swept across his face, her warm breath was on his cheek, her dress exposed her round, smooth shoulder. Conquered, he had half turned back, when suddenly the rich crimson died away from her lips, and she uttered a sharp cry of pain.

The fever which she had struggled against for the past two days had attacked her at this supreme moment. Deathly pale, she reeled to the side of the cabin.

There was another shot, and a violent clashing of arms; and Frere, leaving the miserable woman to her fate, leapt out on to the deck.

The news of the fever had awoke in the convicts a fierce longing for the chance of escape which seemed permitted to freemen. "Let us go out!" they

EIGHT BELLS

said, each man speaking to his particular friend. "We are locked up here to die like sheep." Bye-and-bye, in some inexplicable way, it came to be understood that there was a conspiracy afloat, that they were to be released from their shambles, that some amongst them had been plotting their freedom. The 'tween decks held its foul breath in wondering anxiety.

By seven bells it was found that the prison was divided into three parties—the desperate, the timid, and the cautious. These three parties had arranged themselves in natural sequence. The mutineers, headed by Gabbett, Vetch, and the Moocher, were nearest to the door; the timid—boys, old men, innocent wretches condemned on circumstantial evidence, or rustics condemned to be turned into thieves for pulling a turnip—were at the farther end; and the prudent—that is to say, all the rest, ready to fight or fly, advance or retreat, assist the authorities or their companions, as the fortune of the day might direct—occupied the middle space. The mutineers proper numbered, perhaps, some thirty men, and of these thirty only half a dozen knew what was really about to be done.

Time passed, and the ship's bell had long since struck the half-hour, when Gabbett, who has been leaning with his back against the door, nudges Jemmy Vetch.

"Now, Jemmy," says he in a whisper. "Tell 'em!"

A silence ensues, which gradually spreads like a ripple over the surface of the crowd, reaching even the bunks at the further end.

"Gentlemen," says Mr. Vetch, "myself and my friends here are going to take the ship for you. Those who like to join us had better speak at once, for very soon they will not have the opportunity."

He pauses, and looks round with an impertinently confident air.

"You needn't be afraid," Mr. Vetch continues, "we have arranged it all for you. There are friends waiting for us outside, and the door will be open directly. All we want, gentlemen, is your wote and interest—"

"Gaffing agin!" interrupts the giant, angrily. "Come to business, carn't yer? Tell 'em they may like it or lump it, but we mean to have the ship, and them as refuses to join us we mean to chuck overboard. That's about the plain English of it!"

A grim murmur runs round, and somebody near Mr. Gabbett laughs a laugh of mingled ferocity and amusement, not reassuring to timid people.

"What about the sogers?" asks a voice from out the ranks of the cautious.

"D—— the sogers!" cries the Moocher. "They can but shoot yer, and that's as good as dyin' of typhus anyway!"

The right chord had been struck now, and with a stifled roar the prison admitted the truth of the sentiment. "Go on, old man!" cries Jemmy Vetch to the giant, rubbing his thin hands with glee. "They're all right!" And then, his quick ears catching the jingle of arms, he adds, "Stand by now for the door—one rush'll do it."

It was eight o'clock and the relief guard was coming from the after deck. The crowd of prisoners round the door held their breath to listen. "It's all planned," says Gabbett, in a low growl. "W'en the door hopens we rush, and we're in among the guard afore they know where they are. Drag 'em back into the prison, grab the h'arm rack, and it's all over."

"They're very quiet about it," says the Crow. "I hope it's all right."

"Stand from the door, Miles," says Pine's voice outside, in its usual calm accents.

The Crow was relieved. The tone was an ordinary one, and Miles was the soldier whom Sarah Purfoy had bribed not to fire. All had gone well.

The keys clashed and turned, and the men round the door draw back a little for their rush.

"NOW!" cried Jemmy Vetch, as the iron-plated oak swung back, and with the snarl of a wild boar, Gabbett hurled himself out of the prison.

The red line of light which glowed for an instant through the doorway was blotted out by a mass of figures. All the prison surged forward, and before the eye could wink, twenty of the most desperate were outside. It was as though a sea, breaking against a stone wall, had found some breach through which to pour its waters. Caution was forgotten; and those at the back, seeing Jemmy Vetch raised up on the crest of that human billow, responded to his grin of encouragement by rushing furiously forward.

Suddenly a horrible roar like that of a trapped wild beast was heard. The rushing torrent choked in the doorway, and from out the lantern glow into which the giant had rushed, a flash broke, followed by a groan, as the perfidious sentry fell back shot through the breast. The mass in the doorway hung irresolute, and then by sheer weight of pressure from behind burst forwards, and as it so burst, the heavy door crashed into its jambs, and the bolts were shot into their places.

All this took place so rapidly that the period of time that had elapsed between the opening and the shutting of the door could have been marked by the musket shot.

Another shot, and then confused cries, mingled with the clashing of arms, informed the imprisoned men that the ship had been alarmed. How would it go with their friends on deck? Would they succeed in overcoming the guards, or would they be beaten back? They would soon know; and in the hot dusk, straining their eyes to see each other, they waited for the issue. Suddenly the noises ceased, and a strange rumbling sound fell upon the ears of the listeners.

What had taken place?

This—the men pouring out of the darkness into the sudden glare of the lanterns, rushed, bewildered, across the deck. Miles, true to his promise, did not fire, but the next instant Vickers had snatched the firelock from him, and leaping into the stream, turned about and fired down towards the prison. The attack was more sudden than he had expected, but he did not lose his presence of mind. The shot would serve a double purpose. It would warn the men in the barrack, and perhaps check the rush by stopping up the doorway with a corpse. Amid the storm of hideous faces, his humanity vanished, and he aimed deliberately at the head of Mr. James Vetch; the shot, however, missed its mark, and killed the unhappy Miles.

Gabbett and his companions had by this time reached the foot of the companion ladder, there to encounter the cutlasses of the doubled guard gleaming redly in the glow of the lanterns. A glance up the hatchway showed the giant that the arms he had planned to seize were defended by ten firelocks, and that, behind the open doors of the partition which ran abaft the mizenmast, the remainder of the detachment stood to their arms. Even his dull intellect comprehended that their desperate project had failed, and that he had been betrayed. With a roar of despair, he turned to fight his way back, just in time to see the crowd in the gangway recoil from the flash of the musket fired by Vickers. The next instant, Pine and two soldiers, taking advantage of the momentary cessation of the press, shot the bolts, and secured the prison.

The mutineers were caught in a trap.

The narrow space between the barracks and the barricade was choked with struggling figures. Some twenty convicts, and half as many soldiers struck and stabbed at each other in the crowd. There was barely elbowroom, and attacked and attackers fought almost without knowing whom they struck. Gabbett tore a cutlass from a soldier, shook his huge head, and calling on the Moocher to follow, bounded up the ladder, determined to brave the fire of the watch. The Moocher, close at the giant's heels, flung himself upon the nearest soldier, and grasping his wrist, struggled for the cutlass. A brawny, bull-necked fellow next him dashed his clenched fist in the soldier's face, and the man, maddened by the blow, let go the cutlass, and drawing his pistol, shot his new assailant through the head. It was this second shot that had aroused Maurice Frere.

As the young lieutenant sprang out upon the deck, he saw by the position of the guard that others had been more mindful of the safety of the ship than he. There was, however, no time for explanation, for, as he reached the hatchway, he was met by the ascending giant, who uttered a hideous oath at the sight of this unexpected adversary, and, too close to strike him, locked him in his arms. The two men went down together. The guard on the quarter-deck dared not fire at the two bodies that, twined about each other, rolled across the deck, and for a moment Mr. Frere's cherished existence hung upon the slenderest thread imaginable.

The Moocher, spattered with the blood and brains of his unfortunate comrade, had already set his foot upon the lowest step of the ladder, when the cutlass was dashed from his hand by a blow from a clubbed firelock, and he was dragged roughly backwards. As he fell upon the deck, he saw the Crow spring out of the mass of prisoners who had been, an instant before, struggling with the guard, and, gaining the cleared space at the bottom of the ladder, hold up his hands, as though to shield himself from a blow. The confusion had become suddenly stilled, and upon the group before the barricade had fallen that mysterious silence which had perplexed the inmates of the prison.

They were not perplexed for long. The two soldiers who, with the assistance of Pine, had forced-to the door of the prison, rapidly unbolted that trap-door in the barricade, of which mention has been made in a previous chapter, and, at a signal from Vickers, three men ran the loaded howitzer from its sinister shelter near the break of the barrack berths, and training the deadly muzzle to a level with the opening in the barricade, stood ready to fire.

"Surrender!" cried Vickers. "Surrender, and give up your ringleaders, or I'll blow you to pieces!"

There was no tremor in his voice, and the mutineers perceived, with that acuteness which danger brings to the most stolid of brains that, did they hesitate an instant, he would keep his word. There was an awful moment of silence, broken only by a scurrying noise in the prison, as though a family of rats were scampering to the ship's side for shelter.

This scurrying noise was made by the convicts rushing to their berths to escape the threatened shower of grape; to the twenty desperadoes cowering before the muzzle of the howitzer it spoke more eloquently than words. The charm was broken; their comrades would refuse to join them.

The entrapped men looked up the hatchway, but the guard had already closed in upon it, and some of the ship's crew were peering down upon them. Escape was hopeless.

"One minute!" cried Vickers, confident that one second would be enough—"one minute to go quietly, or——"

"Surrender, mates, for God's sake!" shrieked some unknown wretch from out of the darkness of the prison. "Do you want to be the death of us?"

Jemmy Vetch raised his shrill tones. "We surrender," he said. "It's no use getting our brains blown out!" And raising his hands, he obeyed the motion of Vickers's finger, and led the way towards the barrack.

"Bring the irons forward, there!" shouted Vickers, hastening from his perilous position; and before the last man had filed past, the clink of hammers announced that the Crow had resumed those fetters which had been knocked off his dainty limbs a month previously in the Bay of Biscay.

In another moment the trap-door was closed, the howitzer rumbled back to its cleatings, and the prison breathed again.

In the meantime, a scene almost as exciting had taken place on the upper deck. Gabbett, with the blind fury which the consciousness of failure brings to such brute-like natures, had seized Frere by the throat, determined to put an end to at least one of his enemies. But desperate though he was, and with all the advantages of weight and strength upon his side, he found the young lieutenant a more formidable adversary than he had anticipated.

Maurice Frere was no coward. Brutal and selfish though he might be, his bitterest enemies had never accused him of lack of physical courage. Indeed, he had been—in the rollicking days of old—celebrated for the display of very opposite qualities. He was an amateur at manly sports. He rejoiced in his muscular strength, and, in many a tavern brawl and midnight riot of his own provoking, had proved the fallacy of the proverb which teaches that a bully is *always* a coward. In fact he was, as far as personal vigour went, a Gabbett with the education of a prize-fighter.

Taken by surprise as he was, Maurice Frere did not lose his presence of mind. The convict was so close upon him, that there was no time to strike; but, as he was forced backwards, he succeeded in crooking his knee round the thigh of his assailant and thrust one hand into his collar. Over and over they rolled, the bewildered sentry not daring to fire, until the ship's side brought them up with a violent jerk. Pressing with all the might of his muscles, Frere strove to resist the leverage which the giant was applying to turn him over, but he might as well have pushed against a stone wall. With his eyes protruding, and every sinew strained to its uttermost, he was slowly forced round, and he felt Gabbett releasing his grasp, in order to draw back and aim at him an effectual blow. Disengaging his left hand, Frere suddenly allowed himself to sink, and then drawing up his right knee, struck Gabbett beneath the jaw, and as the huge head was forced backward by the blow, dashed his fist into the brawny throat. Momentarily stunned, the giant was in an instant surrounded by sailors. Ere he could rise he was piniured by twenty hands.

Authority was almost instantaneously triumphant on the upper and lower decks. The mutiny was over.

DISCOVERIES AND CONFESSIONS

The ship, which had been rocking gently on a dull and silent sea, suddenly lurched. The shock was felt all through the vessel, and Pine, who had been watching the ironing of the last of the mutineers, at once divined its cause.

"Thank God!" he cried, "there's a breeze at last!" and as Gabbett, bleeding and bound, was dragged down the hatchway, the triumphant doctor hurried upon deck to find the *Malabar* plunging through the whitening water under the influence of a fifteen-knot breeze.

"Stand by to reef topsails! Away aloft, men, and furl the royals!" cries Best from the quarter-deck; and in the midst of the cheery confusion Maurice Frere briefly recapitulated what had taken place, taking care, however, to pass over his own dereliction of duty as rapidly as possible.

Pine knit his brows. "Do you think that she was in the plot?" he asked.

"Not she!" says Frere—eager to avert inquiry. "How should she be? Plot! She's sickening of fever, or I'm much mistaken."

Sure enough, on opening the door of the cabin, they found Sarah Purfoy lying where she had fallen a quarter of an hour before. The clashing of cutlasses and the firing of muskets had not roused her.

"We must make a sick-bay somewhere," says Pine, looking at the senseless figure with no kindly glance; "though I don't think she's likely to be very bad. Confound her! I believe that she's the cause of all this. I'll find out, too, before many hours are over; for I've told those fellows that unless they confess all about it before to-morrow morning, I'll get them six dozen apiece the day after we anchor in Hobart Town. I've a great mind to do it before we get there. Take her head, Frere, and we'll get her into her cabin before Vickers comes up. What a fool you are, to be sure! I knew what it would be with women aboard ship. Chances are, you've caught the fever, though this breeze will help to blow it out of us, please God. That old jackass, Blunt, too!—he ought to be ashamed of himself, at his age!"

"What do you mean?" asked Frere. "What has Blunt to say about her?"

"Oh, he was smitten, too," returned Pine. "Like a good many more, in fact."

"A good many more!" repeated the other, with a pretence of carelessness.

"Yes!" laughed Pine. "Why, man, she was making eyes at every man in the ship! I caught her kissing a soldier once."

Maurice Frere's cheeks grew hot. The experienced profligate had been taken in, deceived, perhaps laughed at. All the time, the black-eyed maid had been twisting him round her finger, and perhaps imitating his love-making for the gratification of her soldier-lover. It was not a pleasant thought; and yet, strange to say, the idea of Sarah's treachery did not make him dislike her. There is a sort of love which thrives under ill-treatment. Nevertheless, he cursed with some appearance of disgust.

Vickers met them at the door. "Pine, Blunt has the fever. Mr. Best found him in his cabin groaning. Come and look at him."

The commander of the *Malabar* was lying on his bunk in the betwisted condition into which men who sleep in their clothes contrive to get themselves. The doctor shook him, bent down over him, and then loosened his collar. "He's not sick," he said; "he's drunk! Blunt! wake up! Blunt!"

But the mass refused to move.

"Hallo!" says Pine, smelling at the broken tumbler, "what's this? Smells queer. Laudanum! By George, he's been hocussed!"

"Nonsense!"

"I see it," slapping his thigh. "It's that infernal woman! She's drugged him, and meant to do the same for"—(Frere gave him an imploring look)—"for anybody else who would be fool enough to let her do it. Dawes was right, sir. She's in it; I'll swear she's in it."

"What! my wife's maid? Nonsense!" said Vickers.

"Nonsense!" echoed Frere.

"It's no nonsense. That soldier who was shot—what's his name?—Miles, he—oh, it doesn't matter. It's all over now."

"The men will confess before morning," says Vickers, "and we'll see." And he went off to his wife's cabin.

His wife opened the door for him. She had been sitting by the child's bedside, listening to the firing, and waiting for her husband's return without a murmur. Flirt, fribble, and shrew as she was, Julia Vickers had displayed, in times of emergency, that glowing courage which women of her nature at times possess. Though she would shudder at a frog, and scream at a spider, she could sit through a quarter of an hour of such suspense as she had just undergone with as much courage as if she had been the strongest-minded woman that ever denied her sex. "Is it all over?" she asked.

"Yes, thank God!" said Vickers, pausing on the threshold. "All is safe now, though we had a narrow escape. How's Sylvia?"

The child was lying on the bed with her fair hair scattered over the pillow, and her tiny hands moving restlessly to and fro.

"A little better, though she has been talking a good deal."

The red lips parted, and the blue eyes stared vacantly around. The sound of her father's voice seemed to have roused her, for she began to speak a little prayer: "God bless papa and mamma, and God bless me, and make me good girl, for Jesus Christ's sake, our Lord. Amen."

The sound of the child's prayer had something awesome in it, and John Vickers felt his eyes fill with unwonted tears. The contrast was curious. From out of the midst of that desolate ocean—in a fever-smitten prison ship, leagues from land, surrounded by ruffians, thieves, and murderers—the baby voice of an innocent child called confidently on Heaven.

Two hours afterwards—as the *Malabar* plunged cheerily through the rippling water—the mutineers, by their spokesman, Mr. James Vetch, confessed.

"They were very sorry, and hoped that their breach of discipline would be forgiven. It was the fear of the typhus which had driven them to it. They had no accomplices either in the prison or out of it, but they felt it but right to say that the man who had planned the mutiny was Rufus Dawes."

Vetch had guessed from whom the information which had led to the failure of the plot had been derived, and this was his characteristic revenge.

Extracted from the *Hobart Town Courier* of the 12th November, 1827:—

A NEWSPAPER PARAGRAPH

"The examination of the prisoners who were concerned in the attempt upon the Malabar was concluded on Tuesday last. The four ringleaders, Dawes, Gabbett, Vetch, and Sanders, were condemned to death; but we understand that, by the clemency of his Excellency the Governor, their sentence has been commuted to six years at the penal settlement of Macquarie Harbour."

BOOK TWO
Macquarie Harbour~1833

VAN DIEMEN'S LAND

About a hundred and seventy miles to the south of the mill-pond known as Port Phillip Bay lies Van Diemen's Land, fertile, fair, and rich, rained upon by the genial showers from the clouds which, attracted by the Frenchman's Cap, Wyld's Crag, or the lofty peaks of the Wellington and Dromedary range, pour down upon the sheltered valleys their fertilising streams. No parching hot wind—the torment of the continent—blows upon her crops and corn. The cool south breeze ripples gently the blue waters of the Derwent, and fans the curtains of the open windows of the city which nestles in the broad shadow of Mount Wellington. The hot wind, born amid the burning sand of the interior of the vast Australian continent, sweeps over the scorched plains to sink, exhausted with its journey across Bass Strait, at the feet of the terraced slopes of Launceston.

The climate of Van Diemen's Land is one of the loveliest in the world. Launceston is warm, sheltered, and moist; and Hobart Town, protected by Bruny Island and its archipelago of D'Entrecasteaux Channel and Storm Bay from the violence of the southern breakers, preserves the mean temperature of Smyrna; whilst the district between these two towns spreads in a succession of beautiful valleys, through which glide clear and sparkling streams. But on the western coast, from the steeple-rocks of Cape Grim to the scrub-encircled barrenness of Sandy Cape, and the frowning entrance to Macquarie Harbour, the nature of the country entirely changes. Along that iron-bound shore, all is bleak and cheerless. Upon that dreary beach the rollers of the southern sea complete their circuit of the globe, and the storm that has devastated the Cape, and united in its eastern course with the icy blasts which sweep northward from the southern pole, crashes unchecked upon the Huon pine forests, and lashes the grim front of Mount Direction. Navigation is dangerous, and the entrance to the "Hell's Gates" of Macquarie Harbour—at the time of which we are writing (1833), in the height of its ill-fame as a convict settlement—is only to be attempted in calm weather. The sea-line is marked with wrecks. The sunken rocks are dismally named after the vessels they have destroyed. The air is chill and moist, and noxious weeds cling close to the humid, spongy ground. All around breathes desolation; on the face of nature is stamped a perpetual frown. The ship-wrecked sailor, crawling painfully to the summit of basalt cliffs, or the ironed convict, dragging his tree trunk to the edge of some beetling *plateau*, looks down upon a sea of fog, through which rise mountain-tops like islands; or sees through the biting sleet a desert of scrub and crag rolling to the feet of Mount Heemskirk and Mount Zeehan—crouched like two sentinel lions keeping watch over the seaboard.

THE SOLITARY OF "HELL'S GATES"

"Hell's gates," formed by a rocky point which runs abruptly northward, almost touches, on its eastern side, a projecting arm of land which guards the entrance to King's River. In the middle of the gates is a natural bolt—that is to say, an island—which, lying on a sandy bar in the very jaws of the current, creates a double whirlpool, almost impossible to pass in the smoothest weather.

Once through the gates, the convict, chained on the deck of the inward-bound vessel, sees in front of him the bald cone of the Frenchman's Cap, piercing the moist air at a height of five thousand feet; while, gloomed by overhanging rocks, and shadowed by gigantic forests, the black sides of the basin narrow to the mouth of the Gordon. The turbulent stream is the colour of indigo, and, being fed by numerous rivulets which ooze through masses of decaying vegetable matter, is of so poisonous a nature that it is not only undrinkable, but kills the fish, which in stormy weather are driven in from the sea. As may be imagined, the furious tempests which beat upon this exposed coast create a strong surf-line. After a few days of north-west wind, the waters of the Gordon will be found salt for twelve miles up from the bar.

The headquarters of the settlement were placed on an island not far from the mouth of this inhospitable river, called Sarah Island. Though now the whole place is desolate, and a few rotting posts and logs alone remain, in the year 1833 the buildings were numerous and extensive. On Philip's Island, on the north side of the harbour, was a small farm, where vegetables were grown for the use of the officers of the establishment; and on Sarah Island were sawpits, forges, dockyards, gaol, guard-house, barracks, and jetty. The military force numbered about sixty men, who, with convict-warders and constables, took charge of more than three hundred and fifty prisoners. These miserable wretches were employed in the most degrading labour. No beast of burden was allowed on the settlement; all the pulling and dragging was done by human beings. About one hundred "good-conduct" men were allowed the lighter toil of dragging timber to the wharf, to assist in shipbuilding; the others cut down the trees that fringed the mainland, and carried them on their shoulders to the water's edge. The denseness of the scrub and bush rendered it necessary for a "roadway" to be first constructed; and the trunks of trees, stripped of their branches, were rolled together in this roadway, until a "slide" was made, down which the heavier logs could be shunted towards the harbour. The timber thus obtained was made into rafts, and floated to the sheds, or arranged for transportation to Hobart Town.

The convicts were lodged in barracks flanked by a two-storied prison, whose "cells" were the terror of the most hardened. Each morning they received their breakfast of porridge, water, and salt, and then rowed under the protection of their guard, to the wood-cutting stations, where they worked without food, until night. The launching and hewing of the timber compelled them to work up to their waists in water. Many of them were heavily ironed. Those who died were buried on a little plot of ground, called Halliday's Island (from the name of the first man buried there), and a plank stuck into the earth, and carved with the initials of the deceased, was the only monument vouchsafed him.

Sarah Island, situated at the south-east corner of the harbour, is long and low. The commandant's house was built in the centre, having the chaplain's house and barracks between it and the gaol. The hospital was on the west shore, and in a line with it lay the two penitentiaries. Lines of lofty palisades, built for the purpose of warding off the terrific blasts of wind, ran round the settlement, giving it the appearance of a fortified town. The little town was set, as it were, in defiance of Nature, at the very extreme of civilisation, and its inhabitants maintained perpetual warfare with the winds and waves.

But the gaol of Sarah Island was not the only prison in this desolate region.

At a little distance from the mainland is a rock, over the rude side of which the waves dash in rough weather. On the evening of the 3rd December, 1833, as the sun was sinking behind the tree-tops on the left side of the harbour, the figure of a man appeared on the top of this rock. He was clad in the coarse garb of a convict, and wore round his ankles two iron rings, connected by a short and heavy chain. To the middle of this chain a leathern strap was attached, which, splitting in the form of a T, buckled round his waist and pulled the chain high enough to prevent him from stumbling over it as he walked. His head was bare, and his coarse, blue-striped shirt, open at the throat, displayed an embrowned and muscular neck. Emerging from out of a sort of cell, or den, contrived by nature or art in the side of the cliff, he put on a scanty fire, which burned between two hollowed rocks, an iron pot, which contained water. It was evident that the cave was at once his storehouse and larder, and that the two hollowed rocks formed his kitchen.

Having thus made preparations for supper, he ascended a pathway which led to the highest point of the rock. His fetters compelled him to take short steps, and, as he walked, he winced as though the iron bit him. A handkerchief or strip of cloth was twisted round his left ankle, on which the circlet had chafed a sore. Slowly he gained his destination, and flinging himself on the ground, gazed around him. The afternoon had been stormy, and the rays of the setting sun shone redly on the turbid waters of the bay. On the right lay Sarah Island; on the left the bleak shore of the opposite coast, and the tall peak of the Frenchman's Cap. Below him appeared the only sign of life. A brig was being towed up the harbour by two convict-manned boats.

Sinking his chin upon his hand, the solitary man fixed his eyes on the incoming vessel, and immersed himself in moody thought. More than an hour passed, yet he did not move. The ship anchored, the boats detached themselves from her side, the sun sank, and the bay was plunged in gloom. Lights began to twinkle along the shore of the settlement. The little fire died, and the water in the iron pot grew cold; yet the watcher on the rock did not stir. With his eyes staring into the gloom, he lay as motionless as the rock on which he had stretched himself.

The solitary man was Rufus Dawes.

In the house of Major Vickers, Commandant of Macquarie Harbour, there was, on this evening of December 3rd, unusual gaiety.

A SOCIAL EVENING

Lieutenant Maurice Frere, late in command at Maria Island, had unexpectedly come down with news from headquarters. The *Ladybird*, Government schooner, visited the settlement on ordinary occasions twice a year, and such visits were looked forward to with no little eagerness by the settlers. To the convicts the arrival of the *Ladybird* meant arrival of new faces, intelligence of old comrades, news of how the world from which they were exiled was progressing. When the *Ladybird* arrived, the toil-worn felons felt that they were yet human, that there was a world beyond these gloomy forests where men, like themselves, smoked, and drank, and laughed, and were Free. To the Commandant and the "free men" this messenger from the outer life was scarcely less welcome. There was not a man on the island who did not feel his heart grow heavier when her white sails disappeared behind the shoulder of the hill.

On the present occasion business of more than ordinary importance had procured for Major Vickers this pleasurable excitement. It had been resolved by Governor Arthur that the convict establishment should be broken up. A succession of murders and attempted escapes had called public attention to the place, and its distance from Hobart Town rendered it inconvenient and expensive. Arthur had fixed upon Tasman's Peninsula, to the east of Hobart Town, as a future convict depôt, and naming it Port Arthur, in honour of himself, had sent down Lieutenant Maurice Frere with instructions for Vickers to convey the prisoners of Macquarie Harbour thither.

In order to understand the magnitude and meaning of such an order as that with which Lieutenant Frere was entrusted, we must glance at the social condition of the penal colony at this period of its history.

Nine years before, Colonel Arthur, late Governor of Honduras, had arrived at a most critical moment. The former Governor, Colonel Sorrell, was a man of genial temperament, but profligate in his private life; and, encouraged by his example, his officers violated all rules of social decency. It was common for an officer to openly keep a female convict as his mistress. Not only would compliance purchase comforts, but strange stories were afloat concerning the persecution of women who dared to choose their own lovers. To put down this profligacy was the first care of Arthur; and in enforcing a severe attention to etiquette and outward respectability, he perhaps erred on the side of virtue. Honest, brave, and high-minded, he was also penurious and cold, and the ostentatious good humour of the colonist dashed itself in vain against his polite indifference. In opposition to this official society created by Governor Arthur was that of the free settlers and ticket-of-leave men. The latter were more numerous than one would be apt to suppose. On the 2nd November, 1829, thirty-eight free pardons and fifty-six conditional pardons appeared on the books; and the number of persons holding tickets-of-leave, on the 26th of September the same year, was seven hundred and forty-five.

Of the social condition of these people at this time it is impossible to speak without astonishment. According to the recorded testimony of many respectable persons—Government officials, military officers, and free settlers—the profligacy of the settlers was notorious. Drunkenness was a prevailing vice. On Sundays, men and women might be observed standing round the public-house doors, waiting for the expiration of the hours of public worship, in order to continue their carousing. As for the condition of the prisoner population, that, indeed, is indescribable. Notwithstanding the severe punishment for sly grog-selling, it was carried on to a large extent. Men and woman were found intoxicated together and a bottle of brandy was considered to be cheaply bought at the price of twenty lashes. In the factory—a prison for females—the vilest abuses were committed, while the infamies perpetrated in chain gangs and penal settlements were of too horrible a nature to be more than hinted at here. All that the vilest of human creatures could invent and practise, was in this unhappy country invented and practised without restraint.

Seven classes of criminals were established in 1826, when the new barracks for prisoners at Hobart Town were finished. The first class were allowed to sleep out of barracks, and to work for themselves on Saturday; the second had only the last-named indulgence; the third were only allowed Saturday afternoon; the fourth and fifth were "refractory and disorderly characters—to work in irons"; the sixth were "men of the most degraded and incorrigible character—to be worked in irons, and kept entirely separate from the other prisoners"; while the seventh were the refuse of this refuse—the murderers, bandits, and villains, whom neither chain nor lash could tame. They were regarded as socially dead, and shipped to Hell's Gates, or Maria Island.

Hell's Gates was the most dreaded of all these houses of bondage. The discipline at the place was so severe, and the life so terrible, that prisoners would risk all to escape from it. In one year, of eighty-five deaths there, only thirty were from natural causes; of the remaining dead, twenty-seven were drowned, eight killed accidentally, three shot by the soldiers, and twelve murdered by their comrades. During the ten years of its existence, one hundred and twelve men escaped, out of whom sixty-two only were found—dead. The prisoners killed themselves to avoid living any longer, and if so fortunate as to penetrate the desert of scrub, heath, and swamp, which lay between their prison and the settled districts, preferred death to recapture. Successfully to transport the remnant of this desperate band of doubly-convicted felons to Arthur's new prison, was the mission of Maurice Frere.

He was sitting by the empty fire-place, entertaining the company with his usual indifferent air. The six years that had passed since his departure from England had given him a sturdier frame and a fuller face, but in demeanour he was little changed. His five years' residence at Maria Island had increased that brutality and overbearing confidence for which he had been always remarkable, but it had also given him an assured air of authority, which covered the more unpleasant features of his character. He was detested by the prisoners—as he said, "it was a word and a blow with him"—but, among his superiors, he passed for an officer, honest and painstaking, though somewhat bluff and severe.

"Well, Mrs. Vickers," he said, taking a cup of tea from that lady, "I suppose you won't be sorry to get away from this place, eh? Trouble you for the toast, Vickers!"

"No, indeed," says poor Mrs. Vickers, with the old girlishness over-shadowed by six years; "I shall be only too glad. A dreadful place! My dear Mr. Frere, you've no idea of it; I wanted to send Sylvia to Hobart Town, but John would not let her go."

"By the way, how *is* Miss Sylvia?" asked Frere, with the patronising air which men of his stamp adopt when they speak of children.

"Not very well, I'm sorry to say," returned Vickers. "You see, it's lonely for her here. There are no children of her own age, with the exception of the pilot's little girl, and she cannot associate with *her*. But I did not like to leave her behind, and endeavoured to teach her myself."

"Hum! There was a governess, or something, was there not?" said Frere, staring into his tea-cup. "That maid, you know—what was her name?"

"Miss Purfoy," said Mrs. Vickers, a little gravely. "Yes, poor thing! A sad story, Mr. Frere."

Frere's eye twinkled.

"Indeed! I left, you know, shortly after the trial of the mutineers, and never heard the full particulars." He spoke carelessly, but he awaited the reply with keen curiosity.

"A sad story!" repeated Mrs. Vickers. "She was the wife of that wretched man, Rex, and came out as my maid in order to be near him. She would never tell me her history, poor thing, though all through the dreadful accusations made by that horrid doctor—I *always* disliked that man—I begged her almost on my knees. You know how she nursed Sylvia. Really a most superior creature. I think she must have been a governess."

Mr. Frere raised his eyebrows abruptly, as though he would say, *Governess! Of course. Happy suggestion. Wonder it never occurred to me before.* "However, her conduct was most exemplary—really *most* exemplary—and during the six months we were in Hobart Town she taught little Sylvia a great deal. Then she came into a little legacy from an old aunt in England." Mr. Frere gave a little bluff nod, meaning thereby, *Old aunt! Exactly. Just what might have been expected.* "And left my service. She took a little cottage on the New Town road, and Rex was assigned to her as her servant."

"I see. The old dodge!" says Frere, flushing a little. "Well?"

"Well, the wretched man tried to escape, and she helped him. He was to get to Launceston, and so on board a vessel to Sydney; but they took the unhappy creature, and he was sent down here. She was only fined, but it ruined her."

"Ruined her?"

"Well, you see, only a few people knew of her relationship to Rex, and she was rather respected. Of course, when it became known, what with that dreadful trial and the horrible assertions of Dr. Pine, she was quite left alone. She wanted me to bring her down here to teach Sylvia; but John thought that it was only to be near her husband, and wouldn't allow it."

"Of course it was," said Vickers, rising. "Frere, if you'd like to smoke, we'll go on the verandah.—She will never be satisfied until she gets that scoundrel free."

"He's a bad lot, then?" says Frere, opening the glass window, and leading the way to the sandy garden. "You will excuse me, Mrs. Vickers—I have become quite a slave to my pipe. It's wife and child to me!"

"Oh, a very bad lot," returned Vickers, "ready for any villainy. I count him one of the worst men we have."

"Why don't you flog him?" says Frere, lighting his pipe. "By George, I cut the hides off my fellows if they show any nonsense!"

"Well," says Vickers, "I don't care about too much cat myself. Barton, who was here before me, flogged tremendously, but I don't think it did any good. I don't flog more than a man a week, as a rule, and never more than fifty lashes. They're getting quieter now. Then we iron, and dumb-cells, and maroon them."

"Do what?"

"Give them solitary confinement on Grummet Island. When a man gets very bad, we clap him into a boat with a week's provisions, and pull him over to Grummet. There are cells cut in the rock, you see, and the fellow lives there by himself for a month or so. It tames them wonderfully."

"Does it?" said Frere. "By Jove! it's a capital notion."

"I've a fellow there now," says Vickers; "Dawes. You remember him, of course—the ringleader of the mutiny in the *Malabar*. A dreadful ruffian. He was most violent the first year I was here. When I came, in—when was it?—in '29, he'd made a sort of petition to be sent back to the settlement. Said that he was innocent of the mutiny, and that the accusation against him was false."

"The old dodge," said Frere again.

"Of course, I couldn't let him go; but I took him out of the chain-gang, and put him on the *Osprey*. You saw her in the dock as you came in. He worked for some time very well, and then tried to bolt."

"The old trick. Ha! Don't I know it?" says Mr. Frere.

"Well, we caught him, gave him fifty, and sent him to the chain-gang, cutting timber. Then we put him into the boats, but he quarrelled with the coxswain, and we took him back to the timber-rafts. About six weeks ago he made another attempt—together with Gabbett, the man who nearly killed you—but his leg was chafed with the irons, and we took him. Gabbett and three more, however, got away."

"Haven't you found 'em?" asked Frere, puffing at his pipe.

"No. But they'll come to the same fate as the rest," said Vickers, with a sort of dismal pride. "No man ever escaped from Macquarie Harbour."

"When do you think you will be ready to move?" asked Frere.

"As soon as you wish. I don't want to stop a moment longer than I can help. It is a terrible life this."

"Do you think so?" asked his companion, in unaffected surprise. "*I* like it. It's dull, certainly, but there is a sort of satisfaction to me, by George, in keeping the scoundrels in order. I like to see the fellows' eyes glint at you as you walk past 'em!" and he laughed grimly, as though the hate he inspired was a thing to be proud of.

"How shall we go?" asked Vickers. "Have you got any instructions?"

"No," says Frere; "it's all left to you. Get 'em up the best way you can, Arthur said, and pack 'em off to the new peninsula."

"It's a dangerous thing taking so many at once," suggested Vickers.

"Not a bit. Batten 'em down and keep the sentries awake, and they won't do any harm."

"But Mrs. Vickers and the child?"

"I've thought of that. You take the *Ladybird* with the prisoners, and leave me to bring up Mrs. Vickers in the *Osprey*."

"Indeed, that's the best way, I think. I don't like the notion of having Sylvia among those wretches, and yet I don't like to leave her."

"Well," says Frere, confident of his own ability to accomplish anything he might undertake, "*I'll* take the *Ladybird*, and *you* the *Osprey*. Bring up Mrs. Vickers yourself."

"No, no," said Vickers, "that won't do. By the King's Regulations——"

"All right," interjected Frere. " '*The officer commanding is obliged to place himself in charge*'—all right, my dear sir. I've no objection."

"It was Sylvia that I was thinking of," said Vickers.

"Well, then," cries the other, as a door opened, and a little white figure came through into the broad verandah. "Here she is! Ask her yourself. Well, Miss Sylvia, will you come and shake hands with an old friend?"

The bright-haired baby of the *Malabar* had become a child of some eleven years old, and as she stood in her simple white dress in the glow of the lamplight, even the unæsthetic mind of Mr. Frere was struck by her beauty. Her eyes were as bright and as blue as ever, her little figure as upright and supple as a willow rod. Her innocent, delicate face was framed in a nimbus of that fine golden hair, each separate thread shining, with which the dreaming painters of the middle ages glorified their angels.

"Come and give me a kiss, Miss Sylvia!" cries Frere. "You haven't forgotten me, have you?"

But the child surveyed Mr. Frere from head to foot with the charming impertinence of childhood, and then, shaking her lovely hair, inquired—"Who is he, papa?"

"Mr. Frere, darling. Don't you remember kind Mr. Frere, who used to play ball with you on board ship?"

"I remember you," said Sylvia, tossing her head; "but you were nicer then than you are now. I don't like you at all."

"You *don't* remember me," said Frere, affecting to be intensely at his ease. "I am sure you don't. What is my name?"

"Lieutenant Frere. You knocked down a prisoner who picked up my ball. I don't like you."

"You're a forward young lady, upon my word!" says Frere with a great laugh. "Ha! so I did, begad, I recollect now."

"He's here now, isn't he, papa?" went on Sylvia. "Rufus Dawes is his name, and he's always in trouble. Poor fellow, I'm sorry for him. Danny says he's queer in his mind."

"And who's Danny?" asked Frere, with another laugh.

"The cook," replied Vickers. "An old man I took out of hospital. Sylvia, you talk too much with the prisoners."

"But Danny is not prisoner, papa—he's a cook," says Sylvia, "and he's a clever man. He told me all about London, where the Lord Mayor rides in a glass coach, and all the work is done by free men. I should like to see London, papa!"

"So would Mr. Danny, I have no doubt," said Frere.

"No—he didn't say that. But he wants to see his old mother, he says. Fancy Danny's mother! What an ugly old woman she must be! He says he'll see her in heaven. Will he, papa?"

"I hope so, my dear."

"Will Danny wear his yellow jacket in heaven, Papa, or go as a free man?" Frere burst into a roar at this.

"You're an impertinent fellow, sir!" cried Sylvia, her bright eyes flashing. "How dare you laugh at me? Oh, if I was papa, I'd give you half an hour at the triangles!" Crimson with rage, the spoilt little beauty ran from the verandah.

Vickers looked grave, but Frere felt constrained to laugh.

" 'Pon honour, that's good! The little vixen!—Half an hour at the triangles! Ha-ha!"

"She is a strange child," said Vickers, "but you mustn't mind her. She is neither girl nor woman, you see; and her education has been neglected.

What can you expect from a child bred in a convict settlement?"

"My dear sir," says the other, "she's delightful!"

"She must have three or four years at a good finishing school at Sydney. Please God, I will give them to her when we go back—or send her to England if I can."

Just then some one came up the garden path and saluted.

"What is it, Troke?"

"Prisoner given himself up, sir."

"Which of them?"

"Gabbett. He came back to-night."

"Alone?"

"Yes, sir. The rest have died—he says."

"What's that?" asked Frere, suddenly interested.

"The bolter I was telling you about—Gabbett, your old friend. He's returned."

"How long has he been out?"

"Nigh six weeks, sir," said the constable, touching his cap.

"Gad, he's had a narrow squeak for it, I'll be bound. I should like to see him."

"He's down at the sheds," said Troke—a "good conduct" burglar. "You can see him at once, gentlemen, if you like."

"What do you say, Vickers?"

"Oh, by all means."

It was not far to the sheds, and after a few minutes' walk through the wooden palisades they reached a long stone building. Passing between two

THE BOLTER

rows of warders, Troke and the two officers reached a sort of ante-room to the gaol, containing a pine-log stretcher, on which a mass of something was lying. On a stool by the side of this stretcher sat a man, in the grey dress (worn as a contrast to the yellow livery) of "good conduct" prisoners. This man held between his knees a basin containing gruel, and was endeavouring to feed the mass on the pine logs.

"Won't he eat, Steve?" asked Vickers.

And at the sound of the Commandant's voice, Steve arose.

"Dunno what's wrong wi' 'un, sir," he said, jerking up a finger to his forehead. "He seems jest muggy-pated. I can't do nothin' wi' 'un."

"Gabbett!"

Troke, considerately alive to the wishes of his superior officers, dragged the mass into a sitting posture, and woke it.

Gabbett—for it was he—passed one great hand over his face, and scowled, bewildered, at his visitors.

"Well, Gabbett," says Vickers, "you're back again. When will you learn sense, eh? Where are your mates?"

"Dead," says Gabbett.

"All three of them?"

"Ay."

"And how did *you* get back?"

Gabbett, in eloquent silence, held out a bleeding foot.

"We found him on the point, sir," said Troke, jauntily explaining, "and brought him across in the boat. We gave him a basin of gruel, but he didn't seem hungry."

"Are you hungry?"

"Yes."

"Why don't you eat your gruel?"

Gabbett curled his great lips.

"Ain't yer got nuffin better nor that to flog a man on? Ugh! yer a mean lot! Wot's it to be this time, Major? Fifty?"

"I'd flog his soul out of his body," said Frere, "if he spoke to *me* like that!"

Troke and the others, hearing the statement, conceived an instant respect for the new comer. He looked as if he would keep his word.

The giant raised his great head and looked at the speaker, but saw only a strange face—a visitor perhaps. "You may flog, and welcome, master," said he, "if you'll give me a fig o' tibbacky." Frere laughed. The indifference of the rejoinder suited his humour, and, with a glance at Vickers, he took a small piece of cavendish from the pocket of his pea-jacket, and gave it to the convict. Gabbett snatched it as a cur snatches at a bone, and thrust it whole into his mouth.

"How many mates had he?" asked Maurice.

"Three, sir."

"Three, eh? Well, give him thirty lashes, Vickers."

"And if I ha' had three more," growled Gabbett, mumbling at his tobacco, "you wouldn't ha' had the chance."

"What does he say?"

But Troke, shrinking, as it seemed, slightly from the prisoner, said he had not heard either. The wretch himself, munching hard at his tobacco, lapsed into his restless silence, and it was as though he had never spoken.

As he sat there gloomily chewing, he was a spectacle to shudder at. Not so much on account of his tattered and filthy rags, his hare-lip, his torn and bleeding feet and his huge, wasted frame, but also because, in his slavering mouth and his bloodshot, wandering eyes, there lurked a hint of some terror more awful than the terror of starvation—a memory of some tragedy played out in the gloomy depths of that forest which had vomited him forth again.

"Come," said Vickers, "let us go back. I shall have to flog him again, I suppose. Oh, this place! No wonder they call it 'Hell's Gates'. " He sighed as they went out. "I sometimes wonder if kindness would not succeed better than the chain and the cat."

"No, no," laughed Frere. "There's only one way with these fellows. Keep 'em down, sir. If they won't work, flog 'em until they will. If they work well—why, a taste of the cat now and then keeps 'em in mind of what they may expect if they get lazy."

They had reached the verandah now. The rising moon shone softly on the bay beneath them, and touched with her white light the summit of the Grummet Rock.

"That is the general opinion, I know," returned Vickers. "But consider the life they lead. Good God! Since I have been here, ten prisoners have drowned themselves from yonder rock, rather than live on in their misery. Only three weeks ago, two men out wood-cutting, having had words with the overseer, shook hands with the gang, and then, hand in hand, flung themselves over the cliff. It's horrible to think of!"

"They shouldn't get sent here," said practical Frere. "They knew what to expect. Serve 'em right."

"But imagine an innocent man condemned to this place!"

"I can't," said Frere, with a laugh. "Innocent man, be hanged! They're all innocent, if you'd believe their stories. Hallo! what's that red light there?"

"Dawes's fire on Grummet Rock," says Vickers, going in. "Come in and have some brandy-and-water, and we'll shut the door on the place."

"Well," said Frere, as they went in, "you'll be out of it soon. You can be ready to start by the end of the month, and I'll bring on Mrs. Vickers

SYLVIA afterwards."

"What is that you say about me?" asked sprightly Mrs. Vickers. "You wicked men, leaving me alone all this time!"

"Mr. Frere has kindly offered to bring you and Sylvia after us in the *Osprey*."

"You are most kind, Mr. Frere," says Mrs. Vickers, a recollection of her flirtation with a certain young lieutenant, six years before, tinging her cheeks. "It is really most considerate of you. Won't it be nice, Sylvia, to go with Mr. Frere and mamma to Hobart Town?"

"Mr. Frere," says Sylvia, coming up to him, "I am very sorry for what I said just now. Will you forgive me?"

She asked the question in such a prim old-fashioned way that Frere was again inclined to laugh.

"Of course I'll forgive you, my dear," he said. "You didn't mean it, I know."

"Oh, but I *did* mean it, and that's why I'm sorry. I am a very naughty girl sometimes, though you wouldn't think so, especially with Roman history. I don't think the Romans were half as brave as the Carthaginians; do you, Mr. Frere?"

Maurice, somewhat staggered by this question, could only ask, "Why not?"

"Well, I don't like them half so well myself," says Sylvia, with feminine disdain of reason. "They always had so many soldiers, though the others *were* so cruel when they conquered."

"Were they?" says Frere.

"Were they! Didn't they cut poor Regulus's eyelids off, and roll him down hill in a barrel full of nails? What do you call that, I should like to know?"

"You are a great scholar, Miss Sylvia," Mr. Frere remarked, with a consciousness that this self-possessed girl was rapidly taking him out of his depth. "Are you fond of reading?"

"Oh, yes! I have read 'Paul and Virginia', 'Paradise Lost', 'Shakespeare's Plays', 'Robinson Crusoe', 'Blair's Sermons', 'The Tasmanian Almanack', 'The Book of Beauty', and 'Tom Jones'."

"A somewhat miscellaneous collection, I fear," said Mrs. Vickers, with a sickly smile, "but our little library is necessarily limited, and I am not a great reader. John, my dear, Mr. Frere would like another glass of brandy-and-water. Sylvia, my love, say good-night to Mr. Frere, and retire."

"Good night, Miss Sylvia. Will you give me a kiss?"

"No!"

"Sylvia, don't be rude!"

"I'm not rude," cries Sylvia, indignant at the way in which her literary confidence had been received. "*He's* rude! *Kiss* you indeed! My goodness gracious!"

"Won't you, you little beauty?" cried Frere. "Then I must kiss *you!*"

To his astonishment, Sylvia, finding herself kissed despite herself, lifted up her tiny fist and struck him on the cheek with all her force.

The blow was so sudden that Maurice nearly slipped into his native coarseness, and rapped out an oath.

"My *dear* Sylvia!" cried Vickers, in tones of grave reproof.

But Frere laughed, caught the child's hands, and kissed her again and again, despite her struggles. "There!" he said triumphantly. "You got nothing by *that*, you see."

Vickers rose with annoyance visible on his face, to draw the child away; and as he did so, she wrenched her wrist free, and in a storm of childish passion, struck her tormentor again and again. "Man!" she cried, with flaming eyes, "Let me go! I hate you! I hate you!"

"I am very sorry for this, Frere," said Vickers, when the door was closed. "I hope she did not hurt you."

"Not she! I like her spirit. Ha, ha! That's the way with women all the world over. Nothing like showing them that they've got a master."

Vickers hastened to turn the conversation, and, amid recollections of old days, the incident was forgotten. But when, an hour later, Mr. Frere traversed the passage that led to his bedroom, he found himself confronted by a little figure wrapped in a shawl.

"I've waited for you, Mr. Frere," said Sylvia, "to beg pardon. I am a wicked girl. Don't say no, because I am; and if I don't grow better I shall never go to heaven."

Thus addressing him, the child produced a piece of paper from beneath the shawl and handed it to him.

"What's this?" he asked.

"It's a written apology. If you don't accept it, it is not my fault. I have struck you, but I apologise. Being a woman, I can't offer you satisfaction in the usual way."

Mr. Frere made his adversary a low bow.

"I accept your apology, Miss Sylvia," said he.

"Then," returned Miss Sylvia, in a lofty manner, "there is nothing more to be said, and I have the honour to bid you good-night, sir."

The little maiden drew her shawl around her with immense dignity, and marched away down the passage.

Frere, gaining his room, choking with laughter, opened the folded paper by the light of the tallow candle, and read in a quaint, childish hand—

Sir,—I have struck you. I apologise in writing.

Your humble servant to command,
Sylvia Vickers.

"I wonder what book she took that out of?" he said. "Gad, it's a queer life for a child in this place, and no mistake."

A LEAP IN THE DARK

Two or three mornings after the arrival of the *Ladybird*, the solitary prisoner of the Grummet Rock noticed mysterious movements along the shore of the island settlement. The prison boats, which had put off every morning at sunrise to the foot of the timbered ranges on the other side of the harbour, had not appeared for some days. The building of a breakwater, running from the western point of the settlement, was discontinued; and all hands appeared to be occupied with the newly-built *Osprey*, which was lying on the slips. Rufus Dawes, walking his little round each day, in vain wondered what this unusual commotion portended.

A fortnight after this, about the 15th of December, he observed another curious fact. All the boats on the island put off one morning to the opposite side of the harbour, and in the course of the day a great smoke arose along the side of the hills. The next day the same was repeated; and on the fourth day the boats returned, towing behind them a huge raft. This raft, made fast to the side of the *Ladybird*, proved to be composed of planks, beams, and joists, all of which were duly hoisted up, and stowed in the hold of the brig.

This set Rufus Dawes thinking. Could it possibly be that the timber-cutting was to be abandoned, and that the Government had hit upon some other method of utilising its convict labour? Was it possible that some new trade was to be initiated? Before he had settled this point, he was startled by another boat expedition. Three boats' crews went down the bay, and returned, after a day's absence, with four strangers and a quantity of stores and farming implements. Rufus Dawes came to the conclusion that the boats had been to Philip Island, where the "garden" was established, and had taken off the gardeners and garden produce. Rufus Dawes decided that the *Ladybird* had brought a new commandant—his sight, trained by his half-savage life, had already distinguished Mr. Maurice Frere—and that these mysteries were "improvements" under the new rule. Another conjecture followed as a natural consequence. Lieutenant Frere would be a more severe commandant than Major Vickers. Now, severity had already reached its height so far as he was concerned; so the unhappy man took a final resolution—he would kill himself. Before we exclaim against the sin of such a determination, let us endeavour to examine what the sinner had suffered during the past six years.

To do so, we must multiply the infamy of the 'tween decks of the *Malabar* an hundred fold. In that prison was at least some ray of light. Stifling though the prison, infamous the companionship, terrible the memory of past happiness—there was yet ignorance of the future, there was yet hope. But at

Macquarie Harbour was poured out the very dregs of this cup of desolation. The worst had come, and the worst must for ever remain. Death alone kept the keys of that island prison.

We ordinary men, leading ordinary lives—walking, riding, laughing, marrying and giving in marriage—can form no notion of such misery as this. We do not know, and we can never know, how unutterably loathsome life must become when shared with such beings as those who dragged the tree trunks to the banks of the Gordon, and toiled, blaspheming, in their irons, on the dismal sandpit of Sarah Island. No human creature could describe to what depth of personal abasement and self-loathing one week of such a life would plunge him. Imagine such torment endured for six years!

In vain had been Rufus Dawes's first dream of freedom. He had done his best, by good conduct, to win release; but the villainy of Vetch and Rex had deprived him of the fruit of his labour. Instead of gaining credit by his exposure of the plot on board the *Malabar*, he was himself deemed guilty, and condemned. The knowledge of his "treachery"—for so it was deemed among his associates—while it gained for him no credit with the authorities, produced for him the detestation and ill-will of the monsters among whom he found himself. On his arrival at Hell's Gates he was a marked man—a Pariah among those beings who were Pariahs to all the world beside.

Thrice his life was attempted; but he was not then quite tired of living, and he defended it. This defence was construed by an overseer into a brawl, and the irons from which he had been relieved were replaced. His strength made him respected after this, and he was left at peace. At first this treatment was congenial to his temperament; but by-and-by it became almost unendurable. Tugging at his oar, digging up to his waist in slime, or bending beneath his burden of pine-wood, he looked greedily for some excuse to be addressed. In his desolation he agonized for the friendship of robbers and murderers. Then the reaction came, and he hated the very sound of their voices. He never spoke, and refused to answer when spoken to. He would even take his scanty supper alone, did his chain so permit him. He gained the reputation of a sullen, dangerous, half-crazy ruffian. Captain Barton, the superintendent, took pity on him, and made him his gardener. Then, one morning, Barton found the few shrubs pulled up by the roots, the flower-beds trampled into barrenness, and his gardener sitting on the ground among the fragments of his gardening tools. For this act of wanton mischief he was flogged. At the triangles his behaviour was considered curious. He wept and prayed to be released, fell on his knees to Barton and implored pardon. Barton would not listen, and at the first blow the prisoner was silent. From that time he became more sullen than ever, though occasionally he was observed, when alone, to fling himself on the ground and cry like a child. It was generally thought that his brain was affected.

When Vickers came, Dawes sought an interview, and begged to be sent back to Hobart Town. This was refused, of course, but he was put to work on the *Osprey*. After working there for some time, and being released from his irons, he concealed himself on the ship, and in the evening swam across the harbour. He was pursued, retaken, and flogged. Then he ran the dismal round of punishment. He burnt lime, dragged timber, and tugged at the oar. The heaviest and most degrading tasks were always his. Shunned and hated by his companions, feared by the convict overseers, and regarded with unfriendly eyes by the authorities, Rufus Dawes was at the very bottom of that abyss of woe into which he had voluntarily cast himself. Goaded to desperation, he had joined with Gabbett and the unlucky three in their desperate attempt to escape; but, as Vickers stated, he had been captured almost instantly, lamed by the heavy irons he wore. Though Gabbett—with a strange eagerness for which after events accounted—insisted that he could make good his flight, the unhappy man fell in the first hundred yards of the terrible race. For this madness the refractory convict had been condemned to the solitude of the Grummet Rock.

In that dismal hermitage, his mind had become disordered. He saw visions and held converse with imaginary beings. He harangued the rocks, calling upon them to witness his innocence and his sacrifice. Sometimes he thought his present life a dream. Whenever he awoke, however, he was commanded by a voice to leap into the surges which washed the walls of his prison, and to dream these sad dreams no more.

The unusual occurrences along the shore of the settlement roused in him a still fiercer hatred of life, and he read in them threats of an increase of misery. Had he known that the *Ladybird* was preparing for sea, and that he was to be conveyed with the rest for safe passage to Hobart Town, he might have paused; but he knew nothing, save that the burden of life was insupportable, and that the time had come for him to be rid of it.

In the meantime, the settlement was in a fever of excitement. In less than three weeks from the announcement made by Vickers, all had been got ready. Vickers would accompany the *Ladybird* with the main body. His wife and daughter were to remain until the sailing of the *Osprey*, which Mr. Frere was to bring up as soon as possible. "I will leave you a corporal's guard, and ten prisoners as a crew," Vickers said. "You can work her easily with that number." To which Frere had replied that he could do with five prisoners if necessary, for he knew how to get double work out of the lazy dogs.

One incident which took place during the breaking up is necessary to chronicle. Near Philip's Island is situated Coal Head, where a party had been lately at work. This party, hastily withdrawn by Vickers to assist in the business of devastation, had left behind it some tools and timber, and at the eleventh hour a boat's crew was sent to bring away the *débris*. The tools were duly collected, and the pine logs—worth twenty-five shillings apiece in Hobart Town—duly rafted and chained. The timber was secured, and the convicts, towing it after them, pulled for the ship just as the sun sank. But in the general haste, the raft had not been made with as much care as usual, and, in the strong current, the logs began to loosen. Mr. Troke, hooking himself on to the side of the *Ladybird*, saw a huge log slip out from its fellows and disappear into the darkness. Gazing after it with an indignant stare, he thought he heard a cry from the direction in which it had been borne. He would have paused to listen, but all his attention was needed to save the timber.

The cry had proceeded from Rufus Dawes. From his solitary rock he had watched the boat pass him and make for the *Ladybird* in channel, and he had decided—with that childishness into which the mind relapses on such supreme occasions—that at the moment when the gathering gloom swallowed her up, he would plunge into the surge below him. The heavily-labouring boat grew dimmer and dimmer, and presently only the figure of Mr. Troke in the stern sheets was visible. Then that also disappeared, and as the nose of the timber raft rose on the swell of the next wave, Rufus Dawes flung himself into the sea.

He was heavily ironed, and sank like a stone. He had resolved not to attempt to swim, and kept his arms raised above his head, in order to sink the quicker. But, as the agony of suffocation caught him, and the shock of the icy water dispelled the mental intoxication under which he was labouring, he desperately struck out, and, despite the weight of his irons, gained the surface for an instant. As he did so, he became conscious of a huge black mass surging upon him out of the darkness. The huge log, loosened from the raft, was upon him, crushing him beneath its rough and ragged sides. All thoughts of self-murder vanished, and uttering that despairing cry which had been faintly heard by Troke, he flung up his arms to clutch the monster that was pushing him down to death. His hand, scraping along the splintered side, touched the loop of hide rope that yet hung round the mass, and clutched it with the tenacity of a death grip. In another instant he got his head above water, and making good his hold, twisted himself, by a violent effort, across the log.

Exhausted, breathless, and bruised, he closed his eyes, and the drifting log bore him silently away into the darkness.

At daylight the next morning, Mr. Troke, landing on the prison rock, found it deserted. The prisoner's cap was lying on the edge of the little cliff, but the prisoner himself had disappeared. The intelligent Troke pondered on the circumstance, and in delivering his report to Vickers mentioned the strange cry he had heard the night before. "It's my belief, sir, that he was trying to swim the bay," he said. "He must ha' gone to the bottom anyhow, for he couldn't swim five yards with them irons."

Vickers, busily engaged in getting under way, accepted this supposition without question. The prisoner had met his death either by his own act, or by accident. It was either a suicide or an attempt to escape, and the former conduct of Rufus Dawes rendered the latter explanation a more probable one. In any case, he was dead—no man could swim the bay in irons. When the *Ladybird* passed the Grummet Rock an hour later, all on board her believed that the corpse of its late occupant was lying beneath the waves that seethed at its base.

THE LAST OF MACQUARIE HARBOUR

Rufus Dawes was believed to be dead by those on board the *Ladybird*, and not one of the eighteen persons on board the *Osprey* suspected that the boat which had put off for the marooned man had returned without him. Indeed the party had little leisure for thought; Mr. Frere, eager to get away, had kept his unlucky ten so hard at work that within a week from the departure of the *Ladybird* the *Osprey* was ready for sea. On the evening of the 11th of January, Mr. Bates, the pilot, who acted as master, informed the crew that Lieutenant Frere had given orders to weigh anchor at daybreak.

At daybreak accordingly the brig set sail, with a light breeze from the south-west and by three o'clock in the afternoon anchored safely outside the Gates. Unfortunately the wind shifted to the north-west, which caused a heavy swell on the bar and prudent Mr. Bates, having consideration for Mrs. Vickers and the child, ran back ten miles into Wellington Bay, anchoring there early in the evening. The tide was running strongly, and the brig rolled a good deal. Mrs. Vickers kept her cabin, and sent Sylvia to entertain Lieutenant Frere. Sylvia went, but was not entertaining. She had conceived for Frere a violent antipathy, and since the memorable night of the apology had been barely civil to him. In vain did he pet her and compliment her, she was not to be flattered into liking him.

On this particular evening the young lady relaxed her severity of demeanour. Her father away, and her mother sick, the little maiden felt lonely, and as a last resource accepted her mother's commands and went to Frere. He was walking up and down the deck, smoking.

"Mr. Frere, I am sent to talk to you."

"Are you? All right—go on."

"Oh dear no. It is the gentleman's place to entertain!"

"Come and sit down then," said Frere, who was in good humour at the success of his arrangements. "What shall we talk about?"

"As if I knew! It is your place to talk. Tell me a fairy story."

"Jack and the Beanstalk?" suggested Frere.

"Jack and the grandmother! Nonsense! Make one up out of your head, you know."

Frere laughed.

"I can't," he said. "I never did such a thing in my life."

"Then why not begin? I shall go away if you don't begin."

Frere rubbed his brow and, pulling hard at his pipe, plunged into literary reflection.

Sylvia sitting beside him, eagerly watching for the happy thought that never came, finally pouted and said, "What a stupid, stupid man you are! I shall be so glad to get back to papa again. He knows all sorts of stories, nearly as many as old Danny."

"Danny knows some, then?"

"Danny! Of course he does. I suppose now," putting her head on one side with an expression of superiority, "you never heard the story of the Banshee?"

"No, I never did."

"Nor the 'White Horse of the Peppers'?"

"No."

"Nor the 'Changeling'? nor the 'Leprechaun'?"

"No."

Sylvia surveyed the smoking animal beside her with profound contempt.

"Mr. Frere, excuse me if I hurt your feelings; I have no wish to do that; but really you are a *most* ignorant person—for your age, of course."

Maurice Frere grew a little angry. "You are very impertinent, Sylvia," said he.

"Miss Vickers is *my* name, Lieutenant Frere, and I shall go and talk to Mr. Bates."

As Mr. Bates, who had filled the dangerous office of pilot, told her about divers and coral reefs, and some adventures of his—a little apocryphal—in the China seas, Frere resumed his smoking, half angry with himself, and half angry with the provoking little fairy. This elfin creature had a fascination for him which he could not account for.

He saw her no more that evening, and at breakfast the next morning she received him with quaint haughtiness. "When shall we be ready to sail? Mr. Frere, I'll take some marmalade. Thank you."

"I don't know, Missy," said Bates. "It's very rough on the Bar; me and Mr. Frere was a-soundin' of it this marnin', and it ain't safe yet."

"Well," said Sylvia, "I do trust we sha'n't be shipwrecked, and have to swim miles and miles for our lives."

"Ho, ho!" laughed Frere; "don't be afraid. I'll take care of you."

"Can *you* swim, Mr. Bates?" asked Sylvia.

"Yes, Miss, I can."

"Well, then, *you* shall take me; I like you. Mr. Frere can take mamma. We'll go and live on a desert island, Mr. Bates, and grow coco-nuts and bread-fruit, and I'll be Robinson Crusoe and you shall be Man Friday. I'd like to live on a desert island, if I was sure there were no savages, and plenty to eat and drink."

"That would be right enough, my dear, but you don't find them sort of islands every day."

"*Then*," said Sylvia, with a decided nod, "we won't be shipwrecked, will we?"

"Put a biscuit in your pocket, Sylvia, in case of accidents," suggested Frere, with a grin.

There was a short silence.

"Mr. Frere," returned Sylvia, gravely pausing at her mother's cabin door, "if I were Richard the Third, do you know what I'd do with you?"

"No," says Frere, eating complacently; "what would you do?"

"Why, I'd make you stand at the door of St. Paul's Cathedral in a white sheet, with a lighted candle in your hand, until you gave up your wicked aggravating ways—you Man!"

This picture of Mr. Frere was too much for Mr. Bates, and he roared with laughter. "She's a queer child, ain't she, sir? A born natural."

"When shall we be able to get away, Mr. Bates?" asked Frere, whose dignity was wounded by the mirth of the pilot.

Bates felt the change of tone. "I hopes by evening, sir," said he hastily; "if the tide slackens then I'll risk it."

"The men were wanting to go ashore to wash their clothes," said Frere. "If we are going to stop here till evening, you had better let them go this afternoon."

"All right, sir," said Bates.

The afternoon passed off auspiciously. The ten prisoners went ashore in the whaleboat and washed their clothes. Their names were James Barker, James Lesly, John Lyon, Benjamin Riley, William Cheshire, Henry Shiers, William Russen, James Porter, John Fair and John Rex.

This last scoundrel had come on board latest of all. He had behaved himself a little better recently, and during the work attendant upon the departure of the *Ladybird*, had been conspicuously useful. His influence among his fellow prisoners contrived to make him a somewhat important personage, and Vickers had allowed him privileges from which he had hitherto been debarred. Mr. Frere, however, never ceased to hurry and find fault with him. It was "Rex, come here! Do this! Do that!" As the prisoners declared among themselves, it was evident that Mr. Frere had a "down" on the Dandy.

But Rex only redoubled his activity, and—despite all his wish to the contrary—Frere was unable to find fault. He even took credit to himself for "taming" the convict's spirit, and pointed out Rex—silent and obedient—as proof of the excellence of severe measures. To the convicts, however, who knew John Rex better, this silent activity was ominous.

He returned with the rest, however, in the evening of the 13th, in apparently cheerful mood. Indeed Mr. Frere, who had decided to take the whaleboat and catch a few fish before dinner, observed him laughing with some of the others, and again congratulated himself.

The time wore on. Darkness was closing in, and Mr. Bates, walking the deck, kept a look-out for the boat, with the intention of weighing anchor and making for the bar. All was secure. Mrs. Vickers and the child were safely below. The two remaining soldiers (two had gone with Frere) were upon deck, and the prisoners in the forecastle were singing. The wind was fair, and the sea had gone down. In less than an hour the *Osprey* would be safely outside the Harbour.

THE POWER OF THE WILDERNESS

For some time the burden that the drifting log bore was an insensible one. Exhausted with his desperate struggle for life, the convict lay along the rough bark of this Heaven-sent raft without motion, almost without breath. At length a violent shock awoke him to consciousness, and he perceived that the log had become stranded on a sandy point. Painfully rising from his uncomfortable posture, he staggered to his feet, and crawling a few paces up the beach, flung himself upon the ground and slept. When morning dawned, he recognised his position. The log had been cast upon the southern point of Coal Head, and some three hundred yards from him were the mutilated sheds of the coal-gang. For some time he lay still, basking in the warm rays of the rising sun, scarcely caring to move his bruised limbs. The sensation of rest was so exquisite that he did not even trouble himself to conjecture the reason for the apparent desertion of the huts close by him.

While he slept, the *Ladybird*, on her way out, passed him so closely that any one on board her might, with a good glass, have espied his slumbering figure as it lay upon the sand.

When he woke it was past mid-day, and the sun poured its full rays upon him. His clothes were dry, and he rose to his feet refreshed by his long sleep. He scarcely comprehended, as yet, his true position. He had escaped, it was true, but not for long. He was versed in the history of escapes, and knew that a man alone on that barren coast faced starvation or recapture. Glancing up at the sun, he wondered, indeed, how it was that he had been free so long. Then the untenanted coal sheds caught his eye, and he began to tremble with vague apprehension. Entering, he looked around, expecting every moment to see some lurking constable, or armed soldier. Suddenly his glance fell upon some loaves and meat which lay in the corner where the departing convicts had flung them the night before. At that moment, this discovery seemed like a direct revelation from Heaven, and, had he lived in another age, he would have looked round for the angel who had brought them.

By-and-by, having eaten of this miraculous provender, the poor creature began to speculate what had taken place. The coal workings were abandoned; the new Commandant had probably other work for his beasts of burden to execute, and an absconder would be safe here for a few hours at least. But he must not stay. If he thought to escape, it behoved him to commence his journey at once. As he contemplated the meat and bread, something like a ray of hope entered his gloomy soul. Here was provision for his needs. The food before him represented the rations for six men. Was it not possible to cross the desert that lay between him and freedom on such fare? Here was six men's food for one day, or one man's food for six days. He would live on a third of this, and he would have rations for eighteen days. Eighteen days! What could he not do in eighteen days? He could walk thirty miles a day—forty miles a day—that would be six hundred miles and more. Yet stay; he must not be too sanguine; the road was difficult; the scrub was in places impenetrable. He would be moderate, and say twenty miles a day. Twenty miles a day was very easy walking. Eighteen days, and twenty miles a day—three hundred and sixty miles. More than enough to take him to freedom. With prudence, it could be done! He must be careful and abstemious. Abstemious! He had already eaten too much, and he hastily pulled a barely-tasted piece of meat from his mouth, and replaced it with the rest.

Having come to this resolution, the next thing was to disencumber himself of his irons. This was more easily done than he expected. He found in the shed an iron gad, and with that and a stone he drove out the rivets. He packed the meat and the bread together, and then pushing the gad into his belt—it might be needed as a weapon of defence—he set out on his journey.

His intention was to get round the settlement to the coast, reach the settled districts, and, by some tale of shipwreck or of wandering, procure assistance. As to what was particularly to be done when he found himself among free men, he did not pause to consider. At that point his difficulties seemed to him to end. Let him but traverse the desert that was before him, and he would trust to his own ingenuity, or the chance of fortune, to avert suspicion.

Before dawn next morning he had travelled ten miles, and by the night of the fourth day he had succeeded in accomplishing forty more. Footsore and weary, he lay in the thicket of the thorny melaleuca, and felt at last that he was beyond pursuit. The next day he advanced more slowly. Dense scrub impeded his path; barren and stony mountain ranges arose before him. The sea that had hitherto gleamed upon his right hand now shifted to his left. He had mistaken his course, and he must turn again. For two days did this bewilderment last, and on the third he came to a mighty cliff that pierced with its blunt pinnacle the clustering bush. He must go over or round this obstacle, and he decided to go round it. A natural pathway wound about its foot. Here and there branches were broken, and it seemed to the poor wretch, fainting under the weight of his lessening burden, that his were not the first footsteps which had trodden there. The path terminated in a glade, and at the bottom of this glade was something that fluttered. Rufus Dawes pressed forward, and stumbled over a corpse!

Clad in the yellow dress of a convict, flung on the ground as though struck down, the body was hideously mangled. One arm was missing, and the skull had been beaten in by some heavy instrument! Rufus Dawes's first thought—that this heap of rags and bones was a mute witness to the folly of his own undertaking, the corpse of some starved absconder—gave place to a second more horrible suspicion. He recognised the number imprinted on the coarse cloth as that belonging to one of the men who had escaped with Gabbett. He was standing on the place where a murder had been committed! A murder!—and what else? Thank God the food *he* carried was not yet exhausted! He turned and fled, looking back fearfully as he went.

Crashing through the scrub, torn and bleeding, he reached a spur of the Range, and looked around him. The white cone of the Frenchman's Cap was on his right hand and on his left a succession of ranges seemed to bar further progress. The dense scrub through which he had so painfully toiled spread without break below him. He raised his eyes, and there, like a long dull sword, lay the narrow steel-blue reach of the harbour from which he had escaped. A dark speck moved on its waters. It was the *Osprey* making for the Gates. It seemed that he could throw a stone upon her deck. A faint cry of rage escaped him. During the last three days in the bush he must have retraced his steps, and returned upon his own track to the settlement! More than half his allotted time had passed, and he was not yet thirty miles from his prison. Death had waited to overtake him in this barbarous wilderness, had played with him as a cat plays with a mouse. Escape was hopeless now. As the unhappy man raised his despairing eyes, he saw the sinking sun shoot a ray of crimson light into the glade below him. It was as though a bloody finger pointed at the corpse lying there, and Rufus Dawes, shuddering at the dismal omen, plunged again into the forest.

For days he wandered aimlessly through the bush. He had given up all hopes of making the overland journey, and yet, as long as his scanty supply of food held out, he strove to keep away from the settlement. Unable to resist the pangs of hunger, he had increased his daily ration; and though the salted meat had begun to turn putrid, he never looked at it but he was seized with a desire to eat his fill. The lumps of carrion and the hard loaves were to him morsels fit for the table of an emperor. At last, on the twelfth day, he found himself at the foot of Mount Direction at the head of the peninsula which makes the western side of the harbour. His wandering had but led him to make a complete circuit of the settlement, and the next night brought him round the shores of Birches Inlet to the landing-place opposite to Sarah Island. His stock of provisions had been exhausted for two days, and he was savage with hunger. He no longer thought of suicide. His dominant idea was now to get food. He would do as many others had done before him—give himself up to be flogged and fed.

When he reached the landing-place, however, the guard-house was empty. He looked across at the island prison, and saw no sign of life. The settlement was deserted! He struck himself to see if he was not dreaming. He refused to believe his eyesight. He shouted, screamed and waved his tattered garments in the air. Then, exhausted by these paroxysms, he said to himself, quite calmly, that he was mistaken in the place; the island yonder was not Sarah Island, but some other island like it, and that in a second or so he would be able to detect the difference. But the mountains, so hideously familiar for six weary years, made mute reply, and the sea, crawling at his feet, seemed to grin at him with a thin-lipped, hungry mouth.

At last the dreadful truth forced itself upon him; he retired a few paces, and then, with a cry of furious despair, stumbled forward towards the edge of the little reef that fringed the shore. Just as he was about to fling himself for the second time into the dark water, his eyes, sweeping in a last long look around the bay, caught sight of a strange appearance on the left horn of the sea beach. A thin, blue streak, uprising from behind the western arm of the little inlet, hung in the still air. It was the smoke of a fire!

The tiny column of bluish vapour seemed to the dying wretch as glorious as the Pillar of Fire that led the Israelites. There were yet human beings near him! Turning his face from the hungry sea, he tottered with the last of his failing strength towards the blessed token of their presence.

THE SEIZURE OF THE "OSPREY"

Frere's fishing expedition had been unsuccessful, and in consequence prolonged. Though the fast deepening shades of an Australian evening urged him to return, yet obstinately he lingered, unwilling to come back empty-handed. At last a peremptory signal warned him. It was the sound of a musket fired on board the brig: Mr. Bates was getting impatient. With a scowl, Frere drew up his lines, and ordered the two soldiers to pull for the vessel. To the soldiers pulling with their backs to the Osprey, the musket shot seemed the most ordinary occurrence in the world. Eager to quit the dismal prison-bay, they had viewed Mr. Frere's persistent fishing with disgust, and had for the previous half-hour longed to hear the signal of recall which had just startled them. Suddenly, however, they noticed a change of expression on the face of their commander. Frere, sitting with his face to the Osprey, had observed a peculiar appearance on her decks. The bulwarks were every now and then topped by strange figures, who disappeared as suddenly as they came, and a faint murmur of voices floated across the sea. Presently the report of another musket shot echoed among the hills, and something dark fell from the side of the vessel into the water. Frere, with an imprecation, sprang to his feet, and shading his eyes with his hand, looked towards the brig. A moment's anxious pause, and then another musket shot, followed by a woman's shrill scream, explained all. The prisoners had seized the brig!

Mr. Bates, lulled into a sense of false security, had gone below to tell his little playmate that she would soon be on her way to the Hobart Town of which she had heard so much; and, taking advantage of his absence, the soldier not on guard went to the forecastle to hear the prisoners singing. The voices were melodious enough, and the words of the ditty of that character which pleases the soldier nature. Private Grimes forgot all about the unprotected state of the deck, and sat down to listen.

While he listened, absorbed in tender recollections, James Lesly, William Cheshire, William Russen, John Fair, and James Barker slipped to the hatchway and got upon deck. Barker reached the aft hatchway as the soldier who was on guard turned to complete his walk, and passing his arm round his neck, pulled him down before he could utter a cry. Fair, snatching up the guard's weapon, swore to blow his brains out if he raised a finger. Seeing the sentry thus secured, Cheshire, as if in pursuance of a preconcerted plan, leapt down the after-hatchway, and passed up the muskets from the arm-racks to Lesly and Russen. There were three muskets in addition to the one

85

taken from the sentry, and Barker, leaving his prisoner in charge of Fair, seized one of them, and ran to the companion ladder. Russen, left unarmed by this manoeuvre, appeared to know his own duty. He came back to the forecastle, and passing behind the listening soldier, touched the singer on the shoulder. This was the appointed signal, and John Rex, suddenly terminating his song with a laugh, presented his fist in the face of the gaping Grimes. "No noise!" he cried. "The brig's ours." Ere Grimes could reply, he was seized by Lyon and Riley, and bound securely.

"Come on lads!" says Rex, "and pass the prisoner down here. We've got her this time, I'll go bail!" In obedience to this order, the now gagged sentry was flung down the fore hatchway, and the hatch secured. "Stand on the hatchway, Porter," cries Rex again; "and if those fellows come up, knock 'em down with a handspike. Lesly and Russen, forward to the companion ladder! Lyon, keep a look-out for the boat, and if she comes too near, fire!"

As he spoke the report of the first musket rang out. Barker had apparently fired up the companion hatchway.

When Mr. Bates had gone below, he found Sylvia curled upon the cushions of the state-room, reading. "Well, Missy!" he said, "we'll soon be on our way to papa."

Sylvia answered by asking a question altogether foreign to the subject. "Mr. Bates," said she, pushing the hair out of her blue eyes, "what's a coracle?"

"A which?" asked Mr. Bates.

"A coracle. C-o-r-a-c-l-e," said she, spelling it slowly.

Bates shook his head. "Never heard of one, Missy," said he. "What does it say?"

" 'The ancient Britons,' " said Sylvia, reading gravely, " 'painted their bodies with woad,'—that's blue stuff, you know, Mr. Bates—'and, seated in their light coracles of skin stretched upon slender wooden frames, must have presented a wild and savage appearance.' "

"Hah," said Mr. Bates, "a corricle, a cory——," a bright light burst upon him. "A *curricle* you mean, Miss! It's a carriage! I've seen 'em in Hy' Park."

Sylvia, satisfied, returned to the book. It was a little mean-looking volume—a "Child's History of England,"—and after perusing it awhile with knitted brows, she burst into laughter.

"Why, my dear Mr. Bates!" she cried, waving the History above her head in triumph, "what a pair of geese we are! A *carriage*! Oh you silly man! It's a *boat*!"

"Is it?" said Mr. Bates. "Who'd ha' thought that now? Why couldn't they call it a boat at once, then, and ha' done with it?" He was about to laugh also, when, raising his eyes, he saw in the open doorway the figure of James Barker, with a musket in his hand.

"Hallo! What's this? What do you do here, sir?"

"Sorry to disturb yer," says the convict, with a grin, "but you must come along o' me, Mr. Bates."

Bates, at once comprehending that some terrible misfortune had occurred, did not lose his presence of mind. Snatching up a cushion from the couch, he flung it across the cabin full in the face of the prisoner. The soft mass struck the man with force sufficient to blind him for an instant. The musket exploded harmlessly in the air, and ere the astonished Barker could recover his footing, Bates had hurled him out of the cabin, and crying "Mutiny!" locked the cabin door on the inside.

The noise brought out Mrs. Vickers from her berth, and the poor little student of English history ran into her arms.

"Good heavens, Mr. Bates, what is it?"

Bates, furious with rage, so far forgot himself as to swear. "It's a mutiny, ma'am," said he. "Go back to your cabin and lock the door. Those bloody villains have risen on us! Don't move a finger till I tell ye. Maybe it ain't so bad as it looks; I've got my pistols with me, thank God, and Mr. Frere'll hear the shot any way. Mutiny! On deck there!" he cried, and his brow grew damp with dismay when a mocking laugh from above was the only response.

In the meanwhile, Grimes and the other soldier had loosed themselves from their bonds, and encouraged by the firing, which seemed to them a sign that all was not yet lost, made shift to force up the forehatch. Porter, whose courage was none of the fiercest, made but a feeble attempt at resistance, and forcing the handspike from him, the sentry, Jones, rushed aft to help the pilot. As Jones reached the waist, Cheshire, a cold-blooded man, shot him dead. Grimes fell over the corpse, and Cheshire, clubbing the musket—had he another barrel he would have fired,—coolly battered his head as he lay, and then seizing the body of the unfortunate Jones in his arms, tossed it into the sea. "Porter, you lubber!" he cried, exhausted with the effort to lift the body, "come and bear a hand with this other one!" Porter advanced aghast, but just then another occurrence claimed the villain's attention, and poor Grimes's life was spared for that time.

Rex, inwardly raging at the unexpected resistance on the part of the pilot, flung himself on the skylight, and tore it up bodily. As he did so, Barker, who had reloaded his musket, fired down into the cabin. The ball passed through the state-room door, and splintering the wood, buried itself close to the golden curls of poor little Sylvia. It was this hair's breadth escape which drew from the agonised mother that shriek which, pealing through the open stern window, had roused the soldiers in the boat.

Rex, who yet possessed some abhorrence of useless crime, imagined that the cry was one of pain, and that Barker's bullet had taken deadly effect. "You've killed the child, you villain!" he cried.

"What's the odds?" asked Barker sulkily. "She must die any way, sooner or later."

Rex put his head down the skylight, and called on Bates to surrender; but Bates only drew his other pistol. "Would you commit murder?" he asked, looking round with desperation in his glance.

"No, no," cried some of the men, willing to blink the death of poor Jones. "It's no use making things worse than they are. Bid him come up, and we'll do him no harm."

"Come up, Mr. Bates," says Rex, "and I give you my word you sha'n't be injured."

"Will you set the major's lady and child ashore, then?" asked Bates.

"Yes."

"Without injury?" continued the other, bargaining at the very muzzles of the muskets.

"Ay, ay!" returned Russen. "It's our liberty we want, that's all."

"Shut down the skylight, then," said Bates, with the ghost of an authority in his voice, "until I ask the lady."

This, however, John Rex refused to do. "You can ask well enough where you are," he said.

But there was no need for Mr. Bates to put a question. The door of the cabin opened, and Mrs. Vickers appeared, trembling, with Sylvia by her side. "Accept, Mr. Bates," she said, "since it must be so. We should gain nothing by refusing. We are at their mercy—God help us!"

"Put your pistols on the table, and come up, then," says Rex. "Nobody shall hurt you."

Mrs. Vickers, pale with terror, yet sustained by that courage of which we have before spoken, passed rapidly under the open skylight, and prepared to

JOHN REX'S REVENGE

ascend. Sylvia clung to her mother with one hand, and with the other pressed close to her bosom the "English History". In her fear she had forgotten to lay it down.

"Who's to command the brig now?" asked undaunted Bates, as they came up.

"I am," says John Rex; "and with these brave fellows, I'll take her round the world."

This bold project, so boldly avowed, seemed to Bates a sheer absurdity. The "Dandy" and a crew of nine convicts navigate a brig round the world! Preposterous; why, not a man aboard could work a reckoning! He pictured the *Osprey* helplessly rolling on the swell of the Southern Ocean, or hopelessly locked in the ice of the Antarctic Seas, and he dimly guessed at the fate of the deluded ten. Even if they got safe to port, the chances of final escape were all against them, for what account could they give of themselves?

"Fools!" he cried, "do you know what you are about to do? You will never escape. Give up the brig, and I will declare, upon the Bible, that I will say nothing, but give all good characters."

Lesly and another burst into a laugh at this, but Rex, who had weighed his chances well beforehand, answered seriously.

"It's no use talking," he said, shaking his handsome head. "We have got the brig, and we mean to keep her. I can navigate her, though I am no seaman, so you needn't talk further about it. It's liberty we require."

"What are you going to do with us?" asked Bates.

"Leave you behind."

Bates's face blanched. "What, *here?*"

"Yes. Not a picturesque spot, is it? And yet *I've* lived here for some years;" and he grinned.

Bates was silent. The logic of that grin was unanswerable.

"Come!" cried the Dandy, "look alive there! Lower away the jolly-boat. Mrs. Vickers, go down to your cabin and get anything you want. I am compelled to put you ashore, but I have no wish to leave you without clothes." Bates listened, in a sort of dismal admiration, at this courtly convict. *He* could not have spoken like that had life depended on it. "Now, little lady," continued Rex, "go with your mamma, and don't be frightened."

Sylvia flushed burning red at this indignity. "Frightened! If there had been anybody else here but women, you never would have taken the brig. Frightened! Let me pass, *prisoner!*"

Rex—whose politeness was mere bravado—was stung to the quick by the reflection upon his courage, and the bitter accent with which the child had pronounced the word *prisoner* made him bite his lips with rage. Had he had his will, he would have struck the little creature to the deck, but the hoarse laugh of his companions warned him to forbear. There is "public opinion" even among convicts, and Rex dared not vent his passion on so helpless an object. In order to show that he was not moved by the taunt, he smiled upon the taunter more graciously than ever.

"Your daughter has her father's spirit, madam," said he to Mrs. Vickers, with a bow.

As Mrs. Vickers descended the hatchway, the boat with Frere and the soldiers came within musket range, and Lesly, according to orders, fired his musket over their heads, shouting to them to lay to. But Frere had determined not to resign his lost authority without a struggle. Disregarding the summons, he came straight on, with his eyes fixed on the vessel. Suddenly, from out of the darkness a voice hailed him.

"Hold water! back water!" it cried, and was then seemingly choked in its owner's throat.

The voice was Mr. Bates's. Standing near the side, he had observed Rex and Fair bring up a great pig of iron, erst used as ballast, and poise it on the rail. Their intention was but too evident; and honest Bates, like a faithful watch-dog barked, to warn his master. Blood-thirsty Cheshire caught him by the throat, and Frere, unheeding, ran the boat alongside, under the very nose of the revengeful Rex.

The mass of iron fell half in-board upon the now stayed boat, and gave her sternway, with a splintered plank.

"Villains!" cried Frere, "would you swamp us?"

"Aye," laughed Rex, "the brig's ours, can't ye see, and *we*'re your masters now!"

Frere cried to the bow to hook on, but the blow had driven the boat backward, and she was already beyond arm's length of the brig. The two soldiers, exhausted by their long pull, made no effort to stay the progress of the boat, and almost before the swell caused by the plunge of the mass of iron had ceased to agitate the water, the deck of the *Osprey* had become invisible in the darkness.

Frere struck his fist upon the thwart. "The scoundrels!" he said, between his teeth, "they've mastered us. What do they mean to do next?"

The answer came pat to the question. From the dark hull of the brig broke a flash and a report, and a musket ball cut the water beside them.

"Come alongside with ye!" hailed a voice, "or it will be worse for ye!"

"They want to murder us," says Frere. "Give way, men!"

But the two soldiers, exchanging glances one with the other, pulled the boat's head round, and made for the vessel. "It's no use, Mr. Frere," said the man nearest him, "we can't do no good now, and they won't hurt us, I dare say."

"You dogs, you are in league with them," bursts out Frere, purple with indignation. "Do you mutiny?"

"Come, sir," returned the soldier sulkily, "this ain't the time to bully; and as for mutiny, why, one man's about as good as another just now."

This speech from the lips of a man who, but a few minutes before would have risked his life to obey the orders of his officer, convinced Frere of the hopelessness of resistance. His authority had left him. He was now no more than any one else; indeed, he was less than many, for those who held the firearms were the ruling powers. With a groan he resigned himself to his fate.

When they reached the brig, they found that the jolly-boat had been lowered and laid alongside. In her were Bates, with forehead gashed and hands bound, the stunned Grimes, Russen and Fair pulling, Lyon, Riley, Cheshire, and Lesly with muskets, and John Rex in the stern sheets, with Bates's pistols in his trousers belt, and a loaded musket across his knees. Mrs. Vickers and Sylvia huddled together under a large, white shawl.

By the direction of Rex, the whale-boat was brought alongside the jolly-boat, and Cheshire and Lesly boarded her. Frere, catching the malignant eye of John Rex, remembered how easily a twitch of the finger would pay off old scores, and kept silent as Lesly bound his hands. "Step in here, sir, if you please," said Rex, with polite irony. "I am sorry to be compelled to tie you, but I must consult my own safety as well as your convenience." Frere scowled, and, stepping awkwardly into the jolly-boat, fell! Russen pulled him roughly to his feet, with a coarse laugh. In Frere's present frame of mind, that laugh galled him worse than his bonds.

"The wretches!" Mrs. Vickers said under her breath, as Frere was flung down beside her, "to subject you to such indignity!" Sylvia said nothing, and seemed to shrink from the lieutenant. Perhaps in her childish fancy, she had pictured him as coming to her rescue, armed cap-a-pie, and clad in dazzling mail. If she had entertained any such notion the reality must have struck coldly upon her senses. Mr. Frere, clumsy and bound, was not at all heroic.

"Now, my lads," says Rex to the soldiers, "we give you your choice. Stay at Hell's Gates, or come with us!"

The soldiers paused, irresolute. To join the mutineers meant a certainty of hard work, with a chance of ultimate hanging. Yet to stay with the prisoners was to incur the inevitable fate of starvation on a barren coast. As is often the case on such occasions, a trifle sufficed to turn the scale. The wounded

Grimes dimly caught the meaning of the sentence, and in his stupor must needs make comment upon it. "Go with him, ye beggars!" said he, "and leave us honest men! Oh, ye'll get a tying-up for this!"

The phrase "tying-up" brought with it recollection of the worst portion of military discipline, the cat, and revived in the minds of the pair already disposed to break the yoke a train of dismal memories. The life of a soldier on a convict station was a hard one. He was often stinted in rations, and of necessity deprived of all rational recreation, while punishment for offences was prompt and severe. The companies drafted to the penal settlements were not composed of the best material, and the pair had good precedent for the course they were about to take.

"Come," says Rex, "I can't wait here all night. The wind is freshening, and we must make the Bar. Which is it to be?"

"We'll go with *you!*" says the man who had pulled the stroke in the whale-boat, spitting into the water with averted face. Upon which utterance the convicts burst into joyous oaths, and the pair were received with much hand-shaking.

Then Rex, with Lyon and Riley as a guard, got into the whale-boat, and having loosed the two prisoners from their bonds, ordered them to take the places of Russen and Fair. Frere and Bates, in obedience to orders, began to pull the jolly-boat towards the shore; and in this fashion was the dismal little party conveyed to the mainland.

It was night when they reached it, but the clear sky began to thrill with a late moon as yet unarisen, and the waves glimmered with radiance. Frere and Bates, jumping ashore, helped out Mrs. Vickers, Sylvia, and the wounded Grimes. This being done under the muzzles of the muskets, Rex commanded that Bates and Frere should push the jolly-boat as far as they could from the shore, and Riley, catching her by a boat-hook as she came towards them, she was taken in tow.

"Now, boys," says Cheshire, with a savage delight, "three cheers for old England and Liberty!"

Upon which a great shout went up, echoed by the grim hills.

To the wretched five this exultant mirth sounded like a death knell.

"Great God!" Bates cried after the departing boats, "would you leave us here to starve?"

The only answer was the jerk and dip of the retreating oars.

Rejecting Bates's offer of a pea-jacket and Frere's vague tenders of assistance, Mrs. Vickers withdrew behind a rock and, with her daughter in her arms,

LEFT AT "HELL'S GATES"

resigned herself to her torturing thoughts. As a woman and a mother, she owned to a double capacity for suffering. Her feminine imagination pictured all the horrors of death by famine, and having realised her own torments, her maternal love forced her to live them over again in the person of her child. Sylvia, recovered from her terror, was almost content, and, curled in her mother's shawl, slept. To her little soul, this midnight mystery of boats and muskets had all the flavour of a romance. Besides, it was obvious that Papa—the Supreme Being of the settlement—must at once return and severely punish the impertinent prisoners who had dared to insult his wife and child. How they *would* be flogged when Papa came back! In the mean time this sleeping in the open air was rather pleasant.

Honest Bates produced a piece of biscuit, and suggested that this should be set aside for the sole use of the two females, but Mrs. Vickers would not hear of it. "We must all share alike," said she, with something of the spirit that she knew her husband would have displayed under like circumstance. Frere wondered at her apparent strength of mind. Had he been gifted with more acuteness, he would not have wondered; for when a crisis comes to one of two persons who have lived much together, the influence of the nobler spirit makes itself felt.

Aboard the *Osprey*, a discussion had arisen amongst the mutineers as to the propriety of at once making sail, but Barker, who knew the dangers of the Bar, vowed that he would not undertake to steer the brig through the Gates until morning. During the evening—the excitement attendant upon the outbreak having passed away, and the magnitude of the task before them being more fully apparent to their minds—a feeling of pity for the unfortunate party on the mainland took possession of them. It was quite possible that the *Osprey* might be recaptured, in which case five useless murders would have been committed; and however callous were the majority of the mutineers, not one among them could contemplate, without a twinge of remorse, the death of the harmless child. John Rex, seeing how matters were going, made haste to take to himself the credit of mercy.

"I propose," said he, "that we divide the provisions. There are five of them and ten of us. Then nobody can blame us."

"Ay," said Porter, "and if we're taken, they can tell what we have done. Don't let our affair be like that of the *Cypress*, to leave them to starve."

"Ay, ay," says Barker, "you're right! When Fergusson was topped at

Hobart Town, I heard old Troke say that if he'd not refused to set the tucker ashore, he might ha' got off with a whole skin."

Thus urged by self-interest as well as sentiment to mercy, the provision was got upon deck by daylight, and a division made. The soldiers, with generosity born of remorse, were for giving half to the marooned men, but Barker exclaimed against this. "When the *Ladybird* finds they don't get to headquarters, she's bound to come back and look for 'em," said he; "and we'll want all the tucker we can get, maybe, afore we sights land."

This reasoning was admitted and acted upon. There was in the harness-cask about fifty pounds of salt meat, and a third of this quantity, together with half a small sack of flour, some tea and sugar, mixed together in a bag, and an iron kettle and pannikin, was placed in the whale-boat. Rex, fearful of excesses among his crew, also lowered down one of the two small puncheons of rum which the store room contained. Cheshire disputed this, and stumbling over a goat that had been taken on board from Philip Island, caught the creature by the leg, and threw it into the sea, bidding Rex take that with him also. Rex dragged the poor beast into the boat, and with this miscellaneous cargo pushed off to the shore.

Laying off as the water shallowed, Rex called to Bates to come for the cargo. The sight of this almost unexpected succour revived the courage of the five, and they felt grateful. After the horrible anxiety they had endured all that night, they were prepared to look with kindly eyes upon the men who had come to their assistance.

"Men," said Bates, "I didn't expect this. You are good fellows, for there ain't much tucker aboard, I know."

"Yes," affirmed Frere, "you're good fellows."

Rex burst into a savage laugh. "Shut your mouth, you tyrant," said he, forgetting his Dandyism in the recollection of his former suffering. "It ain't for your benefit. You may thank the lady and child for it."

Julia Vickers hastened to propitiate the arbiter of her daughter's fate. "We are obliged to you," she said, with quiet dignity, "and if I ever get back safely, I will take care that your kindness shall be known."

The swindler and forger took off his leather cap with quite an air. It was five years since a lady had spoken to him, and the old time when he was Mr. Lionel Crofton, a "gentleman sportsman", came back again for an instant.

"I sincerely trust, madam," said he, "that you *will* get back safely. May I hope for your good wishes for myself and my companions?"

Bates chuckled. "What a dog it is! John Rex, you were never made to be a convict, man!"

Rex smiled. "Good-bye, Mr. Bates, and God preserve you!"

"Good-bye," says Bates, "and damme, I hope you'll get safe off, for liberty's sweet to every man."

"Good-bye, prisoners!" says Sylvia, "and I hope they won't catch you, too."

So, with cheers and waving of handkerchiefs, the boat departed.

In the emotion which the apparently disinterested conduct of John Rex had occasioned the exiles, all earnest thought of their own position had vanished. But as the boat grew smaller and smaller in the distance, so did their consciousness of their own situation grow more and more distinct; and when at last the boat had disappeared in the shadow of the brig all started, as if from a dream, to the wakeful contemplation of their own case.

A council of war was held, with Mr. Frere at the head, and the possessions of the little party were thrown into common stock. The salt meat, flour, and tea were placed in a hollow rock at some distance from the beach, and Mr. Bates was appointed purser, to apportion to each his stated allowance. The goat was tethered with a piece of fishing line sufficiently long to allow her to browse. The cask of rum, by special agreement, was placed in the innermost recess of the rock, and it was resolved that its contents should not be touched except in case of sickness, or in last extremity. There was no lack of water, for a spring ran bubbling from the rocks within a hundred yards of the spot where the party had landed. They calculated that, with prudence, their provision would last them for nearly four weeks.

It was found, upon a review of their possessions, that they had among them a tinder-box, three pocket knives, a ball of string, two pipes and a fig of tobacco, a portion of fishing line, with hooks, and a big jack-knife which Frere had taken to gut the fish he had expected to catch. But they saw with dismay that there was nothing which could be used axe-wise among the party. Mrs. Vickers had her shawl, and Bates a pea-jacket, but Frere and Grimes were without extra clothing. It was agreed that each should retain his own property, with the exception of the fishing lines, which were confiscated to the commonwealth.

Having made these arrangements, the kettle, filled with water from the spring, was slung over the fire, and a pannikin of weak tea, together with a biscuit, served out to each of the party, save Grimes, who declared himself unable to eat. Breakfast over, Bates made a damper, which was cooked in the ashes, and then another council was held as to future habitation.

It was clearly evident that they could not sleep in the open air. It was the middle of summer, and though no annoyance from rain was apprehended, the heat in the middle of the day was most oppressive. Moreover, it was absolutely necessary that Mrs. Vickers and the child should have some place to themselves. At a little distance from the beach was a sandy rise, on the eastern side of which grew a forest of young trees. Frere proposed to cut down these trees, and make a sort of hut with them. It was soon discovered, however, that the pocket knives were insufficient for this purpose, but by dint of notching the young saplings and then breaking them down, they succeeded, in a couple of hours, in collecting wood enough to roof over a space between the hollow rock which contained the provisions and another rock, in shape like a hammer, which jutted out within five yards of it. Mrs. Vickers and Sylvia were to have this hut as a sleeping place, and Frere and Bates, lying at the mouth of the larder, would at once act as a guard to it and them. Grimes was to make for himself another hut where the fire had been lighted on the previous night.

But when they got back to dinner, inspirited by this resolution, they found Grimes walking about the sea-beach, talking mysteriously, and shaking his fist at an imaginary foe. On going up to him, they discovered that the blow to his skull had affected his brain, for he was delirious. Frere endeavoured to soothe him, without effect; and at last, by Bates's advice, the poor fellow was rolled in the sea. The cold bath quelled his violence, and, being laid beneath the shade of a rock hard by, he fell into a deep sleep.

The damper was then portioned out by Bates, and, together with a small piece of meat, it formed the dinner of the party. Mrs. Vickers reported that she had observed a great commotion on board the brig, and thought that the prisoners were throwing overboard such portions of the cargo as were not absolutely necessary to them, in order to lighten her. Before dinner was over a light breeze sprang up, and the *Osprey*, running up the union-jack reversed, fired a musket, either in farewell or triumph, and spreading her sails, disappeared round the western horn of the harbour.

Mrs. Vickers, taking Sylvia with her, went away a few paces, and leaning against the rugged wall of her future home, wept bitterly. Bates and Frere affected cheerfulness, but each felt that he had never fully realised his own loneliness until now.

The necessity for work, however, admitted of no indulgence of vain sorrow, and Bates setting the example, the pair worked so hard that by nightfall they had dragged together sufficient brushwood to complete Mrs. Vickers's hut. During the progress of this work they were often interrupted by Grimes, who persisted in vague rushes at them, exclaiming loudly against their supposed treachery in leaving him at the mercy of the mutineers. Bates also complained of the pain caused by the wound in his forehead, and that he was afflicted with a giddiness which he knew not how to avert.

Frere applied to him the remedy that had been so successfully tried upon Grimes, but the salt water inflamed Bates's wound, and rendered his condition worse. Mrs. Vickers recommended that a little spirit and water should be used to wash the cut, and the cask was got out and broached for that purpose. Tea and damper formed their evening meal; and by the light of a blazing fire, their condition looked less desperate. Mrs. Vickers dispensed the tea with a dignity which would have been absurd had it not been heart-rending. She had smoothed her hair and pinned the white shawl about her coquettishly; she even ventured to lament to Mr. Frere that she had not brought more clothes. Sylvia was in high spirits, and scorned to confess hunger. When the tea had been drunk, she fetched water from the spring in the kettle, and bathed Bates's head with it. It was resolved that, from the morrow, one of the number should fish daily.

The condition of Grimes now gave cause for the greatest uneasiness. From maundering foolishly, he had taken to absolute violence, and had to be watched by Frere. After much muttering and groaning, the poor fellow at last dropped off to sleep, and Frere, having assisted Bates to his sleeping place, prepared to snatch a few hours' slumber. Wearied by the labours of the day, he slept heavily, but, towards morning, was awakened by a strange noise.

Grimes had succeeded in forcing his way through the rude fence of brushwood, and had thrown himself upon Bates with the ferocity of insanity. Bates, in his weakened condition, was quite unable to cope with his desperate assailant, but calling feebly upon Frere for help, made shift to lay hold upon the jack-knife of which we have before spoken. Frere, starting to his feet, rushed to the assistance of the pilot, but was too late. Grimes tore the knife from Bates's grasp, and before Frere could catch his arm, plunged it twice into the unfortunate man's breast.

"I'm a dead man!" cried Bates faintly.

The sight of the blood, together with the exclamation of his victim, recalled Grimes to consciousness. He looked in bewilderment at the bloody weapon, and then flinging it from him, rushed away towards the sea into which he plunged headlong.

Aghast, Frere gazed after him, and saw from out the placid water, a pair of arms, with outstretched hands, emerge; a black spot, that was a head, rose up between these stiffening arms, and then, with a horrible cry, the whole disappeared, and the bright water sparkled as placidly as before. Then Frere saw, lying on the sand, an object that went far to explain the maniac's sudden burst of fury. The rum cask lay upon its side by the remnants of last night's fire. It was evident that the poor creature had come across the rum cask, drank a quantity of its contents, and been maddened by the fiery spirit.

Hurrying to the side of Bates, Frere strove to staunch the blood that flowed from his chest. Tearing off his neck-handkerchief, he endeavoured to bandage the wound, but found that the strip of silk was insufficient for the purpose. The noise roused Mrs. Vickers, who, stifling her terror, made haste to tear off a portion of her dress, and with this a bandage of sufficient width was made. Frere went to the cask to see if he could obtain from it a little spirit with which to moisten the lips of the dying man, but it was empty. Grimes, after drinking his fill, had overturned the unheaded puncheon, and the greedy sand had absorbed every drop of liquor.

By-and-by it struck Frere, with a curious feeling of pleasant selfishness, that with Grimes gone, the allowance of provisions would be increased, and that if Bates went also, it would be increased still further. He did not give utterance to his thoughts, however, but sat with the wounded man's head on his knees and brushed the flies from his face. He hoped, after all, that the pilot would not die, for he should then be left alone to look after the women. Perhaps some such thought was agitating Mrs. Vickers also. As for Sylvia, she made no secret of her anxiety.

"Don't die, Mr. Bates—oh, don't die!" she cried. "Don't leave mamma and me alone in this dreadful place!"

Frere frowned heavily, and Mrs. Vickers said, reprovingly, "Sylvia!" just as if they had been in the old house on Sarah Island.

In the afternoon Frere went away to gather wood for the fire, and when he returned he found the pilot near his end. Mrs. Vickers had seen more than one death-bed, and was calm enough; but Sylvia, sitting hard by, shook with terror. As the sun sank, Bates rallied; but the two watchers knew that it was but the final flicker of the expiring candle. "He's going!" said Frere at length, under his breath. A tremor shook the once stalwart limbs, and the dying man opened his eyes. For an instant he seemed bewildered, and then, looking from one to the other, intelligence returned to his glance, and it was evident that he remembered all. His gaze rested upon the pale face of Sylvia, and then turned to Frere. There was no mistaking the mute appeal of those eloquent eyes.

"Yes, I'll take care of her," said Frere.

Bates smiled, and then observing that his blood stained the white shawl of Mrs. Vickers, made an effort to move his head. It was not fitting that a lady's shawl should be stained with the blood of a poor fellow like himself. But the fashionable fribble gently drew the head back upon her bosom. In the presence of death the woman was womanly. For a moment all was silent, and they thought he had gone; but all at once he opened his eyes, and looked round for the sea.

"Turn my face to it once more," he whispered. "It's calm enough here,

God bless it, but I can hear the waves a-breaking hard upon the Bar!"

And so his head drooped, and he died.

As Frere relieved Mrs. Vickers from the weight of the corpse, Sylvia ran to her mother. "Oh, mamma, mamma," she cried, "why did God let him die when we wanted him so much?"

As it grew dark, Mrs. Vickers, worn out by the fatigue and excitement of the day, retired to rest; and Sylvia, refusing to speak to Frere, followed her mother. This dislike on the part of the child hurt Maurice more than he cared to own. He felt angry with her for not loving him, and yet he took no pains to conciliate her. It was with pleasure that he remembered how she must soon look up to him as her chief protector. Had Sylvia been a few years older, the young man would have thought himself in love with her.

The following day passed gloomily. Frere spent the morning in scooping a grave in the sand, in which to inter Bates. Awake to his own necessities, he removed such portions of clothing from the body as would be useful to him, but hid them under a stone, not liking to let Mrs. Vickers see what he had done. Having completed the grave by midday, he placed the corpse therein, and rolled as many stones as possible to the sides of the mound. In the afternoon he endeavoured to fish, but caught nothing. Passing by the grave on his return, he noticed that Mrs. Vickers had placed at the head of it a rude wooden cross.

After supper, he lit an economical pipe and tried to talk to Sylvia. "Why won't you be friends with me, Missy?" he asked.

"I don't like you," said Sylvia. "You frighten me."

"Why?"

"You are not kind. You are—oh, I wish papa was here!"

"Wishing won't bring him!" says Frere.

"There! *That's* what I mean. Is that kind?"

"I didn't mean it unkindly," says Frere. "What a strange child you are."

"There are persons," says Sylvia, "who have no Affinity for each other. I read about it in a book, and I suppose that's what it is. I have no Affinity for you. I can't help it, can I?"

"Rubbish!" Frere returned. "Come, I'll tell you a story."

Mrs. Vickers had gone back to her cave, and the two were alone by the fire. The child, with some show of hesitation, came to him, and he caught and placed her on his knee. The moon had not yet risen, and the shadows cast by the flickering fire seemed weird and monstrous. The wicked wish to frighten the child came to Maurice Frere.

"There was once," said he, "a Castle in a wood, and in this Castle there lived an Ogre, with great goggle eyes."

"You silly man!" said Sylvia, struggling to be free. "You are trying to frighten me!"

"And this Ogre lived on the bones of little girls."

"Mr. Frere, let me down!"

"One day a little girl was walking in the wood, and she heard the Ogre coming—"

A piercing scream burst from his companion. "Oh! Oh! What's that?" she cried, and clung to her persecutor.

On the other side of the fire stood the figure of a man. He staggered forward, and then, falling on his knees, stretched out his hands, and hoarsely articulated one word—"Food". It was Rufus Dawes.

The sound of a human voice broke the spell of terror that was on the child, and as the glow from the fire fell upon the tattered yellow garments, she guessed at once the whole story. Not so Maurice Frere. He saw only a new mouth to share the scanty provision, and snatching a brand from the fire he kept the convict at bay. But Rufus Dawes, glaring round with wolfish eyes, caught sight of the damper resting against the kettle, and made a clutch at it. Frere dashed the brand in his face. "Stand back!" he cried. "We have no food to spare!"

The convict uttered a savage cry, and raising the iron gad, plunged forward to attack this new enemy: but the child glided past Frere, and snatching the loaf, placed it in the hands of the starving man, with "Here, poor prisoner, eat!" Then, turning to Frere, she cast upon him a glance so full of horror and indignation that the man blushed and threw down the brand.

As for Rufus Dawes, the sudden apparition of this golden-haired girl seemed to have transformed him. Allowing the loaf to slip through his fingers, he gazed with haggard eyes at the retreating figure of the child, and as it vanished into the darkness outside the circle of firelight, the unhappy man sank his face upon his hands, and burst into tears.

The coarse tones of Maurice Frere roused him. "What do you want!" he asked.

"MR." DAWES

Rufus Dawes, raising his head, contemplated the figure before him, and recognised it. "Is it *you?*" he said slowly.

"What do you mean? Do you know me?" asked Frere. But the convict did not reply. His momentary emotion passed, he greedily seized the piece of damper and began to eat in silence.

"Do you hear, man?" repeated Frere. "What are you?"

"An escaped prisoner. You can give me up in the morning. I've done my best, and I'm beat."

This sentence struck Frere with dismay. The man did not know that the settlement had been abandoned!

"I cannot give you up. There is no one but myself and a woman and child on the settlement." Rufus Dawes stared at him in amazement. "The prisoners have gone away in the schooner. If you choose to remain free, you can do so as far as I am concerned. I am as helpless as you are."

"But how do *you* come here?"

Frere laughed bitterly. To give explanations to convicts was foreign to his experience, and he did not relish the task. "The prisoners mutinied, and seized the brig."

"What brig?"

"The *Osprey.*"

A terrible light broke upon Rufus Dawes, and he began to see how he had again missed his chance. "Who took her?"

"That double-dyed villain, John Rex," says Frere, giving vent to his passion. "May she sink and burn, and ——"

"Have they *gone*, then?" cried the miserable man.

"Yes; two days ago, and left us here to starve."

Rufus Dawes burst into a laugh so discordant that it made the other shudder. "We'll starve together, Maurice Frere," said he; "for while you've a crust, I'll share it. If I don't get liberty, at least I'll have revenge!"

The sinister aspect of this savage, rocking himself to and fro in the firelight, gave Mr. Maurice Frere a new sensation. He felt as might have felt that African hunter who, returning to his camp fire, found a lion there. "Wretch!" cried he, "why should you wish to be revenged on *me?*"

The convict turned upon him with a snarl. "Take care what you say! If I am a wretch, who made me one? If I hate you and myself and the world, who made me hate it? I was born free—as free as you are. Why should I be condemned to this slavery, worse than death? Tell me that, Maurice Frere!"

"I didn't make the laws," says Frere; "why attack me?"

"Because you are what I *was*. You are free! You can love, you can work, you can think. I can only *hate*!" He paused and then continued with a low laugh, "Fine words for a convict, eh! But, never mind, Mr. Frere, we're equal now, and I sha'n't die an hour sooner than you, though you are a 'free man'!"

Frere began to think that he was dealing with another madman. "Die! There's no need to talk of dying," he said, as soothingly as he could. "Time enough for that by-and-by."

"There spoke the *free* man. We convicts have an advantage over you *gentlemen*. You are afraid of death; we pray for it. They were going to hang me once. My God, how I wish they had!"

There was such a depth of agony in this utterance that Frere was appalled. "There, go and sleep, my man," he said. "You are knocked up. We'll talk in the morning."

"Hold on a bit!" cried Rufus Dawes fiercely. "Who's with ye?"

"The Commandant's wife and daughter," replied Frere unwillingly.

"No one else?"

"No."

"Poor souls!" said the convict, "I pity them." And then stretching himself like a dog before the blaze, he went to sleep.

As Maurice Frere gazed upon the sleeping wretch, a horrible prompting made him feel for the jack-knife with which one murder had already been committed. The stock of provisions was so scanty, and, after all, the lives of the woman and child were worth more than that of this unknown desperado! But, to do Frere justice, the thought no sooner shaped itself than he crushed it out. "We'll wait till morning, and see how he shapes," said Frere to himself; and pausing at the brushwood barricade behind which the mother and daughter were clinging to each other, he whispered that he was on guard outside, and that the absconder slept. But when morning dawned, he found that there was no need for alarm. The convict was lying in almost the same position as that in which he had left him, and his eyes were closed. Frere advanced, and shook him by the shoulder.

"Keep off!" cried the wretch, waking with a start, and raising his arm to strike.

"It's all right," said Frere. "No one is going to harm you."

Rufus Dawes glanced around him stupidly, and then remembering what had happened, staggered to his feet. "I thought they'd got me!" he said; "but it's the other way, I see. Come, let's have breakfast, Mr. Frere. I'm hungry."

"You must wait," said Frere. "Do you think there is no one here but yourself?"

Rufus Dawes swayed to and fro from weakness. "I don't know anything about it. I only know I'm hungry."

Frere stopped short. Now or never was the time to settle future relations. Lying awake in the night, he had decided on the course of action that must be adopted. The convict should share with the rest, but no more. If he rebelled, there must be a trial of strength between them. "Look you here," he said. "We have but barely enough food to serve us until help comes—if it does come. I have the care of that poor woman and child, and I will see fair play for their sakes. You shall share with us to our last bit and drop; but, by Heaven, you shall get no more."

The convict looked at him with the uncertain gaze of a drunken man. "I am weak now," he said. "you have the best of me." He sank suddenly down upon the ground. "Give me drink," he moaned feebly.

Frere got him water in the pannikin, and having drunk it, he lay down again. Mrs. Vickers and Sylvia, coming out while he slept, recognised him as the desperado of the settlement.

"He was the most desperate man we had," recalled Mrs. Vickers. "Oh, what shall we do?"

"He won't do much harm," returned Frere, looking at the notorious ruffian with curiosity. "He's as near dead as can be."

Sylvia looked up at him with her clear child's glance. "We mustn't let him die," said she. "That would be murder."

"No, no," returned Frere, hastily; "no one wants him to die. But what can we do?"

"I'll nurse him!" cried Sylvia.

Frere broke into a coarse laugh. "*You* nurse him! By George, that's a good one!" The child felt the contempt in the tone, and burst into a passion of sobs. "Why do you insult me, you wicked man? The poor fellow's ill, and he'll—he'll die, like Mr. Bates. Oh, mamma, mamma, let's go away by ourselves."

Frere swore a great oath, and walked away. He was full of strange thoughts, which he could not express and which he had never owned before. The dislike the child bore him made him miserable, yet he took delight in tormenting her. He was conscious that he had acted the part of a coward the night before in endeavouring to frighten her, and that her detestation was well earned; but he had fully determined to stake his life in her defence, should the savage who had thus come upon them out of the desert attempt violence. It was not fair to be thus misinterpreted. But he had done wrong to swear, and more so in quitting them so abruptly.

Walking along, he came to Bates's grave. Here was another evidence of ill-treatment. She had always preferred Bates. Now that Bates was gone, she must needs transfer her childish affections to a convict. "Oh," said Frere to himself, with pleasant recollections of many coarse triumphs in love-making, "if you were a woman, you little vixen, I'd *make* you love me!" When he had said this, he laughed at himself for his folly—he was "turning romantic"!

When he got back, he found Dawes stretched upon the brushwood, with Sylvia sitting near him.

"He is better," said Mrs. Vickers, disdaining to refer to the scene of the morning. "Sit down and eat, Mr. Frere."

"Are you better?" asked Frere, abruptly.

To his surprise, the convict answered quite civilly, "I shall be strong again in a day or two, and then I can help you, sir."

"Help me? How?"

"To build a hut for the ladies. And we'll live here all our lives, and never go back to the sheds any more."

"He has been wandering a little," said Mrs. Vickers. "Poor fellow, he seems quite well behaved."

The convict began to sing a German song, and Frere looked at him with curiosity. "I wonder what the story of that man's life has been," he said. "A queer one, I'll be bound."

Sylvia smiled up at him. "I'll ask him when he gets well," she said, "and if you are good, I'll tell you, Mr. Frere."

Frere accepted the proffered friendship. "I am a brute, Sylvia, sometimes, ain't I?" he said, "but I don't mean it."

"Let's shake hands and be friends," returned Sylvia. "It's no use quarrelling when there are only four of us, is it?"

And in this way was Rufus Dawes admitted a member of the family circle.

Within a week from the night on which he had seen the smoke of Frere's fire, the convict had recovered his strength, and had become an important personage. The distrust with which he had been at first viewed had worn off, and he was no longer an outcast to be referred to in whispers. He had abandoned his rough manner, and though at times a profound melancholy would oppress him, his spirits were more even than those of Frere, who was often sullen and overbearing. Rufus Dawes was now an active member of society—a society of four—and he began to regain an air of independence and authority. This change had been wrought by the influence of little Sylvia, for Rufus Dawes had experienced for the first time in six years the soothing power of kindness. He had now an object to live for beyond himself. He was of use to somebody, and had he died, he would have been regretted.

By the strange concurrence of circumstances, he had been brought into a position in which his convict experiences gave him authority. He knew how to sustain life on as little food as possible. He could fell trees without an axe, bake bread without an oven, build a weather-proof hut without bricks or mortar. In the semi-savage state to which these four human beings had been brought, Might was Right, and Maurice Frere's authority of gentility soon succumbed to Rufus Dawes's authority of knowledge.

As the time wore on, and the scanty stock of provisions decreased, he found that his authority grew more and more powerful. Did a question arise as to the qualities of a strange plant, it was Rufus Dawes who could pronounce upon it. Were fish to be caught, it was Rufus Dawes who caught them. Did Mrs. Vickers complain of the instability of her brushwood hut, it was Rufus Dawes who produced a wall that defied the keenest wind. He made cups out of pine-knots and plates out of bark-strips. He worked harder than any three men. Nothing daunted him, nothing discouraged him. When Mrs. Vickers fell sick, it was Rufus Dawes who gathered fresh leaves for her couch, who cheered her by hopeful words, who voluntarily gave up half his own allowance of meat that she might grow the stronger on it.

Frere watched all this with dissatisfaction that amounted at times to positive hatred. Yet he could say nothing, and even submitted to take orders from this escaped convict—it was so evident that the escaped convict knew better than he. Sylvia began to look upon Dawes as a second Bates. He was, moreover, all her own. If it had not been for her, this prodigy would not have lived. He felt for her an absorbing affection that was almost a passion. She was his good angel, his protectress, his glimpse of heaven. He would have died for her, and, for love of her, hoped for the vessel which should take *her* back to freedom and give *him* again to bondage.

But the days stole on, and no vessel appeared. Each day they eagerly scanned the horizon—but in vain. Mrs. Vickers's illness increased, and the stock of provisions began to run short.

With blank faces they watched their bag of flour grow smaller and smaller daily. Then the notion of escape was broached. Could they construct a raft? Impossible without nails or ropes. Could they raise a fire sufficient to signal a ship? Easily; but what ship would come within reach of that doubly-desolate spot? Nothing could be done but wait for a vessel, which was sure to come sooner or later; and, growing weaker day by day, they waited.

One day Sylvia was sitting in the sun reading the "English History", which, by the accident of fright, she had brought with her on the night of the mutiny. Suddenly she gave a little scream. The remembrance of the evening when she read about the Ancient Britons to poor Bates came vividly into her mind, and though she had since re-read the passage that had then attracted her attention a hundred times, it had never before presented itself to her in its full significance. Hurriedly turning the well-thumbed leaves, she read aloud the passage which had provoked remark:—

"The Ancient Britons were little better than Barbarians. They painted their bodies with Woad, and, seated in their light coracles of skin stretched upon slender wooden frames, must have presented a wild and savage appearance."

"A coracle! That's a boat! Can't we make a coracle, Mr. Dawes?"

The question gave the marooned party new hope. Maurice Frere, with his usual impetuosity, declared that the project was a most feasible one, and

WHAT THE SEAWEED SUGGESTED

wondered that it had never occurred to him before. "It's the simplest thing in the world!" he cried. But upon taking the matter into more earnest consideration, it became apparent that they were as yet a long way from the realisation of their hopes. To make a coracle of skins seemed sufficiently easy, but how to obtain the skins! The one miserable hide of the unlucky she-goat was utterly inadequate for the purpose. Sylvia—her face beaming with hope—watched the countenance of Rufus Dawes, but she marked no answering gleam of joy in those downcast eyes. "Can't it be done, Mr. Dawes?" she asked, trembling for the reply.

The convict knitted his brows gloomily.

"Come, Dawes!" cried Frere, "can't you suggest something?"

"I don't know," Rufus Dawes said, "I must think. It looks easy, and yet——" He paused as something in the water caught his eye. It was a mass of bladdery seaweed that the returning tide was wafting slowly to the shore. This object, which would have passed unnoticed at any other time, suggested to Rufus Dawes a new idea. "Yes," he added slowly, with a change of tone, "it may be done. I think I see my way."

The others preserved a respectful silence until he should speak again. "How far is it across the bay to the Pilot Station?" he asked Frere.

"About four miles."

The convict sighed. "Too far to swim now, though I might have done it once. But this sort of life weakens a man. It must be done after all."

"What are you going to do?" asked Frere.

"To kill the goat."

Sylvia uttered a little cry; she had become fond of her dumb companion. "Kill Nanny! Oh, Mr. Dawes! What for?"

"I am going to make a boat for you," he said; "and I want hides, and thread, and tallow."

"You can't get more than one hide off a goat, man?" Frere said, with an inquiring tone in his voice—as though it was just possible that Dawes *could* get a second hide, by virtue of some secret process known only to himself.

"I am going to catch other goats."

"Where?"

"At the Pilot Station."

"But how are you going to get there?"

"Float across. Come, there is no time for questioning! Go and cut down some saplings, and let us begin!"

The lieutenant-master looked at the convict prisoner with astonishment, and then did as he was ordered. Before sundown that evening, the carcase of poor Nanny, broken into various most unbutcherly fragments, was hanging on the nearest tree; and Frere, returning with as many young saplings as he could drag together, found Rufus Dawes engaged in a curious occupation. He had killed the goat, and having cut off its head close under the jaws, and its legs at the knee-joint, had extracted the carcase through a slit made in the lower portion of the belly, which slit he had now sewn together with string. This proceeding gave him a rough bag, and he was busily engaged in filling this bag with such coarse grass as he could collect. Frere observed, also, that the fat of the animal was carefully preserved, and the intestines had been placed in a pool of water to soak.

The convict, however, declined to give information as to what he intended to do. "It's my own notion," he said. "Let me alone. I may make a failure of it." Frere scowled, galled to think that a convict brain should contain a mystery which he might not share.

The next day, by Rufus Dawes's directions, Frere cut down some rushes that grew about a mile from the camping ground and brought them in on his back.

"What are they for?" asked Frere, as he flung the bundle down.

His master condescended to reply. "To make a float."

"Well?"

The other shrugged his broad shoulders. "You are very dull, Mr. Frere. I am going to swim over to the Pilot Station and catch some of those goats. *I* can get across on the stuffed skin, but I must float *them* back on the reeds."

"How the doose do you mean to catch 'em?" asked Frere.

The convict motioned to him to approach. He did so, and saw that his companion was cleaning the intestines of the goat. The outer membrane having been peeled off, Rufus Dawes was turning the gut inside out. This he did by turning up a short piece of it, as though it were a coat-sleeve, and dipping the turned-up cuff into a pool of water. The weight of the water pressing between the cuff and the rest of the gut bore down a further portion; and so, by repeated dippings, the whole length was turned inside out. The inner membrane having been scraped away, there remained a fine transparent tube, which was tightly twisted, and set to dry in the sun.

"There is the catgut for the noose," said Dawes. "I learnt *that* trick at the settlement. Now come here."

Frere, following, saw that a fire had been made between two stones, and that the kettle was partly sunk in the ground near it. On approaching the kettle, he found it full of smooth pebbles.

"Take out those stones," said Dawes.

Frere obeyed, and saw in the kettle a quantity of sparkling white powder. "What's that?" he asked.

"Salt."

"How did you get it?"

"I filled the kettle with seawater, and then heating those pebbles red-hot in the fire, dropped them into it. We could have caught the steam in a cloth and wrung out fresh water had we wished to do so. But, thank God, we have plenty."

Frere started. "Did you learn that at the settlement, too?" he asked.

Rufus Dawes laughed bitterly. "Do you think I have been at the 'settlement' all my life? The thing is very simple; it is merely evaporation."

Frere burst out in sudden, fretful admiration: "What a fellow you are, Dawes! What are you—what *have* you been?"

A light came into the other's face, and for an instant he seemed about to make some startling revelation. But the light faded, and he checked himself with a gesture of pain.

"I *am* a convict. Never mind what I *have* been. A sailor, shipbuilder, prodigal, vagabond—what does it matter?"

"If we get safely back," says Frere, "I'll ask for a free pardon for you. You deserve it."

"Come," returned Dawes, with a discordant laugh. "Let us wait until we do get back."

"You don't believe me?"

"I don't want favour at *your* hands," he said, with a return of the old fierceness. "Let us get to work. Bring up the rushes here, and tie them with a fishing-line."

At this instant Sylvia came up.

"Hard at work, Mr. Dawes? Oh! what's this in the kettle?"

The voice of the child acted like a charm upon Rufus Dawes. He smiled quite cheerfully.

"Salt, miss. I am going to catch the goats with that."

"How? Put it on their tails?" she cried merrily.

"Goats are fond of salt, and when I get over to the Pilot Station, I shall set traps for them baited with this salt. When they come to lick it, I shall have a noose of catgut ready to catch them."

"But how will you get across?"

"You will see to-morrow."

A WONDERFUL DAY'S WORK

The next morning Rufus Dawes was stirring by daylight. He first got his catgut wound upon a piece of stick, and then, having moved his frail floats alongside the little rock that served as a pier, he took a fishing-line and a larger piece of stick, and proceeded to draw a diagram on the sand. This diagram when completed represented a rude outline of a punt eight feet long and three broad. At certain distances were eight points—four on each side—into which small willow rods were driven. He then awoke Frere, and showed the diagram to him.

"Get eight stakes of celery-top pine," he said. "You can burn them where you cannot cut them, and drive a stake into the place of each of these willow wands. When you have done that, collect as many willows as you can get. I shall not be back until to-night. Now give me a hand with the floats."

Frere, coming to the pier, saw Dawes strip himself, and piling his clothes upon the stuffed goat-skin, stretch himself upon the reed bundles, and, paddling with his hands, push off from the shore. The clothes floated high and dry, but the reeds, depressed by the weight of the body, sank so that the head of the convict alone appeared above water. In this fashion he gained the middle of the current, and the out-going tide swept him down towards the mouth of the harbour.

Frere, sulkily admiring, went back to prepare the breakfast—they were on half rations now, Dawes having forbidden the slaughtered goat to be eaten lest his expedition should prove unsuccessful—wondering at the chance which had thrown this convict in his way. "Parsons would call it 'a special providence'," he said to himself. "For if it hadn't been for him, we should never have got thus far." The conversation of the previous day occurred to him. "I promised to ask for a free pardon. He wouldn't have it, though. Too proud to accept it at my hands! How confoundedly impudent a little liberty makes these beggars! Wait until we get back. I'll teach him his place." Then a thought came into his head that was in every way worthy of him. "Suppose we took the boat, and left him behind!" The notion seemed so wicked that he laughed involuntarily.

"What is it, Mr. Frere?"

"Oh, it's you, Sylvia, is it? I was thinking of something funny."

"Indeed," said Sylvia, "I am glad. Where's Mr. Dawes?"

Frere was displeased at the interest with which she inquired.

"You are always thinking of that fellow. It's Dawes, Dawes, Dawes, all day long. He has gone."

"Oh!" sorrowfully. "Mamma wants to see him."

"What about?" says Frere roughly.

"Mamma is ill, Mr. Frere."

"Dawes isn't a doctor. What's the matter with her?"

"I don't know but she is worse than she was yesterday."

Frere, somewhat alarmed, strode over to the little cavern.

The poor woman was lying on a bed of rushes and was moaning feebly. The exhaustion and lassitude to which she had partially succumbed soon after Dawes's arrival had now completely overcome her, and she was unable to rise.

"Cheer up, ma'am," said Maurice heartily. "It will be all right in a day or two."

"Is it you? I sent for Mr. Dawes."

"He is away just now. I am making a boat."

"Sylvia told me that *he* was making one."

"Well I—that is *we*—are making it. He will be back again to-night. Can I do anything for you?"

"No, thank you. I only wanted to know how he was getting on. I must go soon—if I am to go. Thank you, Mr. Frere. I am much obliged to you. This is a—he-e—dreadful place to have visitors, isn't it?"

"Never mind," said Frere again, "you will be back in Hobart Town in a few days now. You must cheer up. Have some tea or something."

"No, thank you—I don't feel well enough to eat. Oh, I wish Mr. Dawes was back."

Maurice Frere went out indignant. This "Mr." Dawes was everybody, it seemed, and he was nobody. All that day, working hard to carry out the convict's directions, he meditated a thousand plans by which he could turn the tables. He would accuse Dawes of violence. He would demand that the law take its course, and that the "death" which was the doom of all who were caught in the act of escape from a penal settlement, should be enforced. But if they got safe to land, the courage and ingenuity of the prisoner would tell strongly in his favour. The woman and child would plead for him. Yet there must be some method by which he might claim the credit of the escape, and snatch from the prisoner who had dared to rival him the last hope of freedom.

Rufus Dawes, drifting with the current, had allowed himself to coast along the eastern side of the harbour until the Pilot Station appeared in view on the opposite shore. He landed at a sandy cove, and drawing up his raft, proceeded to unpack from among his garments a piece of damper. Having eaten sparingly, and dried himself in the sun, he replaced the remains of his breakfast, and pushed his floats again into the water. The Pilot Station lay some distance below him, on the opposite shore. He had purposely made his second start from this point, for had he attempted to paddle across at right angles, the strength of the current would have swept him out to sea. At length, breathless and exhausted, he gained the opposite bank, half a mile below the point he had attempted to make, and carrying his floats out of reach of the tide, made off across the hills to the Pilot Station.

Arrived there about mid-day, he set to work to lay his snares. He carefully examined the tracks of the goats, and found that they converged to one point—the track to the nearest water. With much labour, he cut down bushes, so as to mask the approach to the waterhole on all sides save where these tracks immediately conjoined. Close to the water he scattered the salt he had obtained by his rude distillation of sea-water. Between this scattered salt and the points where he judged the animals would be likely to approach, he set his traps.

These he made after the following manner. He took several pliant branches of young trees, having stripped them of leaves and twigs. Then he dug with his knife a succession of holes, about a foot deep. At the thicker end of the saplings he fastened, by a piece of fishing-line, a small cross-bar, which swung loosely. Forcing the ends thus prepared into the holes, he filled in and stamped down the earth all around them. The saplings, anchored as it were by the cross-pieces of stick, not only stood firm, but resisted all his efforts to withdraw them. To the other ends of these saplings he bound tightly the catgut springes, or loops, he had brought from the camping ground. The saplings he then bent double, and secured the gutted ends in the ground.

This was the most difficult part of the business, for it was necessary to discover precisely the amount of pressure that would hold the bent rod without allowing it to spring free, and which would yet "give" to a slight pull on the gut. After many failures, however, this happy medium was discovered; and Rufus Dawes, concealing his springes by means of twigs, smoothed the disturbed sand with a branch, and retired to watch the effect of his labours.

About two hours afterwards, the goats came to drink. There were five goats and two kids, and they trotted calmly along the path to the water. The watcher soon saw that his precautions had been in a manner wasted. The leading goat marched gravely into the springe, which, catching him round the neck, released the bent rod, and sprang him off his legs into the air. He uttered a comical bleat, and then hung kicking. Rufus Dawes, though the success of the scheme was a matter of life and death, burst out laughing at the antics of the beast.

The other goats bounded off at this sudden elevation of their leader, and three more were entrapped at a little distance. Rufus Dawes ran down to the old goat, knife in hand, but before he could reach him, the barely-dried catgut gave way, and the old fellow, shaking his head with grotesque dismay, made off at full speed. The others, however, were secured and killed.

The loss of the springe was not a serious one, for three traps remained unsprung, and before sundown Rufus Dawes had caught four more goats. Removing with care the precious cat-gut, he dragged the carcases to the shore, and proceeded to pack them upon his floats. He discovered, however, that the weight was too great, and that the water, entering through the loops of the stitching in the hide, had rendered the floats no longer buoyant. He was compelled, therefore, to spend two hours in re-stuffing the skin with such material as he could find. Some light and flock-like seaweed, which the action of the water had swathed after the fashion of haybands along the shore, formed an excellent substitute for grass, and having bound his bundle of rushes lengthwise, with the goat-skin as a centre-piece, he succeeded in forming a sort of rude canoe, upon which the carcases floated securely.

He had eaten nothing since the morning, and was exhausted. Still, sustained by the excitement of the task he had set himself, he dismissed with fierce impatience the thought of rest, and dragged his weary limbs along the sand. The tide was now running in, and he knew he must regain the farther shore while the current was in his favour. He could not afford to lose an hour.

It was a clear night, and the risen moon, large and low, flung a rippling streak of silver across the sea. The fire of the exiles, on the other side of the bay, cast a red glow into the air. Rufus Dawes touched the chill water and drew back. For an instant he determined to wait until the beams of morning should illumine the treacherous sea, and then the thought of the helpless child, who was waiting and watching for him on the shore, gave new strength to his wearied frame. Fixing his eyes on the glow that, hovering above the dark tree line, marked her presence, he pushed the raft before him into the sea.

The reeds sustained him bravely, but the current sucked him underneath the water, and for several seconds he feared that he should be compelled to let go his hold. But his muscles, steeled in the slow fire of convict-labour, withstood this last strain upon them, and, with bursting chest and paralysed fingers, he paddled and pushed until the mass, getting out of eddies along the shore-line, drifted steadily down the silvery track that led to the settlement. At last, just when his stiffened limbs refused to obey the impulse of his will, and he began to drift onwards with the onward tide, he felt his feet strike firm ground. The waves, tired of persecuting him, had, with disdainful pity cast him ashore at the goal of his hopes. Looking back, he for the first time realised the peril he had escaped, and shuddered. To this shudder succeeded a thrill of triumph. "Why had he stayed so long, when escape was so easy?"

Dragging the carcases above high-water mark, he made for the fire. The recollection of the night when he had first approached it came upon him, and increased his exultation. How different a man was he now from then! Passing up the sand, he saw the stakes which he had directed Frere to cut, whiten in the moonshine. His officer worked for him! In his brain alone lay the secret of escape! He—Rufus Dawes—the scarred, degraded "prisoner", could alone get these three beings back to civilisation.

He had gained the fire before the solitary watcher there heard his footsteps, and spread his hands to the blaze in silence. He felt as Frere would have felt, had their positions been reversed, disdainful of the man who had stopped at home.

Frere, starting, cried, "It is you! Have you succeeded?"

Rufus Dawes nodded.

"What! Did you catch them?"

"There are seven carcases down by the rocks. You can have meat for breakfast to-morrow!"

The child came running down from the hut. "Oh, Mr. Dawes! I am so glad! We were beginning to despair—mamma and I."

Dawes, bursting into a joyous laugh, swung her up into the air. "Tell me," he cried, "what you will do for me if I bring you and mamma safe home again?"

"Give you a free pardon," says Sylvia, "and papa shall make you his servant!" Frere burst out laughing; Dawes, with a choking sensation in his throat, put the child down and walked away.

This was in truth all he could hope for. All his courage, all his peril, would but result in the patronage of a great man like Major Vickers. He had performed a prodigy of skill and daring, and for his reward he was to be made a servant to the creatures he had protected. Yet what more could a convict expect? Sylvia saw how deeply her unconscious hand had driven the iron, and ran up to the man she had wounded. "And, Mr. Dawes, remember that I shall love you always." The convict, however, motioned her away; and she saw him stretch himself wearily under the shadow of a rock.

In the morning, Rufus Dawes was first at work, and made no allusion to the scene of the previous evening. He had already skinned one of the goats, and

THE CORACLE

he directed Frere to set to work upon another. "Cut down the rump to the hock, and down the brisket to the knee," he said. "I want the hides as square as possible." By dint of hard work they got the seven goats skinned, and the entrails cleaned ready for twisting, by breakfast time; and having broiled some of the flesh, made a hearty meal. Mrs. Vickers being no better, Dawes went to see her, and seemed to have made friends again with Sylvia, for he came out of the hut with the child's hand in his. Frere saw this, and it added fresh fuel to the fire of his jealousy. However, he said nothing, for his enemy had not yet shown him how the boat was to be made. Before mid-day, however, he was a partner in the secret, which, after all, was a very simple one.

Rufus Dawes took two of the straightest and most taper of the celery-top pines which Frere had cut on the previous day, and lashed them tightly together, with the butts outwards. He thus produced a spliced stick about twelve feet long. About two feet from either end he notched the young tree until he could bend the extremities upwards; and having so bent them, he secured the bent portions in their places by means of lashings of raw hide. The spliced trees now presented a rude outline of the section of a boat, having the stem, keel, and stern all in one piece. This having been placed lengthwise between the stakes, four other poles, notched in two places, were lashed from stake to stake, running crosswise to the keel, and forming the knees. Four saplings were now bent from end to end of the upturned portions of the keel that represented stem and stern. Two of these four were placed above, as gunwales; two below as bottom rails. At each intersection the sticks were lashed firmly with fishing-line. The whole framework being complete, the stakes were drawn out, and there lay upon the ground the skeleton of a boat eight feet long by three broad.

Frere would fain have rested; but the convict would not hear of it. "Let us finish," he said; "the skins will be dry if we stop."

"I can work no more," says Frere sulkily. "You've got muscles of iron, I suppose. I haven't."

"There's nothing like work to get rid of aching muscles, Maurice Frere, so they used to tell me."

"Well, what's to be done now?"

"Cover the boat. You can set the fat to melt, and sew these hides together."

"Don't talk to me as if I was a dog!" says Frere. "Be civil, can't you."

But the other, busily trimming the pieces of sapling, made no reply. It is possible that he thought the fatigued lieutenant beneath his notice. About an hour before sundown the hides were ready, and Rufus Dawes, having in the meantime interlaced the ribs of the skeleton with wattles, stretched the skins over it, with the hairy side inwards. Along the edges of this covering he bored holes at intervals, and passing through these holes thongs of twisted skin, he drew the whole to the top rail of the boat. One last precaution remained. Dipping the pannikin into the melted tallow, he plentifully anointed the seams of the sewn skins.

"There!" cried Rufus Dawes, triumphant. "Twelve hours in the sun to tighten the hides, and she'll swim like a duck.

The next day was spent in minor preparations. The jerked goat-meat was packed securely into as small a compass as possible. The rum barrel was filled with water, and water-bags were improvised out of portions of the intestines of the goats. Rufus Dawes also stripped cylindrical pieces of bark, and having sewn each cylinder at the side, fitted it to a bottom of the same material, and caulked the seams with gum and pine-tree resin. Thus four tolerable buckets were obtained. One goatskin yet remained, and out of that it was determined to make a sail. "The currents are strong," said Rufus Dawes, "and we shall not be able to row far with such oars as we have got. If we get a breeze it may save our lives." From thwart to thwart two poles were bound, and the mast, lashed between these poles with thongs of raw hide, was secured by shrouds of twisted fishing-line running fore and aft. Sheets of bark were placed at the bottom of the craft, and made a safe flooring. It was late in the afternoon of the fourth day when these preparations were completed, and it was decided that on the morrow they should adventure the journey. "We will coast down to the Bar," said Rufus Dawes, "and wait for the slack of the tide. I can do no more now."

Sylvia, her childish spirits risen with the hope of safety, called to them. She had wreathed seaweed about her head, and holding in her hand a twig representing a wand, she personified one of the heroines of her books.

"I am the Queen of the Island," she said merrily, "and you are my obedient subjects. Pray, Sir Eglamour, is the boat ready?"

"It is, your Majesty," said poor Dawes.

"Then we will see it. Come, walk in front of me. Mr. Frere, you don't play?"

"Oh, yes!" says Frere, unable to withstand her charming pout. "I'll play. What am I to do?"

"You must walk on *this* side, and be respectful. Now then, the Queen goes to the Seashore surrounded by her Nymphs! There is no occasion to laugh,

Mr. Frere. Of course, Nymphs are very different from *you*, but then we can't help that."

Marching in this ridiculous fashion across the sand, they halted at the coracle. "So that is the boat!" says the Queen, surprised out of her dignity. "You are a Wonderful Man, Mr. Dawes!"

Rufus Dawes smiled sadly. "It is very simple."

"Do you call this simple?" says Frere, who had shaken off his sulkiness. "By George, I don't! I call it sheer hard work."

"Yes!" echoed Sylvia, "sheer hard work by good Mr. Dawes!" And she began to sing a childish chant of triumph, drawing lines and letters in the sand the while, with her sceptre.

> "Good Mr. Dawes!
> Good Mr. Dawes!
> This is the work of Good Mr. Dawes!"

Maurice could not resist a sneer.

> "See-saw, Margery Daw,
> Sold her bed, and lay upon straw!"

"Good Mr. Dawes!" repeated Sylvia. "Why shouldn't I say it? You are disagreeable, sir. I won't play with you any more," and she went off along the sand.

"Poor child," said Rufus Dawes. "You speak too harshly to her."

Frere—now that the boat was made—had regained his self-confidence. "One would think that a boat had never been built before to hear her talk," he said. "If this washing-basket had been one of my old uncle's three-deckers, she couldn't have said much more. By the Lord!" he added, "I ought to have a natural talent for ship-building; for if the old villain hadn't died when he did, I should have been a ship-builder myself."

Rufus Dawes turned his back at the word "died", and busied himself with the fastenings of the hides. Could the other have seen his face, he would have been struck by its sudden pallor.

"Ah!" continued Frere, "that's a sum of money to lose, isn't it?"

"What do you mean?" asked the convict.

"Mean! Why, my good fellow, I should have been left a quarter of a million of money, but the old hunks who was going to give it me died before he could alter his will, and every shilling went to a scapegrace son, who hadn't been near the old man for years. That's the way of the world, isn't it?"

Rufus Dawes caught his breath in astonishment, and then, recovering himself, said in a harsh voice, "A fortunate fellow—that son!"

"Fortunate!" cries Frere. "Yes, he was fortunate! He was burnt to death in the *Hydaspes*, and never heard of his luck. His mother has got the money, though. I never saw a shilling of it." Then he walked away to the fire, musing, doubtless, on the difference between Maurice Frere, with a quarter of a million, disporting himself in the best society; and Maurice Frere, a penniless lieutenant, marooned on a barren coast, and acting as boat-builder to a runaway convict.

Rufus Dawes was also lost in reverie. His eyes were fixed upon the sea, golden in the sunset, but it was evident that he saw nothing of the scene before him. He was looking far away, across the glittering harbour, at the old house at Hampstead, with its well-remembered garden. He pictured himself escaped from this present peril, and freed from sordid thraldom. He saw himself returning, with some plausible story of his wanderings, to take possession of the wealth which was his—saw himself living once more, rich, free and respected, in the world from which he had been so long an exile. He saw his mother's sweet pale face, the light of a happy home circle. A new life opened radiant before him, and he was lost in the contemplation of his own happiness.

So absorbed was he, that he did not hear the light footstep of the child across the sand.

"Mamma has come to see the boat, Mr. Dawes!" cries Sylvia, but Dawes did not reply.

"Mr. Dawes!" Sylvia cried again, pulling at his sleeve.

The touch roused him, and looking down, he saw the pretty, thin face upturned to his. Scarcely conscious of what he did, he caught the little creature in his arms and kissed her. Mr. Frere was astonished at the presumption of the man, and, with Mrs. Vickers on his arm, reproved the apparent insolence of the convict as freely as if they both had been at his own little kingdom of Maria Island. "You insolent beggar!" he cried. "Keep your place, sir!"

That sentence recalled Rufus Dawes to reality. What business had he, a convict, with tenderness for the daughter of his master? He saw the two looking at the boat he had built, marked the flush of hope on the cheek of the poor lady, and the full-blown authority that already hardened the eye of Maurice Frere. All at once he understood the result of what he had done. He had, by his own act, given himself again to bondage. Until now he had been useful, even powerful. Now he had pointed out the way of escape, he had sunk into the beast of burden once again. All at once he turned on his heel, and strode up into the bush.

"A queer fellow," said Frere, as Mrs. Vickers followed the retreating figure with her eyes. "Always in an ill temper."

"Poor man! he has behaved very kindly to us," said Mrs. Vickers. Yet even she felt the change of circumstance, and knew that her blind trust in the convict had been transformed into a patronising kindliness which was quite foreign to esteem or affection.

"Come, let us have some supper," says Frere. "He will come back when his fit of sulks is over."

But he did not come back, and soon Mrs. Vickers and her daughter, rapt in the hopes and fears of the morrow, almost forgot that he had left them. The possession of the boat seemed to them so wonderful that the perils of the voyage they were to make in it were altogether lost sight of. As for Maurice Frere, he rejoiced that the convict was out of the way. He wished that he was out of the way altogether.

THE WRITING ON THE SAND

Having left the ungrateful creatures he had befriended, Rufus Dawes threw himself upon the ground in an agony of rage and regret. For the first time for six years he had tasted the happiness of doing good, had broken through the selfish misanthropy he had taught himself. And this was his reward! He had risked his life, forgone his enmities, almost changed his nature—and his reward was cold looks and harsh words, as soon as his skill had paved the way to freedom. This knowledge coming upon him while the astounding news of his riches yet vibrated in his brain, made him grind his teeth with rage at his own hard fate. Bound by the purest of ties—the affection of a son for his mother—he had condemned himself to social death, rather than buy his libety by a revelation which would shame the gentle creature. By a strange series of accidents, fortune had assisted him to maintain the deception he had practised. His cousin had not recognised him. The very ship in which he was believed to have sailed had been lost with every soul on board. His identity had been completely destroyed—no link remained which could connect Rufus Dawes, the convict, with Richard Devine, the vanished heir to the wealth of the dead ship-builder.

Oh, if he had only known! If, while in the gloomy prison, he had but guessed that death had stepped between Sir Richard and his vengeance, he might have spared himself the sacrifice he had made. He had been tried and condemned as a nameless sailor, who could call no witnesses in his defence, and give no particulars as to his previous history. It was clear to him now that he might have adhered to his statement of ignorance concerning the murder, locked in his breast the name of the murderer, and have yet been free; for it was not impossible that Richard Devine, the millionaire, would have escaped the fate which had overtaken Rufus Dawes, the sailor.

Of little use now was the heritage that he had gained. A convict-absconder, whose hands were hard with menial service, and whose back was scarred with the lash, could never be received among the gently nurtured. Let him lay claim to his name and rights, what then? He was a convicted felon, and his name and rights had been taken from him by the law. Let him go and tell Maurice Frere that he was his lost cousin. He would be laughed at. Let him proclaim aloud his birth and innocence, and the convict-sheds would grin, and the convict overseer set him to harder labour. Let him even get his wild story believed, what would happen? If it was heard in England that a convict claimed to be the heir to an English fortune, with what feeling would the announcement be received? Certainly not with a desire to redeem this ruffian from his bonds and place him in the honoured seat of his dead father. Such intelligence would be regarded as a calamity, a disgrace to an honoured and unsullied name. Let him succeed, let him return again to his mother; he would, at the best, be to her a living shame, scarcely less degrading than that which she had dreaded. Finally, suppose even that he could conceal the name of the real criminal, and show himself guiltless of the crime for which he had been condemned, all the wealth in the world could not buy back the self-respect which had been cut out of him by the lash, or banish from his brain the memory of his degradation.

For hours this agony racked him. It was hopeless to think of freedom and honour. Let him keep silence, and pursue the life fate had marked out for him. He would return to bondage. The law would claim him as an absconder, and would mete out to him such punishment as was fitting.

Yet suppose he did not go back at all, but wandered away into the wilderness and died? Better death than such a doom as his. Yet need he die? He could catch fish, he could build a hut. There was, perchance, at the deserted settlement some remnant of seed corn that, planted, would give him bread. Surely he could contrive to live alone, savage and free. Alone! He had contrived all these marvels alone! Was not the boat he himself had built below upon the shore? Why not escape in her, and leave to their fate those miserable ingrates?

The night had passed during his reverie, and the first faint streaks of dawn began to lighten the sky. Haggard and pale, he rose to his feet, and scarcely daring to think about what he proposed to do, ran towards the boat. As he ran, a voice seemed to encourage him. "Your life is of more importance than theirs. They have been ungrateful and deserve death. You will escape out of this Hell, and return to the loving heart who mourns you. Moreover they may not die. They are sure to be sent for. Think of what awaits you when you return—an absconded convict!"

He was within three feet of the boat, when he suddenly stopped and stood motionless, staring at the sand. He had come upon the sentence traced by Sylvia the evening before.

GOOD MR. DAWES

"Good Mr. Dawes!" What a frightful reproach there was to him in that simple sentence! What a world of baseness and cruelty did not those eleven letters open up to him!

He staggered to the cavern, and shook the sleeping Frere violently. "Awake! awake!" he cried, "and let us leave this place!"

Frere, starting to his feet, looked at the white face and bloodshot eyes of the man before him with astonishment.

"What's the matter with you, man?" he said. "You look as if you'd seen a ghost!"

At these words, Rufus Dawes gave a long, shuddering sigh.

"Come, Sylvia!" shouted Frere, "it's time to get up. I am ready to go!"

The convict's sacrifice was complete. As he turned away, tears rolled down his rugged face and fell upon the sand.

An hour after sunrise, the frail boat drifted with the out-going current towards the mouth of the Harbour. When first launched she had come nigh
AT SEA to swamping, being overloaded, and it was found necessary to leave behind a great portion of the dried meat. With what pangs this was done can be easily imagined, for each atom of food seemed to represent an hour of life. Yet there was no help for it.

That evening they camped at the mouth of the Gates until the slack of the tide, and about ten o'clock adventured to cross the bar. The night was lovely, and the sea calm. It seemed as though Providence had taken pity on them; for, despite the insecurity of the craft and the violence of the breakers, the dreaded passage was achieved. A great misfortune, however, occurred. Two of the bark buckets, left by some oversight uncleated, were washed overboard by a large wave, and with them nearly a fifth of their scanty store of water. But in the face of the greater peril, the accident seemed trifling; and as, drenched and chilled, they gained the open sea, they could not but admit that fortune had almost miraculously befriended them.

Hoisting the goatskin sail, they crept along the coast. It was resolved that the two men should keep watch and watch; and Frere for the second time enforced his authority by giving the first watch to Rufus Dawes. "I am tired," he said, "and shall sleep for a while."

Rufus Dawes, who had not slept for two nights, said nothing. He had suffered so much during the last two days that his senses were becoming dulled to pain.

Frere slept until late in the afternoon, and, when he woke, found Sylvia and her mother both sea-sick. This seemed strange to him. Sea-sickness appeared to be a malady which belonged exclusively to civilisation. Moodily watching the great green waves, he marvelled to think that only twenty-four days had passed since the mutiny. That event had taken place on the 13th of January; it was now the 6th of February. "Surely," thought he, "the *Ladybird* might have returned by this time." There was no one to tell him that the *Ladybird* had been driven into Port Davey by stress of weather, and detained there for seventeen days.

That night the wind fell, and they had to take to their oars. Rowing all night, they made but little progress, and Rufus Dawes suggested that they should put in to the shore and wait until the breeze sprang up. But, upon getting under the lee of a line of rocks which rose abruptly out of the sea, they found the waves breaking furiously upon a horse-shoe reef, six or seven miles in length. There was nothing for it but to coast again.

They coasted for two days, and on the third day a great wind drove them back thirty miles. The coracle began to leak, and required constant baling.

Almost as bad, the rumcask, that held the best part of their water, had leaked also, and was now half empty. They caulked it, by cutting out the leak, and plugging the hole with linen.

"It's lucky we ain't in the tropics," said Frere.

Mrs. Vickers, lying at the bottom of the boat, chilled to the bone with the bitter wind, had not the heart to speak. Surely the stifling calm of the tropics could not be worse than this bleak sea.

The position of the four poor creatures was now almost desperate. It was evident that Mrs. Vickers could not long survive the continued exposure to the weather. The child was in somewhat better case. Rufus Dawes had wrapped her in his woollen shirt, and, unknown to Frere, had divided with her daily his allowance of meat. She lay in his arms at night, and in the day crept by his side. As long as she was near him she felt safe. They spoke little to each other, but when Rufus Dawes felt the pressure of her tiny hand in his, he almost forgot the cold and his gnawing hunger.

So two more days passed, and yet no sail! On the tenth day after their departure from Macquarie Harbour, they came to the end of their provisions. The salt water had spoiled the goat-meat, and soaked the bread into a nauseous paste. The wind, having veered to the north, was blowing with increased violence. The wretched craft to which they had entrusted themselves was leaking in four places. If caught in one of the frequent storms which ravaged that iron-bound coast, she could not live an hour. The two men, wearied, hungry, and cold, almost hoped for the end to come quickly. To add to their distress, the child was now seized with fever. She was hot and cold by turns, and talked deliriously. Rufus Dawes, holding her in his arms, watched the suffering he was unable to alleviate with a savage despair at his heart. Was she to die after all?

So another day and night passed, and the eleventh morning saw the boat still rolling in the trough of the same deserted sea. The four exiles lay in her almost without breath.

All at once Dawes uttered a cry, and seizing the sheet, put the clumsy craft about. "A sail! a sail!" he cried.

Frere's hungry eyes ranged the dull water in vain.

"There is no sail, fool!" he said. "You mock us!"

The boat, no longer following the coast, was running due south, straight into the great Southern Ocean. Frere tried to wrest the thong from the hand of the convict, and bring the boat back to her course. "Are you mad," he shouted, "to run us out to sea?"

"Sit down!" returned the other, with a menacing gesture. "I tell you I see a sail!"

Frere, overawed by the strange light which gleamed in the eyes of his companion, shifted sulkily back to his place. "Have your own way," he said, "madman! It serves me right for putting off to sea in such a devil's craft as this!"

After all, what did it matter? As well be drowned in mid-ocean as in sight of land.

The long day wore out, and no sail appeared. The wind freshened towards evening, and the boat, plunging clumsily on the waves, staggered as though drunk with the water she had swallowed. The coast had altogether disappeared, and the vast ocean heaved and hissed all around them. It seemed impossible that they should live until morning. But Rufus Dawes, with his eyes fixed on some object visible alone to him, hugged the child in his arms, and drove the quivering coracle into the black waste of night and sea. To Frere, it began to seem that privation and anxiety had driven the unhappy convict mad.

Thinking over his fate, he fell—as it seemed to him—into a momentary sleep, in the midst of which some one called to him. Starting up, he saw that the day had broken, and the dawn, in one long pale streak of sickly saffron, lay low on the left hand. Between this streak of saffron-coloured light and the bows of the boat gleamed for an instant a white speck.

"A sail! a sail!" cried Rufus Dawes, a wild light gleaming in his eyes. "Did I not tell you that I saw a sail?"

Frere, confounded, looked again, and again did the white speck glimmer. For an instant he felt almost safe, and then a blanker despair than before fell upon him. From that distance, it was impossible for the ship to sight the boat.

"They will never see us!" he cried. "Do you hear, Dawes? They will never see us!"

Rufus Dawes started as if from a trance. Lashing the sheet to the pole which served as a gunwale, he laid the sleeping child by her mother, and tearing up the strip of bark on which he had been sitting, moved to the bows of the boat. "They will see this! Tear up that board! Now, place it thus across the bows. Hack off that sapling end! Now that dry twist of osier! Never mind the boat, man; we can afford to leave her now. Tear off that outer strip of hide! See, the wood beneath is dry! Quick—you are too slow."

"What are you going to do?" cried Frere, aghast, as the convict tore up all the dry wood he could find.

"Make a fire! See!"

Frere began to comprehend. "I have three matches left," he said, fumbling in his pocket. "I wrapped them in one of the leaves of the book to keep them dry."

The word "book" was a new inspiration. Rufus Dawes seized upon the "English History", tore out the drier leaves in the middle of the volume, and carefully added them to the little heap of touchwood.

"Now, steady!"

The match was struck and lighted. The paper, after a few obstinate curlings, caught fire, and the bark began to burn. He piled upon the fire all that was combustible, the hides began to shrivel, and a great column of black smoke rose up over the sea.

"Sylvia!" cried Rufus Dawes, "Sylvia! You are saved!"

She opened her blue eyes and looked at him, but gave no sign of recognition. Delirium had hold of her, and in the hour of safety the child had forgotten her preserver. Rufus Dawes, overcome by this last cruel stroke of fortune, sat down in the stern of the boat, with the child in his arms, speechless. Frere, feeding the fire, knew that the chance he had so longed for had come. With the mother at the point of death, and the child delirious, who could testify to this hated convict's skilfulness? No one but Mr. Maurice Frere, and Mr. Maurice Frere, as commandant of convicts, could not but give up an "absconder" to justice.

The ship changed her course, and came towards this strange fire in the middle of the ocean. The boat, the fore part of her blazing like a pine torch, could not float above an hour. The convict and the child remained motionless. Mrs. Vickers was lying senseless, ignorant of the approaching succour.

The ship—a brig, with American colours flying—came within hail of them. Frere could almost distinguish figures on her deck. He made his way aft to where Dawes was sitting with the child in his arms, and stirred him roughly with his foot.

"Go forward," he ordered, "and give the child to me."

With a low laugh, full of unutterable bitterness, Rufus Dawes placed the burden he had borne so tenderly in the arms of the lieutenant, and moved to the blazing bows.

The brig was close upon them. From her bulwarks peered bearded, eager faces, looking with astonishment at this burning boat and its haggard company, alone on that stormy ocean.

Frere, with Sylvia in his arms, waited for her.

BOOK THREE
Port Arthur~1838

"Society in Hobart Town, in this year of grace, 1838, is, my dear lord, composed of very curious elements." So ran a passage in the letter which the

A LABOURER IN THE VINEYARD

Rev. Mr. Meekin, newly-appointed chaplain, and seven-days' resident in Van Diemen's Land, was carrying to the post-office, for the delectation of his patron in England. As the reverend gentleman tripped daintily down the summer street that lay between the blue river and the purple mountain, he cast his mild eyes hither and thither upon human nature, and the sentence he had just penned recurred to him with pleasurable appositeness. Elbowed by well-dressed officers of garrison, bowing sweetly to well-dressed ladies, shrinking from ill-odoured ticket-of-leave men, or hastening across a street to avoid being run down by the hand-carts that, driven by gangs of convicts, rattled at him unexpectedly from behind corners, he certainly felt that the society through which he moved was composed of curious elements.

Clad in glossy black of the most fashionable clerical cut, with dandy boots and gloves of lightest lavender,—a white silk overcoat hinting that its wearer was not wholly free from sensitiveness to sun and heat,—the Reverend Meekin tripped daintily to the post-office, and deposited his letter. Two ladies met him as he turned.

"Mr. Meekin!"

Mr. Meekin's elegant hat was raised from his brow and hovered in the air, like a courteous black-bird, for an instant. "Mrs. Jellicoe! Mrs. Protherick! My dear leddies, this *is* an unexpected pleasure! And where, pray, are you going on this lovely afternoon? Ah! what a climate—but the Trail of the Serpent, my dear Mrs. Protherick—the Trail of the Serpent—" and he sighed.

"It must be a great trial to you to come to the colony," said Mrs. Jellicoe, sighing sympathetically.

Meekin smiled, as a gentlemanly martyr might have smiled. "The Lord's work, dear leddies—the Lord's work. I am but a poor labourer in the vineyard, toiling through the heat and burden of the day." The sight of him, with his faultless tie, airy coat, natty boots, and his self-satisfied Christian smile, was so unlike a poor labourer, that good Mrs. Jellicoe, the wife of an orthodox Comptroller of Convicts' Stores, felt a horrible thrill of momentary heresy. "I would rather have remained in England," continued Mr. Meekin, smoothing one lavender finger with the tip of another, "but I felt it my duty not to refuse the offer made me through the kindness of his lordship. Here is a field, leddies—a field for the Christian pastor. They appeal to me, leddies, these lost and outcast lambs of our Church."

Mrs. Jellicoe shook her gay bonnet ribbons at Mr. Meekin. "You don't know our convicts," she said. "They are horrible creatures. And as for servants—my goodness, I have a fresh one every week. When you have been here a little longer, you will know them better, Mr. Meekin."

"They are unbearable at times," said Mrs. Protherick, the widow of a Superintendent of Convicts' Barracks. "I am ordinarily the most patient creature breathing, but the stupid, vicious wretches that one gets are enough to put a saint out of temper."

"We have all our crosses, dear leddies," said Mr. Meekin piously. "Heaven send us strength to bear them! *Good*-morning."

"Why, you are going our way," said Mrs. Jellicoe. "We can walk together."

"Delighted! I am going to call on Major Vickers."

"What a charming little creature the Major's daughter is, isn't she?" said Mrs. Protherick.

"I have only met Major Vickers at Government House," said Meekin. "I haven't yet had the pleasure of seeing his daughter."

"A sad thing," said Mrs. Jellicoe. "Quite a romance, if it was not so sad, you know. His wife, poor Mrs. Vickers."

"Indeed! What of her?" asked Meekin.

"She is dead, poor soul," sighed Mrs. Jellicoe. "You mean to say you haven't heard the story, Mr. Meekin?"

"Dear leddies, I have only been in Hobart Town a week."

"The mutiny, you know, the mutiny at Macquarie Harbour. The prisoners took the ship, and put Mrs. Vickers and Sylvia ashore. Captain Frere was with them, too. The poor things had a dreadful time, and nearly died. Captain Frere made a boat at last, and they were picked up by a ship. Poor Mrs. Vickers only lived a few hours, and little Sylvia—she was only twelve years old then—was quite light-headed. They thought she wouldn't recover."

"How dreadful! And has she recovered?"

"Oh, yes, she's quite strong now, but her memory's gone."

"Her memory?"

"Yes," struck in Mrs. Protherick. "She doesn't remember anything about the time they were ashore—at least, not distinctly."

"It's a great mercy!" interrupted Mrs. Jellicoe. "Who wants her to remember these horrors? From Captain Frere's account, it was positively awful!"

"You don't say so!" warbled Mr. Meekin.

"A 'bolter'—an escaped prisoner, Mr. Meekin—happened to be left behind, and he found them out, and insisted on sharing the provisions—the wretch! Captain Frere was obliged to watch him constantly for fear he should murder them. Even in the boat he tried to run them out to sea and escape. He was one of the worst men in the Harbour, they say."

"And where is he now?" asked Mr. Meekin, with interest.

"Oh, goodness, I don't know—at Port Arthur, I think. I know that he was tried for bolting, and would have been hanged but for Captain Frere's exertions."

"Dear, dear!" said Mr. Meekin. "And so the young lady doesn't know anything about it?"

"Only what she has been told, of course, poor dear. She's engaged to Captain Frere."

"Really! How charming—quite a romance!"

"Isn't it? And Captain Frere's so much older than she."

"But her girlish love clings to her heroic protector," said Meekin. "Quite the—hem!—the ivy and the oak, dear leddies. Ah, in our fallen nature, what sweet spots—I think *this* is the gate."

A convict-servant—a pickpocket of note in days gone by—left the clergyman to repose in a handsomely furnished drawing-room, whose windows revealed a bright garden outside. The Major was out, it seemed, but Miss Vickers was in the garden, and could be called in at once. The Reverend Meekin, wiping his heated brow, laid himself back on the soft sofa, soothed by the elegant surroundings no less than by the coolness of the atmosphere. So charmed, indeed, was he, that he commenced to turn a fresh sentence for the Bishop, and to sketch out an elegant description of this oasis in his desert of a vineyard. While at this occupation, he was disturbed by the sound of some one near at hand crying. Softly stepping on to the broad verandah, he saw on the grass-plot two persons, an old man and a young girl. The sobbing proceeded from the old man.

"'Deed, miss, it's the truth! I've but jest come back to yez this morning. O my! it's a cruel thrick to play an ould man."

He was a white-haired old fellow, in grey convict garb.

"But it is your own fault, Danny; we all warned you against her," said the young girl softly. "How long was it this time?"

"Six months, miss. She said I was a drunkard, and beat her. Beat her, God help me!" stretching forth two trembling hands. "And they believed her, o' coorse. Now, when I kem back, she's away wid a ship's captain, saving your presence, miss, dhrinking in the George the Fourth. O my, but it's hard on an ould man!"

The girl sighed. "I can do nothing for you, Danny. I dare say you can work about the garden as you did before. I'll speak to the Major when he comes home."

Danny, lifting his bleared eyes to thank her, caught sight of Mr. Meekin, and saluted abruptly. Miss Vickers turned, and Mr. Meekin became conscious that the young lady was about seventeen years old, that her eyes were large and soft, her hair plentiful and bright, and that the hand which held the book she had been reading was white and small.

"Miss Vickers, I think. I am the Reverend Arthur Meekin."

"How do you do, Mr. Meekin?" said Sylvia, putting out one of her small hands. "Papa will be in directly."

"His daughter more than compensates for his absence, my dear Miss Vickers."

"I don't like flattery, Mr. Meekin, so don't use it. At least," she added, with a delicious frankness, "not *that* sort of flattery. Young girls *do* like flattery, of course. Don't you think so?"

Disconcerted, Mr. Meekin could only bow and smile at the self-possessed young lady. "Go into the kitchen, Danny, and ask for some tobacco. Say *I* sent you. Mr. Meekin, won't you come in?"

"A strange old gentleman that, Miss Vickers. A faithful retainer, I presume?"

"An old convict servant of ours," said Sylvia. "He has got into trouble lately, though, poor old man." She sighed. "He married a free woman much younger than himself, and she makes him drink, and then gives him in charge for insubordination."

"For insubordination!"

"Yes, insubordination. He is her assigned servant, you know," said Sylvia, as if such a condition of things was the most ordinary in the world; "and if he misbehaves himself, she sends him back to the road-gang."

The Reverend Mr. Meekin opened his mild eyes wide. "What an

extraordinary anomaly! I am beginning, my dear, Miss Vickers, to find myself indeed at the antipodes."

"Society here is different from society in England, I believe. Most new arrivals say so," returned Sylvia quietly.

"But for a wife to imprison her husband, my dear young lady!"

"She can have him flogged if she likes. Indeed, Danny has been flogged at his wife's instigation. He was very silly to marry her; but you can't reason with an old man in love, Mr. Meekin."

Mr. Meekin's Christian brow had grown crimson. To hear a young lady talk in such an open way! Why, in reading the Decalogue from the altar, Mr. Meekin was accustomed to soften one indecent prohibition lest its uncompromising plainness of speech might offend the delicate sensibilities of his female souls! He turned quickly from the dangerous theme.

"You have been reading?"

"'Paul et Virginie.' I have read it before in English."

"Ah, you read French, then, my dear young lady?"

"Not very well. I had a master for some months, but then he went back to gaol. He stole papa's silver tankard."

"A French master! Stole—!"

"He was a prisoner, you know. A clever man. He wrote for the 'London Magazine'. I have read his writings. Some of them are quite above the average."

"And how did he come to be transported?" asked Mr. Meekin a little hesitantly.

"Poisoning his niece, I think, but I forget the particulars. He was a gentlemanly man, but oh, such a drunkard!"

Mr. Meekin, more astonished than ever at this strange country where young ladies talked casually of poisoning and flogging, and murderers taught French, perfumed the air with his cambric handkerchief in silence.

"You have not been here long, Mr. Meekin," said Sylvia, after a pause.

"No, only a week. A lovely climate, but, as I said just now to Mrs. Jellicoe, the Trail of the Serpent—the Trail of the Serpent—my dear young lady."

"If you send all the wretches in England here, you must expect the Trail of the Serpent," said Sylvia. "It isn't the fault of the colony."

"Oh, no; certainly not," returned Meekin hastily.

"You gentlemen should make it better. I don't know what the penal settlements are like, but the prisoners in the town have not much inducement to become good men."

"They have the Liturgy of our Holy Church read to them twice every week, my dear lady," said Mr. Meekin, as if to say, "if that doesn't reform them, what will?"

"Oh, yes," returned Sylvia, "they have that, certainly; but that is only on Sundays. But don't let us talk about this, Mr. Meekin. Papa says that I am not to talk about these things, because they are all done according to the Rules of the Service, as he calls it."

"An admirable notion of papa's," said Meekin, much relieved as the door opened and Vickers and Frere entered.

Vickers's hair had grown white, but Frere carried his thirty years as easily as some men carry two-and-twenty.

"My dear Sylvia," began Vickers, "here's an extraordinary thing!" Then, becoming conscious of the presence of the agitated Meekin, he paused.

"You know Mr. Meekin, papa?" said Sylvia. "Mr. Meekin, Captain Frere."

"I have that pleasure," said Vickers. "Glad to see you, sir. Pray sit down." Upon which Mr. Meekin beheld Sylvia unaffectedly kiss both gentlemen; but become strangely aware that the kiss bestowed upon her father was warmer than that which greeted her affianced husband.

"Warm weather, Mr. Meekin," said Frere. "Sylvia, my darling, I hope you have not been out in the heat."

"It's not hot at all," said Sylvia, pettishly. "Nonsense! I'm not made of butter—I sha'n't melt." And then, as though angry with herself for her irritation, she added, "You are always thinking of me, Maurice," and gave him her hand affectionately.

"It's very oppressive, Captain Frere," said Meekin; "and to a stranger, quite enervating."

"Have a glass of wine," said Frere, as if the house was his own. "One wants bucking up a bit a day like this."

"Ay, to be sure," repeated Vickers. "Sylvia dear, some sherry. I hope she has not been attacking you with her strange theories, Mr. Meekin?"

"Oh, dear no; not at all," returned Meekin, sensing that this young lady was regarded as a creature not to be judged by ordinary rules. "We got on famously, my dear Major, quite famously."

"She is very plain-spoken, is my little girl, and strangers can't understand her sometimes," said Vickers. "Can they, Poppet?"

Poppet tossed her head saucily. "I don't know," she said. "Why shouldn't they? But you were going to say something extraordinary when you came in. What is it, dear?"

"Ah," said Vickers with grave face. "Yes, a most extraordinary thing. They've caught those villains."

"What, you don't mean—? No, papa!" said Sylvia, turning round with alarmed face.

In that little family there were, for conversational purposes, but one set of villains in the world—the mutineers of the *Osprey.*

"They've got four of them in the bay at this moment—Rex, Barker, Shiers, and Lesly. They are on board the *Lady Jane.* The most extraordinary story I ever heard. The fellows got to China and passed themselves off as shipwrecked sailors. The merchants in Canton got up a subscription, and sent them to London. They were recognised there by old Pine, who had been surgeon on board the ship they came out in."

Sylvia sat down on the nearest chair, with heightened colour. "And where are the others?"

"Two were executed in England; the other six have not been taken. These fellows have been sent out for trial."

"To what are you alluding, dear sir?" asked Meekin, eyeing the sherry with the gaze of a fasting saint.

"The piracy of a convict brig five years ago," replied Vickers. "The scoundrels put my poor wife and child ashore, and left them to starve. If it hadn't been for Frere—God bless him!—they would have died. But it's a long story to tell now — Mr. Meekin, your health!"

"I have heard of it already," said Meekin, sipping the sherry elegantly, "and of your gallant conduct, Captain Frere."

"Oh, that's nothing," said Frere, reddening. "We were all in the same boat. Poppet, have a glass of wine?"

"No," said Sylvia, "I don't want any."

She was staring at the window, as though the bright light might enable her to remember something. "What's the matter?" asked Frere, frowning.

"I was trying to recollect, but it is all so confused. I only remember a great shore and a great sea, and two men, one of whom—that's you, dear—carried me in his arms."

"Dear, dear," said Mr. Meekin.

"She was quite a baby," said Vickers hastily, as if unwilling to admit that her illness had caused her forgetfulness.

"Oh, no; I was twelve years old," said Sylvia; "that's not a baby you know. But I think the fever made me stupid."

Frere, looking at her uneasily, shifted in his seat.

"Maurice," asked she suddenly, "what became of the other man?"

"Which other man?"

"The man who was with us; the other one, you know."

"Poor Bates?"

"No, not Bates. The prisoner. What was his name?"

"Oh, ah—the prisoner," said Frere, as if he, too, had forgotten. "Why, you know, darling, he was sent to Port Arthur."

"Ah!" said Sylvia, with a shudder. "And is he there still?"

"I believe so," said Frere, frowning again.

"By-the-bye," said Vickers, "I suppose we shall have to get that fellow up for the trial. We have to identify the villains."

"Can't you and I do that?" asked Frere, uneasily.

"I am afraid not. I wouldn't like to swear to a man after five years."

"By George," said Frere, "*I'd* swear to him! When once I see a man's face—that's enough for me."

"We had better get up a few prisoners from Port Arthur who were at the Harbour at the time," said Vickers, as if wishing to terminate the discussion. "I wouldn't let the villains slip through my fingers for anything."

"Ah, Port Arthur—I have heard of it," said Meekin.

"It's our place for 'colonial sentence' men," said Vickers. "The worst we have are there—most of them are Lifers. It has taken the place of Macquarie Harbour."

"And do they never leave the place when sentenced for life?" said Meekin, nibbling a biscuit. "How distressing!"

"Never, except when they die," answered Frere, with a laugh; "and then they are buried on an island. You should come down with me and have a look at it, Mr. Meekin. Picturesque, I can assure you."

"My dear Maurice," says Sylvia, rising abruptly and going to the piano, "how can you talk like that?"

"I should much like to see it," said Meekin, still nibbling, "for the Governor, Sir John Franklin, was saying something about a chaplaincy there, and I understand that the climate is quite endurable."

The convict-servant in attendance stared at the dainty clergyman, and Maurice laughed again. "Oh, it's a stunning climate," he said; "and nothing to do. Just the place for you. There's a regular little colony there. All the scandals in Van Diemen's Land are hatched at Port Arthur."

Perhaps Sylvia found this chatter not to her taste, for she struck a few chords, which, compelling the party, out of sheer politeness, to cease talking for the moment, caused the conversation to flag, and hinted to Mr. Meekin that it was time for him to depart.

"Good afternoon, dear Miss Vickers," he said, rising with his sweetest smile. "Thank you for your delightful music. That piece is an old favourite of mine. It was quite a favourite of the Bishop's, too. Pray excuse me, my dear Captain Frere, but this strange occurrence—of the capture of the wreckers, you know—must be my apology for touching on a delicate subject. How charming to contemplate! Yourself and your dear young lady! 'None but the brave', you know, 'deserve the fair'!"

"It's rather a long invitation," said Vickers, always well disposed to anyone who praised his daughter, "but if you've nothing better to do, come and dine with us on Christmas Day, Mr. Meekin. We usually have a little gathering then."

"Charmed," said Meekin, "charmed, I am sure. It *is* so refreshing to meet with persons of one's own tastes. Indeed yes. Once more—*good* afternoon."

Sylvia burst into laughter as the door closed. "What a ridiculous creature!" she said. "Bless the man, with his gloves and his umbrella, and his hair and his scent! Fancy that mincing noodle showing me the way to Heaven!"

"My dear Sylvia," said Vickers, seriously, "Mr. Meekin is a clergyman, you know."

"Oh, I know," said Sylvia, "but then, a clergyman can talk like a man, can't he? Why do they send such people here? Oh, by the way, papa, poor old Danny's back again. I told him he might go into the kitchen. May he, dear?"

"You'll have the house full of these vagabonds, you little puss," said Vickers, kissing her. "I suppose I must let him stay. What has he been doing now?"

"His wife," said Sylvia, "locked him up, you know, for being drunk. Wife! What do people want with wives, I wonder."

"Ask Maurice!" said her father, smiling.

Sylvia moved away, and tossed her head.

"What does he know about it? Maurice, you are a great bear; and if you hadn't saved my life, you know, I shouldn't love you a bit. There, you may kiss me. This convict business has brought it all back; and I *should* be ungrateful if I didn't love you, dear."

Maurice Frere, with suddenly crimsoned face, accepted the proffered caress, and then turned away to the window. A grey-clothed man was working in the garden, and whistling as he worked. "They're not so badly off," said Frere, under his breath.

"What's that, sir?" asked Sylvia.

"That I am not half good enough for you," cried Frere, with sudden vehemence. "I—I——"

"It's *my* happiness you've got to think of, Captain Bruin," said the girl. "You've saved my life, haven't you, and I should be wicked if I didn't love you! No, no more kisses," she added, putting out her hand. "Come, papa, it's cool now, let's walk in the garden, and leave Maurice to think of his own unworthiness."

Maurice watched the retreating pair with a puzzled expression. "She always leaves me for her father," he said to himself. "I wonder if she really *loves* me, or if it's only gratitude, after all?"

He had often asked himself the same question during the five years of his wooing, but he had never satisfactorily answered it.

The evening passed as it had passed a hundred times before; and having smoked a pipe at the barracks, Captain Frere returned home. His home was

SARAH PURFOY'S REQUEST

a cottage on the New Town road—a cottage which he had occupied since his appointment as Assistant Police Magistrate, an appointment given to him as a reward for his exertions in connection with the *Osprey* mutiny. Captain Maurice Frere had risen in life. Quartered in Hobart Town, he had assumed a position in society, and had held several of those excellent appointments which in the year 1834 were bestowed upon officers of garrison. He had been Superintendent of Works at Bridgewater, and when he got his captaincy, Assistant Police Magistrate at Bothwell. The affair of the *Osprey* made a noise; and it was tacitly resolved that the first "good thing" that fell vacant should be given to the gallant preserver of Major Vickers's child.

Major Vickers also prospered. He had always been a careful man, and having saved some money, had purchased land on favourable terms. The "assignment system" enabled him to cultivate portions of it at a small expense, and, following the usual custom, he stocked his run with cattle and sheep. He had sold his commission, and was now a comparatively wealthy man. He owned a fine estate; the house he lived in was purchased property. He was in good odour at Government House, and his office of Superintendent of Convicts caused him to take an active part in that local government which keeps a man constantly before the public.

Major Vickers had become one of the leading men in Van Diemen's Land. His daughter was a good match for any man; and many ensigns and lieutenants, many sons of settlers living on their fathers' stations among the mountains, and many dapper clerks envied Maurice Frere his good fortune. Some went so far as to say that the beautiful daughter of "Regulation Vickers" was too good for the coarse red-faced Frere, who was noted for his fondness for low society, and his almost brutal demeanour. No one denied, however, that Captain Frere was a valuable officer. It was said that, in consequence of his tastes, he knew more about the tricks of convicts than any man on the island. It was said, even, that he was wont to disguise himself, and mix with the pass-holders and convict-servants, in order to learn their signs and mysteries. When in charge at Bridgewater it had been his delight to rate the chain-gangs in their own hideous jargon, and to astound a new comer by his knowledge of his previous history. The convict population hated him, for, with his brutality and violence, he mingled a ferocious good humour that resulted sometimes in tacit permission to go without the letter of the law. Yet, as the convicts themselves said, "a man was never safe with the Captain;" for, after drinking and joking with them, as the Sir Oracle of some public-house whose hostess he delighted to honour, he would disappear through a side door just as the constables burst in at the back, and show himself as remorseless, in his next morning's sentence of the captured, as if he had never entered a tap-room in all his life. His superiors called this "zeal;" his inferiors "treachery."

As the time for his marriage approached, however, he had in a measure given up these exploits, and strove to make his acquaintances forget several remarkable scandals concerning his private life. When Commandant at the Maria Island, and for the first two years after his return from the unlucky expedition to Macquarie Harbour, he had not suffered any fear of society's opinion to restrain his vices, but, as the affection for the young girl who looked upon him as her saviour increased, he had resolved to shut up those dark pages in his colonial experience. He was not remorseful, he was not even disgusted. He had merely "had his fling, like all young men;" perhaps he had been foolish, but no reproachful ghost of past misdeeds haunted him.

One of these ghosts, however, was very close to him at this moment. His convict servant had, according to his instructions, sat up for him, and as he entered, the man handed him a letter addressed to him in a female hand.

"Who brought this?" asked Frere, hastily tearing it open.

"The groom, sir. He said that there was a gentleman at the 'George the Fourth' who wished to see you."

Frere smiled in admiration of the intelligence which had dictated such a message, and then frowned at the contents of the letter. "You needn't wait," he said to the man. "I shall have to go back again, I suppose." Changing his forage cap for a soft hat, he prepared to retrace his steps. "What does she want now?" he asked himself fiercely as he strode down the moonlit road.

The "George the Fourth" was a long, low house, painted a dull red, in Elizabeth-street. Its narrow-paned windows and red curtains gave to it a spurious appearance of old English jollity.

Pushing open the side-door with the manner of one well acquainted with the house, Frere made his way along a narrow passage to a glass door at the further end. A tap upon this door brought a pock-pitted Irish girl, who curtsied with servile recognition of the visitor and ushered him upstairs. The room into which he was shown was large and handsomely furnished. The carpet was soft, the candles bright, and the supper tray gleamed invitingly from a table between the windows. As Frere entered, he became conscious of a rich, heavy perfume, and, rounding the promontory of an ottoman, found himself face to face with Sarah Purfoy.

"Thank you for coming," she said. "Pray sit down."

Frere sat down in obedience to a motion of a plump hand that twinkled with rings.

The eleven years that had passed since we last saw this woman had dealt gently with her. Her hand was as white as of yore, her hair as glossy, and her eyes as dangerously bright. Her figure was coarser, however, and the white arm that gleamed through a muslin sleeve showed an outline that a fastidious artist might wish to modify. The most noticeable change was in her face. The cheeks owned no longer that delicate purity which they once boasted, but had become thicker, while here and there showed those faint red streaks which are the first signs of the decay of "fine" women.

Maurice Frere spoke first; he was anxious to bring his visit to as speedy a termination as possible. "What do you want of me?" he asked.

Sarah Purfoy laughed; a laugh so unnatural that Frere turned to look at her. "I want you to do me a favour—a very great favour."

"What do you mean?" asked Frere roughly. "Favour! What do you call *this?*" striking the sofa on which he sat. "Isn't *this* a favour? What do you call your precious house and all that's in it? Isn't *that* a favour? What do you mean?"

To his utter astonishment the woman replied by shedding tears. For some time he regarded her in silence, as if unwilling to be softened by such shallow device, but eventually felt constrained to speak. "Have you been drinking again?" he asked. "Tell me what it is you want, and have done with it. I don't know what possessed me to come here at all."

Sarah dashed away her tears with a passionate hand.

"I am ill, can't you see, you fool!" said she. "The news has unnerved me. If I have been drinking, what then? It's nothing to you, is it?"

"Oh, no," returned the other, "it's nothing to me. If you choose to bloat yourself with brandy, do it by all means."

"*You* don't pay for it, at any rate!" said she, with a quickness of retaliation which showed that this was not the only occasion on which they had quarrelled.

"Come," said Frere, "get on. I can't stop here all night."

She suddenly rose, and crossed to where he was sitting.

"Maurice, you were very fond of me once."

"Once," said Maurice. "But that was before you took to drinking and swearing, and going raving mad with passion."

"Well, dear," said she, with her great glittering eyes belying the soft tones of her voice, "I suffered for it, didn't I? Didn't you turn me out into the streets? Didn't you lash me with your whip like a dog? Didn't you put me in gaol for it, eh? It's hard to struggle against you, Maurice."

The compliment to his brutality seemed to please him, and he smiled.

"Well, there; let old times be old times, Sarah. You haven't done badly, after all," and he looked round the well-furnished room. "What do you want?"

"There was a transport came in this morning."

"Well?"

"*You* know who was on board her, Maurice!"

Maurice slapped his fist into the palm of his hand.

"Oh, that's it, is it! 'Gad, what a flat I was not to think of it before! You want to see him, I suppose?"

She came close to him, and, in her earnestness, took his hand. "I want to save his life!"

"Save his life! It can't be done."

"You can do it, Maurice."

"I save John Rex's life?" cried Frere. "Why, you must be mad!"

"He is the only creature that loves me, Maurice—the only man who cares for me. He has done no harm. He only wanted to be free—was it not natural? You can save him if you like. What does it matter to you? A miserable prisoner—let him live, Maurice."

Maurice laughed. "What have I to do with it?"

"You are the principal witness against him. If you say that he behaved well—and he *did* behave well: many men would have left you to starve—they won't hang him."

"Oh, won't they! That won't make much difference."

"Ah, Maurice, be merciful!"

She tried to retain his hand, but he withdrew it.

"You're a nice sort of woman to ask me to help your lover—a man who left me on that cursed coast to die. Save him! Confound him, not I!"

"Ah, Maurice," she said with a sob, "what is it to you? You don't care for me now. This man was a husband to me—long before I met you. He will bless you if you save him, Maurice."

Frere jerked his head impatiently. "*Bless* me!" he said. "I don't want his blessings. Let him swing. Who cares?"

At this, Sarah Purfoy's pent-up passion broke forth, and she poured upon him a torrent of abuse. "You! Who are you, that you dare to speak to me like that? His little finger is worth your whole body. He is a brave man, not a coward like you. Yes, a coward! You are very brave with defenceless men and weak women. You have beaten me until I was bruised black, you cur; but who ever saw you attack a man unless he was chained or bound? You will be murdered one of these days, Maurice Frere—take my word for it. Men are flesh and blood, and flesh and blood won't endure the torments you lay on it!"

"There, that'll do," says Frere, growing pale.

"I know you, you brutal coward. I have not been your mistress—God forgive me!—without learning you by heart. I've seen your ignorance and your conceit. One of your dogs has more brain than you, and twice as much heart. And such an animal as you has life and death in his hands! He may hang, may he? I'll hang with him, then, for I will kill *you!*"

At the scream which accompanied the last words, Frere raised his arm as if to strike her.

"Strike me! You daren't! I defy you! Bring up the wretched creatures who learn the way to Hell in this cursed house, and let them see you do it. Call them! They are old friends of yours. They all know Captain Frere."

"Sarah!"

"You remember Lucy Barnes—poor little Lucy Barnes that stole sixpennyworth of calico. She is downstairs now. But she isn't the bright-faced baby she was when they sent her here to 'reform,' and when Lieutenant Frere wanted a new housemaid from the Factory! Call! do you hear? Ask any one of those beasts whom you lash for Lucy Barnes. He'll tell you all about her—ay, and about many more poor souls that are at the bidding of any drunken brute that has stolen a pound note to fee the Devil with! Oh, God in Heaven, will you not judge this man?"

Frere trembled. He had often witnessed this creature's whirlwinds of passion, but never had he seen her so violent as this. Her frenzy frightened him. "Woman, be quiet, or by Heaven—"

"By Heaven! I'll go to this girl you want to marry, and tell her all I know of you. I have seen her in the streets—have seen her gather up her muslin skirts when my silks touched her—I that heard her say her baby-prayers. I know what she thinks of women like me. She would shudder if she knew what I know of you. You will be *respectable*, will you? Wait till I tell her my story. You kill my love; I'll blight yours!"

Frere seized her brutally by both wrists. "Don't speak *her* name," he said hoarsely, "or I'll do you a mischief. Men have murdered women like you, and, by God, now I know how they came to do it!"

A silence fell upon the pair, and at last, Frere, releasing her hands, fell back from her.

"I'll do what you want, on one condition—that you leave this place."

"Where for?"

"Anywhere—the farther the better. I'll pay your passage to Sydney, and you go or stay there as you please."

"May I see *him*?"

"You can see him in the dock if you like," says Frere, with a laugh cut short by a flash of her eyes. "There, I didn't mean to offend you."

"Offend me! Go on."

"Listen here," said he, "if you go away, and promise never to interfere with me or mine, I'll do what you want. I will not say all I know about this man. I will say he befriended me. I will do my best to save his life."

"You *can* save it if you like."

"I will try. On my honour, I will try."

"I must believe you, I suppose," said she, doubtfully. "You are not deceiving me, Maurice?"

"Why should I? You keep your promise, and I'll keep mine. Is it a bargain?"

"Yes."

He eyed her steadfastly for a moment, and then, without another word, got up and left the room.

Getting into the cool street directly, and seeing the calm stars shining, he strove to cast off the fear that was on him. It was hard that, just as he had turned over a new leaf this old blot should come through to the clean page. It was cruel that, having comfortably forgotten the past, he should be thus rudely reminded of it.

The reader of the foregoing pages has doubtless asked himself—"What is the link between John Rex and Sarah Purfoy?"

THE STORY OF TWO BIRDS OF PREY

In the year 1825 there lived, at St. Heliers, Jersey, a watchmaker named Urban Purfoy. He was a hard-working man, and had amassed a little money—sufficient to give his grand-daughter an education above the common in those days. At sixteen, Sarah Purfoy was a strong-willed, precocious girl, with big brown eyes and an immense admiration for handsome members of the opposite sex. She was brimful of vitality, with strong passions and little religious sentiment, and her distaste for her humdrum life found expression in a rebellion against social usages. She was the sort of girl of whom women say—"It is a pity she has no mother;" and men, "It is a pity she does not get a husband;" and who say to themselves, "When shall I have a lover?"

Though she adored the soldiery quartered on the island, Sarah's first lover was a civilian. Walking one day on the cliff, she met a young man, tall, well-looking, and well-dressed. His name was Lemoine, he was the son of a wealthy resident of the island, and had come from London to recruit his health and to see his friends. They got into conversation—about scenery, lonely walks, and the dullness of St. Heliers. "Did she often walk there?" "Sometimes." "Would she be there to-morrow?" "She might." Mr. Lemoine lifted his hat, and went back to dinner, rather pleased with himself.

They met next day, and the day after that. Lemoine was not a gentleman, but he had lived among gentlemen and had caught something of their manner. He said that, after all, virtue was a mere name, and that when people were powerful and rich, the world respected them more than if they had been honest and poor. He told Sarah of London and the great ladies there, and hinting that *they* were not always virtuous, drew himself up with a moody air as though *he* had been unhappily the cause of their fatal lapse into wickedness. Sarah did not wonder at this in the least. Had she been a great lady, she would have done the same. She began to coquet with this seductive fellow, and to hint to him that she had too much knowledge of the world to set a fictitious value upon virtue. He mistook her artfulness for innocence, and thought he had made a conquest. Moreover, the girl was pretty, and when dressed properly, would look well. Only one obstacle stood in the way of their loves—the dashing profligate was poor. He had been living in London above his means, and his father was not inclined to increase his allowance.

Sarah liked him better than anybody else she had seen, but there are two sides to every bargain. Sarah Purfoy must go to London. In vain her lover sighed and swore. But unless he would promise to take her away with him, Diana was not more chaste. His desire to possess her increased in proportionate ratio to her resistance, and at last he borrowed two hundred pounds from his father's confidential clerk, and acceded to her wishes. There was no love on either side—Lemoine did not like to be beaten; Sarah sold herself for a passage to England and an introduction into the "great world."

We need not describe her career at this epoch. Suffice it to say that she discovered that vice is not always conducive to happiness. Sated and disappointed, she soon grew tired of her life and longed to escape from its wearying dissipations. At this juncture she fell in love.

The object of her affections was one Mr. Lionel Crofton. Crofton was tall, well made, and with an insinuating address. His eyes were the best part of his face, and, like his hair, were jet black. With this man, barely four years older than herself, Sarah, at seventeen, fell violently in love. This was the more strange as, though fond of her, he would tolerate no caprices, and possessed an ungovernable temper, which found vent in curses, and even blows. He seemed to have no profession or business, and though he owned a good address, he was even less of a gentleman than Lemoine. Yet Sarah was devoted to him. Touched by her affection, and rating her intelligence and unscrupulousness at their true value, he told her who he was. He was a swindler, a forger, and a thief, and his real name was John Rex. When she heard this she experienced a sinister delight. "I am glad you found me," she said. "Two heads are better than one. We will work together."

John Rex, known among his intimate associates as Dandy Jack, was the putative son of a man who had been for many years valet to Lord Bellasis, and who retired from the service of that profligate nobleman with a sum of money and a wife. John Rex was sent to as good a school as could be procured for him and, at sixteen was given, by the interest of his mother with his father's former master, a clerkship in an old-established banking-house. Mrs. Rex was intensely fond of her son, and imbued him with a desire to shine in aristocratic circles. He was a clever lad, without any principle; he would lie unblushingly, and steal deliberately, if he thought he could do so with impunity. He soon found that his fellow clerks were not of that "gentlemanly" stamp which his mother thought so admirable, and therefore he despised them. And to be tied all day to a desk was beyond endurance.

But John Rex, senior, told him to "wait and see what came of it." He did so, and in the mean time he got into bad company and forged the name of a customer of the bank to a cheque for twenty pounds. The fraud was a clumsy one, and was detected in twenty-four hours. Forgeries by clerks, however, are not considered to add to the attractions of a banking-house, and the old-established firm decided not to prosecute, but dismissed Rex from their service. The ex-valet, who never liked his legalised son, was at first for turning him out of doors, but by the entreaties of his wife, was at last induced to place the promising boy in a draper's shop in the City Road.

This employment was not a congénial one, and John Rex planned to leave it. He lived at home, and had his salary—about thirty shillings a week—for pocket money. Though he displayed considerable skill with the cue, and not unfrequently won considerable sums, his expenses averaged more than his income; and having borrowed all he could, he found himself again in difficulties. Just then one of those "lucky chances" which blight so many lives occurred. The "shop-walker" died, and Messrs. Baffaty & Co. made the gentlemanly Rex act as his substitute for a few days. Shop-walkers have opportunities not accorded to other folks, and on the evening of the third day Mr. Rex went home with a bundle of lace in his pocket. Unfortunately, he owed more than the worth of his petty theft, and was compelled to steal again. This time he was detected. One of his fellow-shopmen caught him in the act of concealing a roll of silk, and, to his astonishment, cried "Halves! I saw you take it and if you won't share, I'll tell old Baffaty." This argument was irresistible, and they shared. Having become good friends, the self-made partner lent Rex a helping hand with the disposal of the booty, and introduced him to a purchaser, who kept a second-hand clothes warehouse in the City Road, and was supposed to have branch establishments all over London.

Mr. Blick purchased the stolen goods for about a third of their value, and, encouraged by success, Rex and his companion took more articles of value. John Rex paid off his debts, and began to feel himself quite a "gentleman" again. Just as Rex had arrived at this pleasing state of mind, Baffaty discovered the robbery. He did not suspect Rex—he was such a gentlemanly young man—but having had his eye for some time upon Rex's partner, who was vulgar and squinted, he sent for him. Rex's partner stoutly denied the accusation, and old Baffaty, who was a man of merciful tendencies, gave him until the next morning to confess, hinting at the persuasive powers of a constable at the end of that time. The shopman, with tears in his eyes, hastened to Rex, and informed him that all was lost. He did not want to confess, because he must implicate his friend Rex, but if he did not confess, he would be given in charge. Flight was impossible, for neither had money.

But Rex soon found a way out of their dilemma. The shop-walker was allowed half an hour in the middle of the day for lunch. John Rex took advantage of this half-hour to hire a cab and drive to Blick's. That worthy man received him cordially, for he saw that he was bent upon great deeds. John Rex rapidly unfolded his plan of operations. He would remain behind after the warehouse doors were locked, and open them at a given signal. A light cart or cab could be stationed in the lane at the back; three men could fill it with valuables in as many hours. Did Blick know of three such men? Blick's one eye glistened. He thought he did know. At half-past eleven they should be there. Was that all? No, said Mr. Rex. The booty was worth at least £5,000—he must have £100 cash when the cart stopped at Blick's door. Blick at first refused point blank, but Rex was firm; it was his only chance, and at last he got a promise of £80. That night "The Great Silk Robbery" took place, and two days afterwards, John Rex and his partner, dining comfortably at Birmingham, read an account of the transaction in a London paper.

John Rex was now, after his fashion, a "gentleman." As long as the £80 lasted, he lived in luxury, and by the time it was spent he had established himself in his profession—that of a swindler. Gifted with a handsome person and ready wit, he had added to these natural advantages some skill at billiards, some knowledge of gamblers' legerdemain, and the consciousness that he must prey or be preyed on. John Rex was no common swindler; he saw that to successfully swindle mankind, one must not aim at comparative, but superlative, ingenuity. Examining, moreover, the history of detected crime, John Rex discovered one thing. At the bottom of all these robberies and swindles was some lucky fellow who profited by the folly of his confederates. This gave him an idea. Suppose he could not only make use of his own talents to rob mankind, but utilise those of others also? Very well, then. He would plan the robberies; others—dull clods who could break locks, burst doors and "neddy" constables—should execute them.

Working through many channels, John Rex, in a few years, became the head of a society of ruffians. Mixing with fast clerks and unsuspecting middle-class profligates, he found out particulars of houses ill guarded and shops insecurely fastened, and "put up" Blick's ready ruffians to the more dangerous work. Rich spendthrifts who affected male society asked him to their houses, and Mr. Anthony Croftonbury, Captain James Craven, and Mr. Lionel Crofton were names remembered, sometimes with pleasure, oftener with regret, by many a broken man of fortune.

Thus he had lived for three years when he met Sarah Purfoy, and thus he proposed to live for many more. With this woman as coadjutor, he thought he could defy the law. She was the net spread to catch his "pigeons;" she was the well-dressed lady who ordered goods in London for her husband at Canterbury, and *paid* half the price down, "which was all this letter authorised her to do," and where a less beautiful or clever woman might have failed, she succeeded. Her husband saw fortune before him, and believed that, with prudence, he might carry on his lucrative employment of "gentleman" until he chose to relinquish it. Alas for human weakness! He one day did a foolish thing, and the law he had so successfully defied got him in the simplest way imaginable.

Under the names of Mr. and Mrs. Skinner, John Rex and Sarah Purfoy were living in quiet lodgings in the neighbourhood of Bloomsbury. Their landlady was a respectable woman, and had a son who was a constable. This son, coming in to supper one night, told his mother that on the following evening an attack was to be made on a gang of coiners in the Old Street Road. The mother came the next day to Mrs. Skinner in the parlour, and, under a pledge of profound secrecy, told her of the dreadful expedition in which her son was engaged. John Rex was out at a pigeon-match with Lord Bellasis, and when he returned, at nine o'clock, Sarah told him what she had heard.

Now, 4, Bank-place, Old Street Road, was the residence of a man named Green, who had for some time carried on the lucrative trade of "counterfeiting." This man was one of the most daring of that army of ruffians whose master was Blick, and his liberty was valuable. John Rex, eating his dinner more nervously than usual, ruminated on the intelligence, and thought it would be wise to warn Green of his danger. Not that he cared much for Green personally, but it was bad policy to miss doing a good turn to a comrade, and, moreover, Green, if captured, might wag his tongue too freely. But how to do it? If he went to Blick's, it might be too late; he would go himself. He went out—and was captured.

When Sarah heard of the calamity she set to work to help him. She collected all her money and jewels, paid Mrs. Skinner's rent, went to see Rex, and arranged his defence. Blick was hopeful, but Green—who came very near hanging—admitted that the man was an associate of his, and the Recorder, being in a severe mood, transported him for seven years.

Vowing that she would follow him, Sarah Purfoy saw Mrs. Vickers's advertisement for a "lady's-maid," and answered it. It chanced that Rex was shipped in the *Malabar*, and Sarah, discovering this before the vessel had been a week at sea, conceived the bold project of inciting a mutiny for the rescue of her lover. We know the result of that scheme, and the story of the scoundrel's subsequent escape from Macquarie Harbour.

"THE NOTORIOUS DAWES"

The mutineers of the *Osprey* had been long since given up as dead, and the story of their desperate escape had become indistinct to the general public mind. Now that they had been recaptured in a remarkable manner, popular belief invested them with all sorts of strange fictions. John Rex, the ringleader, was related, it was said, to a noble family, and a special message had come out to Sir John Franklin concerning him. He had every prospect of being hung, however, for even the most outspoken admirers of his skill and courage could not but admit that he had committed an offence which meant death by the law. The Crown would leave nothing undone to convict him, and to the already crowded prison were added half a dozen life sentence men brought up from Port Arthur to identify the prisoners. Amongst this number was stated to be "the notorious Dawes."

This statement gave fresh food for recollection and invention. It was remembered how sullen and morose the wretch had been on his trial for "bolting" five years before, and how he had laughed when the commutation of his death sentence was announced to him. The *Hobart Town Gazette* published a short biography of this horrible villain, setting forth the facts as it saw them, and painting a colourful picture of him nowadays as double-ironed at Port Arthur, after two more ineffectual attempts to regain his freedom.

Miss Sylvia Vickers also received a share of public attention. Her romantic rescue by the heroic Frere, who was shortly to reap the reward of his devotion in the good old fashion, made her almost as famous as the villain Dawes, or the monster John Rex. It was reported that her lover was most anxious that she should not give evidence, as she was affected deeply by the suffering she had undergone, and in a state of pitiable mental confusion as to the whole business.

These reports caused the Court, on the day of the trial, to be crowded with spectators; and as the various particulars were detailed, the excitement grew more intense. At first it was thought that the four heavily ironed prisoners would throw themselves on the mercy of the Crown, but a little study of the demeanour of the chief prisoner, John Rex, dispelled that conjecture. Calm, placid, and defiant, he seemed prepared to accept his fate. Only when he heard the indictment, setting forth that he had "feloniously pirated the brig *Osprey*", he smiled a little.

Mr. Meekin, sitting in the body of the Court, felt his religious prejudices sadly shocked by that smile. "A perfect wild beast, my dear Miss Vickers," he said, on his return to the little room where Sylvia and her father were waiting. "He has quite a tigerish look about him."

"Poor man!" said Sylvia, with a shudder.

"Poor! My *dear* young lady, you do not pity him?"

"I do," said Sylvia, twisting her hands together as if in pain. "I pity them all, poor creatures."

"Charming sensibility!" says Meekin. "The true woman's heart, my dear Major."

The Major tapped his fingers impatiently at this ill-timed twaddle. "Come here, Poppet," he said, "and look through this door. You can see them from here, and if you do not recognise any of them, I can't see what is the use of putting you in the box; though, of course, if it is necessary, you must go."

The girl had never before seen the ceremony of trying a man for his life, and the solemnities of the business affected her, as it affects all who see it for the first time. The atmosphere was heavy, the chains of the prisoners clanked ominously. Familiar faces seemed to her evilly transfigured. Even the countenance of her promised husband, bent eagerly forward, showed tyrannous and bloodthirsty. Her eyes hastily followed the pointing finger of her father, and sought the men in the dock. Two of them lounged, sullen and inattentive; one nervously pawed the dock with restless hand; the fourth scowled across the Court at the witness-box, which she could not see. The four faces were all strange to her.

"No, papa," she whispered, "I can't recognise them at all."

As she was turning from the door, a voice from the witness-box made her suddenly grow pale and pause to look again. The notorious criminal Rufus Dawes, the desperado of Port Arthur, had just entered the witness-box. He was a man of thirty, with a torso whose muscular grandeur not even the ill-fitting yellow jacket could altogether conceal, and a pair of fierce, black eyes that roamed over the Court hungrily.

Not all the frowning faces bent upon him could frown an accent of respect into the contemptuous tones in which he answered to his name, "Rufus Dawes, prisoner of the Crown."

"Come away, my darling," said Vickers, alarmed at his daughter's blanched face and eager eyes.

"Wait," she said, impatiently, listening for the voice whose owner she could not see. "Rufus Dawes! Oh, I have heard that name before!"

"You are a prisoner of the Crown at the penal settlement of Port Arthur?"

"Yes."

"For life?"

"For life."

Sylvia turned to her father with breathless inquiry in her eyes. "Oh, papa, who is that speaking? I know the name! I know the voice!"

"That is the man who was with you in the boat, dear," says Vickers, gravely. "The prisoner."

The eager light died out of her eyes, and in its place came a look of pain. "I thought it was a good man," she said. "It sounded like a good voice." And then she pressed her hands over her eyes and shuddered.

The colloquy in the Court went on. "Do you know the prisoners in the dock?"

"Yes."

"Who are they?"

"John Rex, Henry Shiers, James Lesly, and, and—I'm not sure about the last man."

"You are not sure about the last man. Will you swear to the three others?"

"Yes."

"You remember them well?"

"I was in the chain-gang at Macquarie Harbour with them for three years." Sylvia, hearing this hideous reason for acquaintance, gave a low cry and fell into her father's arms.

"Oh, papa, take me away! I feel as if I was going to remember something terrible!"

At the cry of the poor girl, all heads turned to the door. In the general wonder no one noticed the change that passed over Rufus Dawes. His face flushed scarlet, great drops of sweat stood on his forehead, and his black eyes glared in the direction from whence the sound came. Maurice Frere sprang up and pushed his way through the crowd. "What's this?" he said to Vickers angrily. "What did you bring her here for? She is not wanted. I told you that."

"It was my duty, sir," says Vickers, with stately rebuke.

"What has frightened her? What has she heard? What has she seen?" asked Frere, with a strangely white face.

She opened her eyes at the sound of his voice. "Take me home, papa; I'm ill. Oh, what thoughts!"

"What does she mean?" cried Frere in alarm.

"That ruffian Dawes frightened her," said Meekin. "A gush of recollection, poor child."

"Frightened her, eh?"

"Yes," said Sylvia, faintly, "he frightened me, Maurice. I needn't stop any longer, dear, need I?"

"No," says Frere, the cloud passing from his face. "Major, I beg your pardon. Please take her home at once. This sort of thing is too much for her." And he went back to his place, wiping his brow as one who had just escaped from some near peril.

Rufus Dawes had remained in the same attitude until the figure of Frere, passing through the doorway, roused him. "Who is she?" he said, in a low, hoarse voice, to the constable behind him.

"Miss Vickers," said the man shortly.

"Miss Vickers!" repeated the convict, staring in disbelief. "They told me she was dead!"

The constable sniffed contemptuously. "You thort she was, I've no doubt. You did your best to make her so, I've heard."

The convict raised his hands as though he would seize the other, despite the loaded muskets; but checking himself with sudden impulse, wheeled round to the Court. "Your Honour!—Gentlemen! I want to speak."

The sudden exclamation made the faces, hitherto bent upon the door through which Mr. Frere had passed, turn round again. In place of the upright and defiant villain who stood there an instant back, was a white-faced, agitated creature, bending forward in an attitude almost of supplication. "Your Honour, there has been some dreadful mistake made. I want to explain about myself. I explained before, when I first was sent to Port Arthur, but the letters were never forwarded by the Commandant; of course, that's the rule, and I can't complain. I've been sent there unjustly, your Honour. *I* made that boat, your Honour. *I* saved the Major's wife and daughter. *I* was the man; I did it all myself, and my liberty was sworn away by a villain who hated me. I thought, until now, that no one knew the truth, for they told me that she was dead." His rapid utterance took the Court so much by surprise that no one interrupted him. "I was sentenced to death for bolting, sir, and they reprieved me because I helped them in the boat. Helped them! Why, I *made* it! She will tell you so. I nursed her! I carried her in my arms! I starved myself for her! She was fond of me, sir. She was, indeed. She called me 'Good Mr. Dawes.'"

At this, a coarse laugh broke out, which was instantly checked. The judge bent over to ask, "Does he mean Miss Vickers?" and in this interval, Rufus Dawes, looking down into the Court, saw Maurice Frere staring up at him with terror in his eyes.

"I see you, Captain Frere, coward and liar! Put him in the box, gentlemen, and make him tell his story. She'll contradict him, never fear. Oh, and I thought she was dead all this while!"

The judge had got his answer from the clerk by this time. "Miss Vickers had been seriously ill, had fainted just now in the Court. Her only memories of the convict who had been with her in the boat were those of terror and disgust. The sight of him just now had most seriously affected her. The convict himself was an inveterate liar and schemer, and his story had been already disproved by Captain Frere."

The judge shook his head.

"This is not the place for an accusation against Captain Frere, nor the place to argue upon your alleged wrongs. If you have suffered injustice, the authorities will hear your complaint, and redress it. I can't listen to you. Mr. Mangles, have you any more questions to ask the witness?"

But Mr. Mangles not having any more, some one called "Matthew Gabbett," and Rufus Dawes, still endeavouring to speak, was clanked away with, amid a buzz of remark and surmise.

The trial progressed without further incident. Sylvia was not called, and, to the astonishment of many of his enemies, Captain Frere went into the witness-box and generously spoke in favour of John Rex. "He might have left us to starve," Frere said—"he might have murdered us; we were completely in his power. The stock of provisions on board the brig was not a large one, and I consider that, in dividing it with us, he showed great generosity for one in his situation."

The defence set up by Rex, moreover, was most ingenious. He was guilty of absconding, but his only object was his freedom, and having gained it, he had lived honestly for nearly three years, as he could prove. He was charged with piratically seizing the brig Osprey, and he urged that the brig Osprey, having been built by convicts at Macquarie Harbour, and never entered in any shipping list, could not be said to be "piratically seized," in the strict meaning of the term. The Court admitted the force of this objection, and, influenced doubtless by Captain Frere's evidence, the fact that five years had passed since the mutiny, and that the two men most guilty (Cheshire and Barker) had been executed in England, sentenced Rex and his three companions to transportation for life to the penal settlements of the colony.

At this happy conclusion to his labours, Frere went to comfort the girl for whose sake he had suffered Rex to escape the gallows. On his way he

MAURICE FRERE'S GOOD ANGEL

was met by a man who touched his hat, and asked to speak with him an instant. Past middle-age, with a brandy-beaten face, the man had in his gait and manner that nameless something that denotes the seaman.

"Well, Blunt," says Frere impatiently, "what is it now?"

"Only to tell you that it is all right, sir," says Blunt. "She's come aboard again this morning."

"Come aboard again!" ejaculated Frere. "Why I didn't know that she had been ashore. Where did she go?" He spoke with an air of confident authority, and Blunt—no longer the bluff tyrant of old—seemed to quail before him. The trial of the mutineers of the *Malabar* had ruined Phineas Blunt. Make what excuses he might, there was no concealing the fact that Pine found him drunk in his cabin when he ought to have been attending to his duties on deck; and the "authorities" could not, or would not, pass over such a heinous breach of discipline. Thus Captain Blunt was deprived of the honour of bringing His Majesty's prisoners to His Majesty's colonies. He gradually sank lower and lower, becoming a drunkard, and being known as a man with a "grievance against the Government." Captain Frere had become in a manner his patron, and had got him the command of a schooner trading from Sydney. On getting this command—not without some wry faces on the part of the owner resident in Hobart Town—Blunt had taken the temperance pledge for the space of twelve months, and was a miserable dog in consequence. He was, however, a faithful henchman, for he hoped by Frere's means to get some "Government billet"—the grand object of all colonial sea captains of that epoch.

"Well, sir, she went ashore to see a friend," says Blunt, looking at the sky and then at the earth.

"What friend?"

"The—the prisoner, sir."

"And she saw him, I suppose?"

"Yes, but I thought I'd better tell you, sir," says Blunt.

"Of course; quite right," returned the other; "you had better start at once. It's no use waiting."

"As you wish, sir. I can sail this evening, if you like."

"Very good," says Frere.

"There's a situation in Sydney I've been looking after," said the other, uneasily, "if you could help me to it."

"What is it?"

"The command of one of the Government vessels, sir."

"Well, keep sober, then," says Frere, "and I'll see what I can do. And keep that woman's tongue still if you can."

The pair looked at each other, and Blunt grinned slavishly.

"I'll do my best."

"Take care you do," returned his patron, leaving him without further ceremony.

Frere found Vickers in the garden, and at once begged him not to talk about the "business" to his daughter.

"You saw how bad she was to-day, Vickers. For goodness' sake don't make her ill again."

"My dear sir," says poor Vickers, "I won't refer to the subject. She's been very unwell ever since. Go in and see her."

Frere went in and held the nervous girl in his arms, with real sorrow at her suffering.

"It's all right now, Poppet," he said to her. "Don't think of it any more. Put it out of your mind, dear."

"It was foolish of me, Maurice, I know, but I could not help it. The sound of that man's voice seemed to bring back to me some great pity for something or some one. I don't explain what I mean, I know, but I felt that I was just on the verge of remembering a story of some great wrong, just about to hear something that should make me turn from all the people whom I ought most to love. Do you understand?"

"I think I know what you mean," says Frere, with averted face. "But that's all nonsense, you know."

"Of course," returned she, with a touch of her old childish manner of disposing of questions out of hand. "Everybody knows it's all nonsense. But then we do think such things. It seems to me that I have lived somewhere before, and have had another life—a dream-life."

"What a romantic girl you are," said the other. "How could you have a dream-life?"

"Of course not really, stupid. But in thought, you know. I dream such strange things now and then. I am always falling down precipices and into cataracts, and being pushed into great caverns in enormous rocks. Horrible dreams!"

"Indigestion," returned Frere. "You don't take exercise enough. Have a good five-mile walk."

"And in these dreams," continued Sylvia, ignoring his interruption, "there is one strange thing. You are always there."

"Come, that's all right," says Maurice.

"Ah, but not kind and good as you *are*, Captain Bruin, but scowling and threatening, and angry."

"But that is only a dream, darling."

"Yes, but——but you looked just so to-day in the Court, Maurice, and I think that's what made me so silly."

"My darling! There! Hush—don't cry!"

But she had burst into a passion of sobs and tears that shook her slight figure in his arms.

"Oh, Maurice, I am a wicked girl! I don't know my own mind. I think sometimes I don't love you as I ought—you who have saved me and nursed me."

"There, never mind about that," muttered Frere.

She grew more composed presently, and said, after a while, lifting her face—"Tell me, Maurice, did you ever, in those days—when you nursed me, and fed me, and starved for me—did you ever think we should be married?"

"I don't know," says Maurice. "Why?"

"I think you must have thought so, because—it's not vanity, dear—you would not else have been so kind and devoted."

"Nonsense, Poppet," he said, with his eyes resolutely averted.

"No, but you have been, and I am very pettish, sometimes. Papa has spoiled me. Those worrying ways of yours, which I get angry at, all come from love for me, don't they?"

"I hope so," said Maurice, with an unwonted moisture in his eyes.

"Well, you see, that is the reason why I am angry with myself for not loving you as I ought. I want you to like the things I like, and to love the books and the music and the pictures and the—the World I love; and I forget that you are a man, you know, and I am only a girl; and I forget how nobly you behaved. Why, what is the matter, dear?"

He had put her away from him suddenly, and gone to the window, gazing across the sloping garden at the bay below. The schooner which had brought the witnesses from Port Arthur lay off the shore, and the yellow flag at her mast fluttered gently in the cool evening breeze. As his eyes fell on the flag, he uttered an impatient exclamation.

"Maurice!" she cried, "I have wounded you!"

"No, no. It is nothing," said he, with the air of a man surprised in a moment of weakness. "I—I did not like to hear you talk in this way—about not loving me."

"Ah, forgive me, dear; I did not mean to hurt you. How could I do otherwise than love you—after all you have done?"

A sudden desperate whim caused him to exclaim, "But suppose I had not acted thus, would you not love me still?"

Her eyes, raised to his face with anxious tenderness, fell at this speech.

"What a question! I don't know. I suppose I should; yet—but what is the use, Maurice, of *supposing*? I know you *have* done it, and that is enough. How can I say what I might have done if something else had happened? Why, you might not have loved *me*."

If there had been for a moment any sentiment of remorse in his heart, the hesitation of her answer went far to dispel it.

"To be sure, that's true," and he placed his arm round her.

She lifted her face again with a bright laugh.

"We are a pair of geese—supposing! How can we help what is past? We have the Future, darling—the Future, in which I am to be your little wife, and we are to love each other all our lives, like the people in the story-books."

Frere sighed. What hopes had he not built upon her love; what good resolutions had he not made by reason of the purity she was to bring to him? As she said, the past was beyond recall; the future—in which she was to love him all her life—was before them. With the hypocrisy of selfishness which deceives even itself, he laid the little head upon his heart with a sensible glow of virtue.

"God bless you, darling! You are my good angel."

"I *will* be your good angel, dear, if you will let me," returned the girl.

Rex told Mr. Meekin, who, the next day, did him the honour to visit him, that, "under Providence, he owed his escape from death to the kind

MR. MEEKIN ADMINISTERS CONSOLATION

manner in which Captain Frere had spoken of him."

"I hope your escape will be a warning to you, my man," said Mr. Meekin, "and that you will endeavour to make the rest of your life an atonement for your early errors."

"Indeed I will, sir," said John Rex, who had taken Mr. Meekin's measure very accurately, "and it is very kind of you to condescend to speak to a wretch like me."

"Not at all," said Meekin, with affability; "it is my duty. I am a Minister of the Gospel."

"Ah! sir, I wish I had attended to the Gospel's teachings when I was younger. I might have been saved from all this."

"You might, indeed, poor man; but the Divine Mercy is infinite and will be extended to all of us—to you as well as to me." (This with the air of saying, "What do you think of *that*!") "Remember the penitent thief, Rex,—the penitent thief."

"Indeed I do, sir."

"And read your Bible, Rex, and pray for strength to bear your punishment."

"I will, sir. I need it sorely—physical as well as spiritual sir—for the Government allowance is sadly insufficient."

"I will speak to the authorities about a change in your dietary scale," returned Meekin patronisingly. "In the mean time, just collect together in your mind those particulars of your adventures of which you spoke, and have them ready for me when next I call. Such a remarkable history ought not to be lost."

"Thank you, sir. I will, sir. Ah! I little thought when I occupied the position of a gentleman, Mr. Meekin, that I should be reduced to this. But it is only just, sir."

"The mysterious workings of Providence are always just, Rex," returned Meekin. "I am glad to see you so conscious of your errors. Good morning."

"Good morning, and Heaven bless you, sir," said Rex, with his tongue in his cheek for the benefit of his yard mates; and so Mr. Meekin tripped away, convinced that he was labouring most successfully in the vineyard.

"I will send Rex's narrative to the Bishop," said he to himself. "It will surely amuse him."

Just then his eye fell upon the "notorious Dawes," who, while waiting for the schooner to take him back to Port Arthur, had been permitted to amuse himself by breaking stones. The prison-shed which Mr. Meekin was visiting was long and low, roofed with iron, and terminating at each end in the stone wall of the gaol. At one side rose the cells, at the other the outer wall of the prison. From the outer wall projected a weatherboard under-roof, and beneath this were seated forty heavily-ironed convicts. Two constables with loaded carbines walked up and down the clear space in the middle, and another watched from a sort of sentry-box built against the main wall. Every half-hour a third constable went down the line and examined the irons.

The other inmates of the prison were at work on the roads, or otherwise bestowed in the day time, but these forty were judged too desperate to be let loose. They sat, three feet apart, in two long lines, each man with a heap of stones between his outstretched legs. Rufus Dawes was seated last of the line—his back to the cells, his face to the gaol wall. This was the place nearest the watching constable, and was allotted on that account to the most ill-favoured.

"Well, Dawes," says Mr. Meekin, regarding him as one might regard some ferocious dog. "How are you this morning, Dawes?"

Dawes, scowling in a parenthesis between the cracking of two stones, was understood to say that he was very well.

"I am afraid, Dawes," said Mr. Meekin, "that you have done yourself no good by your outburst in court. I understand that public opinion is quite incensed against you."

Dawes, slowly arranging one large fragment of bluestone in a comfortable basin of smaller fragments, made no reply.

"I am afraid you lack patience, Dawes. You do not repent of your offences against the law, I fear."

The only answer vouchsafed by the ironed man was a savage blow, which split the stone into sudden fragments, and made the clergyman skip a step backward.

"You are a ruffian, sir! Do you not hear me speak?"

"I hear you," said Dawes, picking up another stone.

"Then listen respectfully, sir," said Meekin, roseate with celestial anger. "You have all day to break those stones."

"Yes, I have all day," returned Rufus Dawes, with a dogged look upward, "and all next day, for that matter."

"I came to console you, man—to console you," says Meekin indignantly. "I wanted to give you some good advice!"

The self-importance of the tone seemed to appeal to whatever vestige of appreciation for the humorous still lingered in the convict's brain, for a faint smile crossed his features.

"I beg your pardon, sir," he said. "Pray go on."

"I was going to say, my good fellow, that you have done yourself a great deal of injury by your ill-advised accusation of Captain Frere, and the use you made of Miss Vickers's name."

A frown, as of pain, contracted the prisoner's brows, and he seemed with difficulty to put a restraint upon his speech. "Is there to be no inquiry, Mr. Meekin?" he asked, at length. "What I stated was the truth—the truth, so help me God!"

"No blasphemy, sir," said Meekin solemnly. "No blasphemy, wretched man. Do not add to the sin of lying the greater sin of taking the name of the Lord thy God in vain."

"Are they not going to ask her for *her* story?" asked Dawes, with a pitiful change of manner. "They told me that she was to be asked. Surely they will ask her."

"I am not, perhaps, at liberty," says Meekin, placidly unconscious of the agony of despair that made the voice of the strong man before him quiver, "to state the intentions of the authorities, but I can tell you that Miss Vickers will not be asked anything about you. You are to go back to Port Arthur on the 24th, and to remain there."

A groan burst from Rufus Dawes; a groan so full of torture, that even the comfortable Meekin was thrilled by it.

"It is the Law, you know, my good man. I can't help it," he said. "You shouldn't break the Law, you know."

"Curse the Law!" cries Dawes. "It's a Bloody Law; it's—there, I beg your pardon," and he fell to cracking his stones again, with a laugh terrible in its bitter hopelessness.

"Come," says Meekin, feeling uneasily constrained to bring forth some of his London-learnt platitudes. "You can't complain. You have broken the Law, and you must suffer. Civilised Society says you sha'n't do certain things, and if you do thém you must suffer the penalty Civilised Society imposes."

Rufus Dawes cast his eyes round the yard with a glance that seemed to ask grimly if Civilised Society was progressing quite in accordance with justice, when its civilisation created such places as that stone-walled, carbine-guarded prison-shed, and filled it with such creatures as those forty human beasts, doomed to spend the best years of their manhood cracking pebbles in it.

"You don't deny *that*, Dawes?" asked the smug parson.

"It's not my place to argue with you, sir," said Dawes, in a tone of such indifference that Meekin could not tell whether he had made a convert, or subjected himself to an impertinence; "but I'm a prisoner for life, and don't look at it in the same way that you do."

This view of the question did not seem to have occurred to Mr. Meekin, for his mild cheek flushed. Certainly, the fact of being a prisoner for life did make some difference. The sound of the noonday bell, however, warned him to cease argument.

With a great clanking and clashing of irons, the forty rose and stood each by his stone-heap. The third constable came round, rapping the leg-irons of each man and roughly pulling up the coarse trousers (made with buttoned flaps at the sides, like Mexican *calzoneros*, in order to give free play to the ankle fetters) so that he might assure himself that no tricks had been played since his last visit. As each man passed this ordeal he saluted, and clanked, with wide-spread legs, to his place in the double line. Mr. Meekin found himself reminded of a blacksmith picking up horses' feet to examine the soundness of their shoes.

"Upon my word," he said to himself, with a momentary pang of genuine compassion, "it *is* a dreadful way to treat human beings. I don't wonder at that wretched creature groaning under it. But, bless me, it is near one o'clock, and I promised to lunch with Major Vickers at two. How time flies, to be sure!"

That afternoon, while Mr. Meekin was digesting his lunch, Rufus Dawes began to brood over a desperate scheme. The intelligence that the inves-

RUFUS DAWES'S IDYLL

tigation he had hoped for was not to be granted to him had rendered doubly bitter those galling fetters of self-restraint which he had laid upon himself. For five years he had waited for a chance which might bring him to Hobart Town, and enable him to denounce the treachery of Maurice Frere. He had, by an almost miraculous accident, obtained that chance and, having obtained it, had found that he was not allowed to speak. All the hopes he had formed were dashed to earth. The whole world was his foe: there was no honesty or truth in any living creature—save one.

During his convict life at Port Arthur one bright memory shone upon him like a star—the memory of the child whom he had saved, and who loved him. When Frere, handing him over to the authorities as an absconder, ingeniously twisted the details of the boat-building to his own glorification, the belief that Sylvia would expose these pretences had given him courage to keep silence. So strong was his belief in her gratitude that he scorned to *beg* for the pardon he had taught himself to believe that she would ask for him. So utter was his contempt for the coward who bore false witness against him that, when he heard his sentence of life banishment, he disdained to make known the true part he had played in the matter, preferring to wait for the more exquisite revenge which would follow upon the recovery of the child from her illness.

But when, at Port Arthur, day after day passed and brought no word, he began, with a sickening feeling of despair, to comprehend that something strange had happened. He was told by new comers that the child of the Commandant lay still sick and near to death. Then he heard that she and her father had left the colony, and that all prospect of her righting him by her evidence was at an end. This news gave him a terrible pang; and at first he was inclined to break out into upbraidings of her selfishness. But, with that depth of love which was in him, he found excuses for her even then. She was ill. She was in the hands of friends who regarded her entreaties as childish babblings. She would free him if she had the power. Then he began to write "statements," agonised to see the Commandant, pestered the gaolers and warders and inundated the Government with letters, which, containing as they did denunciations of Maurice Frere, were never suffered to reach their destination. The authorities grew weary of this perpetual iteration of what they believed to be malicious falsehoods, and ordered him heavier tasks and more continuous labour. They mistook his gloom for treachery, his impatient outbursts of passion at his fate for ferocity, his silent endurance for dangerous cunning. As he had been at Macquarie Harbour, so did he become at Port Arthur—a marked man.

Despairing of winning his liberty by fair means, he twice attempted to escape, but escape was even more hopeless than it had been at Hell's Gates. The Peninsula of Port Arthur was admirably guarded. Signal stations drew a chain round the prison, an armed boat's crew watched each bay, and across the narrow isthmus which connected it with the mainland was a cordon of watch-dogs, in addition to the soldier guard. He was retaken, of course, flogged, and weighted with heavier irons. The second time, they sent him to the Coal Mines, where the prisoners lived undergound, worked half-naked, and dragged their inspecting gaolers in waggons upon iron tramways, when such great people condescended to visit them. The day on which he started for this place he heard that Sylvia was dead, and his last hope went from him.

Now, instead of the phantoms of his vanished youth which were once wont to visit him, he saw but one vision—that of the child who had loved him. Around her figure, he grouped every image of happiness and love. He pictured to himself some quiet nook at the world's end—a deep-gardened house in a German country town, or remote cottage by the English seashore, where he and his dream-child might have lived together, happier in a purer affection than the love of man for woman. He could see her—in his visions—reading by a cheery fireside, wandering in summer woods, or lingering by the marge of the slumbering mid-day sea. He could feel—in his dreams—her soft arms about his neck, her innocent kisses on his lips, he could hear her light laugh, and see her sunny ringlets float, back-blown, as she ran to meet him. Conscious that she was dead, and that he did to her gentle memory no disrespect by linking her fortunes to his, he loved to think of her as still living, and to plot out for her and for himself impossible plans of future happiness. Thus dreaming, he had shaped out for himself a sorrowful comfort, and found a compensation for the terrible affliction of living.

Indifference to his present sufferings took possession of him; only at the bottom of this indifference lurked a fixed hatred of the man who had brought these sufferings upon him. It was in this mood that he had intended to make the revelation which he had made in court, but the intelligence that Sylvia lived unmanned him, and his prepared speech had been usurped by a torrent of invective which convinced no one and gave Frere the very argument he needed. But he would defeat them yet. He had planned a method of escape, and he would break from his bonds, fling himself at her feet, and pray her to speak the truth for him, and so save him. "If she knew I was alive, she would come to me," he said. "I am sure she would. Perhaps they told her that I was dead."

Meditating that night in the solitude of his cell he almost wept to think of the cruel deception that had doubtless been practised on her. "Five years! She must be a woman now. My little child a woman! Yet she is sure to be childlike, sweet and gentle. How she will grieve when she hears of my sufferings. Oh! my darling, my darling, you are not dead!" And then, looking hastily about him in the darkness, as though fearful of being seen, he pulled from his breast a little packet, and felt it lovingly with his coarse, toil-worn fingers, reverently raising it to his lips.

A few days after this—on the the 23rd of December—Maurice Frere was alarmed by a piece of startling intelligence. The notorious Dawes had

AN ESCAPE

escaped from gaol!

Captain Frere had inspected the prison that very afternoon, and it had seemed to him that the hammers had never fallen so briskly, nor the chains clanked so gaily, as on the occasion of his visit. "Thinking of their Christmas holiday, the dogs!" he had said to the patrolling warder. "Thinking of their Christmas pudding, the luxurious scoundrels!" Moreover, he had—by way of a pleasant stroke of wit—tormented Rufus Dawes with his ill-fortune. "The schooner sails to-morrow, my man," he had said: "you'll spend *your* Christmas at the mines." And congratulated himself upon the fact that Rufus Dawes merely touched his cap, and went on with his stone-cracking in silence. Certainly double irons and hard labour were fine things to break a man's spirit. So that afternoon, when he heard the astounding news that Rufus Dawes had freed himself from his fetters, climbed the gaol wall in broad daylight, run the gauntlet of Macquarie-street, and was now supposedly safely hidden in the mountains, he was dumbfounded.

"How the deuce did he do it, Jenkins?" he asked, as soon as he reached the yard.

"Well, I'm blessed if I rightly know, your honour," says Jenkins. "He was over the wall before you could say 'knife.' Scott fired and missed him, and then I heard the sentry's musket, but he missed him, too."

"Missed him!" cries Frere. "Pretty fellows you are, all of you! Why, the man wasn't three feet from the end of your carbine!"

The unlucky Scott muttered something about the sun having been in his eyes. "I don't know how it was, sir. I ought to have hit him. I think I did touch him, too, as he went up the wall."

A stranger to the customs of the place might have imagined that he was listening to a conversation about a pigeon match.

"Tell me about it," says Frere, with an angry curse.

"I was just turning, your honour, when I hears Scott sing out 'Hallo!' and when I turned round I saw Dawes's irons on the ground, and him a-scrambling up the heap o' stones yonder. The two men on my right jumped up, and I thought it was a made-up thing among 'em, so I covered 'em with my carbine and called out that I'd shoot the first that stepped out. Then I heard Scott's piece, and the men gave a shout. When I looked round, he was gone."

"Nobody else moved?"

"No, your honour; and they all swore later they knowed nothing of it. I know Dawes's irons was all right when he went to dinner."

Frere stooped and examined the empty fetters. "If you don't know your duty better than this, the sooner you go somewhere else the better, my man. Look here!"

The two ankle fetters were severed. One had been evidently filed through, and the other broken transversely. The latter was bent, as from a violent blow.

"Don't know where he got the file from," said Warder Short.

"Don't know—with things like *this* lying about? I wonder the whole yard isn't loose and dining with the Governor."

"*This*" was a fragment of delft which Frere's quick eye had detected among the broken metal.

"Well, Captain Frere, it's an accident," says Short, "and can't be helped now."

"An accident!" roared Frere. "What business have you with *accidents*? How, in the devil's name, you let the man get over the wall, I don't know."

"He ran up that stone heap," says Scott, "and seemed to me to jump at the roof of the shed. I fired at him, and he swung his legs over the top of the wall and dropped."

Frere measured the distance from his eye, and an irrepressible feeling of admiration took possession of him for the instant.

"By the Lord Harry, but it's a big jump!" he said; and then the memory of the hideous wrong he had done the escaped convict made him add—"A desperate villain like that wouldn't stick at a murder if you pressed him hard. Which way did he go?"

"Right up Macquarie-street, and then made for the Mountain. Mr. Mays of the Star Hotel tried to stop him, and was knocked head over heels. He says the fellow runs like a deer."

"We'll have the reward out if we don't get him to-night," says Frere; "and you'd better put on an extra warder. This sort of game is catching;" and he strode away to the Barracks.

Through the prison city flew the signal of alarm, and the patrol clattering out along the road to New Norfolk made haste to strike the trail of the fugitive. But night came and found him yet at large. Meanwhile the usual message ran through the island and, before noon of the next day, there was not a signal station on the coast but knew that No. 8942, prisoner for life, was illegally at large. This intelligence, further aided by a paragraph in the *Gazette* anent the "Daring Escape," noised abroad, the world cared little that the *Mary Jane*, Government schooner, had sailed for Port Arthur without Rufus Dawes.

But two or three persons cared a good deal. Major Vickers, for one, was indignant that his boasted security should have been so easily defied, and in proportion to his indignation was the grief of Messieurs Jenkins, Scott, and Co., threatened with dismissal. Sylvia had shown symptoms of nervous terror, none the less injurious because carefully repressed; and Captain Maurice Frere was a prey to the most cruel anxiety. He had ridden off at a hand-gallop within ten minutes after he had reached the barracks, and had spent the few hours of remaining daylight scouring the country along the road to the North. At dawn the next day he was away to the Mountain, and with a black-tracker at his heels, explored as much of that wilderness as nature permitted to him. He had offered to double the reward, and had examined a number of suspicious persons. "Our dear friend feels his reputation at stake," the future chaplain of Port Arthur said to Sylvia at the Christmas dinner. "He is so proud of his knowledge of these unhappy men that he dislikes to be outwitted by any of them."

Notwithstanding all this, however, Dawes had completely disappeared.

The "little gathering" of which Major Vickers had spoken to Mr. Meekin, had grown into something larger than he had anticipated. Instead of a

JOHN REX'S LETTER HOME

quiet dinner at which his own household, his daughter's betrothed, and the clergyman should be present, the Major found himself entangled with Mesdames Protherick and Jellicoe, Mr. McNab of the garrison, and Mr. Pounce of the civil list. His quiet Christmas dinner had grown into an evening party.

The conversation was on the usual topic.

"Heard anything about that fellow Dawes?" asked Mr. Pounce.

"Not yet," says Frere, sulkily; "but he won't be out long."

"I suppose it is not easy for a prisoner to make good his escape?" says Meekin.

"Oh, he mightn't be caught," says Frere, "but he'll starve instead. It's a precious poor look-out for any man to live upon luck in the bush."

"Indeed, yes," says Mr. Pounce, lapping his soup. "This island seems specially adapted by Providence for a convict settlement; for with an admirable climate, it carries little indigenous vegetation which will support human life."

"Indeed," says Mrs. Protherick, "poor Protherick used often to say that it seemed as if some Almightly Hand had planned the Penal Settlements round the coast, the country is so delightfully barren."

"Ay, Port Arthur couldn't have been better if it had been made on purpose," says Frere; "and all up the coast from Tenby to St. Helen's there isn't a scrap for a human being to make a meal on. The West Coast is worse."

"By the way," says Meekin, "I've got something to show you. Rex's confession. I brought it down on purpose."

"Rex's confession!"

"His account of his adventures after he left Macquarie Harbour. I am going to send it to the Bishop."

"Oh, I should like to see it," said Sylvia, with heightened colour. "The story of these unhappy men has a personal interest for me, you know."

"A forbidden subject, Poppet."

"No, papa, not altogether forbidden; for it does not affect me now as it used to do."

"A pack of lies, I expect," said Frere, with a scowl. "That scoundrel Rex couldn't tell the truth to save his life."

"You misjudge him, Captain Frere," said Meekin. "All prisoners are not hardened in iniquity like Rufus Dawes. Rex is, I believe, truly penitent, and has written a most touching letter to his father."

"A letter!" said Vickers. "You know that, by the King's—no, the Queen's regulations, all letters must first pass through the hands of the authorities."

"I am aware of that, Major," returned Meekin, producing a packet, "and for that reason have brought it with me, that you may read it for yourself. It seems to me to breathe a spirit of true piety."

Frere, turning the packet between his fingers, read the address:

> John Rex, sen.,
> Care of Mr. Blick,
> 38, Bishopsgate Street Within,
> London.

"Who is Blick, I wonder?" said he.

"A worthy merchant, I am told, in whose counting-house the unfortunate Rex passed his younger days. He had a tolerable education, as you are aware."

"Educated prisoners are always the worst," said Vickers. "James, some more wine. We don't drink toasts here, but as this is Christmas Eve—'Her Majesty the Queen!'"

Having drunk this loyal toast with due fervour, Vickers proposed, "His

Excellency Sir John Franklin," which toast was likewise duly honoured.

"Here's a Merry Christmas and a Happy New Year to you, sir," said Frere. "God bless us all."

"Amen," says Meekin piously. "Let us hope He will; and now, leddies, the letter. I will read the Confession afterwards." Opening the packet with the satisfaction of a Gospel vineyard labourer who sees his first vine sprouting, the good creature began:

"'Hobart Town, Dec. 27th, 1838.

" 'MY DEAR FATHER,—Through all the chances, changes, and vicissitudes of my chequered life, I never had a task so painful to my mangled feelings as the present one, of addressing you from this doleful spot—my sea-girt prison, on the beach of which I stand a monument of destruction; driven by the adverse winds of fate to the confines of black despair, and into the vortex of galling misery.'"

"Poetical!" said Frere.

" 'I am just like a gigantic tree of the forest which has stood many a wintry blast and stormy tempest, but now, alas! I am become a withered trunk, with all my greenest and tenderest branches lopped off. Though fast attaining middle age, I am not filling an envied and honoured post with credit and respect. No—I shall be soon wearing the garb of degradation, and the badge and brand of infamy at P.A., which is, being interpreted, Port Arthur, the "Villain's Home." ' "

"Poor fellow!" said Sylvia.

"Touching, is it not?" assented Meekin, continuing,—

" 'I am, with heartrending sorrow and anguish of soul, ranged and mingled with the Outcasts of Society. My present circumstances and picture you will find well and truly drawn in the 102nd Psalm, commencing with the 4th verse to the 12th inclusive, which, my dear father, I request you will read attentively before you proceed any further.'"

"Hullo!" said Frere, pulling out his pocket-book, "what's that? Read those numbers again."

Mr. Meekin complied, and Frere grinned.

"Go on," he said. "I'll show you something in that letter directly."

" 'Oh, my dear father, avoid, I beg of you, the reading of profane books. Let your mind dwell upon holy things, and assiduously study to grow in grace, Psalm lxxiii, 2. Yet I have hope even in this my desolate condition. Psalm xxxv, 18. "For the Lord our God is merciful, and inclineth His ear unto pity."'"

"Blasphemous dog!" said Vickers. "You don't believe all that, Meekin, do you?"

The parson reproved him gently.

"Wait a moment, sir, until I have finished."

"'Party spirit runs very high, even in prison in Van Diemen's Land. I am sorry to say that a licentious press invariably evinces a very great degree of contumely, while the authorities are held in respect by all well-disposed persons, though it is often endeavoured by some to bring on them the hatred and contempt of prisoners. But I am glad to tell you that all their efforts are without avail; but, nevertheless, do not read in any colonial newspaper. There is so much scurrility and vituperation in their productions. I am aware that you will hear accounts of cruelty, said, by the evil-minded haters of the Government, to have been inflicted by gaolers on convicts. To be candid, this is not the dreadful place it has been represented to be by vindictive writers. Severe flogging and heavy chaining is sometimes used, no doubt, but only in rare cases; and nominal punishments are marked out by law for slight breaches of discipline. So far as I have an opportunity of judging, the lash is never bestowed unless merited.'"

"As far as he is concerned, I don't doubt it!" said Frere, cracking a walnut.

"'The texts of Scripture quoted by our chaplain have comforted me much, and I have much to be grateful for; for after the rash attempt I made to secure my freedom, I have reason to be thankful for the mercy shown to me. Death—dreadful death of soul and body—would have been my portion; but, by the mercy of Omnipotence, I have been spared to repentance—John iii. I have now come to bitterness. The chaplain, a pious gentleman, says it never really pays to steal. "Lay up for yourselves treasures in Heaven, where neither moth nor rust doth corrupt." Honesty is the best policy, I am convinced, and I would not for £1,000 repeat my evil courses—Psalm xxxviii, 14. When I think of the happy days I once passed with good Mr. Blick, in the old house in Blue Anchor Yard, and reflect that since that happy time I have recklessly plunged in sin, and stolen goods and watches, studs, rings, and jewellery, become, indeed, a common thief, I tremble with remorse, and fly to prayer—Psalm v. Oh what sinners we are! Let me hope that now I, by God's blessing placed beyond temptation, will live safely, and that some day I even may, by the will of the Lord Jesus, find mercy for my sins. Some kind of madness has method in it, but madness of sin holds us without escape.

Such is, dear father, then, my hope and trust for my remaining life here—Psalm c. 74. I owe my bodily well-being to Captain Maurice Frere, who was good enough to speak of my conduct in reference to the *Osprey*, when, with Shiers, Barker, and others, we captured that vessel. Pray for Captain Frere, my dear father. He is a good man, and though his public duty is painful and trying to his feelings, yet, as a public functionary, he could not allow his private feelings, whether of mercy or revenge, to step between him and his duty.'"

"Confound the rascal!" said Frere, growing crimson.

"'Remember me most affectionately to Sarah and little William, and all friends who yet cherish the recollection of me, and bid them take warning by my fate, and keep from evil courses. A good conscience is better than gold, and no amount can compensate for the misery incident to a return to crime. Whether I shall ever see you again, dear father, is more than uncertain; for my doom is life, unless the Government alter their plans concerning me, and allow me an opportunity to earn my freedom by hard work.

"'The blessing of God rest with you, my dear father; and that you may be washed white in the blood of the Lamb is the prayer of your

"'Unfortunate Son,

" 'John Rex.

" 'P.S.—Though your sins be as scarlet they shall be whiter than snow.' "

"A touching letter, is it not?" beamed Meekin.

"So it is," said Frere. "Now let me have it a moment."

He took the paper, and referring to the numbers of the texts which he had written in his pocket-book, began to knit his brows over Mr. John Rex's production. "I thought so," he said at length. "Those texts were never written for nothing. It's an old trick, but cleverly done."

"What do you mean?" said Meekin.

"Mean!" cries Frere. "This precious composition contains a very gratifying piece of intelligence for Mr. Blick, whoever he is. Some receiver, I've no doubt. Look here, Mr. Meekin. Take the letter and this pencil, and begin at the first text. The 102nd Psalm, from the 4th verse to the 12th inclusive, doesn't he say? Very good; that's nine verses, isn't it? Well, now, underscore nine consecutive words from the second word immediately following the next text quoted, '*I have hope*,' etc. Have you got it?"

"Yes," says Meekin, astonished, while all heads bent over the table.

"Well, now, his text is the eighteenth verse of the thirty-*fifth* Psalm, isn't it? Count eighteen words on, then underscore *five* consecutive ones. You've done that?"

"A moment—sixteen—seventeen—eighteen, '*authorities*.'"

"Count and score in the same way until you come to the word '*Texts*' somewhere."

"Yes," said Meekin after a pause. "Here it is—'the texts of Scripture quoted by our chaplain.' But surely, Mr. Frere——"

"Hold on a bit now," cries Frere. "What's the next quotation?—John iii. That's every third word. Score every third word beginning with 'I' immediately following the text, now, until you come to a quotation. Got it? How many words in it?"

"'Lay up for yourselves treasures in Heaven, where neither moth nor rust doth corrupt,'" said Meekin, bewildered. "Fourteen words."

"Count fourteen words on, then, and score the fourteenth. I'm up to this text-quoting business."

"The word '£1,000,'" said Meekin. "Yes."

"Then there's another text. Thirty-eighth—isn't it?—Psalm and the fourteenth verse. Do that the same way as the other—count fourteen words, and then score eight in succession. Where does that bring you?"

"The fifth Psalm."

"Every fifth word then. Go on, my dear sir—go on. 'Method' of 'escape,' yes. The *hundredth* Psalm means a full stop. What verse? Seventy-four. Count seventy-four words and score."

There was a pause for a few minutes while Mr. Meekin counted.

"Read out your marked words now, Meekin. Let's see if I'm right."

Mr. Meekin read with gradually crimsoning face:—

"'I have hopes even in this my desolate condition ... in prison Van Diemen's Land ... the authorities are held in ... hatred and contempt of prisoners ... read in any colonial newspaper ... accounts of cruelty and tyranny ... inflicted by gaolers on convicts ... severe flogging and heavy chaining ... for slight breaches of discipline ... I ... come ... the pious ... it ... pays ...£1,000 ... in the old house in Blue Anchor Yard ... stolen goods and watches studs rings and jewellery ... are ... now ... placed ... safely ... I ... will ... find ... some ... method of ... escape ... then ... for ...revenge.'"

"Well," said Maurice, looking round with a grin, "what do you think of that?"

"Most remarkable!" said Mr. Pounce.

Mr. Meekin arose in wrath.

"It's very ungracious on your part, Captain Frere. A capital joke, I have no doubt; but permit me to say I do not like jesting on such matters. This poor fellow's letter to his aged father was confided to me in my sacred character as a Christian pastor."

"That's just it. The fellows play upon the parsons, excuse me, don't you know, and under cover of your 'sacred character,' play all kinds of pranks."

"Captain Frere," protested Mr. Meekin, "your interpretation is, I am convinced, an incorrect one. How could the poor man compose such an ingenious piece of cryptography?"

"If you mean, fake up that paper," returned Frere, unconsciously dropping into prison slang, "I'll tell you. He had a Bible, I suppose, while he was writing?"

"I certainly permitted him the use of the Sacred Volume, Captain Frere. I should have judged it inconsistent with the character of my Office to have refused it to him."

"Of course. And that's just where you parsons are always putting your foot into it. If you'd put your 'Office' into your pocket and open your eyes a bit——"

"Maurice! My dear Maurice!"

"I beg your pardon, Meekin," says Maurice, with clumsy apology; "but I *know* these fellows. I've lived among 'em, and I'm down to all their moves, don't you see. The Bible is the only book they get hold of, and being chockfull of villainy, what other book should they make use of to aid their infernal schemes *but* the one that the chaplain has made a text-book of for 'em?" And Maurice rose in disgust, not unmixed with self-laudation.

"Dear me, it is really very terrible," said Meekin, shaken—"very terrible indeed."

"But unhappily true," said Mr. Pounce. "An olive? Thanks."

"Upon me soul!" burst out honest McNab, "the hail seestem seems to be maist ill-calculated tae advance the wark o' reeformation."

"Mr. McNab, I'll trouble you for the port," said equally honest Vickers, bound hand and foot in the chains of the rules of the service. And so, what seemed likely to become a dangerous discussion upon convict discipline, was stifled judiciously at the birth. But Sylvia, prompted, perhaps by curiosity, perhaps by a desire to modify the parson's chagrin, in passing Mr. Meekin, took up the "confession," that lay unopened beside his wine glass, and bore it off.

"Come, Mr. Meekin," said Vickers, when the door closed behind the ladies, "help yourself. I am sorry the letter turned out so strangely, but you may rely on Frere, I assure you. He knows more about convicts than any man on the island."

"I see, Captain Frere, that you have made a study of the criminal classes."

"So I have, my dear sir, and know every turn and twist among 'em. I tell you my maxim—*divide to conquer*. Set all the dogs spying on each other. Why, if the prisoners were as faithful to each other as we are, we couldn't hold the island a week. It's just because no man can trust his neighbour that every mutiny falls to the ground."

"I suppose it must be so," said poor Meekin.

"It is so; and, by George, if I had my way, I'd have it so that no prisoner should say a word to his right hand man, but his left hand man should tell me of it. I'd promote the men that peached, and make the beggars their own warders."

"But such a course, Captain Frere, would surely excite the worst passions of our fallen nature, and lead to endless lying and tyranny."

"Wait a bit," cries Frere. "Perhaps one of these days, I'll get a chance, and then I'll try it. Convicts! By the Lord Harry, sir, there's only one way to treat 'em; give 'em tobacco when they behave 'emselves, and flog 'em when they don't."

"Terrible!" exclaimed the clergyman. "You speak of them as if they were wild beasts."

"So they are," said Maurice Frere, calmly.

At the bottom of the garden was a rustic seat abutting upon a low wall. The branches of the English trees (planted long ago) hung above it, and between the boughs one could see the silver river. Sitting with her face to the bay and her back to the house, Sylvia opened the manuscript she had carried off, and began to read. It was written in a firm, large hand, and headed—

HAT BECAME OF THE "OSPREY" MUTINEERS

A NARRATIVE

OF THE SUFFERINGS AND ADVENTURES OF CERTAIN OF THE TEN CONVICTS WHO SEIZED THE BRIG "OSPREY," AT MACQUARIE HARBOUR, IN VAN DIEMEN'S LAND, RELATED BY ONE OF THE SAID CONVICTS WHILE LYING UNDER SENTENCE FOR THIS OFFENCE IN THE GAOL AT HOBART TOWN.

Sylvia, having read this grandiloquent sentence, paused for a moment. Longing, and yet fearing, to proceed, she held the paper, half unfolded, in her hand, as, in her childhood, she had held ajar the door of some dark room, into which she longed and yet feared to enter. Her timidity lasted but an instant.

"When orders arrived from head-quarters to break up the penal settlement of Macquarie Harbour, the Commandant (Major Vickers, —th Regiment) and most of the prisoners embarked on board a colonial vessel, and set sail for Hobart Town, leaving behind them a brig that had been built at Macquarie Harbour, to be brought round after them, and placing Captain Maurice Frere in command. Left aboard her was Mr. Bates, who had acted as pilot at the settlement, also four soldiers, and ten prisoners, as a crew to work the vessel. The Commandant's wife and child were also aboard."

"How strangely it reads," thought the girl.

"On the 12th of January, 1834, we set sail, and in the afternoon anchored safely outside the Gates; but a breeze setting in from the north-west, caused a swell on the Bar, and Mr. Bates ran back to Wellington Bay. We remained there all next day; and in the afternoon Captain Frere took two soldiers and a boat, and went a-fishing. There were then only Mr. Bates and the other two soldiers aboard, and it was proposed by William Cheshire to seize the vessel. I was at first unwilling, thinking that loss of life might ensue; but Cheshire and the others, knowing that I was acquainted with navigation— having in happier days lived much on the sea—threatened me if I refused to join. A song was started in the folksle, and one of the soldiers coming to listen to it, was seized, and Lyon and Riley then made prisoner of the sentry. Forced thus into a project with which I had at first but little sympathy, I felt my heart leap at the prospect of freedom, and would have sacrificed all to obtain it. From that moment I assumed the command of my wretched companions; and honestly think, that however culpable I may have been in the eyes of the law, I prevented them from the display of a violence to which their savage life had unhappily made them but too accustomed."

"Poor fellow," said Sylvia, beguiled by Master Rex's specious paragraphs, "I think he was not to blame."

"Mr. Bates was below in the cabin, and on being summoned by Cheshire to surrender, with great courage attempted a defence. Barker fired at him through the skylight, but, fearful of the lives of the Commandant's wife and child, I struck up his musket, and the ball passed through the mouldings of the stern windows. At the same time, the soldiers whom we had bound in the folksle forced up the hatch and came on deck. Cheshire shot the first one, and struck the other with his clubbed musket. The wounded man lost his footing, and the brig, lurching with the rising tide; he fell into the sea. This was—by the blessing of God—the only life lost in the whole affair.

"Mr. Bates, seeing now that we had possession of the deck, surrendered, upon promise that the Commandant's wife and child should be put ashore in safety. I directed him to take such matters as he needed, and prepared to lower the jolly-boat.

"As she swung off the davits, Captain Frere came alongside in the whale-boat, and gallantly endeavoured to board us, but the boat drifted past the vessel. I was now determined to be free, and, hailing the whale-boat, swore to fire into her unless she surrendered. Captain Frere refused, and was for boarding us again, but the two soldiers joined with us, and prevented his intention. Having now got the prisoners into the jolly-boat, we transferred Captain Frere into her, and being ourselves in the whale-boat, compelled Captain Frere and Mr. Bates to row ashore. We then took the jolly-boat in tow, and returned to the brig, a strict watch being kept for fear that they should rescue the vessel from us.

"At break of day every man was upon deck, and a consultation took place concerning the parting of the provisions. Cheshire was for leaving them to starve, but Lesly, Shiers, and I held out for an equal division. After a long controversy, Humanity gained the day, and the provisions were put into the whale-boat, and taken ashore. Upon the receipt of the provisions, Mr. Bates thus expressed himself: 'Men, I did not for one moment expect such kind treatment from you, regarding the provisions you have now brought ashore for us, out of so little which there was on board. When I consider your present undertaking, without a competent navigator, and in a leaky vessel, your situation seems most perilous; therefore I hope God will prove kind to you, and preserve you from the manifold dangers you may have to encounter on the stormy ocean.' Mrs. Vickers also was pleased to say that I had behaved kindly to her, that she wished me well, and that when she returned to Hobart Town she would speak in my favour. Then they cheered us on our departure, wishing we might be prosperous on account of our humanity in sharing provisions with them.

"Having had breakfast, we commenced throwing overboard the light cargo which was in the hold, which employed us until dinner-time. After dinner we ran out a small kedge-anchor with about one hundred fathoms of line, and having weighed anchor, and the tide being slack, we hauled on the kedge-line and succeeded in this manner by kedging along, and we came to two islands, called the Cap and Bonnet. The whole of us then commenced heaving the brig short, sending the whale-boat to take her in tow, after we had tripped the anchor. By this means we got her safe across the bar. Scarcely was this done than a light breeze sprang up from the south-west, and firing a musket to apprise the party we had left of our safety, we made sail and put out to sea."

Having read thus far, Sylvia paused in an agony of recollection. She remembered the firing of the musket, and that her mother had wept over her. But beyond this all was uncertainty. Memories slipped across her mind like shadows—she caught at them, and they were gone. Yet the reading of this strange story made her nerves thrill. The very barrenness of the narration was hideously suggestive, and the girl felt her heart beat quicker as her poetic intellect rushed to complete the terrible picture sketched by the convict. She saw it all—the blue sea, the slowly moving ship, the wretched company on the shore; she heard——Was that a rustling in the bushes below her? A bird! How nervous she was growing!

"Being thus fairly rid—as we thought—of our prison life, we cheerfully held consultation as to our future course. It was my intention to get among the islands in the South Seas, and scuttling the brig, to pass ourselves off among the natives as shipwrecked seamen, trusting to God's mercy that some homeward bound vessel might at length rescue us. With this view, I made James Lesly first mate, he being an experienced mariner, and prepared myself, with what few instruments we had, to take our departure from Birches Rock. Having hauled the whale-boat alongside, we stove her, together with the jolly-boat, and cast her adrift. This done, I parted the landsmen with the seamen, and, steering east south-east, at eight p.m. we set our first watch. In little more than an hour after this, came on a heavy gale from the south-west. I, and others of the landsmen, were violently sea-sick, and Lesly had some difficulty in handling the brig, as the boisterous weather called for two men at the helm. In the morning, getting upon deck with difficulty, I found that the wind had abated, but upon sounding the well discovered much water in the hold. Lesly rigged the pumps, but the starboard one only could be made to work. From that time there were but two businesses aboard—from the pump to the helm. The gale lasted two days and a night, the brig running under close-reefed topsails, we being afraid to shorten sail, lest we might be overtaken by some pursuing vessel, so strong was the terror of our prison upon us.

"On the 16th, at noon, I again forced myself on deck, and taking a meridian observation, altered the course of the brig to east and by south, wishing to run to the southward of New Zealand, out of the usual track of shipping; and having a notion that, should our provisions hold out, we might make the South American coast, and fall into Christian hands. This done, I was compelled to retire below, and for a week lay in my berth as one at the last gasp. At times I repented of my resolution, Fair urging me to bestir myself, as the men were not satisfied with our course. On the 21st a mutiny occurred, led by Lyon, who asserted we were heading for the Pacific, and must infallibly perish. This disaffected man, though ignorant of navigation, insisted upon steering to the south, believing that we had run to the northward of the Friendly Islands, and was for running the ship ashore and beseeching the protection of the natives. Lesly in vain protested that a southward course would bring us into icefields. Barker, who had served on board a whaler, strove to convince the mutineers that the temperature of such latitudes was too warm for such an error to escape us. After much noise, Lyon rushed to the helm, and Russen, drawing one of the pistols taken from Mr. Bates, shot him dead, upon which the others returned to their duty. This dreadful deed was, I fear, necessary to the safety of the brig; and had it occurred on board a vessel manned by freemen, would have been applauded as a stern but needful measure.

"Forced by these tumults upon deck, I made a short speech to the crew, and convinced them that I was competent to perform what I had promised to do, though at the time my heart inwardly failed me, and I longed for some sign of land. Supported at each arm by Lesly and Barker, I took an observation, and altered our course to north by east, the brig running eleven knots an hour under single-reefed topsails, and the pumps hard at work. So we ran until the 31st of January, when a white squall took us, and nearly proved fatal to all aboard.

"For nine days and nights the storm continued, the men being utterly exhausted. One of the two soldiers was washed overboard and drowned. Our provision was now nearly done, but the gale abating on the ninth day, we hastened to put provisions on the launch. The sea was heavy, and we were compelled to put a purchase on the fore and main yards, with preventers to windward, to ease the launch in going over the side. We got her fairly afloat at last, the others battening down the hatches in the brig. Having dressed ourselves in the clothes of Captain Frere and the pilot, we left the brig at sun-down, lying with her channel plates nearly under water.

"The wind freshening during the night, our launch, which might, indeed, be termed a long-boat, having been fitted with mast, bowsprit, and main boom, began to be very uneasy, shipping two seas one after the other. The plan we could devise was to sit, four of us about, in the stern sheets, with our backs to the sea, to prevent the water pooping us. This itself was enough to exhaust the strongest men. The day, however, made us some amends for the dreadful night. Land was not more than ten miles from us; approaching as nearly as we could with safety, we hauled our wind, and ran along in, trusting to find some harbour. At half-past two we sighted a bay of very curious appearance, having two large rocks at the entrance, resembling pyramids. Shiers, Russen, and Fair landed, in hopes of discovering fresh water, of which we stood much in need. Before long they returned, stating that they had found an Indian hut, inside of which were some rude earthenware vessels. Fearful of surprise, we lay off the shore all that night, and putting into the bay very early in the morning, killed a seal. This was the first fresh meat I had tasted for four years. It seemed strange to eat it under such circumstances. We cooked the flippers, heart, and liver for breakfast, giving some to a cat which we had taken with us out of the brig, for I would not, willingly, allow even that animal to perish. After breakfast, we got under way; and we had scarcely been out half an hour when we had a fresh breeze, which carried us along at the rate of seven knots an hour, running from bay to bay to find inhabitants. Steering along the shore, as the sun went down, we suddenly heard the bellowing of a bullock, and James Barker, whom, from his violent conduct, I though incapable of such sentiment, burst into tears.

"In about two hours we perceived great fires on the beach and let go the anchor in nineteen fathoms of water. We lay awake all that night. In the morning, we rowed further inshore, and moored the boat to some seaweed. As soon as the inhabitants caught sight of us, they came down to the beach. I distributed needles and thread among the Indians, and on saying 'Valdivia,' a woman instantly pointed towards a tongue of land to the southward, holding up three fingers, and crying '*leaghos!*' which I conjectured to be three leagues; the distance we afterwards found it to be.

"About three o'clock in the afternoon, we weathered the point pointed out by the woman, and perceived a flagstaff and a twelve-gun battery under our lee. I now divided among the men the sum of six pounds ten shillings that I had found in Captain Frere's cabin, and made another and more equal distribution of the clothing. There were also two watches, one of which I gave to Lesly, and kept the other for myself. It was resolved among us to say that we were part crew of the brig *Julia*, bound for China and wrecked in the South seas. Upon landing at the battery, we were received with the greatest civility by the Spaniards, and were heartily entertained, though we did not understand one word of what they said. Next morning, it was agreed that Lesly, Barker, Shiers, and Russen should pay for a canoe to convey them to the town, and that day they took their departure.

"On the 9th March, a boat, commanded by a lieutenant, came down with orders that the rest of us should be conveyed to town; and we accordingly launched the boat under convoy of the soldiers, and reached the town the same evening, in some trepidation. I feared lest the Spaniards had obtained a clue as to our real character, and so it was—the surviving soldier having betrayed us. This fellow was thus doubly a traitor—first, in deserting his officer, and then in betraying his comrades.

"We were immediately escorted to prison, where we found our four companions. Some of them were for brazening out the story of shipwreck, but knowing how confused must necessarily be our accounts, were we examined separately, I persuaded them that open confession would be our best chance of safety. On the 14th we were taken before the Intendente or Governor, who informed us that we were free, on condition that we chose to live within the limits of the town. At this intelligence I felt my heart grow light, and only begged in the name of my companions that we might not be given up to the British Government; 'rather than which,' said I, 'I would beg to be shot dead in the palace square.' The Governor regarded us with tears in his eyes, and spoke as follows: 'My poor men, do not think that I would take that advantage over you. Do not make an attempt to escape, and I will be your friend; and should a vessel come to-morrow to demand you, you shall find I will be as good as my word.'

"The following day we all procured employment in launching a vessel of three hundred tons burden, and my men showed themselves so active that the owner said he would rather have us than thirty of his own countrymen. After she was launched, the seamen amongst us helped to fit her out, being paid fifteen dollars a month, with provisions on board. As for myself, I speedily obtained employment in the shipbuilder's yard, and subsisted by honest industry, almost forgetting, in the unwonted pleasures of freedom, the sad reverse of fortune which had befallen me. To think that I, who had mingled among gentlemen and scholars, should be thankful to labour in a shipwright's yard by day, and sleep on a bundle of hides by night! But this is personal matter, and need not be obtruded.

"In the same yard with me worked the soldier who had betrayed us, and I could not but regard it as a special judgment of Heaven, when he one day fell from a great height and died in much torment in a few hours. The days thus passed on in comparative happiness until the 20th of May, 1836, when the old Governor took his departure, regretted by all the inhabitants of Valdivia, and the *Achilles*, a one-and-twenty-gun brig of war, arrived with the new Governor. One of the first acts of this gentleman was to sell our boat, which was moored at the back of Government-house. This proceeding looked to my mind indicative of ill-will; and, fearful lest the Governor should deliver us again into bondage, I resolved to make my escape from the place. Having communicated my plans to Barker, Lesly, Riley, Shiers, and Russen, I offered the Governor to get built for him a handsome whale-boat, making the iron work myself. The Governor consented, and in a little more than a fortnight we had completed a four-oared whale-boat. We fitted her with sails and provisions in the Governor's name, and on the 4th of July, being a Saturday night, we took our departure from Valdivia, dropping down the river shortly after sunset. Whether the Governor, disgusted at the trick we had played him, decided not to pursue us, or whether—as I rather think—our absence was not discovered until the Monday morning, I know not, but we got out to sea without hazard, and, taking accurate bearings, ran for the Friendly Islands, as had been agreed upon among us.

"But it now seemed that the good fortune which had hitherto attended us, had deserted us, for after crawling for four days in sultry weather, there fell a dead calm, and we lay like a log upon the sea for forty-eight hours. For three days we remained in the midst of the ocean, exposed to the burning rays of the sun, in a boat without water or provisions. On the fourth day, just as we had resolved to draw lots to determine who should die for the sustenance of the others, we were picked up by an opium clipper returning to Canton. The captain, an American, was most kind to us, and on our arrival at Canton, a subscription was got up for us by the British merchants of that city, and a free passage to England obtained for us. Russen, however, getting in drink, made statements which brought suspicion upon us. I had imposed upon the Consul with a fictitious story of a wreck, but had stated that my name was Wilson, forgetting that the sextant which had been preserved in the boat had Captain Bates's name engraved upon it. These circumstances together caused sufficient doubts in the Consul's mind to cause him to give directions that, on our arrival in London, we were to be brought before the Thames Police Court. There being no evidence against us, we should have escaped, had not a Dr. Pine, who had been surgeon on board the *Malabar* transport, being in the Court, recognised me and swore to my identity. We were remanded, and, to complete the chain of evidence, Mr. Capon, the Hobart Town gaoler, was, strangely enough, in London at the time, and identified us all. Our story was then made public, and Barker and Lesly, turning King's evidence against Russen, he was convicted of the murder of Lyon, and executed. We were then placed on board the *Leviathan* hulk, and remained there until shipped in the *Lady Jane*, which was chartered, with convicts, for Van Diemen's Land, in order to be tried in the colony, where the offence was committed, for piratically seizing the brig *Osprey*, and arrived here on the 15th December, 1838."

Coming, breathless, to the conclusion of this narrative, Sylvia suffered her hand to fall into her lap, and sat meditative. She had never before realised among what manner of men she had lived. Her imagination pictured the voyage in the leaky brig, the South American slavery, the midnight escape, the desperate rowing, the slow agony of starvation, and the heart-sickness that must have followed upon recapture. Surely the punishment of "penal servitude" must have been made very terrible for men to risk such peril. Surely John Rex, who had quelled a mutiny and navigated a vessel through a storm-ravaged ocean, must possess qualities which could be put to better use than stone-quarrying. Was the opinion of Maurice Frere the correct one after all, and were these convict monsters gifted with unnatural powers of endurance, only to be subdued by inhuman punishments of lash and chain? Her fancies growing amid the fast gathering gloom, she shuddered as she guessed to what extremities of evil might such men proceed did an opportunity ever come to them to retaliate upon their gaolers. What if the whole island was but one smouldering volcano of revolt and murder! Terrible to think of—yet not impossible.

Oh, how strangely must the world have been civilised, that this most lovely corner of it must needs be set apart as a place of banishment for the monsters that civilisation had brought forth! She cast her eyes around, and all beauty seemed blotted out from the scene before her. The river seemed to flow sluggishly, as though thickened with blood and tears. The shadow of the trees seemed to hold lurking shapes of cruelty and danger. Even the whispering breeze bore with it sighs and threats. Oppressed by sudden terror, she hastily caught up the manuscript, and turned to seek the house, when, as if summoned from the earth by the power of her fears, a ragged figure barred her passage.

To the excited girl this apparition seemed the embodiment of the unknown evil she had dreaded. She recognised the yellow clothing, and marked the eager hands outstretched to seize her. Instantly upon her flashed the story that three days since had set the prison-town agog. The desperado of Port Arthur, the escaped mutineer and murderer, was before her!

"Sylvia! Oh, at last! I have escaped, and come to ask—What? Do you not know me?"

She stepped back a pace, speechless with terror, as he caught her hand.

"I am Rufus Dawes," he said, looking in her face for the grateful smile of recognition that did not come—"Rufus Dawes."

The party at the house was sitting on the broad verandah, listening to some gentle dulness of the clergyman, when there broke upon their ears a cry.

"What's that?" said Vickers.

Frere sprang up, and looked down the garden. He saw two figures that seemed to struggle together. With a shout, he leapt the flower-beds, and made straight at the escaped prisoner.

Rufus Dawes saw him coming, but, secure in the protection of the girl who owed him so much, advanced a step nearer, and, loosening his respectful clasp of her hand, caught her dress.

"Oh, help, Maurice, help!" cried Sylvia again.

Into the face of Rufus Dawes came an expression of horror and bewilderment. Having made an unparalleled escape from the midst of his warders, he had crept to the place where lived the idol of his dreams, braving recapture, that he might hear from her two words of justice and gratitude. Not only did she shrink from him as from one accursed, but, at the sound of his name, she summoned his deadliest foe to capture him. Such monstrous ingratitude was almost beyond belief. *She*, too—the child for whom he had given up his hard-earned chance of freedom and fortune, the child whose image he had worshipped—she, too, against him! Then there was no justice, no heaven, no God! He loosed his hold of her dress, and regardless of the approaching footsteps, stood speechless, shaking from head to foot. In another instant Frere and McNab flung themselves upon him, and he was borne to the ground. Though weakened by starvation, he shook them off with scarce an effort, and, despite the servants who came hurrying from the alarmed house, might even then have turned and made good his escape. But he seemed unable to fly.

His chest heaved, great drops of sweat beaded his white face, and from his eyes tears seemed about to break. For an instant his features worked convulsively, as if he would fain invoke upon the girl some hideous curse. But no words came, and, thrusting his hand into his breast, with a supreme gesture of horror and aversion, he flung something from him. Then a profound sigh escaped him, and he held out his hands to be bound.

There was something so pitiable about this silent grief, that as they led him away, the little group instinctively averted their faces, lest they should seem to triumph over him.

"You must try and save him from further punishment," said Sylvia next day to Frere. "I did not mean to betray the poor creature, but I had made myself nervous by reading that convict's story."

"You shouldn't read such rubbish," said Frere. "I don't suppose a word of it's true."

A RELIC OF MACQUARIE HARBOUR

"It must be true. I am sure it's true. Oh, Maurice, these are dreadful men. I thought I knew all about convicts, but I had no idea that such men as these were among them."

"Thank God, you know very little," said Maurice.

"Oh, Maurice, I am so tired of this place—I wish I was somewhere out of the sight of chains and yellow cloth."

"Come to Sydney," said Frere. "There are not so many convicts there. It was arranged that we should go to Sydney, you know."

"For our honeymoon? Yes," said Sylvia, simply. "I know it was. But we are not married yet."

"That's easily done," said Maurice.

"Oh, nonsense, sir! But I want to speak to you about this poor Dawes. I don't think he meant any harm. It seems to me now that he was rather going to ask for food, or something. They won't hang him, Maurice, will they?"

"No," said Maurice. "I spoke to your father this morning. If the fellow is tried for his life, you may have to give evidence, and so we came to the conclusion that Port Arthur again, and heavy irons, will meet the case. We gave him another life sentence this morning. That will make the third he has had."

"What did he say?"

"Nothing. I sent him down aboard the schooner at once. He ought to be out of the river by this time."

"Maurice, I have a strange feeling about that man."

"Eh?" said Maurice.

"I seem to fear him, as if I know some story about him, and yet didn't know it."

"That's not very clear," said Maurice, forcing a laugh; "but don't let's talk about him any more. We'll soon be far from Port Arthur and everybody in it."

"Maurice," said she, caressingly, "I love you, dear. You'll always protect me against these men, won't you?"

Maurice kissed her. "You have not got over your fright, Sylvia," he said. "I see I shall have to take a great deal of care of my wife."

Suddenly her eye caught something. "What's that—there, on the ground by the fountain?" They were near the spot where Dawes had been seized the night before. Under the lip of the fountain lay a small packet. Frere picked it up. It was made of soiled yellow cloth, and stitched evidently by a man's fingers. "It looks like a needle-case," said he.

"Let me see. What a strange-looking thing! Yellow cloth, too. Why, it must belong to a prisoner. Oh, Maurice, the man who was here last night!"

"Ay," says Maurice, turning over the packet, "it might have been his, sure enough."

"He seemed to fling something from him, I thought. Perhaps this is it?" said she, peering over his arm. Frere, with a scowl, tore off the outer covering of the mysterious packet, and displayed a second envelope of grey cloth—the "good-conduct" uniform. Beneath this was a small piece of discoloured merino, that had once been blue.

"Hullo!" says Frere. "Why, what's this?"

"It is a piece of a dress," says Sylvia.

It was Rufus Dawes's talisman,—a portion of the frock she had worn at Macquarie Harbour, and which the unhappy convict had cherished as a sacred relic for five weary years.

Frere flung it into the water. The running stream whirled it away. "Why did you do that?" cried the girl, with a sudden pang of remorse for which she could not account. The shred of cloth, caught by a weed, lingered for an instant on the surface of the water. Almost at the same moment, the pair, raising their eyes, saw the schooner which bore Rufus Dawes back to bondage glide past the opening of the trees and disappear. When they looked again for the strange relic of the desperado of Port Arthur, it also had vanished.

The usual clanking and hammering was prevalent upon the stone jetty of Port Arthur when the schooner bearing the returned convict, Rufus Dawes,

AT
PORT
ARTHUR

ran alongside. On the heights above the esplanade rose the grim front of the soldiers' barracks; beneath the soldiers' barracks was the long range of prison buildings, with their workshops and tan-pits; to the left lay the Commandant's house, authoritative by reason of its embrasured terrace and guardian sentry.

Rufus Dawes had seen this prospect before, had learnt by heart each beauty of rising sun, sparkling water, and wooded hill. But there was no charm for him in the exquisite blue of the sea, the soft shadows of the hills, or the soothing ripple of the waves. He sat with his head bowed down, and his hands clasped about his knees, disdaining to look until they roused him.

"Hallo, Dawes!" says Warder Troke, halting his train of ironed yellow-jackets. "So you've come back again! Glad to see yer, Dawes! It seems an age since we had the pleasure of your company, Dawes!" At this pleasantry the train laughed, so that their irons clanked more than ever. They found it often inconvenient not to laugh at Mr. Troke's humour. "Step down here, Dawes, and let me introduce you to your h'old friends. They'll be glad to see yer, won't yer, boys? Why, bless me, Dawes, we thort we'd lost yer!"

"Take care, Mr. Troke," said a warning voice, "you're at it again! Let the man alone!"

By virtue of an order transmitted from Hobart Town, they had begun to attach the dangerous prisoner to the last man of the gang, riveting the leg-irons of the pair by means of an extra link. At the sound of the friendly tone, Dawes looked up, and saw a tall, gaunt man, dressed in a shabby pepper-and-salt raiment, and wearing a black handkerchief knotted round his throat. He was a stranger to him.

"I beg yer pardon, Mr. North," said Troke, sinking at once the bully in the sneak. "I didn't see yer reverence."

"A parson!" thought Dawes with disappointment.

"I know that," returned Mr. North coolly. "If you had, you would have been all butter and honey. Don't trouble yourself to tell a lie; it's quite unnecessary."

Dawes looked up again. This was a strange parson.

"What's your name, my man?" said Mr. North, suddenly, catching his eye.

Rufus Dawes had intended to scowl, but the tone, sharply authoritative, roused his automatic convict second nature, and he answered, almost despite himself, "Rufus Dawes."

"Oh," said Mr. North, eyeing him with a curious air of expectation that had something pitying in it. "This is the man, is it? I thought he was to go to the Coal Mines."

"So he is," said Troke, "but we hain't a goin' to send there for a fortnit, and in the mean time I'm to work him on the chain."

"Oh!" said Mr. North again. "Lend me your knife, Troke."

And then this curious parson took a piece of tobacco out of his ragged pocket, and cut off a "chaw" with Mr. Troke's knife. Rufus Dawes stared at the parson in unaffected astonishment. Mr. North perhaps mistook the meaning of his fixed stare, for he held out the remnant of tobacco to him.

The chain line vibrated at this, and bent forward to enjoy the vicarious delight of seeing another man chew tobacco. "Here," said Mr. North, holding out the dainty morsel. Rufus took the tobacco; looked at it hungrily for an instant, and then—to the astonishment of everybody—flung it away with a curse.

"I don't want your tobacco," he said; "keep it."

From convict mouths went out a respectful roar of amazement, and Mr. Troke's eyes snapped with pride of outraged janitorship. "You ungrateful dog!" he cried, raising his stick.

Mr. North put up a hand. "That will do, Troke," he said; "I know your respect for the cloth. Move the men on again."

"Get on!" said Troke, rumbling oaths beneath his breath, and Dawes felt his newly-riveted chain tug. It was some time since he had been in a chain gang, and the sudden jerk nearly overbalanced him. He caught at his neighbour, and looking up, met a pair of black eyes which gleamed recognition. His neighbour was John Rex.

Mr. North, watching them, was struck by the resemblance the two men bore to each other. Their height, eyes, hair, and complexion were similar.

Despite the difference in name they might be related. "They might be brothers," thought he. "Poor devils! I never knew a prisoner refuse tobacco before." And he looked on the ground for the despised portion. But in vain. John Rex had picked it up and put it in his mouth.

So Rufus Dawes was relegated to his old life again, and came back to his prison with the hatred of his kind increased a hundred-fold. He was at first unable to apprehend the details of his misery. He knew only that his dream-child was alive and shuddered at him, that the only thing he loved and trusted had betrayed him, that all hope of justice and mercy had gone from him for ever. He went about his work, unheedful of the jests of Troke, ungalled by his irons, unmindful of the groans and laughter about him. He did not complain, he did not laugh, he did not weep. His "mate" Rex tried to converse with him, but did not succeed. In the midst of one of Rex's tales of London dissipation, Rufus Dawes would sigh wearily. "There's something on that fellow's mind," thought Rex. "He has some secret which weighs upon him."

It was in vain that Rex attempted to discover what this secret might be. To all questions concerning his past life, Rufus Dawes was dumb. In vain did Rex endeavour to win his confidence. Rufus Dawes met his advances with a cynical carelessness that revealed nothing; and when not addressed, held a gloomy silence. Galled by this indifference, Rex attempted to practise those ingenious arts of torment by which Gabbett, Vetch, or other leading spirits of the gang asserted their superiority over their quieter comrades. But he soon ceased. "I have been longer in this hell than you," said Rufus Dawes, "and I know more of the devil's tricks than you can show me. You had best be quiet." Rex neglected the warning, and Rufus Dawes took him by the throat one day, and would have strangled him, but that Troke beat off the angered man with a favourite bludgeon. Rex had a wholesome respect for personal prowess, and had the grace to admit the provocation to Troke. Even this instance of self-denial did not move the stubborn Dawes. He only laughed.

Then Rex came to a conclusion. His mate was plotting an escape. He himself cherished a notion of the kind, as did Gabbett and Vetch, but by common distrust no one ever gave utterance to thoughts of this nature. It would be too dangerous. "He would be a good comrade for a rush," thought Rex, and resolved more firmly than ever to ally himself to his silent companion.

One question Dawes had asked which Rex had been able to answer: "Who is that North?"

"A chaplain. He is only here for a week or so. There is a new one coming.

North goes to Sydney. He is not in favour with the Bishop."

"How do you know?"

"By deduction," says Rex. "He wears coloured clothes and smokes, and doesn't patter Scripture. The Bishop dresses in black, detests tobacco, and quotes the Bible like a concordance. North is sent here for a month, as a warming-pan for that ass Meekin. *Ergo*, the Bishop don't care about North." Then, catching the eye of the overseer upon him, Rex fell silent.

As the days rolled on, Rufus Dawes almost longed for the Coal Mines. To be sent from the settlement to the Coal Mines, and from the Coal Mines to the settlement, was to these unhappy men a "trip." At Port Arthur one went to an out station, as more fortunate people go to Queenscliff or the Ocean Beach now-a-days for "change of air."

Rufus Dawes had been a fortnight at the settlement when a new comer appeared on the chain-gang. This was a young man of about twenty years of

THE COMMANDANT'S BUTLER

age, thin, fair, and delicate. His name was Kirkland, and he belonged to what were known as the "educated" prisoners. He had been a clerk in a banking house, and was transported for embezzlement, though, by some, grave doubts as to his guilt were entertained. The Commandant, Captain Burgess, had employed him as butler in his house, and his fate was considered a "lucky" one. So, doubtless, it might have been, had not an untoward accident occurred. Captain Burgess, who was a bachelor of the "old school," confessed to an amiable weakness for blasphemy, and was given to condemning the convicts' eyes and limbs with indiscriminate violence. Kirkland belonged to a Methodist family and owned a piety utterly out of place in that region. The language of Burgess made him shudder, and one day, he so far forgot himself as to raise his hands to his ears. "My blank!" cried Burgess. "You blank blank, is that your blank game? I'll blank soon cure you of that!" and forthwith ordered him to the chain-gang for "insubordination."

He was received with suspicion by the gang, who did not like white-handed prisoners. Troke, by way of experiment in human nature, perhaps, placed him next to Gabbett. The day was got through in the usual way, and Kirkland felt his heart revive.

The toil was severe, and the companionship uncouth, but despite his blistered hands and aching back, he had not experienced anything so very terrible after all. When the muster bell rang, and the gang broke up, Rufus Dawes, on his silent way to his separate cell, observed a notable change of custom in the disposition of the new convict. Instead of placing him in a cell by himself, Troke was turning him into the yard with the others.

"I'm not to go in there?" says Kirkland, drawing back in dismay from the cloud of foul faces which lowered upon him.

"By the Lord, but you are, then!" says Troke. "The Governor says a night in there'll take the starch out of yer."

"But, Mr. Troke——"

"Stow your gaff," says Troke impatiently. "I can't argue here all night. Get in." So Kirkland, the son of Methodist parents, went in.

About dawn the next morning, Mr. North—who, amongst other vagaries not approved of by his bishop, had a habit of prowling about the prison at unofficial hours—was attracted by a dispute at the door of the dormitory.

"What's the matter here?" he asked.

"A prisoner refractory, your reverence," said the watchman. "Wants to come out."

"Mr. North! Mr. North!" cried a voice, "for the love of God, let me out of this place!"

Kirkland, ghastly pale, bleeding, with his shirt torn, and his blue eyes wide with terror, was clinging to the bars.

"Oh, Mr. North! Oh! for God's sake, Mr. North!"

"What, Kirkland!" cried North, who was ignorant of the vengeance of the Commandant. "What do you do here?"

But Kirkland could do nothing but cry,—"Oh, Mr. North! For God's sake, Mr. North!"

"Let him out, watchman!" said North.

"Can't, sir, without an order from the Commandant."

"Mr. North!" screamed Kirkland. "Would you see me perish, body and soul, in this place? Oh, you ministers of Christ—wolves in sheep's clothing—you shall be judged for this!"

"Let him out!" cried North again, stamping his foot.

"It's no good," returned the gaoler. "I *can't*. If he was dying, I can't."

North rushed away to the Commandant, and the instant his back was turned, the watchman flung open the door and darted into the dormitory.

"Take that!" he cried, dealing Kirkland a blow on the head that stretched him senseless. "There's more trouble with you bloody aristocrats than enough. Lie quiet!"

The Commandant, roused from slumber, told Mr. North that Kirkland might stop where he was, and that he'd thank the chaplain not to wake him up in the middle of the night because a blank prisoner set up a blank howling.

"But, my good sir," protested North, restraining his impulse to overstep the bounds of modesty in his language to his superior officer, "you know the character of the men in that ward. You can guess what that unhappy body has suffered."

"Impertinent young beggar!" said Burgess. "Do him good, curse him! *Will* you let me go to sleep?"

North returned to the prison disconsolately, found the dutiful Hailes at his post, and all quiet.

"What's become of Kirkland?" he asked.

"Fretted hisself to sleep, yer reverence," said the watchman. "Poor young chap! It's hard for such young 'uns as he, sir."

In the morning, Rufus Dawes, coming to his place on the chain-gang, was struck by the altered appearance of Kirkland. His face was of a greenish tint, and wore an expression of bewildered horror.

"Cheer up, man!" said Dawes, touched with momentary pity. "It's no good being in the mopes, you know."

"What do they do if you try to bolt?" whispered Kirkland.

"Kill you," returned Dawes laconically.

"Thank God!" said Kirkland.

"Now, then, Miss Nancy," said one of the men, "what's the matter with *you!*"

Kirkland shuddered, and his pale face grew crimson.

"Oh," he said, "that such a wretch as I should live!"

"Silence!" cried Troke. "No. 44, if you can't hold your tongue, I'll give you something to talk about. March!"

The work of the gang that day was the carrying of some heavy logs to the water-side, and Rufus Dawes observed that Kirkland was exhausted long before the task was accomplished. "They'll kill you, little beggar!" said he, not unkindly. "What have you been doing to get into this scrape?"

"Have you ever been in that—that place I was in last night?" asked Kirkland.

Rufus Dawes nodded.

"Does the Commandant know what goes on there?"

"I suppose so. What does he care?"

"Care! Man, do you believe in a God?"

"No," said Dawes, "not here. Hold up, my lad. If you fall, we must fall over you, and then you're done for."

He had hardly uttered the words, when the boy flung himself beneath the log. In another instant the train would have been scrambling over his crushed body, had not Gabbett stretched out an iron hand, and plucked the would-be suicide from death.

"Hold on to me, Miss Nancy," said the giant, "I'm big enough to carry double."

Spurning the offered hand, Kirkland uttered a cry, and then, holding up his irons with his hands, started to run for the water.

"Halt! you young fool," roared Troke, raising his carbine. But Kirkland kept steadily on for the river. Just as he reached it, however, the figure of Mr. North rose from behind a pile of stones. Kirkland jumped for the jetty, missed his footing, and fell into the arms of the chaplain.

"You young vermin—you shall pay for this," cries Troke.

"Oh, Mr. North," says Kirkland, "why did you stop me? I'd be better dead than stay another night in that place."

"You'll get it, my lad," said Gabbett, when the runaway was brought back. "Your blessed hide'll feel for this, see if it don't."

Kirkland only breathed harder, and looked round for Mr. North, but Mr. North had gone. The new chaplain was to arrive that afternoon, and it was incumbent on the old one to be present at the reception.

Troke reported the ex-bank clerk that night to Burgess, and Burgess, who was about to go to dinner with the new chaplain, disposed of his case out of hand. "Tried to bolt, eh! Must stop that. Fifty lashes, Troke. I'll break the young devil's spirit, blank him."

"Yes, sir," said Troke. "Good evening, sir."

"Troke—pick out some likely man, will you? That last fellow you had ought to have been tied up himself. His flogging wouldn't have killed a flea."

"You can't get 'em to *warm* one another, your honour," says Troke. "They *won't* do it."

"Oh, yes, they will, though," says Burgess, "or I'll know the reason why. I won't have my men knocked up with flogging these rascals."

"Very good, your honour," says Troke.

Kirkland was put into a separate cell that night; and Troke, by way of assuring him a good night's rest, told him that he was to have fifty in the morning. "And Dawes'll lay it on," he added. "He's one of the smartest men I've got, and he won't spare yer, yer may take your oath of that."

"You will find this a terrible place, Mr. Meekin," said North to his supplanter, as they walked across to the Commandant's to dinner. "It has made me heart-sick."

MR. NORTH'S INDISPOSITION

"I thought it was a little paradise," said Meekin. "Captain Frere says that the scenery is delightful."

"So it is," returned North, looking askance; "but the prisoners are not delightful."

"Poor, abandoned wretches," says Meekin, "I suppose not. How sweet the moonlight sleeps upon that bank! Eh!"

"Abandoned, indeed, by God and man—almost."

"Mr. North, Providence never abandons the most unworthy of His servants. In the valley of the shadow of death, you know, Mr. North. Really, the Commandant's house is charmingly situated!"

Mr. North sighed again. "You have not been long in the colony, Mr. Meekin. I doubt if you quite know our convict system."

"An admirable one! A most admirable one!" said Meekin. "There were a few matters I noticed in Hobart Town that did not please me—the use of profane language for instance—but on the whole I was delighted with the scheme. It is so complete."

North pursed up his lips. "Yes, it is very complete," he said; "almost too complete. But I am always in a minority when I discuss the question, so we will drop it, if you please."

"If you please," said Meekin, gravely. He had heard from the Bishop that Mr. North was an ill-conditioned sort of person, who smoked clay pipes, had been detected in drinking beer out of a pewter pot, and had been heard to state that white neck-cloths were of no consequence.

The dinner went off successfully. Burgess—desirous, perhaps, of favourably impressing the chaplain whom the Bishop delighted to honour—shut off his blasphemy for a while, and was urbane enough. "You'll find us rough, Mr. Meekin," he said, "but you'll find us 'all there' when we're wanted. This is a little kingdom in itself. Some wine, Mr. North?"

"Thank you, none," said North, filling a tumbler with water. "I have a headache."

His manner of speech was so awkward that a silence fell upon the party, caused by each one wondering why Mr. North should grow confused, and drum his fingers on the table, and stare everywhere but at the decanter. Meekin—ever at his ease—was the first to speak. "Have you many visitors, Captain Burgess?"

"Very few. Sometimes a party comes over with a recommendation from the Governor, and I show them over the place; but, as a rule, we see no one but ourselves."

"I asked," said Meekin, "because some friends of mine were thinking of coming."

"And who may they be?"

"Do you know Captain Frere?"

"Frere! I should say so!" returned Burgess. "I was quartered with him at Sarah Island. So he's a friend of yours, eh?"

"I had the pleasure of meeting him in society. He is just married, you know."

"Is he?" said Burgess. "The devil he is!"

"Miss Vickers, a charming young person. They are going to Sydney, where Captain Frere has some interest, and Frere thinks of taking Port Arthur on his way down."

"A strange fancy for a honeymoon trip," said North.

"Captain Frere takes a deep interest in all relating to convict discipline," went on Meekin, unheeding the interruption.

"Yes, one oughtn't to leave the colony without seeing it," says Burgess; "it's worth seeing."

"So Captain Frere thinks. A romantic story, Captain Burgess. He saved her life, you know."

"Ah! that was a queer thing, that mutiny," said Burgess. "We've got the fellows here, you know."

"I saw them tried at Hobart Town," said Meekin. "In fact, the ringleader, John Rex, gave me his confession, and I sent it to the Bishop."

"A dangerous, cold-blooded villain," put in North.

"Well, now!" said Meekin, with asperity, "I don't agree with you. Everybody seems to be against that poor fellow—Captain Frere tried to make me think his letters contained a hidden meaning, but I don't believe they did. He seems to me to be truly penitent for his offences."

"I hope he is," said North. "I wouldn't trust him."

"Oh! there's no fear of him," said Burgess, cheerily; "if he grows uproarious, we'll soon give him a touch of the cat."

"I suppose severity is necessary," returned Meekin; "though to my ears a flogging sounds such a brutal punishment."

"It's a punishment for brutes," said Burgess, and laughed, pleased with his wit. Here attention was called by the strange behaviour of Mr. North. He had risen, and, without apology, flung wide the window, as though he gasped for air. "Hullo, North! what's the matter?"

"Nothing," said North, recovering himself with an effort. "A spasm. I have these attacks at times."

"Have some brandy," said Burgess.

"No, no, it will pass. No, I say. Well, if you insist." And seizing the tumbler offered to him, he half-filled it with raw spirit, and swallowed the fiery draught at a gulp.

The Reverend Meekin eyed his clerical brother with horror. He was not accustomed to clergymen who drank neat brandy out of tumblers.

"Ha!" said North, looking wildly round upon them, "That's better."

"Let us go on to the verandah," said Burgess. "It's cooler than in the house."

So they went on to the verandah, and looked down upon the lights of the prison, and listened to the sea lapping the shore. The Reverend Mr. North, in this cool atmosphere, seemed to recover himself, and the conversation resumed.

By-and-by, a short figure, smoking a cheroot, came up out of the dark, and proved to be Dr. Macklewain, who had been prevented from attending the dinner by reason of an accident to a constable at Norfolk Bay, which had claimed his professional attention.

"Well, how's Forest?" cried Burgess. "Mr. Meekin—Dr. Macklewain."

"Dead," said Dr. Macklewain. "Delighted to see you, Mr. Meekin."

"Confound it—another of my best men," grumbled Burgess. "Macklewain, have a glass of wine."

"I must be thinking of repose," said Meekin; "the journey—though most enjoyable—has fatigued me."

"Come on, then," said North. "Our roads lie together."

"You won't have a nip of brandy before you start?" asked Burgess. "No? Then I shall send round for you in the morning, Mr. Meekin. Good night. Macklewain, I want to speak with you a moment."

Before the two clergymen had got very far from the Commandant's house, Macklewain joined them.

"Another flogging to-morrow," said he, grumblingly. "Up at daylight, I suppose, again."

"Whom is he going to flog now?"

"That young butler-fellow of his."

"What, Kirkland?" cried North.

"Insubordination," says Macklewain. "Fifty lashes."

"Oh, this must be stopped," cries North, in great alarm. "He can't stand it. I tell you he'll die, Macklewain."

"Perhaps you'll have the goodness to allow me to be the best judge of that," returned Macklewain crisply.

"My dear sir," replied North, alive to the importance of conciliating the surgeon, "you haven't seen him lately. He tried to drown himself this morning."

Mr. Meekin expressed some alarm; but Dr. Macklewain re-assured him. "*That* sort of nonsense must be stopped," said he. "A nice example to set."

"He was put into the long dormitory," said North; "you surely know what sort of place that is."

"Well, he'll be put into the hospital for a week or so to-morrow," said Macklewain, "and that'll give him a spell."

"If Burgess flogs him I'll report it to the Governor," cries North. "The condition of those dormitories is infamous."

"If the boy has anything to complain of, why don't he complain? We can't do anything without evidence."

"Complain! Would his life be safe if he did? Besides, he's not the sort of creature to complain."

"That's all nonsense," says Macklewain. "We can't flog a whole dormitory on suspicion. *I* can't help it. The boy's made his bed, and he must lie on it."

"I'll go back and see Burgess," said North. "Mr. Meekin, here's the gate, and your room is on the right hand."

"Pray don't hurry back," said Meekin politely. "You are on an errand of mercy, you know. I shall find my portmanteau in my room, you said."

"Yes, yes. Call the servant if you want anything. He sleeps at the back," and North hurried off.

"An impulsive gentleman," murmured Meekin to Macklewain. Macklewain shook his head.

"There is something wrong about him, but I can't make it out. He has the strangest fits at times. Unless it's a cancer in the stomach, I don't know what it can be."

"Cancer in the stomach! dear me, how dreadful!" says Meekin. "Ah! Doctor, we all have our crosses, have we not? How delightful the grass smells! This seems a very pleasant place, and I think I shall enjoy myself very much. Good-night."

"Good-night, sir. I hope you will be comfortable."

"And let us hope Mr. North will succeed in his labour of love," said Meekin, shutting the gate. "Good-night, once more."

Captain Burgess was shutting his verandah-window when North hurried up. "Captain Burgess, I have come to beg you not to flog young Kirkland, sir. The lad has been cruelly punished already. He attempted suicide to-day—unhappy creature."

"Well, that's just what I'm flogging him for. I'll teach my prisoners to attempt suicide!"

"But he can't stand it, sir. He's too weak."

"That's Macklewain's business."

"Captain Burgess," protested North, "I assure you that he does not deserve punishment."

"Look here, Mr. North, I don't interfere with what you do to the prisoners' souls—don't you interfere with what I do to their bodies."

"Captain Burgess, do you persist in having this boy flogged?"

"I've given my orders, sir."

"Then, Captain Burgess," cried North, his pale face flushing, "I tell you the boy's blood will be on your head. I am a minister of God, sir, and I forbid you to commit this crime."

"Damn your impertinence, sir!" burst out Burgess. White with rage, he rang the bell that summoned his convict servant. "Show Mr. North out," he said, "and go down to the barracks, and tell Troke that Kirkland is to have *a hundred* lashes to-morrow. I'll show you who's master here, my good sir."

"I'll report this to the Government," said North, aghast. "This is murderous."

"The Government may go to——, and you, too!" roared Burgess. "Get out!"

North returned home in great agitation. "They shall not flog that boy," he said. "I'll shield him with my own body if necessary. I'll report this to the Government. I'll see Sir John Franklin myself. I'll have the light of day let into this den of horrors." He reached his cottage, and lighted the lamp in the little sitting-room. All was silent save that from the adjoining chamber came the sound of Meekin's gentlemanly snore.

North took down a book from the shelf and tried to read, but the letters ran together. "I wish I hadn't taken that brandy," he said. "Fool that I am." Then he began to walk up and down, to fling himself on the sofa, to read, to pray. "O God, give me strength! Help me! I struggle, but I am weak! O Lord, look down upon me!"

To see him rolling on the sofa in agony, to hear his moans and muttered prayers, one would have thought him suffering from the pangs of some terrible disease. He opened the book again, and forced himself to read, but his eyes wandered to the cupboard. There lurked something that fascinated him. He got up at length, went into the kitchen, and found a packet of red pepper. He mixed a teaspoonful of this in a pannikin of water and drank it. It relieved him for a while.

"I *must* keep my wits for to-morrow. The life of that lad depends upon it."

He went to his bedroom and flung himself on the bed, but only to toss from side to side. In vain he repeated texts of Scripture; in vain counted imaginary sheep, or listened to imaginary clock-tickings. Sleep would not come to him. It was as though he had reached the crisis of a disease which had been for days gathering force. "I *must* have a teaspoonful," he said, "to allay the craving."

Twice he paused on his way to the sitting-room, and twice was he driven on by a power stronger than his will. He reached it at length, and opening the cupboard, pulled out what he sought. A bottle of brandy.

With this in his hand, all moderation vanished. He raised it to his lips and eagerly drank. Then, ashamed, he thrust the bottle back, and made for his room. Still he could not sleep. He saw in the darkness the brandy bottle, saw its amber fluid sparkle, smelt its nutty aroma. He pictured it standing in the cupboard, and imagined himself seizing it and quenching the fire that burned within him. He wept, he prayed, he fought with his desire as with a madness. He told himself that another's life depended on his exertions, that to give way to his fatal passion was unworthy of an educated man and a reasoning being, that it was degrading, disgusting, and bestial. That, at all times debasing, at this particular time it was infamous. In vain. In the midst of his arguments he found himself at the cupboard, with the bottle at his lips, in an attitude that was at once ludicrous and horrible.

He had no cancer. His disease was a more terrible one. The Reverend James North—gentleman, scholar, and Christian priest—was what the world calls "a confirmed drunkard."

The bright morning sun looked down upon a curious sight. In a stone-yard was a little group of persons—Troke, Burgess, Macklewain, Kirkland, and Rufus Dawes.

ONE HUNDRED LASHES

Three wooden staves, seven feet high, were fastened together in the form of a triangle. The structure looked not unlike that made by gipsies to boil their kettles. To this structure Kirkland was bound. His feet were fastened to the base of the triangle; his wrists, bound above his head, at the apex. His white back shone in the sunlight.

"Now, prisoner," said Troke to Dawes, "do your duty."

Rufus Dawes looked from the three stern faces to Kirkland's white back, and his face grew purple. In all his experience he had never been asked to flog before.

"You don't want me to flog him, sir?" he said to the Commandant.

"Pick up the cat, sir!" ordered Burgess, astonished.

Rufus Dawes picked up the heavy cat, and drew its knotted lashes between his fingers.

"Go on, Dawes," whispered Kirkland, without turning his head. "You are no more than another man."

"What does he say?" asked Burgess.

"Telling him to cut light, sir," said Troke, eagerly lying.

"Cut light, eh! We'll see about that. Get on, my man, and look sharp, or I'll tie you up and give you fifty for yourself."

"Go on, Dawes," whispered Kirkland again, "I don't mind." Rufus Dawes lifted the cat, swung it round his head, and brought its knotted cords down upon the white back.

"Wonn!" cried Troke.

The white back was instantly striped with six crimson bars. Kirkland stifled a cry. It seemed to him that he had been cut in half.

"Now, then you scoundrel!" roared Burgess; "separate your cats! What do you mean by flogging a man that fashion?"

Rufus Dawes drew his fingers through the entangled cords, and struck again. This time the blood beaded on the skin.

"Tew!"

"That's better," said Burgess.

The third blow sounded as though it had been struck upon a piece of raw beef, and the crimson turned purple.

"My God!" said Kirkland, faintly, and bit his lips.

The flogging proceeded in silence for ten strokes, and then Kirkland gave a screech like a wounded horse.

"Oh! ... Captain Burgess! ... Dawes! ... Mr. Troke! ... Oh, my, God!
... Oh! oh! ... Mercy!"

"Ten!" cried Troke impassively.

The lad's back, swollen into a hump, now presented the appearance
of a ripe peach which a wilful child has scored with a pin. Dawes, turning
away from his bloody handiwork, drew the cats through his fingers twice.
They were beginning to get clogged a little.

"Go on," said Burgess, with a nod.

Roused by the morning sun streaming in upon him, Mr. North opened his
bloodshot eyes, rubbed his forehead with hands that trembled, and
suddenly awakening to a consciousness of his promised errand, rolled off the
bed and rose to his feet. His brain seemed on fire, his hands were hot and
dry, his tongue clove to the roof of his mouth. He shuddered as he viewed
his pale face and red eyes in the little looking-glass, and hastily tried the
door. He had retained sufficient sense in his madness to lock it, and his
condition had been unobserved. Stealing into the sitting-room, he saw that
the clock pointed to half-past six. The flogging was to have taken place at
half-past five. Unless accident had favoured him he was already too late.
Fevered with remorse, he hurried past the room where Meekin yet
slumbered, and made his way to the prison. As he entered the yard,
Kirkland had just got his fiftieth lash.

"Stop!" cried North. "Captain Burgess, I call upon you to stop."

"You're rather late, Mr. North," retorted Burgess. "The punishment is
nearly over."

"Wonn!" cried Troke again; and North stood by, biting his nails and
grinding his teeth, during six more lashes.

Kirkland had ceased to yell now, and merely moaned. His back was like a
bloody sponge, which, in the interval between the lashes, twitched like that
of a new-killed bullock. Suddenly Macklewain saw his head droop on his
shoulder. "Throw him off! Throw him off!" he cried, and Troke hurried to
loosen the thongs.

"Fling some water over him!" said Burgess, "he's shamming."

A bucket of water made Kirkland open his eyes. "I thought so," said
Burgess. "Tie him up again."

"No. Not if you are Christians!" cried North.

He met with an ally where he least expected one. Rufus Dawes flung down
the dripping cat. "I'll flog no more," said he.

"What?" roared Burgess, furious at this gross insolence.

"I'll flog no more. Get some one else to do your bloody work."

"Tie him up!" cried Burgess, foaming. "Here, constable, fetch a man here with a fresh cat. I'll give you that beggar's fifty, and fifty more on top of 'em; and he shall look on while his back cools."

Rufus Dawes, with a glance at North, pulled off his shirt and stretched himself at the triangles. His back was not white and smooth, like Kirkland's had been, but hard and seamed. He had been flogged before. Troke appeared with Gabbett—grinning. Gabbett liked flogging. It was his boast that he could flog a man to death on a place no bigger than the palm of his hand.

Rufus Dawes planted his feet firmly on the ground, took fierce grasp of the staves, and drew in his breath.

Macklewain spread the garments of the two men upon the ground, and, placing Kirkland upon them, turned to watch this new phase in the morning's amusement. He grumbled a little below his breath, for he wanted his breakfast, and when the Commandant once began to flog, there was no telling where he would stop. Rufus Dawes took five-and-twenty lashes without a murmur, and then Gabbett "crossed the cuts." This went on up to fifty lashes, and North felt himself stricken with admiration at the courage of the man. "If it had not been for that cursed brandy," thought he bitterly, "I might have saved all this." At the hundredth lash, the giant paused, but Burgess was determined to "break the man's spirit."

"I'll make you speak, you dog, if I cut your heart out!" he cried. "Go on, prisoner."

For twenty lashes more Dawes was mute, and then the agony forced from his breast a hideous cry. But it was not a cry for mercy, as Kirkland's had been. Having found his tongue, the wretched man gave vent to his boiling passion in a torrent of curses. He shrieked imprecations upon Burgess, Troke, and North. He cursed all soldiers for tyrants, all parsons for hypocrites. He blasphemed his God and his Saviour. He foamed, raved and tugged at his bonds until the strong staves shook. North, with his hands to his ears, crouched against the corner of the wall, palsied with horror. He would fain have fled, but a horrible fascination held him back.

In the midst of this, North saw Kirkland look at him with what he thought a smile. Was it a smile? He leapt forward, and uttered a cry of dismay so loud that all turned.

"Hullo!" says Troke, running to the heap of clothes, "the young un's slipped his wind!"

Kirkland was dead.

"Throw him off!" says Burgess, aghast; and Gabbett reluctantly untied the thongs that bound Rufus Dawes. Two constables were alongside him in an instant, for sometimes newly tortured men grew desperate. This one, however, was silent with the last lash, only in taking his shirt from under the body of the boy, he muttered "Dead!" and in his tone there seemed to be a touch of envy. Then flinging his shirt over his bleeding shoulders, he walked out—defiant to the last.

"Game, ain't he?" said one constable to the other, as they pushed him into an empty cell, there to wait for the hospital guard. The body of Kirkland was taken away in silence, and Burgess turned pale when he saw North's threatening face.

"It isn't my fault," he said. "I didn't know that the lad was chicken-hearted." But North turned away in disgust, and Macklewain and Burgess pursued their homeward route together.

"Strange, that he should drop like that," said the Commandant.

"Yes, unless he had any internal disease," said the surgeon.

"Disease of the heart for instance," said Burgess.

"I'll *post-mortem* him and see."

"Come in and have a nip, Macklewain. I feel quite qualmish," said Burgess.

Mr. North, slowly, and with head bowed down, as one bent on a painful errand, went to see the prisoner who had survived. He found him kneeling on the ground.

"Rufus Dawes."

At the low tone Rufus Dawes looked up, and seeing who it was, waved him off.

"Don't speak to me," he said. "You're nothing but a hypocrite, who stands by while a man is cut to pieces, and then comes and whines religion to him."

North stood in the centre of the cell, with his head bent low.

"You are right," he said. "I must seem to you a hypocrite. *I* a servant of Christ? A besotted beast rather! I am not come to whine religion to you. I am come to—to ask your pardon. I might have saved you from punishment,—saved that poor boy from death. But I have a vice; I am a drunkard, I yielded to my temptation, and—I was too late. I come to you as one sinful man to another, to ask you to forgive me." And North suddenly flung himself down beside the convict, and catching his blood-bespotted hands in his own, cried, "Forgive me, brother!"

Rufus Dawes, too astonished to speak, bent his black eyes upon the man who crouched at his feet, and a ray of pity penetrated his gloomy soul. He seemed to catch a glimpse of misery more profound than his own, and his stubborn heart felt human sympathy with this erring brother. "Then in this hell there is yet a man," said he; and a hand-grasp passed between these two unhappy beings. North arose, and, with averted face, passed quickly from the cell. Rufus Dawes looked at the hand which his strange visitor had taken, and something glittered there. It was a tear. He broke down at the sight of it, and when the guard came to fetch him, they found him on his knees in a corner, sobbing like a child.

The morning after this, Mr. North departed in the schooner for Hobart Town. Between the officious chaplain and the Commandant, the events of

KICKING AGAINST THE PRICKS

the previous day had fixed a great gulf. Burgess knew that North meant to report the death of Kirkland, and guessed that he would also relate the story to such persons in Hobart Town as would most readily repeat it. "Blank awkward the fellow's dying," he confessed to himself. "If he hadn't died, nobody would have bothered about him." A sinister truth. North, on the other hand, comforted himself with the belief that the convict's death under the lash would cause indignation and subsequent inquiry. "The truth must come out if they only *ask*," thought he. Self-deceiving North! Four years a Government chaplain, and not yet a knowledge of a Government's method of "asking" about such matters! Kirkland's mangled flesh would have fed the worms before the ink on the last "minute" from deliberating Authority was dry.

Burgess, however, determined to baulk the parson at the outset. He would send down an official "return" of the unfortunate occurrence by the same vessel that carried his enemy, and thus get the ear of the Office. Meekin, walking on the evening of the flogging past the wooden shed where the body lay, saw Troke bearing buckets filled with dark coloured water, and heard a great splashing and sluicing going on inside the hut.

"What is the matter?" he asked.

"Doctor's bin post morticing the prisoner what was flogged this morning, sir," said Troke, "and we're cleanin' up."

Meekin, sickened, walked on. He had heard that Kirkland possessed unknown disease of the heart, and had unhappily died before receiving his allotted punishment. His duty was to comfort Kirkland's soul—he had nothing to do with Kirkland's slovenly unhandsome body—and so he went for a walk on the pier, that the breeze might blow his momentary sickness away from him. On the pier he saw North talking to Father Flaherty, the Roman Catholic chaplain. Meekin had been taught to look upon a priest as a shepherd might look upon a wolf, and passed with a distant bow. The pair were apparently talking of Kirkland's death, for he heard Father Flaherty say, with a shrug of his round shoulders, "He woas not one of moi people, Mr. North, and the Government would not suffer me to interfere with mathers relating to Prhotestint prisoners."

"The wretched creature was a Protestant," thought Meekin. "At least then his immortal soul was not endangered by belief in the damnable heresies of the Church of Rome." So he passed on, giving Flaherty a wide berth lest he should pounce down upon him unawares, and with Jesuitical argument and silken softness of speech, convert him by force to his own state of error. North, on his side, left Flaherty with regret. He had spent many a pleasant hour with him, and knew him for a narrow-minded, conscientious, yet laughter-loving creature, whose God was neither his belly nor his breviary, but sometimes in one place and sometimes in the other. Or such was North's reflection as Port Arthur faded into indistinct beauty behind the swift-sailing schooner. "God help those poor villains, for neither parson nor priest can."

North, on his arrival, went straight to Major Vickers. "I have a formal complaint to make, sir," he said. "A prisoner has been flogged to death at Port Arthur. I saw it done."

Vickers frowned. "A serious accusation, Mr. North. I must, of course, receive it with respect, coming from you, but I trust that you have fully considered the circumstances of the case. I always understood Captain Burgess was a most humane man."

North shook his head. He would let events speak for themselves. "I only ask for an inquiry," said he.

"Yes, my dear sir, I know. Very proper indeed on your part, if you think any injustice has been done; but have you considered the expense and the immense trouble all this will give?"

"No trouble or expense should stand in the way of humanity and justice," cried North.

"Of course not. But will justice be done? Are you sure you can prove your case? Supposing your charge to be true, can you prove it?"

"Yes. If the witnesses speak the truth."

"Who are they?"

"Myself, Dr. Macklewain, the constable, and two prisoners, one of whom was flogged himself. *He* will speak the truth, I believe. The other man I have not much faith in."

"Very well; then there is only a prisoner and Dr. Macklewain; for if there has been foul play the convict-constable will not accuse the authorities. Moreover, the doctor does not agree with you."

"No!" cried North, amazed.

"No. You see, then, my dear sir, how necessary it is not to be hasty in matters of this kind. I really think—pardon me for my plainness—that your goodness of heart has misled you. Captain Burgess sends a report of the case. He says the man was sentenced to a hundred lashes for gross insolence and disobedience of orders, that the doctor was present during the punishment, and that the man was thrown off by his directions after he had received fifty-six lashes. That, after a short interval, he was found to be dead, and that the doctor made a *post-mortem* examination of the body and found disease of the heart."

North started. "A *post-mortem?* I never knew there had been one held."

"Here is the medical certificate," said Vickers, holding it out, "accompanied by the copies of the evidence of the constable and a letter from the Commandant."

North took the papers and read them slowly. They were straightforward enough. Aneurism of the ascending aorta was given as the cause of death; and the doctor frankly admitted that had he known the deceased to be suffering from that complaint he would not have permitted him to receive more than twenty-five lashes.

"I think Macklewain is an honest man," said North, doubtfully. "He would not dare to return a false certificate. Yet the circumstances of the case—"

"I cannot enter into these questions, Mr. North. My position here is to administer the law to the best of my ability, not to question it."

North bowed his head. "I can say no more, sir. Then I see that the evidence is against me; but it is my duty to carry my efforts as far as I can, and I will do so." Vickers bowed stiffly, and wished him good morning. Authority, however well-meaning, has a natural dislike to those dissatisfied persons who persist in pushing inquires to extremities.

North, going out with saddened spirits, met in the passage a beautiful young girl. It was Sylvia, coming to visit her father. He lifted his hat and looked after her. He guessed that she was the daughter of the man he had left—the wife of the Captain Frere concerning whom he had heard so much. North was a man prone to strange fancies; and it seemed to him that beneath the clear blue eyes that flashed upon him for a moment, lay a hint of future sadness in which, in some strange way, he himself was to bear part. He stared after her until she disappeared; and long after the dainty presence of the young bride—trimly-booted, tight-waisted, and neatly-gloved—had faded from his mental vision, he still saw those blue eyes and that cloud of golden hair.

Sylvia had become the wife of Maurice Frere. The alliance was entered into with due pomp of ball and supper; bride and bridegroom departing through

CAPTAIN AND MRS. FRERE

the golden afternoon to the nearest of Major Vickers's stations. Thence it had been arranged they should return after a fortnight, and take ship for Sydney.

Major Vickers, affectionate though he was to the man whom he believed to be the saviour of his child, had no notion of allowing him to live on Sylvia's fortune. He had settled his daughter's portion—ten thousand pounds—upon herself and children, and had informed Frere that he expected him to live upon an income of his own earning. After many consultations between the pair, it had been arranged that a civil appointment in Sydney would suit the bridegroom, who was to sell out of the service. This notion was Frere's own. He never cared for military duty, and had, moreover, considerable private debts. By selling his commission he would be enabled at once to pay these, and render himself eligible for any well-paid post under the Colonial Government that the interest of his father-in-law, and his own reputation as a convict disciplinarian, might procure.

Vickers would fain have kept his daughter with him, but he unselfishly acquiesced in the scheme, admitting that the society of Sydney would be far more congenial to her.

"You can come over and see us when we get settled, papa," said Sylvia, "and we can come and see you. Hobart Town is very pretty, but I want to see the World."

"You should go to London, Poppet," said Maurice, "that's the place. Isn't it, sir?"

"Oh, London!" cries Sylvia, clapping her hands. "And Westminster Abbey, and Hyde Park, and Fleet-street! 'Sir,' said Dr. Johnson, 'let us take a walk down Fleet-street.' Do you remember, in Mr. Croker's book, Maurice? No, you don't, I know, because you only looked at the pictures, and then read Pierce Egan's account of the Topping Fight between Bob Gaynor and Ned Neal, or some such person."

"Little girls should be seen and not heard," said Maurice, laughing. "You have no business to read my books."

"Why not?" she asked, with a gaiety which already seemed a little strained; "husband and wife should have no secrets from each other, sir. Besides, I want you to read my books. I am going to read Shelley to you."

"Don't, my dear," said Maurice simply. "I can't understand him."

This little scene took place at the dinner-table of Frere's cottage in New Town, to which Major Vickers had been invited, in order that future plans might be discussed.

"I don't want to go to Port Arthur," said the bride, later in the evening. "Maurice, there can be no necessity to go there."

"Well," said Maurice, "I want to have a look at the place. I ought to be familiar with all phases of convict discipline, you know."

"There is likely to be a report ordered upon the death of a prisoner," said Vickers. "The chaplain, a fussy but well-meaning person, has been memorialising about it. You may as well do it as anybody else, Maurice."

"Ay. And save the expenses of the trip," said Maurice.

"But it is so melancholy," cried Sylvia.

"The most delightful place in the island, my dear. I was there for a few days once, and I really was charmed."

It was remarkable—so Vickers thought—how each had caught something of the other's manner of speech. Sylvia was less choice in her mode of utterance, Frere more so. He caught himself wondering which of the two methods both would finally adopt.

"But those dogs, and sharks, and things. Oh, Maurice, haven't we had enough of convicts?"

"Enough! Why, I'm going to make my living out of 'em," said Maurice, with his most natural manner.

Sylvia sighed.

"Play something, darling," said her father; and so the girl, sitting down to the piano, trilled and warbled in her pure young voice, until the Port Arthur question floated itself away and was heard of no more for that time. But upon pursuing the subject, Sylvia found her husband firm. He wanted to go, and he would go. Having once assured himself that it was advantageous to him to do a certain thing, his native obstinacy urged him to do it despite all opposition, and Sylvia, having had her first "cry", gave up the point. This was the first difference of their short married life, and she hastened to condone it.

In the light of Maurice's love for her—which curbed the worst part of him, and bestowed upon him an unaccustomed gentleness—Sylvia's fears melted away. Yet by-and-by out of this very sentiment arose a new and strange source of anxiety. Having accepted her position as a wife, and put away from her all doubts as to her own capacity for loving the man to whom she had allied herself, she began to be haunted by a dread lest *he* might do something which would lessen the affection she bore him. On one or two occasions she had been forced to confess that her husband was more of an egotist than she cared to think. He demanded of her no great sacrifices, but he now and then intruded on her that disregard for the feelings of others which was part of his character. He was fond of her—almost too passionately fond—but he was unused to thwart his own will in anything. Did she want to read when he wanted to walk, he good-humouredly put aside her book; did she want to walk when he wanted to rest, he laughingly set up his laziness as an all-sufficient plea for her remaining within doors. He was at no pains to conceal his weariness when she read her favourite books to him. If he felt sleepy when she sang or played, he slept without apology. He would not have wittingly offended her; but it seemed to him natural to yawn when he was weary, to sleep when he was fatigued, and to talk only about those subjects which interested him. Had anybody told him that he was selfish, he would have been astonished.

Thus it came about that Sylvia one day discovered that she led two lives—one in the body, and one in the spirit—and that with her spiritual existence her husband had no share. This discovery alarmed her, but then she smiled at it. "A man's thoughts are different from a woman's," she said; "he has his business and his worldly cares, of which a woman knows nothing. I must comfort him, and not worry him with my follies."

As for Maurice, he also grew sometimes rather troubled. He could not understand his wife. Her nature was an enigma to him. He had loved her from a child, and had committed a cruel crime to obtain her; but having got her, he was no nearer to the mystery of her than before. She was all his own, he thought. Her golden hair was for his fingers, her lips were for his caress, her eyes looked love upon him alone. Yet there were times when her lips were cold to his kisses, and her eyes looked disdainfully upon his coarser passion. He would catch her musing when he spoke to her, much as she would catch him sleeping when she read to him,—but she awoke with a start and a blush at her forgetfulness, which he never did. He was not a man to brood over these things; and after some reflective pipes and ineffectual rubbings of his head, he "gave it up."

It was enough that he had finally obtained his treasure, and he was in daily wonderment at it. He marvelled at her feminine devices of dress and adornment. Her dainty garments seemed to him perfumed with the odour of sanctity.

The fact was, that the patron of Sarah Purfoy had not met with many virtuous women, and had but just discovered what a dainty morsel modesty was.

IN THE HOSPITAL

The hospital of Port Arthur was not a cheerful place, but to Rufus Dawes it seemed a paradise. There at least—despite the roughness and contempt with which his gaolers ministered to him—he was free from the enforced companionship of the men whom he loathed, and to whose level he felt that he was daily sinking. Throughout his long term of degradation he had, as yet, aided by the memory of his sacrifice and his love, preserved something of his self-respect, but he felt that he could not preserve it long. Since his capture in the garden at Hobart Town, he had given loose rein to his rage and his despair. "I am forgotten or despised; I have no name in the world; what matter if I become like one of these?"

It was under the influence of this feeling that he had picked up the cat at the command of Captain Burgess. As the unhappy Kirkland had said, "As well you as another;" and truly, what was *he* that he should cherish sentiments of honour or humanity? But he had miscalculated his own capacity for evil. When he flung down the cat and stripped his own back for punishment, he felt a fierce joy in the thought that his baseness would be atoned for in his own blood. Even when, faint from the hideous ordeal, he flung himself upon his knees in the cell, he regretted only the impotent, blasphemous ravings that the torture had forced from him—not because they were blasphemous, but because their utterance, by revealing his agony, gave triumph to his tormentors. When North found him, he was in the very depth of this abasement, and he repulsed his comforter—not so much because he had seen him flogged, as because North had heard him cry. The self-reliance which had hitherto sustained him through his self-imposed trial had failed him when he needed it most; and he who had faced the gallows, the desert, and the sea, confessed his debased humanity beneath the physical torture of the lash. He had been flogged before, but he now for the first time comprehended how the agony of the wretched body can force the soul to quit its last poor refuge of assumed indifference, and *confess itself conquered.*

Not many months before, one of the companions of the chain had killed his mate when at work with him, and carrying the body on his back to the nearest gang, had surrendered himself—going to his death thanking God he had at last found a way of escape from his miseries. Dawes had been filled with horror at a deed so bloody, and he had, with others, commented on the cowardice that would thus shirk the responsibility of that state of life in which it had pleased man and the devil to place him. Now he understood how and why the crime had been committed, and felt only pity. Lying awake with a back that burned beneath its lotioned rags, when lights were low, in the breathful silence of the hospital, he registered in his heart a terrible oath that he would die ere he would again be made such hideous sport for his enemies.

In this frame of mind he bethought him of the strange man who had deigned to clasp his hand and call him "brother." He had been touched with sympathy at the confession of weakness made to him, in a moment when his own weakness had overcome him. Soothed by the brief rest that his fortnight of hospital seclusion had afforded him, he had begun, in a speculative way, to turn his thoughts to religion. He had read of martyrs who had borne agonies unspeakable, upheld by their confidence in Heaven and God. In his old wild youth he had scoffed at prayers and priests; in the hate that had grown upon him with his later years he had despised a creed that told men to love one another. "God is love, my brethren," said the chaplain on Sundays, and all the week the thongs of the overseer cracked, and the cat hissed and swung. Of what practical value was a piety that preached but did not practise? As one hardened prisoner had said, "God's terrible far from Port Arthur."

Rufus Dawes had smiled at the spectacle of priests admonishing men, who knew what *he* knew and had seen what *he* had seen, for the trivialities of lying and stealing. He had believed all priests impostors or fools, all religion a mockery and a lie. But now, broken in spirit and weakened in body, with faith in his own will shaken, he longed for something to lean upon, and turned—as all men turn when in such case—to the Unknown. Had now there been at hand some Christian priest, some Christian-spirited man even, no matter of what faith, to pour into his ears words of comfort and grace, he might have been saved from his after fate; but there was no such man. He asked for the Chaplain. North was fighting the Convict Department, seeking vengeance for Kirkland, and was being pushed hither and thither, referred here, snubbed there, bowed out in another place. Rufus Dawes, half ashamed of himself for his request, waited a long morning, and then saw, respectfully ushered into his cell as his soul's physician—Meekin.

"Well, my good man," said Meekin, soothingly, "so you wanted to see me."

"I asked for the chaplain," said Rufus Dawes, his anger with himself growing apace.

THE CONSOLATIONS OF RELIGION

"I am the chaplain," returned Meekin, with dignity, as if to say,—"none of your brandy-drinking, pea-jacketed Norths, but a Respectable chaplain who is the friend of a Bishop!"

"I thought that Mr. North was——"

"Mr. North has left, sir," said Meekin, dryly, "but I will hear what you have to say. There is no occasion to go, constable; wait outside the door."

Rufus Dawes smiled bitterly. "Don't be afraid, sir; I am not going to harm you," he said. "I only wanted to talk a little."

"Do you read your Bible, Dawes?" asked Meekin by way of reply. "It would be better to read your Bible than to talk, I think. You must humble yourself in prayer, Dawes."

"I have read it," said Dawes.

"But is your mind softened by its teachings? Do you realise the Infinite Mercy of God, who has compassion, Dawes, upon the greatest sinners?"

The convict made a move of impatience.

"Do you believe that there is a God, Mr. Meekin?"

"Abandoned sinner! How do you ask such a question?"

"Because I think that if there is, He must often be dissatisfied at the way things are done here," said Dawes.

"I can listen to no mutinous observations, prisoner," said Meekin. "Do not add blasphemy to your other crimes. I fear that all conversation with you, in your present frame of mind, would be worse than useless. I will mark a few passages in your Bible, that seem to me appropriate to your condition, and beg you to commit them to memory. Hailes, the door, if you please."

So, with a bow, the "consoler" departed.

Rufus Dawes felt his heart grow sick. North had gone, then. The only man who had seemed to have a heart in his bosom had gone. The only man who had dared to clasp his hand, and call him "brother," had gone. Turning his head, he saw through the window—unbarred, for Nature, at Port Arthur, had no need of bars—the lovely bay glittering in the afternoon sun, the long quay spotted with groups of parti-coloured chain-gangs, and heard, mingling with the murmur of the waves and the rustling of the trees, the never-ceasing clashing of irons, and the eternal click of hammers. Was he to be for ever buried in this whitened sepulchre, shut out from the face of Heaven and mankind?

The appearance of Hailes broke his reverie. "Here's a book for you," said he, with a grin. "Parson sent it."

Rufus Dawes took the Bible, and, placing it on his knee, turned to the places indicated by slips of paper. There were some three or four of these slips of paper, embracing some twenty marked texts.

"Parson says he'll come and hear·you to-morrer, and you're to keep the book clean."

"Keep the book clean!" and "hear him!" Did Meekin think that he was a charity school boy? The utter incapacity of the chaplain to understand his wants was so sublime that it was nearly ridiculous enough to make him laugh. He turned to the texts. Good Meekin had selected the fiercest denunciations of bard and priest. The most notable of the Psalmist's curses upon his enemies, the most terrible thunderings of apostle and evangelist against idolatry and unbelief, were grouped together and presented to Dawes to soothe him. The miserable man, seeking for consolation and peace, turned over the leaves of the Bible only to find "the pains of Hell," "the never-dying worm," "the unquenchable fire," "the bubbling brimstone," the "bottomless pit," from out of which the "smoke of his torment" should ascend for ever and ever.

Repelled by this unlooked-for ending to his hopes, he let the book fall to the ground. "Is there, then, nothing but torment for me in this world or the next?" he groaned. Presently his eyes sought his right hand, resting upon it as though it had some secret virtue which made it different from the other. "*He* would not have done this! *He* would not have thrust upon me these dreadful threats of Hell and Death. He called me 'Brother!' " And he fell to nursing the hand on which North's tears had fallen, moaning and rocking himself to and fro.

Meekin, coming in the morning, found his pupil more sullen than ever. "Have you learned these texts, my man?" said he cheerfully to his unpromising convert.

Rufus Dawes pointed with his foot to the Bible, which still lay on the floor as he had left it the night before. "No!"

"No! Why not?"

"I would learn no such words as those. I would rather forget them."

"Forget them! My good man, I——"

Rufus Dawes sprang up in sudden wrath, and pointing to his cell door, cried, "What do you know about the feelings of such as I? Take your book and yourself away. When I asked for a priest, I had no thought of *you*. Begone!"

Meekin, despite the halo of sanctity which he felt should surround him, found his gentility melt all of a sudden. Adventitious distinctions had disappeared for the instant. The pair had become simply man and man, and the sleek priest quailing before the convict, picked up his Bible and backed out.

"That man Dawes is very insolent," said the chaplain to Burgess later. "He was brutal to me to-day—quite brutal."

"Was he?" said Burgess. "Had too long a spell, I expect. I'll send him back to work to-morrow."

"It would be well," said Meekin, "if he had some employment."

The "employment" at Port Arthur consisted chiefly of agriculture, ship-building, and tanning. Dawes, who was in the chain-gang, was put to work bringing down logs from the forest, or "lumbering" timber on the wharf. This work was not light. An ingenious calculator has discovered that the pressure of the log upon the shoulder was wont to average 125 lbs. Members of the chain-gang were dressed in yellow, and— by way of encouraging the others—had the word "Felon" stamped upon conspicuous parts of their raiment.

"A NATURAL PENITENTIARY"

In the summer time Rufus Dawes rose at half-past five in the morning, and worked until six in the evening, getting three-quarters of an hour for breakfast, and one hour for dinner. Once a week he had a clean shirt, and once a fortnight clean socks. If he felt sick, he was permitted to "report his case to the medical officer." If he wanted to write a letter he could ask permission of the Commandant, and send the letter, open, through that Almighty Officer, who could stop it if he thought necessary. If he felt himself aggrieved by any order, he was "to obey instantly, but might complain afterwards, if he thought fit, to the Commandant." In making any complaint against an officer or constable, it was strictly ordered that a prisoner "must be most respectful in his manner and language, when speaking of or to such officer or constable." He was held responsible only for the safety of his chains, and for the rest was at the mercy of his gaoler. These gaolers—owning right of search, entry into cells at all hours, and other *droits* of seigneury—were responsible only to the Commandant, who was responsible only to the Governor, that is to say, to nobody but God and his own conscience. The jurisdiction of the Commandant included the whole of Tasman's Peninsula, with the islands and waters within three miles thereof; and save the making of certain returns to head-quarters, his power was unlimited.

A word as to the position and appearance of this place of punishment. Tasman's Peninsula is in the form of an earring with a double drop. The lower drop is the larger, and is ornamented, so to speak, with bays. At its southern extremity, is a deep indentation called Maingon Bay, bounded east and west by the organ-pipe rocks of Cape Raoul, and the giant form of Cape Pillar. From Maingon Bay an arm of the ocean cleaves the rocky walls in a northerly direction. On the Western coast of this sea-arm was the settlement; in front of it was a little island where the dead were buried, called The Island of the Dead. Ere the in-coming convict passed the purple beauty of this convict Golgotha, his eyes were attracted by a point of grey rock covered with white buildings, and swarming with life. This was Point Puer, the place of confinement for boys from eight to twenty years of age.

From the extremity of Long Bay, as the extension of the sea-arm was named, a convict-made tramroad ran due north, through the nearly impenetrable thicket to Norfolk Bay. In the mouth of Norfolk Bay was Woody Island. This was used as a signal station, and an armed boat's crew was stationed there. To the north of Woody Island lay One-tree Point—the southernmost projection of the drop of the earring; and the sea that ran between narrowed to the eastward, until it struck on the sandy bar of Eaglehawk-Neck. Eaglehawk-Neck was the link that connected the two drops of the earring, being a strip of sand four hundred and fifty yards across. On its eastern side the waters of the Southern Ocean poured their unchecked force. The isthmus emerged from a wild coast-line, into whose bowels the ravenous sea had bored strange caverns. At one spot in this wilderness the ocean had penetrated the wall of rock for two hundred feet, and in stormy weather the salt spray rose through a perpendicular shaft more than five hundred feet deep. This place was called the Devil's Blow-hole. The upper drop of the earring was named Forrestier's Peninsula, and was joined to the mainland by another isthmus called East Bay Neck. Forrestier's Peninsula was an almost impenetrable thicket, growing to the brink of a perpendicular cliff of basalt.

Eaglehawk-Neck was the door to the prison, and it was kept bolted. On the narrow strip of land was built a guard-house, and on stages, set out in the water in either side, watch-dogs were chained. The station officer was charged to "pay especial attention to the feeding and care" of these useful beasts, being ordered "to report to the Commandant whenever any one of them became useless." It may be added that the Bay was not innocent of sharks. Westward from Eaglehawk-Neck and Woody Island, lay the dreaded Coal Mines. Sixty of the "marked men" were stationed here under a strong guard. At the Coal Mines was the northernmost of that ingenious series of semaphores which rendered escape almost impossible. The wild and mountainous character of the peninsula offered peculiar advantages to the signalmen. On the summit of the hill which overlooked the guard tower of the settlement was a gigantic gum-tree stump, upon the top of which was placed a semaphore. This semaphore communicated with the two wings of the prison—Eaglehawk-Neck and the Coal Mines—by sending a line of signals right across the peninsula. Thus, the settlement communicated with Mount Arthur, Mount Arthur with One-tree Hill, One-tree Hill with Mount Communication, and Mount Communication with the Coal Mines. On the other side, the signals would run thus—the settlement to Signal Hill,

Signal Hill to Woody Island, Woody Island to Eaglehawk. Did a prisoner escape from the Coal Mines, the guard at Eaglehawk-Neck could be aroused, and the whole island informed of the "bolt" in less than twenty minutes.

With these advantages of nature and art, the prison was held to be the most secure in the world. Colonel Arthur reported to the Home Government that the spot which bore his name was a "natural penitentiary." The worthy disciplinarian probably took as a personal compliment the polite forethought of the Almighty, in thus considerately providing for the carrying out of the celebrated "Regulations for Convict Discipline."

One afternoon the ever active semaphores transmitted a piece of intelligence which set the peninsula agog. Captain Frere, having arrived from headquarters with orders to hold an inquiry into the death of Kirkland, was to make a progress through the stations, and it behoved the keepers of the Natural Penitentiary to produce their Penitents in good case. Burgess was in high spirits at finding so congenial a soul selected for the task of reporting upon him.

A VISIT OF INSPECTION

"It's only a nominal thing, old man," Frere said to his former comrade, when they met. "That parson has made meddling, and they want to close his mouth."

"I am glad to have the opportunity of showing you and Mrs. Frere the place," returned Burgess. "I must try and make your stay as pleasant as I can, though I'm afraid that Mrs. Frere will not find much to amuse her."

"Frankly, Captain Burgess," said Sylvia, "I would rather have gone straight to Sydney. My husband, however, was obliged to come, and of course I accompanied him."

"You will not have much society," said Meekin, who was of the welcoming party. "Mrs. Datchett, the wife of one of our stipendiaries, is the only lady here, and I hope to have the pleasure of making you acquainted with her this evening at the Commandant's. Mr. McNab, whom you know, is in command at the Neck, and cannot leave, or you would have seen him."

"I have planned a little party," said Burgess, "but I fear that it will not be so successful as I could wish."

"You wretched old bachelor," said Frere, "you should get married, like me."

"Ah!" said Burgess, with a bow, "that would be difficult."

Sylvia was compelled to smile at the compliment, made in the presence of some twenty prisoners, who were carrying the various trunks and packages up the hill, and she remarked that the said prisoners grinned at the Commandant's clumsy courtesy.

"I don't like Captain Burgess, Maurice," she said, in the interval before dinner. "I dare say he did flog that poor fellow to death. He looks as if he could do it."

"Nonsense!" said Maurice, "he's a good fellow enough. Besides, I've seen the doctor's certificate. I can't understand your absurd sympathy with prisoners."

"Don't they sometimes deserve sympathy?"

"No, certainly not, the lying scoundrels. You're always whining over them, Sylvia, and I don't like it, as you well know."

Sylvia said nothing. Maurice was often guilty of these small brutalities, and she had learnt that the best way to meet them was by silence. Unfortunately silence did not mean indifference, for the reproof was unjust, and nothing stings a woman's fine sense like an injustice.

Burgess had prepared a feast, and the "Society" of Port Arthur was present. Father Flaherty, Meekin, Doctor Macklewain, and Mr. and Mrs. Datchett had been invited, and the dining-room was resplendent with glass and flowers.

"I've a fellow who was a professional gardener," said Burgess to Sylvia during the dinner, "and I make use of his talents."

"We have a professional artist also," said Macklewain, with a sort of pride. "That picture of the 'Prisoner of Chillon' yonder was painted by him Quite fine, is is not?"

"I've got the place full of curiosities," said Burgess; "quite a collection. I'll show them to you to-morrow. Those napkin rings were made by a prisoner."

"Ah!" cried Frere, taking up the daintily-carved bone, "very neat!"

"That is some of Rex's handiwork," said Meekin. "He is very clever at these trifles."

"We will go down to the Neck to-morrow or next day, Mrs. Frere," said Burgess, "and you shall see the Blow-hole. It is a curious place."

"Is it far?" asked Sylvia.

"Oh, no! We shall go in the train."

"The train!"

"Yes—don't look so astonished. You'll see it to-morrow. Oh, you Hobart Town ladies don't know what we can do here."

"What about this Kirkland business?" Frere asked. "I suppose I can have half an hour with you in the morning, and take the depositions?"

"Any time you like, my dear fellow," said Burgess. "It's all the same to me."

"I don't want to make more fuss than I can help," Frere said apologetically—the dinner had been good—"but I must send these people up a 'full, true, and particular,' don't you know."

"Of course," cried Burgess, with friendly nonchalance. "That's quite all right."

The next two days were devoted to sight-seeing. Sylvia was taken through the Hospital and the Workshops, shown the semaphores, and shut up by Maurice in a "dark cell." Her husband and Burgess seemed to treat the prison like a tame animal, whom they could handle at their leisure, and whose natural ferocity was kept in check by their superior intelligence. This bringing of a young and pretty woman into immediate contact with bolts and bars had about it an incongruity which pleased them. Maurice penetrated everywhere, questioned the prisoners, jested with the gaolers, even, in the munificence of his heart, bestowed tobacco on the sick.

With such graceful rattlings of dry bones, they got by-and-by to Point Puer, where a luncheon had been provided.

An unlucky accident had occurred at Point Puer that morning, however, and the place was in a ferment. A refractory thief named Peter Brown, aged twelve years, had jumped off the high rock and drowned himself in full view of the constables. These "jumpings off" had become rather frequent lately, and Burgess was enraged at one happening on this particular day. If he could by any possibility have brought the corpse of poor little Peter Brown to life again, he would have soundly whipped it for its impertinence.

"It is most unfortunate," he said to Frere, as they stood in the cell where the little body was laid, "that it should have happened to-day."

"Oh," says Frere, frowning down upon the young face. "It can't be helped. I know those young devils. They'd do it out of spite. What sort of a character had he?"

"Very bad—Johnson, the book."

Johnson bringing it, the two saw Peter Brown's iniquities set down in the neatest of running hand, and ornamented in quite an artistic way with flourishes of red ink.

"20th November, disorderly conduct, 12 lashes. 24th November, insolence to hospital attendant, diet reduced. 4th December, stealing cap from another prisoner, 12 lashes. 15th December, absenting himself at roll call, two days' cells. 23rd December, insolence and insubordination, two days' cells. 8th January, insolence and insubordination, 12 lashes. 20th January, insolence and insubordination, 12 lashes. 22nd February, insolence and insubordination, 12 lashes and one week's solitary. 6th March, insolence and insubordination, 20 lashes."

"That was the last?" asked Frere.

"Yes, sir," says Johnson.

"And then he—hum—did it?"

"Just so, sir. That was the way of it."

Just so! The magnificent system starved and tortured a child of twelve until he killed himself. That was the way of it.

After luncheon the party made a progress. Everything was most admirable. There was a long schoolroom, where Meekin taught how Christ loved little children; and behind the schoolroom were the cells and the constables and the little yard where they gave their "twenty lashes." Sylvia shuddered at the array of faces. From the stolid nineteen years old booby of the Kentish hop-fields, to the wizened, shrewd, ten years old Bohemian of the London streets, all degrees and grades of juvenile vice grinned in untamable wickedness, or snuffled in affected piety.

After the children had stood up and sat down, and sung a hymn, and told how many twice five were, and repeated their belief in "One God the Father Almighty, maker of Heaven and Earth," the party reviewed the workshops, and saw the church, and went everywhere but into the room where the body of Peter Brown, aged twelve, lay starkly on its wooden bench, staring at the gaol roof which was between it and Heaven.

Just outside this room, Sylvia met with a little adventure. Meekin had stopped behind, and Burgess, being suddenly summoned for some official duty, Frere had gone with him, leaving his wife to rest on a bench that, placed at the summit of the cliff, overlooked the sea. While resting thus, she became aware of the presence of a small boy, with his cap in one hand and a hammer in the other. The appearance of the little creature, clad in a uniform of grey cloth that was too large for him, and holding in his withered little hand a hammer that was too heavy for him, had something pathetic about it.

"What is it, you mite?" asked Sylvia.

"We thought you might have seen him, mum," said the little figure, opening its blue eyes with wonder at the kindness of the tone.

"Him! Whom?"

"Cranky Brown, mum," returned the child; "him as did it this morning. Me and Billy knowed him, mum; he was a mate of ours, and we wanted to know if he looked happy."

"What do you mean, child?" said she, with a strange terror at her heart; and then, filled with pity at the aspect of the little being, she drew him to her and kissed him.

He looked up at her with joyful surprise.

"Oh!" he said.

Sylvia kissed him again.

"Does nobody ever kiss you, poor little man?" said she.

"Mother used to," was the reply, "but she's at home. Oh, mum," with a sudden crimsoning of the little face, "may I fetch Billy?"

And taking courage from the bright young face, he gravely marched to an angle of the rock, and brought out another little creature in grey uniform.

"This is Billy, mum," he said. "Billy never had no mother. Kiss Billy."

The young wife felt the tears rush to her eyes. "You two poor babies!" she cried. And then, forgetting that she was a lady, dressed in silk and lace, she fell on her knees in the dust, and, folding the friendless pair in her arms, wept over them.

"What is the matter, Sylvia?" said Frere, when he came up. "You've been crying."

"Nothing, Maurice; at least, I will tell you by-and-by."

When they were alone that evening, she told him of the two little boys, and he laughed.

"Artful little humbugs," he said, and supported his argument by so many illustrations of the precocious wickedness of juvenile felons, that his wife was half convinced against her will.

Unfortunately, when Sylvia went away, Tommy and Billy put into execution a plan which they had carried in their heads for some weeks.

"I can do it now," said Tommy. "I feel strong."

"Will it hurt much, Tommy?" said Billy, who was not so courageous.

"Not so much as a whipping."

"I'm afraid! Oh, Tom, it's so deep! Don't leave me, Tom!"

The bigger boy took his little handkerchief from his neck, and with it bound his own left hand to his companion's right.

"Now I *can't* leave you."

"What was it the lady that kissed us said, Tommy?"

"Lord, have pity of them two fatherless children!" repeated Tommy.

"Let's say it, Tom."

And so the two knelt on the brink of the cliff, and raising the bound hands together, looked up at the sky, and ungrammatically said, "Lord, have pity on we two fatherless children!" And then they kissed each other, and "did it."

The intelligence, transmitted by the ever-active semaphore, reached the Commandant in the midst of dinner, and in his agitation he blurted it out.

"These are the two poor things I saw in the morning," cried Sylvia. "Oh, Maurice, these two poor babies driven to suicide!"

"Condemning their young souls to everlasting fire," said Meekin, piously.

"Mr. Meekin! How can you talk like that! Oh, it's horrible!" And she burst into a passion of weeping.

"*I* can't help it, ma'am," says Burgess, rudely, ashamed. "It ain't my fault."

"She's nervous," says Frere, leading her away. "You must excuse her. Come and lie down, dearest."

"I will not stay here longer," said she. "Let us go to-morrow."

"We can't," said Frere.

"Oh, yes, we can. Maurice, if you love me, take me away."

"Well," said Maurice, moved by her evident grief, "I'll try."

He spoke to Burgess. "Burgess, this matter has unsettled my wife so that she wants to leave at once. I must visit the Neck, you know. How can we do it?"

"Well," says Burgess, "if the wind only holds, the brig could go round to Pirates' Bay and pick you up. You'll only be a night at the barracks."

"I think that would be best," said Frere. "We'll start to-morrow, please, and if you'll give me a pen and ink I'll be obliged."

"I hope you are satisfied," said Burgess.

"Oh, quite," said Frere. "I must recommend more careful supervision at Point Puer, though. It will never do to have these young blackguards slipping through our fingers in this way."

So a neatly written statement of the occurrence was appended to the ledgers in which the names of William Tomkins and Thomas Grove were entered. Macklewain held an inquest, and nobody troubled about them any more. Why should they? The prisons of London were full of such Tommys and Billys.

Sylvia passed through the rest of her journey in a dream of terror. The incident of the children had shaken her nerves, and she longed to be away from the place and its associations. She shuddered as she gazed into the boiling abyss of the Blow-hole, and shook with fear as the Commandant's "train" rattled over the dangerous tramway that wound across the precipice to Long Bay.

This "train" was composed of a number of low wagons pushed and dragged up the steep inclines by convicts, who drew themselves up in the wagons when the trucks dashed down the slope, and acted as drags. Sylvia felt degraded at being thus drawn by human beings, and trembled when the lash cracked. Moreover, there was among these beasts of burden a face that had dimly haunted her girlhood, and only lately vanished from her dreams.

This face looked on her—she thought—with bitterest loathing and scorn, and she felt relieved when at the mid-day halt its owner was ordered to fall out from the rest, and was with four others re-chained for the homeward journey. Frere, struck with the appearance of the five said, "By Jove, Poppet, there are our old friends Rex and Dawes, and the others." Sylvia comprehended now: the face was the face of Dawes; and as she looked after him, she suddenly saw him raise his hands above his head with a motion that terrified her. She felt for an instant a great shock of pitiful recollection. Staring at the group, she strove to recall when and how Rufus Dawes had ever merited her pity, but her clouded memory could not complete the picture, and as the wagons swept round a curve, and the group disappeared, she awoke from her reverie with a sigh.

"Maurice," she whispered, "how is it that the sight of that man always makes me sad?"

Her husband frowned, and then caressing her, bade her forget the place and her fears. "I was wrong to have insisted on your coming," he said. They stood on the deck of the Sydney-bound vessel the next morning, and watched the "Natural Penitentiary" grow dim in the distance. "You were not strong enough."

"Dawes," said John Rex, "you love that girl! Now that you've seen her another man's wife, and have been harnessed like a beast to drag him along the road, while he held her in his arms!—now that you've seen and suffered that, perhaps you'll join us."

Rufus Dawes made a movement of agonised impatience.

"You'll never get out of this place any other way. Come, be a man; join us!"

"No!"

"It is your only chance. Why refuse it? If you think to get any good out of that 'inquiry,' you are mightily mistaken," said he. "Frere has put a stopper upon that, you'll find."

He spoke truly. Nothing more was heard of it, only that, some six months afterwards, Mr. North, when at Parramatta, received an official letter (in which the expenditure of wax and printing and paper was as large as it could be made) which informed him that the "Comptroller-General of the convict department had decided that further inquiry concerning the death of the prisoner named in the margin was unnecessary," and that some gentleman with an utterly illegible signature "had the honour to be his most obedient servant."

Maurice found his favourable expectations of Sydney fully realised. His notable escape from death at Macquarie Harbour, his alliance with the

GATHERING IN THE THREADS

daughter of Major Vickers, and his reputation as a convict disciplinarian, rendered him a man of note. He received a vacant magistracy, and became even more noted for hardness of heart and artfulness of prison knowledge than before. The convict population spoke of him as "that —— Frere" and registered vows of vengeance against him, which he laughed—in his bluffness—to scorn.

One of the first things that this useful officer did upon his arrival in Sydney was to inquire for Sarah Purfoy. To his astonishment, he discovered that she was the proprietor of large export warehouses in Pitt-street, owned a neat cottage on one of the points of land which jutted into the bay, and was reputed to possess a considerable banking account. He in vain applied his brains to solve this mystery. His cast-off mistress had not been rich when she left Van Diemen's Land—at least, so she had assured him, and appearances bore out her assurance. How had she accumulated this sudden wealth? Above all, why had she thus invested it? He made inquiries at the banks, but was snubbed for his pains. Sydney banks in those days did some queer business.

"Mrs. Purfoy had come to them fully accredited," said the manager with a smile.

"But where did she get the money?" asked the magistrate. "I am suspicious of these sudden fortunes. The woman was a notorious character in Hobart Town, and when she left hadn't a penny."

"My dear Captain Frere," said the banker, "it is not the custom of our bank to make inquiries into the previous history of its customers. The bills were good, you may depend, or we should not have honoured them. Good morning!"

"The bills!" Frere saw but one explanation. Sarah had received the proceeds of some of Rex's rogueries. Rex's letter to his father, and the mention of the sum of money "in the old house in Blue Anchor Yard," flashed across his memory. But why invest it in an oil and tallow warehouse? Convinced that there was some plot hatching, he determined to discover the secret and bring it to light. The name of the man to whom Rex's letter had been addressed was "Blick." He would find out if any of the convicts under his care had heard of Blick. Prosecuting his inquiries in the proper direction, he soon obtained a reply. Blick was a London receiver of stolen goods, known to at least a dozen of the black sheep of the Sydney fold. He was reputed to be enormously wealthy, had often been tried, but never convicted. Frere was thus not much nearer enlightenment than before, and an incident occurred a few months afterwards which increased his bewilderment.

He had not been long established in his magistracy, when Blunt came to claim payment for the voyage of Sarah Purfoy. "There's that schooner going begging, one may say, sir," said Blunt, when the office door was shut.

"What schooner?"

"The *Franklin*."

Now the *Franklin* was a vessel of three hundred and twenty tons, which plied between Norfolk and Sydney, as the *Osprey* had plied in the old days between Macquarie Harbour and Hobart Town.

"I am afraid that is rather stiff, Blunt," said Frere. "That's one of the best billets going, you know. I doubt if I have enough interest to get it for you. Besides," he added, eyeing the sailor critically, "you are getting oldish for that sort of thing, ain't you?"

Phineas Blunt stretched his arms wide, and opened his mouth, full of sound white teeth. "I am good for twenty years more yet, sir," he said. "My father was trading to the Indies at seventy-five years of age. *I'm* hearty enough, thank God; for, barring a drop of rum now and then, I've no vices to speak of. However, I ain't in a hurry, Captain, for a month or so; only I thought I'd jog your memory a bit, d'ye see."

"Oh, you're not in a hurry; where are you going then?"

"Well," said Blunt, shifting on his seat, uneasy under Frere's convict disciplined eye, "I've got a job on hand."

"Glad of it, I'm sure. What sort of a job?"

"A job of whaling," said Blunt, more uneasy than before.

"Oh, that's it, is it? Your old line of business. And who employs you now?" There was no suspicion in the tone, but Blunt replied as one who had anticipated such questioning, and had been advised how to answer it.

"Mrs. Purfoy."

"What!" cried Frere, scarcely able to believe his ears.

"She's got a couple of ships now, Captain, and she made me skipper of one of 'em. We look for beshdellamare,[1] and take a turn at harpooning sometimes."

Frere stared at Blunt, who stared at the window.

"Oh," said Frere eventually. "And when do you start?"

"I'm expecting to get the word every day," returned Blunt, apparently relieved, "and I thought I'd just come and see you first, in *case* of anything

[1] Bêche-de-la-mer.

falling in." Frere played with a penknife on the table in silence for a while, and then he said, "Where does she get the money from?"

"Blest if I know!" said Blunt, in unaffected simplicity. "That's beyond me. She says she saved it."

"*You* don't know anything about it, then," cried Frere, suddenly fierce.

"No, not I."

"Because, if there's any game on, she'd better take care. She knows me. Tell her that I've got my eyes on her. Let her remember her bargain." In his suspicious wrath he so savagely struck downwards with the open penknife that it shut upon his fingers, and cut him to the bone.

"I'll tell her," said Blunt, wiping his brow. "I'm sure she wouldn't go to sell you. But I'll look in when I come back, sir." When he got outside he drew a long breath. "By the Lord Harry, but it's a ticklish game to play," he said to himself, "and there's only one woman in the world I'd be fool enough to play it for."

Maurice Frere, oppressed with suspicions, ordered his horse and rode down to see the cottage which the owner of "Purfoy Stores" had purchased. He found it a low white building, situated four miles from the city, at the extreme end of a tongue of land which ran into the deep waters of the harbour. A garden, carefully cultivated, stood between the roadway and the house, and in this garden he saw a man digging.

"Does Mrs. Purfoy live here?" he asked, pushing open one of the iron gates.

The man replied in the affirmative, staring at the visitor with some suspicion.

"Is she at home?"

"No."

"You are sure?"

"If you don't believe me, ask at the house," was the reply.

Frere pushed his horse through the gate, and walked up the well-kept carriage drive. A man-servant in livery, answering his ring, told him that Mrs. Purfoy had gone to town, and then shut the door in his face. Frere, more astonished than ever at these signs of independence, paused indignant, feeling half inclined to enter despite opposition. As he looked through the break of the trees, he saw the masts of a brig lying at anchor off the point, and understood that the cottage commanded communication by water as well as by land. Could there be a special motive in choosing such a situation? He was uneasy, but strove to dismiss his alarm.

Sarah had kept faith with him so far. She had entered upon a new and more reputable life, and why should he seek to imagine evil where perhaps no evil was? It was likely that, after all, some wealthy merchant was the real owner of house and garden, pleasure yacht, and tallow warehouse, and that he had no cause for fear.

The experienced convict disciplinarian did not rate the ability of John Rex high enough.

From the instant the convict had heard his sentence of life, he had determined upon escaping, and had brought all the powers of his intellect to the consideration of the best method of achieving his purpose. His first care was to procure money. This he thought to do by writing to Blick, but when informed by Meekin of the fate of his letter, he adopted the less pleasant alternative of procuring it through Sarah Purfoy.

It was peculiar to the man's hard and ungrateful nature that, despite the attachment of the woman who had made it the object of her life to set him free, he cherished for her no affection. During the twelve years which had passed since his rashness had delivered him into the hands of the law at the house of Green, the coiner, he had been oppressed with no regrets for her fate. When, on his return from London, he heard that Sarah Purfoy was still in Hobart Town, he was glad, for he knew that she would do her utmost to help him—she had shown that on board the *Malabar*. But he was also sorry, for he remembered that the price she would demand for her services was his affection, and that had cooled long ago. However, he would make use of her. There might be a way to discard her if she proved troublesome.

His pretended piety had, despite Frere's exposure of his cryptograph, won the confidence of Meekin; and into that worthy creature's ear he poured a strange history. He was the son, he said, of a clergyman of the Church of England, whose real name, such was his reverence for the cloth, should never pass his lips. He was transported for a forgery which he did not commit. Sarah Purfoy was his wife—his erring, lost, and yet loved wife. She, an innocent and trusting girl, had determined to follow her husband to his place of doom, and had hired herself as lady's-maid to Mrs. Vickers. Alas! fever prostrated that husband on a bed of sickness, and Maurice Frere, the profligate and the villain, had taken advantage of the wife's unprotected state to ruin her! Rex darkly hinted how the seducer made his power over the helpless husband a weapon against the virtue of the wife and so terrified poor Meekin that, had it not "happened so long ago," he would have thought it necessary to look with disfavour upon the son-in-law of Major Vickers.

"I bear him no ill-will, sir," said Rex. "I did at first. There was a time when I could have killed him, but when I had him in my power, I—as you know—forbore to strike. No, sir, I could not permit murder!"

"Very proper," says Meekin, "very proper indeed."

"God will punish him in His own way, and His own time," continued Rex. "My great sorrow is for the poor woman. She is in Sydney, I have heard, living respectably, sir; and my heart bleeds for her." Here Rex heaved a sigh that would have made his fortune on the boards.

"My poor fellow," said Meekin. "Do you know where she is?"

"I do, sir."

"You might write to her."

John Rex appeared to hestitate, to struggle with himself, and finally to take a deep resolve. "No, Mr. Meekin, I will not write."

"Why not?"

"You know the orders, sir—the Commandant *reads* all the letters sent. Could I write to my poor Sarah what other eyes were to read?" and he watched the parson slyly.

"N—no, you could not," said Meekin, at last.

The next day, Meekin, conscious that what he was about to do was wrong, said to his penitent, "If you will promise to write nothing that the Commandant *might* not see, Rex, I will send your letter to your wife."

"Heaven bless you, sir," said Rex, and took two days to compose an epistle which should tell Sarah Purfoy how to act. The letter was a model of composition in one way. It stated everything clearly and succinctly. Not a detail that could assist was omitted—not a line that could embarrass was suffered to remain. He brought his letter unsealed to Meekin. Meekin looked at it with an interest that was half suspicion. "Have I your word that there is nothing in this that might not be read by the Commandant?"

John Rex was a bold man, but at the sight of the deadly thing fluttering open in the clergyman's hand, his knees knocked together. Strong in his knowledge of human nature, however, he pursued his plan. "Read it, sir," he said, turning away his face reproachfully. "You are a gentleman. I can trust *you*."

"No, Rex," said Meekin, walking loftily into the pitfall; "I do not read private letters." It was sealed, and John Rex felt as if somebody had withdrawn a match from a powder barrel.

In a month, Mr. Meekin received a letter, beautifully written, from "Sarah Rex," stating briefly that she had heard of his goodness, that the enclosed letter was for her husband, and that if it was against the rules to give it him, she begged it might be returned to her unread. Of course Meekin gave it to Rex, who next morning handed to Meekin a most touching and pious production, begging him to read it. Meekin did so, and any suspicions he may have had were at once disarmed. He was ignorant of the fact that the pious letter had contained a private one intended for John Rex only, which letter John Rex thought so highly of, that, having read it twice, he *ate* it.

The plan of escape was a simple one. Sarah Purfoy was to obtain from Blick the moneys he held in trust, and to embark the sum thus obtained in any business which would suffer her to keep a vessel hovering round the southern coast of Van Diemen's Land without exciting suspicion. The escape was to be made in the winter months, if possible, in June or July. The watchful vessel was to be commanded by some trustworthy person, who was to frequently land on the south-eastern side, and keep a look-out for any extraordinary appearance along the coast. Rex himself must be left to run the gauntlet of the dogs and guards unaided. "This seems a desperate scheme," wrote Rex, "but it is not so wild as it looks. I will wait eighteen months to give you time to make all arrangements." The eighteen months had now nearly passed over, and the time drew near. Faithful to his cruel philosophy, John Rex had provided scape-goats to assist him to his salvation.

He had discovered that of the twenty men in his gang eight had already determined on an effort for freedom. These were Gabbett, Vetch, Bodenham, Cornelius, Greenhill, Sanders, called the "Moocher," Cox, and Travers. The leading spirits were Vetch and Gabbett, who, with profound reverence, requested the "Dandy" to join. John Rex by degrees allowed himself to appear to be drawn into the scheme. He would urge these men to their fate, and take advantage of the excitement attendant on their absence to effect his own escape. He wished, however, to have a companion. A strong man, who, if pressed hard, would turn and keep the pursuers at bay, and this comrade-victim he sought in Rufus Dawes.

Beginning from a purely selfish motive, John Rex gradually found himself attracted into something like friendliness by the sternness with which his overtures were repelled. Always a keen student of human nature, the scoundrel saw, beneath the roughness, how faithful a friend and how undaunted a spirit was concealed. There was, moreover, a mystery about Rufus Dawes which Rex longed to fathom.

"Have you *no* friends whom you would wish to see?" he asked, one evening, when Rufus Dawes had proved more than usually deaf to his arguments.

"No," said Dawes. "My friends are all dead to me."

"What, all?" asked the other. "Most men have *some one* whom they wish to see."

Rufus Dawes laughed heavily. "I am better here."

"Then, are you content to live this dog's life?"

"Enough, enough," said Dawes, "I am resolved."

"Pooh! Pluck up a spirit," cried Rex. "It can't fail."

"Who are going?" asked the other, eyes on the ground.

John Rex enumerated the eight, and Dawes raised his head. "I won't go. I have had two trials at it; I don't want another. I would advise you not to attempt it either."

"Why not?"

"Gabbett bolted twice before," said Dawes, shuddering at the remembrance of what he had seen in the sunlit glen at Hell's Gates. "Others went with him, but each time he returned *alone*."

"What do you mean?" asked Rex, struck by the tone of his companion.

"What became of the others?"

"Died, I suppose," said the Dandy, with a forced laugh.

"Yes; but how? They were all without food. How came he to live six weeks?"

John Rex grew paler and did not reply. He recollected the legend that pertained to Gabbett's rescue. But he did not intend to make the journey in his company, so, after all, he had no cause for fear. "Come with me then," he said, at length. "We will try our luck together."

"No. I have resolved. I stay here."

"And leave your innocence unproved."

"How can I prove it?" cried Rufus Dawes, roughly impatient. "There are crimes committed which are never brought to light, and this is one of them."

"Well," said Rex, rising, as if weary of the discussion, "have it your own way, then. You know best. The private detective game *is* hard work. I, myself, have gone on a wild-goose chase before now. There's a mystery about a certain ship-builder's son which took me four months to unravel, and *then* I lost the thread."

"A *ship-builder's son!* Who was he?"

John Rex paused in wonderment at the eager interest with which the question was put, and then hastened to take advantage of this new opening. "A queer story. A well-known character in my time—Sir Richard Devine. A miserly old curmudgeon, with a scapegrace son."

Rufus Dawes bit his lips to avoid showing his emotion. "I think I remember something of him," he said, with a voice that sounded strangely calm in his own ears.

"A curious story," said Rex. "Amongst other matters, I dabbled a little in the Private Inquiry line of business, and the old man came to me. He had a son who had gone abroad, and he wanted particulars of him."

"Did you get them?"

"To a certain extent. I hunted him through Paris into Brussels, from Brussels to Antwerp, from Antwerp back to Paris. I lost him there. A miserable end to a long and expensive search. I got nothing but a portmanteau with a lot of letters from his mother. I sent the particulars to the ship-builder, and by all accounts the news killed him, for he died not long after."

"And the son?"

"Came to the queerest end of all. The old man had left him his fortune—a large one, I believe—but he'd left Europe, it seems, and was lost in the *Hydaspes*. Frere was his cousin."

"Ah!"

"By Gad, it annoys me when I think of it," continued Rex, feeling, by force of memory, once more the adventurer of fashion. "With the resources I had too! Oh, a miserable failure! The days and nights I've spent walking about looking for Richard Devine, and never catching a glimpse of him. The old man gave me his son's portrait, and I suppose I carried that ivory gimcrack in my breast for nearly three months, pulling it out to refresh my memory every half-hour. By Gad, if he was anything like his picture, I could have sworn to him if I'd met him in Timbuctoo."

"Do you think you'd know him again?" asked Rufus Dawes in a low voice, turning away his head.

There may have been something in the subdued eagerness of the tone, contrasting so strangely with the inconsequence of the theme, that caused John Rex's brain to perform one of those feats of automatic synthesis at which we afterwards wonder. The profligate son—the likeness to the portrait—the mystery of Dawes's life! These were the links of a galvanic chain. He closed the circuit, and a vivid flash revealed to him—THE MAN.

Warder Troke, coming up, put his hand on Rex's shoulder. "Dawes," he said, "you're wanted at the yard;" and then, seeing his mistake, added with a grin, "Curse you two; you're so much alike one can't tell t'other from which."

Rufus Dawes walked off moodily; but John Rex turned pale, and a strange hope made his heart leap.

"Gad, Troke's right, we are alike. *I'll not press him to escape any more.*"

The *Pretty Mary*—as ugly and evil-smelling a tub as ever pitched under a southerly burster—had been lying on and off Cape Surville for nearly three

RUNNING
THE
GAUNTLET

weeks. Captain Blunt was getting wearied. He made strenuous efforts to find the oyster-beds of which he was ostensibly in search, but with no success. In vain did he take boat and pull into every cove between the Hippolyte Reef and Schouten's Island. In vain did he run the *Pretty Mary* near to the rugged cliffs and make perpetual expeditions to the shore. He never found an oyster. "If I don't find something in three or four days more," said he to his mate, "I shall go back again. It's too dangerous cruising here."

On the same evening that Captain Blunt made this resolution, Jones, the watchman at Signal Hill, saw the arms of the semaphore at the settlement make three motions.

"By George, Harry," cried Jones, "there's a bolt!"

The semaphore signalled again.

"With arms!" Jones said, translating as he read. "Come here, Harry! here's a go!"

But Harry did not reply, and looking down, the watchman saw a dark figure suddenly fill the doorway. The boasted semaphore had failed *this* time at all events. The "bolters" had arrived as soon as the signal!

The man sprang at his carbine, but the intruder had already possessed himself of it. "It's no use making a fuss, Jones! There are eight of us. Oblige me by attending to your signals."

Jones knew the voice. It was that of John Rex. "Reply, can't you?" said Rex coolly. "Captain Burgess is in a hurry." The arms of the semaphore at the settlement were, in fact, gesticulating with comical vehemence.

Jones, with his signal-book open before him, was about to acknowledge the message, when Rex stopped him. "Send *this* message," he said. "NOT SEEN! SIGNAL SENT TO EAGLEHAWK!"

Jones paused irresolutely. He was himself a convict, and dreaded the cat that he knew would follow this false message. "If they find me out——" he said. Rex cocked the carbine with so decided a meaning that Jones began to signal eagerly. There came up a clinking of metal, and a murmur from below. "What's keeping yer, Dandy?"

"All right. Get those irons off, and then we'll talk, boys. I'm putting salt on old Burgess's tail." The rough jest was received with a roar, and Jones, looking momentarily down, saw, in the waning light, a group of men freeing themselves from their irons with a hammer taken from the guard house; while two, already freed, were casting buckets of water on the beacon wood-pile. The sentry was lying bound at a little distance.

"Now," said the leader of this surprise party, "signal to Woody Island." Jones perforce obeyed. "Say, 'AN ESCAPE AT THE MINES! WATCH ONE-TREE POINT! SEND ON TO EAGLEHAWK!' Quick now."

Jones—comprehending at once that this manoeuvre would distract attention from the Neck—executed the order with a grin. "You're a knowing one, Dandy Jack," said he.

John Rex acknowledged the compliment by uncocking the carbine. "Hold out your hands!—Jemmy Vetch!" "Ay, ay," replied the Crow, from beneath. "Come up and tie our friend Jones. Gabbett, have you got the axes?" "There's only one," said Gabbett with an oath. "Then bring that, and any tucker you can lay your hands on. Have you tied him? On we go then." And in the space of five minutes from the time when unsuspecting Harry had been surprised, the Signal Hill Station was deserted.

At the settlement Burgess was foaming. Nine men to seize the Long Bay boat, and get half-an-hour's start of the alarm-signal, was an unprecedented achievement! What could Warder Troke have been about! Warder Troke, however, found eight hours afterwards, disarmed, gagged and bound in the scrub, had been guilty of no negligence. How could he tell that the nine men he had taken to Stewart's Bay would "rush" him; and, before he could draw a pistol, truss him like a chicken? The worst of the gang, Rufus Dawes, had volunteered for the hated duties of pile-driving, and Troke had felt himself secure. How could he possibly guess that there was a plot, in which Rufus Dawes, of all men, had refused to join?

Constables, mounted and on foot, were despatched to scour the bush round the settlement. Burgess, confident that the alarm had been given at Eaglehawk Isthmus, promised himself the re-capture of the gang before many hours; and retired to dinner. His convict-servants had barely removed the soup when the result of John Rex's ingenuity became manifest.

The semaphore at Signal Hill had stopped working.

Burgess stamped with rage. "Get me my boat's crew ready; and tell the Mines to signal to Woody Island." As he stood on the jetty, a breathless messenger brought the reply. "A BOAT'S CREW GONE TO ONE-TREE POINT! FIVE MEN SENT FROM EAGLEHAWK IN OBEDIENCE TO ORDERS!" Burgess understood it at once. The fellows had decoyed the Eaglehawk guard. "Give way, men!" And the boat, shooting into the darkness, made for Long Bay. "I won't be far behind 'em," said the Commandant, "at any rate."

Between Eaglehawk and Signal Hill were, for the absconders, other
dangers. Along the indented coast of Port Bunche were four constables'
stations. These stations—mere huts within signalling distance of each
other—fringed the shore, and to avoid them it would be necessary to make a
circuit into the scrub. Unwilling as he was to lose time, John Rex saw that to
attempt to run the gauntlet of these four stations would be destruction. The
safety of the party depended upon the reaching of the Neck while the guard
was weakened by the absence of some of the men along the southern shore,
and before the alarm could be given from the eastern arm of the peninsula.
With this view, he ranged his men in single file, and made straight for the
Neck. The night had set in with a high westerly wind, and threatened rain.
It was pitch dark; and the fugitives were guided only by the dull roar of the
sea as it beat upon Descent Beach.

The Crow walked first, as guide, carrying a musket taken from Harry.
Then came Gabbett with the axe; followed by the other six, sharing between
them such provisions as they had obtained at Signal Hill. John Rex, with
the carbine, and Troke's pistols, walked last. It had been agreed that if
attacked they were to run each one his own way.

After nearly two hours of painful progress, Jemmy Vetch stopped, and
whispered them to approach. They were on a sandy rise. To the left was a
black object;—a constable's hut; to the right was a dim white line;—the
ocean; in front was a row of lamps, and between every two lamps leapt and
ran a dusky indistinct body. Jemmy Vetch pointed with his lean forefinger.

"The dogs!"

Instinctively they crouched down.

"Well, bo's," said Gabbett, "what's to be done now?"

As he spoke, a long low howl broke from one of the chained hounds, and
the whole kennel burst into hideous outcry.

John Rex, who perhaps was the bravest of the party, shuddered. "They
have smelt us," he said. "We must go on."

Gabbett spat in his palm, and took firmer hold of the axe-handle. "Right
you are," he said. "I'll leave my mark on some of them before this night's
out!"

On the opposite shore lights began to move, and the fugitives could hear
the hurrying tramp of feet.

"Make for the right-hand side of the jetty," said Rex in a fierce whisper. "I
think I see a boat there. It is our only chance now. We can never break
through the station. Are we ready? Now! All together!"

Gabbett was outstripping the others by some distance. There were eleven
dogs, two of whom were placed on stages set out in the water, and they were

so chained that their muzzles nearly touched. The giant leapt into the line, and with a blow of his axe split the skull of the beast on his right hand. This action unluckily took him within reach of the other dog, who seized him by the thigh.

"Fire!" cried McNab from the other side of the lamps.

The giant uttered a cry of rage and pain, and fell with the dog under him. It was, however, the dog who had pulled him down, and the musket-ball intended for him struck Travers in the jaw. The unhappy villain fell—like Virgil's Dares—"spitting blood, teeth, and curses."

Gabbett clutched the mastiff's throat with iron hand, and forced him to loose his hold; then bellowing with fury, seized his axe and sprang forward, mangled as he was, upon the nearest soldier. Jemmy Vetch had been beforehand with him. Uttering a low snarl of hate, he fired, and shot the sentry through the breast. The others rushed through the now broken cordon, and made headlong for the boat.

"Fools!" cried Rex behind them. "You have wasted a shot! Look to your left!"

Burgess had tarried at Signal Hill only long enough to loose the surprised guard from their bonds, and taking the Woody Island boat was pulling with a fresh crew to the Neck. The reinforcement was not ten yards from the jetty.

The Crow saw the danger, and flinging himself into the water, desperately seized McNab's boat.

"In with you for your lives!" he cried.

Another volley from the guard spattered the water around the fugitives, but in the darkness the ill-aimed bullets fell harmless. Gabbett swung himself over the sheets and seized an oar.

"Cox, Bodenham, Greenhill! Now, push her off! Jump, Tom, jump!" and as Burgess leapt to land, Cornelius was dragged over the stern, and the whale-boat floated into deep water.

McNab, seeing this, ran down to the water side to aid the Commandant.

"Lift her over the Bar, men!" he shouted. "With a will—So!" And raised in twelve strong arms, the pursuing craft slid across the isthmus.

"We've five minutes' start," said Vetch, coolly, as he saw the Commandant take his place in the stern sheets. "Pull away, my jolly boys, and we'll best 'em yet."

The soldiers on the Neck fired again almost at random, but the blaze of their pieces only served to show the Commandant's boat a hundred yards astern of that of the mutineers, which had already gained the deep water of Pirates' Bay.

Then, for the first time, the six prisoners became aware that John Rex was not among them.

John Rex had put into execution the first part of his scheme. At the moment when, seeing Burgess's boat near the sand-pit, he had uttered the warning

IN THE NIGHT

cry heard by Vetch, he turned back into the darkness, and made for the water's edge at a point some distance from the Neck. His desperate hope was that, the attention of the guard being concentrated on the escaping boat, he might, favoured by the darkness and the confusion—*swim* to the peninsula. Once safe on the peninsula, his plans were formed.

But, owing to the incoming tide upon the isthmus, it was necessary for him to attain some point sufficiently far to the south to enable him to be assisted, not impeded, by the current. With this view, he hurried over the sandy hummocks at the entrance to the Neck, and ran backwards towards the sea. In a few strides he had gained the shore, and, pausing to listen, heard behind him the sound of footsteps. He was pursued. The footsteps stopped, and then a voice cried:

"Surrender!"

It was McNab, who, seeing Rex's retreat, had followed him. John Rex drew from his breast Troke's pistol and waited.

"Surrender!" cried the voice again, and the footsteps advanced.

At the instant that Rex raised the weapon to fire, a vivid flash of lightning over the ocean showed him two boats, the hindermost one apparently within a few yards of him. The men looked like corpses. In the distance rose Cape Surville, and beneath Cape Surville was the hungry sea. The scene vanished in an instant, but the shock it gave him made him miss his aim, and flinging away the pistol with a curse, he turned and fled. McNab followed.

The path had been made by frequent passage from the Station, and Rex found it tolerably easy running. He had acquired—like most men who live much in the dark—that cat-like perception of obstacles, which is due rather to increased sensitiveness of touch than increased acuteness of vision. His pursuer was not so fortunate. Twice did John Rex laugh mentally, at a crash and scramble that told of a fall, and once—in a valley where trickled a little stream that he had cleared almost without an effort—he heard a splash that made him laugh outright. The track now began to go uphill, and Rex redoubled his efforts, then paused to listen. The crashing of branches behind him had ceased, and it seemed that he was alone.

He had gained the summit of the cliff. The lights of the Neck were invisible. Below him lay the sea. From the north side of the bay was borne the hoarse roar of the breakers as they dashed against the perpendicular cliffs which guarded Forrestier's Peninsula. At his feet arose a frightful shrieking and whistling, broken at intervals by reports like claps of thunder.

Where was he? Exhausted and breathless, he sank down into the rough scrub and listened. All at once he heard a sound that made him bound to his feet in deadly fear—the bay of a dog!

He thrust his hand to his breast for the remaining pistol, and uttered a cry of alarm. He had dropped it. Sweat began to run down his face. With staring eyeballs he stared into the darkness, as if he would dissipate it by the very intensity of his gaze. The noise was repeated, and seemed to be close at hand. He heard a man's voice cheering the dog in accents that the gale blew away from him before he could recognise them. It was probable that some of the soldiers had been sent to the assistance of McNab. Capture, then, was certain. The dog, crashing through the underwood, gave one short, sharp howl, and then ran mute.

The darkness had increased with the gale, the white and raging waters were blotted out by a dark mist, and even the lightning seemed unable to penetrate its intensity. A large, warm drop of rain fell upon Rex's outstretched hand, and far overhead rumbled a wrathful peal of thunder. The shrieking which he had heard a few moments ago had ceased, but every now and then immense shocks reverberated around him, and shook the ground where he stood. He looked towards the ocean and a tall misty Form—white against the all-pervading blackness—beckoned and bowed to him. He saw it distinctly for an instant, and then it sank and vanished. Maddened with a terror he could not define, the hunted man turned to meet the material peril that was so close at hand.

With a ferocious gasp, the dog flung himself upon him. John Rex was borne backwards, but, in his desperation, he clutched the beast by the throat, and exerting all his strength, flung him off. The brute uttered one howl, and seemed to lie where he had fallen; while above his carcass again hovered that white and vaporous column. It was strange that McNab and the soldier did not follow up the advantage they had gained. With a thrill of renewed hope, he ran forward. A few steps more, and he should gain the summit of the cliff. He could *feel* the sea roaring in front of him in the gloom. The column disappeared; and in a lull of wind, uprose from the place where it had been, such a hideous medley of shrieks, laughter, and exultant wrath, that John Rex paused in horror. Too late.

The ground gave way—it seemed—beneath his feet. He was falling—clutching, in vain, at rocks, shrubs, and grass. The cloud-curtain lifted, and by the lightning that leaped and played about the ocean, John Rex found an explanation of his terrors, more terrible than they themselves had been. The track he had followed led to that portion of the cliff in which the sea had excavated the tunnel-spout known as the Devil's Blow-Hole.

Clinging to a tree that, growing half way down the precipice, had arrested his course, he stared into the abyss. Before him—already high above his head—was a gigantic arch of cliff. Through this arch he saw, at an immense distance below him, the raging ocean. Beneath him was an abyss splintered with black rocks and tortured water. Suddenly the bottom of this abyss seemed to advance to meet him; the chasm belched a volume of leaping, curling water, which mounted to drown him. Was it fancy that showed him, on the surface of the rising column, the mangled carcass of the dog?

The chasm into which John Rex had fallen was shaped like a huge funnel set up on its narrow end. The sides of this funnel were rugged rock, and in the banks of earth lodged here and there upon projections, a scrubby vegetation grew. The scanty growth paused abruptly half way down the gulf, and the rock below was perpetually damp from the upthrown spray. Accident had lodged him on the lowest of these banks of earth. In calm weather he would have been out of danger, but the lightning flash revealed a black patch of dripping rock some ten feet above his head. It was evident that upon the next rising of the water-spout the place where he stood would be covered with water.

The roaring column mounted swiftly. Rex felt it rush at him and swing him upward. With both arms round the tree, he clutched the sleeves of his jacket with either hand. Perhaps if he could maintain his hold he might out-live the shock of that suffocating torrent. He felt his feet rudely seized, as though by the hand of a giant, and plucked upwards. Water gurgled in his ears. His arms seemed about to be torn from their sockets. Had the strain lasted another instant, he must have loosed his hold; but then the column sank, and left him gasping, half drowned, but alive.

It was impossible that he could survive another shock, and he unclasped his stiffened fingers, determined to resign himself to his fate. At that instant, however, he saw on his right hand a red and lurid light, in the midst of which fantastically bobbed hither and thither the gigantic shadow of a man. He cast his eyes upwards and saw, slowly descending into the gulf, a blazing bush tied to a rope. McNab was taking advantage of the pause in the spouting to examine the sides of the Blow-hole.

A despairing hope seized John Rex. In another instant the light would reveal his figure, clinging like a limpet to the rock, to those above. He must be detected in any case; but if they could lower the rope quickly, he might be saved. His dread of the horrible death that was beneath him overcame his resolution to avoid recapture. He had already drawn in his breath for a shout which should make itself heard above the roar of the wind and water, when a strange appearance on the face of the cliff made him pause.

About six feet from him—glowing like gold in the light cast by the burning tree—a stream of water slipped from the rock into the darkness, like a serpent from its hole. Above this stream a dark spot defied the torchlight, and John Rex comprehended that close to him was one of those tortuous caves which is carved by the worm-like action of the sea. The stream ceased to let itself out of its crevice; it was then likely, he realised, that the rising column of water did not penetrate far into this wonderful hiding-place.

Endowed with a wisdom which in a less desperate situation would have been madness, John Rex shouted to his pursuers, "The rope! the rope!" The words, projected against the sides of the enormous funnel, were pitched high above the blast, and, reduplicated by a thousand echoes, reached the ears of those above.

"He's alive!" cried McNab, peering into the abyss. "I see him. Look!"

The soldier whipped the end of the bullock-hide lariat round the tree to which he held, and began to oscillate it, so that the blazing bush might reach the ledge on to which convict clung. The groan which preceded the fierce belching forth of the torrent was cast up to them from below.

"God be gude to the puir felly!" said the pious young Scotchman, catching his breath.

A white spume was visible at the bottom of the gulf, and John Rex, eyeing the blazing pendulum, looked up to the black heaven for the last time, with a muttered prayer. The bush—the flame fanned by the motion—flung a crimson glow upon his frowning features. "Slack out! Slack out!" he cried; and then, drawing the burning bush towards him, attempted to stamp out the fire with his feet.

The soldier set his body against the tree trunk, and gripped the rope hard, turning his head away from the pit below. "Hold tight," he muttered to McNab. "She's coming!"

The groan changed into a roar, and with a gust of wind and spray, the seething sea leapt up out of the gulf.

John Rex, unable to extinguish the flame, twisted his arm about the rope, and the instant before the surface of the rising water made a momentary floor to the mouth of the cavern, he flung himself across the chasm. He had already clutched the rock, and thrust himself forward, when the tremendous volume of water struck him. McNab and the soldier felt the sudden pluck of the rope and saw the light swing across the abyss. Then the fury of the waterspout burst with a triumphant scream, the tension ceased, the light was blotted out, and when the column sank, there dangled at the end of the lariat nothing but the drenched and blackened skeleton of the she-oak bough. At their feet was the black abyss of the Blow-hole—empty.

They pulled up the useless rope in silence.

"God rest his puir soul," said McNab, shuddering. "He's oot o' our han's."

THE FLIGHT

Gabbett, guided by the Crow, had determined to beach the captured boat on the southern point of Cape Surville. Nothing but the desperate nature of the attempt could have justified so desperate a measure. The perpendicular cliffs seemed to promise certain destruction; but Vetch, who had been employed in building the pier at the Neck, knew that on the southern point of the promontory was a strip of beach upon which the company might, by good fortune, land in safety. The Crow determined at once that in their desperate plight this was the only measure, and setting his teeth as he seized the oar that served as a rudder, put the boat's head straight for the huge rock that formed the northern horn of Pirates' Bay.

Save for the faint phosphorescent radiance of the foaming waves, the darkness was intense, and Burgess for some minutes pulled almost at random in pursuit. Then the same flash of lightning which had saved the life of McNab, by causing Rex to miss his aim, showed to the Commandant the whale-boat balanced on the summit of an enormous wave, and apparently about to be flung against the wall of rock. The next instant the boat glided down into the depths, and the whole phantasmagoria was swallowed up in the tumultuous darkness of the tempest.

Burgess—his hair bristling with terror—shouted to put the guard-boat about, but he might with as much reason have shouted at an avalanche. The wind blew his voice away, and a snarling billow jerked the oar from his hand. Despite the desperate efforts of the soldiers, the boat was whirled up the mountain of water like a leaf on a water-spout, and a second flash of lightning showed them what seemed a group of dolls struggling in the water, and a walnut-shell bottom upwards driven by the recoil of the waves towards them.

For an instant all thought that they must share the fate which had overtaken the unlucky convicts; but Burgess succeeded in trimming the boat, and awed by the peril he had so narrowly escaped, gave the order to return. As the men set the boat's head to the welcome line of lights that marked the Neck, a black spot balanced upon a black line was swept under their stern and carried out to the sea. As it swooped past them, this black spot emitted a cry, and they knew that it was one of the shattered boat's crew clinging to an oar.

"He was the only one of 'em alive," said Burgess, bandaging his sprained wrist two hours afterwards at the Neck, "and he's food for the fishes by this time!"

He was mistaken, however. Aided by the lightning, Vetch had managed to bring the boat close enough to the shore for the party, bruised and bleeding, to struggle towards safety. Of all this number only Cox was lost. He was pulling stroke-oar, and being something of a laggard, stood in the way of the Crow, who, seeing the importance of haste in preserving his own skin, plucked the man backwards by the collar, and passed over his sprawling body to the shore.

Cox, grasping at anything to save himself, clutched an oar, and the next moment found himself borne out with the overturned whale-boat by the under-tow. He was drifted past the guard-boat with a velocity that forbade all attempts at rescue, and almost before the poor scoundrel had time to realise his condition, he was in the best possible way of escaping the hanging that his comrades had so often humorously prophesied for him. Being a strong and vigorous villain, however, he clung tenaciously to his oar, and unbuckling his leather belt, passed it round the slip of wood that was his salvation, girding himself to it as firmly as he was able. In this condition, he was descried by the helmsman of the *Pretty Mary*, a few miles from Cape Surville, at daylight next morning.

Blunt, with a wild hope that this stray might be the lover of Sarah Purfoy, *dead*, lowered a boat and picked him up. Nearly bisected by the belt, gorged with salt water, and frozen with cold, the victim of Vetch's murderous quickness retained sufficient life to survive Blunt's remedies for nearly two hours. During that time he stated that his name was Cox, that he had escaped from Port Arthur with eight others, that John Rex was the leader of the expedition, that the others were all drowned, and that he believed John Rex had been retaken. Having placed Blunt in possession of these particulars, he further cursed Jemmy Vetch, the settlement, and the sea, and so impenitently died.

Blunt smoked three pipes, and then altered the course of the *Pretty Mary* and ran for the coast. It was possible that the man for whom he was searching had not been retaken, and was now awaiting his arrival.

"I'll take one more look along," said he to himself.

The *Pretty Mary*, hugging the coast as closely as she dared, crawled in the thin breeze all day, and saw nothing. It would be madness to land at Cape Surville, for the whole station would be on the alert; so Blunt, as night was falling, stood off a little across the mouth of Pirates' Bay. He was walking the deck, groaning at the folly of the expedition, when a strange appearance on the southern horn of the bay made him come to a sudden halt. There was a furnace blazing in the bowels of the mountain! Blunt rubbed his eyes and called to the man at the helm.

"Do you see anything yonder, Jem?"

Jem—a Sydney man, who had never been round that coast before—briefly remarked, "Lighthouse."

Blunt stumped into the cabin and got out his charts. No lighthouse was laid down there, only a mark like an anchor, and a note, "Remarkable Hole at this Point." A remarkable hole indeed, he thought.

Blunt called up his mate, William Staples, a fellow whom Sarah Purfoy's gold had bought body and soul. Staples looked at the glow for a while, and then said, in tones trembling with greed, "It's a fire. Lie to, and lower away the jolly-boat. That's our bird for a thousand pounds!"

The *Pretty Mary* shortened sail, and Blunt and Staples got into the jolly-boat.

"Goin' a hoysterin', sir?" said one of the crew, with a grin, as Blunt threw a bundle into the stern-sheets.

Staples thrust his tongue into his cheek. The object of the voyage was now pretty well understood among the carefully picked crew. Blunt had not chosen men who were likely to betray him, though, for that matter, Rex had suggested a precaution which rendered betrayal almost impossible.

"What's in the bundle, old man?" asked Will Staples, after they had got clear of the ship.

"Clothes," returned Blunt. "We can't bring him off, if it *is* him, in his canaries. He puts on these duds, d'ye see, sinks Her Majesty's livery, and comes aboard, a 'shipwrecked mariner.'"

"That's well thought of. Madam's notion, I'll be bound."

"Ay."

"She's a knowing one."

And his sinister laughter floated across the violet water.

"Go easy, man," said Blunt, as they neared the shore. "They're all awake at Eaglehawk; and if those cursed dogs give tongue, there'll be a boat out in a twinkling."

Staples lay on his oar and listened. The night was moonless, and the ship had already disappeared from view. They were approaching the promontory from the south-east, and the isthmus of the guarded Neck was hidden by the outlying cliff. In the south-western angle of this cliff, about midway between the summit and the sea, was an arch, which vomited a red light that faintly shone upon the sea in the track of the boat. The light was lambent and uncertain, now sinking almost into insignificance, and now leaping up with a fierceness that caused a deep glow to throb in the very heart of the mountain. Sometimes a black figure would pass across this gigantic furnace-mouth, stooping and rising, as though feeding the fire. One might have imagined that a door in Vulcan's Smithy had been left inadvertently open, and that the old hero was forging arms for a demigod.

Blunt turned pale. "It's no mortal," he whispered. "Let's go back."

"And what will Madam say?" returned dare-devil Will Staples, who would have plunged into Mount Erebus had he been paid for it. Thus appealed to in the name of his ruling passion, Blunt turned his head and the boat sped onward.

THE WORK OF THE SEA

The lift of the water-spout had saved John Rex's life. At the moment when it struck him he was on his hands and knees at the entrance of the cavern. The wave, gushing upwards, at the same time expanded laterally, and this lateral force drove him into the mouth of the passage. For some seconds he was rolled over and over, the rush of water wedging him at length into a crevice between two enormous stones, which overhung a still more formidable abyss. It was evident that the two stones acted as breakwaters to the torrent poured in from the outside, and repelled the main body of the stream in the fashion he had observed from his position on the ledge. In a few seconds the cavern was empty.

Painfully extricating himself, and feeling as yet doubtful of his safety, John Rex essayed to climb the twin blocks that barred the unknown depths below him. The first movement he made caused him to shriek aloud. His left arm—with which he clung to the rope—hung powerless. Ground against the ragged entrance, it was momentarily paralysed. For an instant he sank despairingly on the wet floor of the cave; then a gurgling beneath his feet warned him of the approaching torrent, and collecting all his energies, he scrambled up the incline. Though nigh fainting with pain and exhaustion, he pressed desperately higher and higher. He heard the hideous shriek of the whirlpool which was beneath him grow louder and louder. He saw the darkness grow darker as the rising water-spout covered the mouth of the cave. He felt the salt spray sting his face, and the wrathful tide lick the hand that hung over the shelf on which he fell. But that was all. He was out of danger at last! And as the thought blessed his senses, his eyes closed, and the exhausted wretch fell into a stupor.

When he awoke the cavern was filed with the soft light of dawn. Raising his eyes, he beheld, high above his head, a roof of rock, on which the reflection of the sunbeams, playing upwards through a pool of water, cast flickering colours. On his right hand was the mouth of the cave, on his left a terrific abyss, at the bottom of which he could hear the sea faintly lapping and washing.

He raised himself and stretched his stiffened limbs. It was imperative that he should bestir himself. He knew not if his escape had been noticed, or if the cavern had another inlet, by which McNab returning might penetrate. Moreover, he was wet and famished.

He examined the crevice by which he had entered. It was shaped like an irregular triangle, hollowed at the base by the action of the water forced into it by the stormy sea. John Rex dared not crawl too near the edge, lest he should slide out of the damp and slippery orifice, and be dashed upon the rocks at the bottom of the Blow-hole. Craning his neck, he could see, a hundred feet below him, the sullenly frothing water occasionally leaping upwards. It was impossible to get down that way. He turned back into the cavern, and began to explore in that direction

The twin-rocks against which he had been hurled were, in fact, pillars which supported the roof of his hiding place. Beyond them lay emptiness, faintly illumined by the sea-light cast up through the bottom of the gulf. The immense promontory, which, viewed from the outside, seemed as solid as a mountain, was in reality split into a thousand fissures by the unsuspected action of the sea for centuries. The Blow-hole was but an insignificant cranny compared with this enormous chasm.

Descending with difficulty the steep incline, he found himself on the brink of a gallery of rock, which bore on its moist and weed-bearded edges signs of submersion. It must be low tide without, he realised. John Rex crept round the projection of the gallery, and passed at once from dimness to daylight. There was a broad loop-hole in the side of the honey-combed and wave-perforated cliff. The cloudless heaven expanded above him; a fresh breeze kissed his cheek, and sixty feet below him, the sea sparkled in myriad wavelets.

He turned from the opening, and prepared to descend still farther into the rocky pathway. The sunshine had revived and cheered him, but fine weather would be an additional inducement to McNab and Burgess to satisfy themselves as to the fate of their late prisoner. It grew darker as he descended, and twice he almost turned back in dread of the gulfs on either side of him. It seemed to him, also, that the gullet of weed-clad rock through which he was crawling doubled upon itself, and led only into the bowels of the mountain. Gnawed by hunger, and conscious that in a few hours the rising tide would fill the subterranean passage and cut off his retreat, he pushed desperately onwards, looking for egress onto the rocky shore. He had descended some ninety feet when he was rewarded by a glimpse of sunshine striking upwards. He parted two enormous masses of seaweed, whose bubble-beaded fronds hung curtainwise across his path, and found himself in the very middle of the narrow cleft of rock through which the sea was driven to the Blow-hole.

The narrow strip of rock at the base of the cliff was as flat as a table. Here and there were enormous hollows, which the retreating tide had left full of clear, still water. The crannies of the rocks were inhabited by small white crabs, and John Rex found to his delight that there was on this little shelf abundance of mussels, which, though lean and acrid, were sufficiently grateful to his famished stomach. Attached to the flat surfaces of the numerous stones, moreover, were coarse limpets. These, however, John Rex found too salt to be palatable, and was compelled to reject them. A larger variety, however, having a succulent body as thick as a man's thumb, contained in long razor-shaped shells, were in some degree free from this objection, and he soon collected the materials for a meal.

Having eaten and sunned himself, he began to examine the enormous rock, to the base of which he had so strangely penetrated. Rugged and worn, it raised its huge breast against wind and wave, secure upon a broad pedestal, which probably extended as far beneath the sea as the massive column itself rose above it. Standing upon the broad platform where surely no human foot but his had ever stood in life, the convict saw many feet above him, pitched into a cavity of the huge sun-blistered boulders, an object which his sailor eye told him at once was part of the top hamper of some large ship. Crusted with shells, and its ruin so overrun with the ivy of the ocean, that its ropes could barely be distinguished from the weeds with which they were encumbered, this relic of human labour attested to some past tragedy when a doomed vessel, with her crew of shrieking souls, had splintered and gone down upon the giant rock.

John Rex, however, gazing up at this memento of a forgotten agony, felt a sensation of the most vulgar pleasure. "There's wood for my fire!" thought he, and mounting to the spot, he essayed to fling down the splinters of timber upon the platform. Long exposed to the sun, the timber had dried to the condition of touch-wood, and would burn fiercely. It was precisely what he required.

Striking the disintegrated mass with his iron-shod heel, John Rex broke off convenient portions; and making a bag of his shirt by tying the sleeves and neck, he was speedily staggering into the cavern with a supply of fuel. He made two trips, flinging down the wood in the floor of the gallery that overlooked the sea, and was returning for a third, when his quick ear caught the dip of oars. He had barely time to lift the sea-weed curtain that veiled the entrance to the chasm, when the Eaglehawk boat rounded the promontory.

Burgess was in the stern-sheets, and seemed to be making signals to some one on the top of the cliff. Rex, grinning behind his veil, divined the manoeuvre. McNab and his party were to search above, while the Commandant examined the gulf below. The boat headed direct for the passage, and, for an instant, John Rex's undaunted soul shivered at the thought that, perhaps after all, his pursuers might be aware of the existence of the cavern. Yet that was unlikely. He kept his ground, and the boat passed within a foot of him, gliding silently into the gulf. He observed that Burgess's usually florid face was pale, and that his left sleeve was cut open, showing a bandage on the arm. There had been some fighting, then, and it was not unlikely that his fellow-desperadoes had been captured! He chuckled at his own ingenuity and good sense. The boat, emerging from the arch-way, entered the pool of the Blow-hole, and, held with the full strength of the party, remained stationary. John Rex watched Burgess scan the rocks and eddies, saw him signal to McNab, and then, with much relief, beheld the boat's head brought round to the sea-board.

His gaolers were convinced of his death, and would search for him no more. So far, so good. Now for the last desperate venture—the escape from the wonderful cavern which was at once his shelter and his prison. Piling his wood together, and succeeding after many efforts, by aid of a flint and the ring which yet clung to his ankle, in lighting a fire, and warming his chilled limbs in its cheering blaze, he set himself to meditate upon his course of action. He was safe for the present, and the supply of food that the rock afforded was amply sufficient for many days, but it was impossible that he could remain for many days concealed. He had no fresh water, and the salt and acrid mussels had induced a raging thirst, which he could not alleviate. It was imperative that within forty-eight hours at farthest he should be on his way to the peninsula. He remembered the little stream into which—in his flight of the previous night—he had so nearly fallen, and hoped, under cover of the darkness, to steal round the reef and reach it unobserved. His desperate scheme was to run the gauntlet of the dogs and guards, gain the peninsula, and await the rescuing vessel. He confessed to himself that the chances were terribly against him.

If Gabbett and the others had been recaptured—as he devoutly trusted—the coast would be comparatively clear; but if they had escaped, he knew Burgess too well to think that he would give up the chase while hope of taking the absconders remained to him. If indeed all fell out as he had wished, he had still to sustain life until Blunt found him—if haply Blunt had not already departed, wearied with waiting.

As night came on, and the firelight showed strange shadows waving from the corners of the enormous vault, while the dismal abysses beneath him murmured and muttered, John Rex tried to drive away his gloomy thoughts by sketching out for himself a plan of action—but in vain. In vain he strove to picture in its completeness that—as yet vague—design by which he had promised himself to wrest from the vanished son of the wealthy ship-builder his name and heritage. His mind, filled with forebodings, could not give to the subject the calm consideration which it needed. In the midst of his schemes for the baffling of the jealous love of the woman who was to save him, and the getting to England, in ship-wrecked and foreign guise, as the long-lost heir to the fortune of Sir Richard Devine, there arose ghastly shapes of death and horror.

He heaped fresh wood upon his fire, that the bright light might drive out the gruesome things that lurked above, below, and around him. He became afraid to look behind him, lest some shapeless mass of mid-sea birth—some voracious polype, with far-reaching arms and jellied mouth ever open to devour—might slide up over the edge of the dripping caves below, and fasten upon him in the darkness. All creatures that could be engendered by slime and salt crept forth into the firelight to stare at him. Bloodless and bladdery things ran hither and thither noiselessly. Strange carapaces crawled from out of the rocks. All the horrible unseen life of the ocean seemed to be rising up and surrounding him. He retreated to the brink of the gulf, and the glare of the upheld brand fell upon a rounded hummock, whose coronal of silky weed out-floating in the water looked like the head of a drowned man. He rushed to the entrance of the gallery, and his shadow, thrown into the opening, took the shape of an avenging phantom, with arms upraised to warn him back.

The naturalist, the explorer, or the ship-wrecked seaman would have found nothing frightful in this exhibition of the harmless life of the Australian ocean. But the convict's guilty conscience, long suppressed and derided, asserted itself in this hour when it was alone with Nature and Night. The bitter intellectual power which had so long supported him succumbed beneath imagination—the unconscious religion of the soul. If ever he was nigh repentance it was then. Phantoms of his past crimes gibbered at him, and covering his eyes with his hands, he fell shuddering upon his knees. The brand, loosening from his grasp, dropped into the gulf, and was extinguished with a hissing noise. As if the sound had called up some spirit that lurked below, a whisper ran through the cavern.

"John Rex!"

The hair of the convict's flesh stood up, and he cowered to the earth.

"John Rex!"

It was a *human* voice! Whether of friend or enemy he did not pause to think.

His terror over-mastered all other considerations.

"Here! here!" he cried, and sprang to the opening of the vault.

Arrived at the foot of the cliff, Blunt and Staples found themselves in almost complete darkness for the light of the mysterious fire, which had hitherto guided them, had necessarily disappeared. Calm as was the night, the sea yet ran with dangerous strength through the channel which led to the Blow-hole; and Blunt, instinctively feeling the boat drawn towards some unknown peril, held off the shelf of rocks out of reach of the current. A sudden flash of fire, as from a flourished brand, burst out above them, and floating downwards through the darkness came an atom of burning wood. Surely no one but a hunted man would lurk in such a retreat.

Blunt determined to risk all upon one venture. "John Rex!" he shouted up through his rounded hands. The light flashed again at the eye-hole of the mountain, and on the point above them appeared a wild figure.

"Here! here!" cried Rex, his voice shrill.

"The poor devil seems half-crazy," said Will Staples, under his breath; and then aloud, "We're friends!"

The terrors which had oppressed John Rex disappeared in human presence, and the villain's coolness returned. Kneeling on the rock platform, he held parley.

"It is impossible for me to come down now," he said. "The tide covers the only way out of the cavern."

"Can't you dive through it?" said Will Staples.

"No, nor you neither," said Rex, shuddering at the thought of trusting himself to that horrible whirlpool.

"What's to be done? You can't come down that *wall*."

"Wait until morning," returned Rex coolly. "It will be dead low tide at seven o'clock. You must send a boat at six, or thereabouts. It will be low enough for me to get out, I dare say, by that time."

"But the Guard?"

"——Won't come here, my man. They've got their work to do in watching the Neck and exploring after my mates. They won't come here. Besides, I'm dead."

"Dead!"

"Thought to be so, which is as well—better for me, perhaps. If they don't see your ship, or your boat, you're safe enough."

"Well," says Blunt, "I'll try it."

"You wouldn't like to stop here till morning? It is rather lonely," suggested Rex, making a jest of his late terrors.

Will Staples laughed. "You're a bold boy!" said he. "We'll come at daybreak."

"Have you got the clothes as I directed?"

"Yes."

"Then good-night. I'll put my fire out, in case somebody else might see it, who wouldn't be as kind as you are."

"Good-night."

"Not a word for the Madam," said Staples, when they reached the vessel.

"Not a word, the ungrateful dog," assented Blunt; adding, with some heat, "That's the way with women. They'll go through fire and water for a man that doesn't care a snap of his fingers for 'em; but for any poor fellow who risks his neck to pleasure 'em they've nothing but sneers! I wish I'd never meddled in the business."

"There are no fools like old fools," thought Will Staples, but he did not utter his thoughts aloud.

At eight o'clock the next morning the *Pretty Mary* stood out to sea with every stitch of canvas set, alow and aloft. The skipper's fishing had come to an end. He had caught a ship-wrecked seaman, who had been brought on board at daylight, and was then at breakfast in the cabin. The crew winked at each other when the haggard mariner, attired in garments that seemed remarkably well preserved, mounted the side. But they, none of them, were in a position to controvert the skipper's statement.

"Where are we bound for?" asked John Rex, smoking Staples' pipe in lingering puffs of delight. "I'm entirely in your hands, my worthy Blunt."

"My orders are to cruise about the whaling grounds until I meet my consort," returned Blunt, sullenly, "and put you aboard her. She'll take you back to Sydney. I'm victualled for a twelvemonth's trip."

"Right!" cried Rex, clapping his preserver on the back. "I'm bound to get to Sydney somehow; but, as the Philistines are abroad, I may as well tarry in Jericho till my beard be grown. Don't stare at my scriptural quotation,

Mr. Staples," he added. "I assure you that I've had the very best religious instruction. Indeed, it is chiefly owing to my worthy spiritual pastor and master that I am enabled to smoke this very villainous tobacco of yours at the present moment!"

It was not until they had scrambled up the beach to safety that the absconders became fully aware of the loss of another of their companions.

THE VALLEY OF THE SHADOW OF DEATH

As they stood on the break of the beach, Gabbett, counting their number, missed the stroke oar.

"Where's Cox?"

"The fool fell overboard," said Jemmy Vetch, shortly. "He never had much sense in that skull of his."

Gabbett scowled. "That's three of us gone," he said, in the tones of a man suffering some personal injury.

They summed up their means of defence against attack. Sanders and Greenhill had knives. Gabbett still retained the axe in his belt. Vetch had dropped his musket at the Neck; and Bodenham and Cornelius were unarmed.

"Let's have a look at the tucker," said Vetch.

There was one bag of provisions. It contained a piece of salt pork, two loaves, and some uncooked potatoes. Signal Hill Station was not rich in edibles.

"That ain't much," said Crow. "Is it, Gabbett?"

"It must do, any way," returned the giant carelessly.

The six proceeded up the shore, and camped under a rock. Bodenham was for lighting a fire, but Vetch, who by tacit consent had been chosen leader of the expedition, forbade it, saying that the light might betray them. So all that night the miserable wretches crouched fireless together.

Morning breaks clear and bright, and—free for the first time in ten years—they comprehend that their terrible journey has begun. "Where are we to go? How are we to live?" asks Bodenham, scanning the barren bush that stretches to the barren sea. "Gabbett, you've been out before—how's it done?"

"We'll make the shepherds' huts, and live on their tucker till we get a change o' clothes," said Gabbett. "We can follow the coast line."

"Steady, lads," said prudent Vetch; "we must sneak round yon sandhills, and so creep into the scrub. If they've a good glass at the Neck, they can see us."

Vetch divides the provisions, and they travel all that day until dark night. The scrub is prickly and dense. Their clothes are torn, their hands and feet bleeding. Already they feel wearied. No one pursuing, they light a fire and sleep. The second day they come to a sandy spit that runs out into the sea, and find that they have got too far to the eastward, and must follow the shore line to East Bay Neck. Back through the scrub they drag their heavy feet. That night they eat the last crumb of the loaf. The third day, at noon, they see the upper link of the earring, the isthmus of East Bay Neck, at their feet. Passing the isthmus, they strike into the bush along the shore, and tightening their belts over their gnawing bellies, camp under some low-lying hills.

The fourth day is notable for the indisposition of Bodenham, who is a bad walker, and falling behind, delays the party by frequent cooeys. Gabbett threatens him with a worse fate than sore feet if he lingers. That evening Greenhill espies a hut, but not trusting to the friendship of the occupant, they wait until he quits it in the morning, and then send Vetch to forage. Vetch returns bending under half a bag of flour.

"You'd better carry the flour," said he to Gabbett, "and give me the axe." Gabbett eyes him for a while, as if struck by his puny form, but finally gives the axe to his mate Sanders. That day they creep cautiously along between the sea and the hills, camping at a creek. Vetch, after much search, finds a handful of berries, and adds them to the main stock. Half of this handful is eaten at once, the other half reserved for "to-morrow." That evening they reach the camping ground by twos and threes; and each wonders—between the paroxysms of hunger—if his face is as haggard, and his eyes as bloodshot, as those of his neighbour.

On the seventh day, Bodenham says his feet are so bad he can't walk, and Greenhill, with a greedy look at the berries, bids him stay behind. Being in a very weak condition he takes his companion at his word, and drops off about noon the next day. Gabbett, discovering this defection, however, goes back, and in an hour or so appears, driving the wretched creature before him with blows, as a sheep is driven to the shambles. Greenhill remonstrates at another mouth being thus forced upon the party, but the giant silences him with a hideous glance. Jemmy Vetch remembers that Greenhill accompanied Gabbett once before, and feels uncomfortable. He gives hint of his suspicions to Sanders, but Sanders only laughs. It is horribly evident that there is an understanding among the three.

The ninth sun of their freedom, rising upon sandy and barren hillocks, bristling thick with cruel scrub, sees the six famine-stricken wretches cursing their God, and yet afraid to die. All around is the fruitless, shadeless, shelterless bush. Above, the pitiless heaven. It the distance, the remorseless sea. Vetch suggests that Oyster Bay cannot be far to the eastward—the line of ocean is deceitfully close—and though it is out of their course, they resolve to make for it. After hobbling five miles, they seem no nearer than before, and, nigh dead with fatigue and starvation, sink despairingly upon the ground.

On the tenth day Bodenham refuses to stir, and the others, being scarce able to drag along their limbs, sit on the ground about him. Greenhill, eyeing the prostrate figure, said, slowly, "I am so weak that I could eat a piece of a man."

Vetch, hearing his comrade give utterance to a thought all had secretly cherished, speaks out, crying, "It would be murder to do it, and then, perhaps we couldn't eat it."

"Oh," said Gabbett, with a grin, "I'll warrant you that, but you must all have a hand in it."

Gabbett, Sanders, and Greenhill then go aside, and presently Sanders, coming to the Crow, said, "He consented to act as flogger. He deserves it."

"So did Gabbett, for that matter," shudders Vetch.

"Ay, but Bodenham's feet are sore," said Sanders, "and 'tis a pity to leave him."

Having no fire, they made a little breakwind; and Vetch, half-dozing behind this at about three in the morning, hears some one cry out "Christ!" and awakes, sweating ice.

No one but Gabbett and Greenhill would eat that night. That pair, however, make a fire, fling ghastly fragments on the embers. In the morning the frightful carcass is divided.

That day's march takes place in silence, and at the mid-day halt Cornelius volunteers to carry the billy, affecting great restoration from the food. Vetch gives it to him, and in half an hour afterwards Cornelius is missing. Gabbett and Greenhill pursue him in vain, and return with curses. "He'll die like a dog," said Greenhill, "alone in the bush." Jemmy Vetch, with his intellect acute as ever, thinks that Cornelius prefers such a death to the one in store for him, but says nothing.

The twelfth moring dawns wet and misty, but Vetch, seeing the provision running short, strives to be cheerful, telling stories of men who have escaped greater peril. Vetch feels with dismay that he is the weakest of the party, but has some consolation in remembering that he is also the leanest. They come to a creek that afternoon, and look, until nightfall, in vain for a crossing-place. The next day Gabbett and Vetch swim across and cut a long sapling, which, being stretched across the water, is seized by Greenhill and the Moocher, who are dragged over.

"What would you do without me?" said the Crow with a ghastly grin.

They cannot kindle a fire, for Greenhill, who carries the tinder, has allowed it to get wet. The giant swings his axe in savage anger at enforced cold, and Vetch takes an opportunity to remark privately to him, what a *big* man Greenhill is.

On the fourteenth day they can scarcely crawl. Greenhill, who is the weakest, sees Gabbett and the Moocher go aside to consult, and crawling to the Crow, whimpers: "For God's sake, Jemmy, don't let 'em murder me!"

"I can't help you," says Vetch, looking about in terror. "Think of poor Tom Bodenham."

"But he was no murderer. If they kill me, I shall go to hell with Tom's blood on my soul."

Gabbett bids Vetch bring wood for the fire. Vetch, going, sees Greenhill clinging to Gabbett's knees, and Sanders calls after him, "You will hear it presently, Jem."

Crow puts his hands to his ears, but is conscious, nevertheless, of a dull crash and a groan. When he comes back, Gabbett is putting on the dead man's shoes, which are better than his own.

"We'll stop here a day or so and rest," said he, "now we've got provisions."

Two more days pass, and the three resume their march. The third day—the sixteenth of their journey—such portions of the carcass as they have with them prove unfit to eat. They look into each other's famine-sharpened faces, and wonder "who next?"

"We must all die together," said Sanders quickly, "before anything else must happen."

Vetch marks the terror concealed in the words, and when the dreaded giant is out of earshot, says, "For God's sake, let's go on alone, Alick. You see what sort of a cove that Gabbett is—he'd kill his father before he'd fast one day."

They made for the bush, but the giant turned and strode towards them. Vetch skipped nimbly on one side, but Gabbett struck the Moocher on the forehead with the axe. "Help! Jem, help!" cried the victim, cut, but not fatally, and in the strength of his desperation he tore the axe from Gabbett and flung it to Vetch. "Keep it, Jemmy," he cried, "let's have no more murder done!"

At nightfall Vetch called the giant to him.

"He must die."

"Either you or he," laughs Gabbett. "Give me the axe."

"No, no," said the Crow, his thin, malignant face distorted by a horrible resolution. "*I'll* keep the axe. Stand back! You shall hold him, and I'll do the job."

Sanders, seeing them approach, knew his end was come, and submitted, crying, "Give me half an hour to pray for myself." They consent, and the bewildered wretch knelt down and folded his hands like a child. "I can't think o' the words, Jem!"

"Pah," snarled the cripple, swinging the axe, "we can't starve here all night."

Four days passed, and the two survivors sat watching each other. The gaunt giant sat sentinel over the dwarf. The dwarf, chuckling at his superior sagacity, clutched the fatal axe. For two days they had not spoken to each other. For two days each had promised himself that on the next his companion must *sleep*—and die. Gabbett watched to snatch the weapon from his companion, and make the odds even for once and for ever. Vetch held aloof. In the day-time they travelled on, seeking each a pretext to creep behind the other. In the night-time when they feigned slumber, each stealthily raising a head caught the wakeful glance of his companion.

On the fifth day, Vetch, creeping behind a tree, takes off his belt and makes a noose. He will hang himself. He gets one end of the belt over a bough, and then his cowardice bids him pause. Gabbett approaches; he tries to steal away into the bush. In vain. The insatiable giant is not to be shaken off. Vetch tries to run, but his legs bend under him. The axe feels heavy as lead. He will fling it away. No—he dares not.

Night falls again. Vetch must rest, or go mad. His limbs are powerless. His eyelids are glued together. He sleeps as he stands. This horrible thing must be a dream. He is at Port Arthur, or will wake on his pallet in the penny lodging-house he slept at when a boy. Is that the Deputy come to wake him to the torment of living? It is not time—surely not time yet. He sleeps—and the giant, grinning with ferocious joy, approaches on clumsy tiptoe and seizes the coveted axe.

On the north-east coast of Van Diemen's Land is a place called St Helen's Point, and a certain skipper, being in want of fresh water, landing there with a boat's crew, found on the banks of the creek a gaunt and blood-stained man, clad in tattered yellow, who carried on his back an axe and a bundle. When the sailors came within sight of him, he made signs to them to approach, and opening his bundle with much ceremony offered them some of its contents. Filled with horror at what the maniac displayed, they seized and bound him. At Hobart Town he was recognised as the only survivor of the nine desperadoes who had escaped from Colonel Arthur's "Natural Penitentiary."

BOOK FOUR
Norfolk Island-1846

In turning over the pages of my journal, to note the good fortune that has just happened to me, I am struck by the utter desolation of my life for the last seven years.

FROM THE DIARY OF MR. JAMES NORTH

Can it be possible that I, James North, the college-hero, the poet, the prizeman, have been content to live on at this dreary spot—an animal, eating and drinking, for to-morrow I die? Yet it has been so. My world, that world of which I once dreamt so much, has been—here. My fame—which was to reach the ends of the earth—has penetrated to the neighbouring stations. I am considered a "good preacher" by my sheep-feeding friends. It is kind of them.

Yet, on the eve of leaving it, I confess that this solitary life has been not without its charms. I have had my books and my thoughts—though at times the latter were but grim companions. I have striven with my familiar sin, and have not always been worsted. Melancholy reflection. I vowed, however, that I would not cheat myself in this diary of mine, and I will not. No evasions, no glossings over of my own sins. This journal is my confessor, and I bare my heart to it.

I tell to your cold blue pages these stories, longings, remorses, which I would fain tell to human ear could I find a human being as discreet as thou. It has been said that a man dare not *write* all his thoughts and deeds; the words would blister the paper. Yet a man *must* confess. One reads of wretches who have carried secrets in their bosoms for years, and blurted them forth at last. I, shut up here without companionship, without sympathy, without letters, cannot lock up my soul, and feed on my own thoughts. They will not, and so I will whisper them to thee.

Hobart Town, *Jan.* 12th.

"Dear North—I have much pleasure in informing you that you can be appointed Protestant chaplain at Norfolk Island, if you like. It seems that they did not get on well with the last man, and when my advice was asked, I at once recommended you for the office. The pay is small, but you have a house and so on. It is certainly better than Bathurst, and indeed is considered rather a prize in the clerical lottery.

"There is to be an investigation into affairs down there. Poor old Pratt—who went down, as you know, at the earnest solicitation of the Government—seems to have become absurdly lenient with the prisoners, and it is reported that the island is in a frightful state. Sir Eardley is looking out for some disciplinarian to take the place in hand.

"In the mean time, the chaplaincy is vacant, and I thought of you."

February 19th.—I accept. There is work to be done among those unhappy men that may be my purgation.

February 27th, 11.30 p.m.—Nine Creeks Station. I like to be accurate in names, dates, etc. Accuracy is a virtue. To exercise it, then. Station ninety miles from Bathurst. I should say about 4,000 head of cattle. Luxury without refinement. Plenty to eat, drink, and read. Hostess' name—Carr. She is a well-preserved creature, about thirty-four years of age, and clever—not in a poetical sense, but in the widest worldly acceptation of the term. At the same time, I should be sorry to be her husband. Women have no business with a brain like hers—that is, if they wish not to be sexual monsters. Mrs. Carr is not a lady, though she might have been one. I don't think she is a good woman either. It is possible that she has known the factory before now. There is a mystery about her, for I was informed that she was a Mrs. Purfoy, the widow of a whaling captain, and had married one of her assigned servants, who had deserted her five years ago, as soon as he obtained his freedom. A word at dinner set me thinking. She had received some English papers, and, accounting for her pre-occupied manner, grimly said, "I think I have news of my husband." I should not like to be in Carr's shoes if she *has* news of him! I don't think she would suffer indignity calmly. After all, what business is it of mine? I was beguiled into taking more wine at dinner than I needed. Confessor, do you hear me? But I will not allow myself to be carried away. You grin, you fat familiar! So may I, but I shall be eaten with remorse to-morrow.

March 20th.—Sydney. At Captain Frere's. The last week has made a new man of me. I am no longer morose, and bitter, but genial, and on good terms with fortune. It is strange that accident should have induced me to stay a week under the same roof with that vision of brightness which has haunted me so long. A meeting in the street, an introduction, an invitation—the thing is done.

Circumstances are certainly curious things. I had thought never again to meet the bright young face to which I felt so strange an attraction—and lo! here it is smiling on me daily. Captain Frere should be a happy man. Yet there is a skeleton in this house also. That young wife, by nature so lovable and so mirthful, ought not to have the sadness on her face that twice to-day has clouded it. He seems a passionate and boorish creature, this convict disciplinarian. His convicts—poor devils—are doubtless disciplined enough. Charming little Sylvia, with your wit and beauty, he is not good enough for you—and yet it was a love match.

March 22nd.—This unromantic Captain Frere has had some romantic incidents in his life, and he is fond of dilating upon them. It seems that in early life he expected to have been left a large fortune by an uncle who had quarrelled with his heir. But the uncle dies on the day fixed for the altering of the will, the son disappears, and is thought to be drowned. The widow, however, steadfastly refuses to believe in the young man's death, and having a life-interest in the property, holds it against all comers. My poor host in consequence comes out here on his pay, and, three years ago, just as he is hoping that the death of his aunt may give him opportunity to claim some portion of the property, the long-lost son returns, is recognised by his mother and the trustees, and installed in due heirship!

The other romantic story is connected with Frere's marriage. He told me after dinner to-night, how his wife had been wrecked when a child, and how he had saved her life, and defended her from the rude hands of an escaped convict—one of the monsters that our monstrous system breeds. "That was how we fell in love," said he, tossing off his wine complacently.

"An auspicious opportunity," said I. To which he nodded. He is not overburdened with brains, I fancy.

Let me see if I can set down some account of this lovely place and its people.

A long low white house, surrounded by a blooming garden. Wide windows opening on a lawn. The ever glorious, ever changing sea beneath. It is evening. I am talking with Mrs. Frere of theories of social reform, of picture galleries, of sunsets, and new books. There comes a sound of wheels on the gravel. It is the magistrate. We hear him come briskly up the steps, but we go on talking. (I fancy there was a time when the lady would have run to meet him.) He enters, coldly kisses his wife, and disturbs at once the current of our thoughts.

"It has been hot to-day. What, still no letter from Head-quarters, Mr. North! I saw Mrs. Golightly in town, Sylvia, and she asked for you. There is to be a ball at Government House. We must go." Then he departs, and is heard in the distance indistinctly cursing because the water is not hot enough, or because Dawkins has not brushed his trousers sufficiently. We resume our chat, but he returns all hungry, and bluff, and whisker-brushed.

"Dinner. Ha-ha! I'm ready for it. North, take Mrs. Frere." By-and-by it is, "North, some sherry? Sylvia, the soup is spoilt again. Did you go out to-day? No?" His eyebrows contract here, and I know he says inwardly, "Reading some trashy novel, I suppose."

After dinner the disciplinarian and I converse—of dogs and horses, gamecocks and convicts. I remember old college feats, and strive to keep pace with him in the relation of athletics. What hypocrites we are!—for all the time I am longing to get to the drawing-room, and finish my criticism of the new poet, Mr. Tennyson, to Mrs. Frere. Frere does not read Tennyson—nor anybody else. Adjourned to the drawing-room, we chat—Mrs. Frere and I—until supper. (He eats supper.) She is a charming companion, and when I talk my best—I *can* talk, you must admit, O Familiar—her face lightens up with an interest I rarely see upon it at other times. I feel cooled and soothed by this companionship. The quiet refinement of this house, after bullocks and Bathurst, is like the shadow of a great rock in a weary land.

Mrs. Frere is about five-and-twenty. She is not tall, and has a slight, girlish figure. This girlish appearance is enhanced by bright fair hair and blue eyes. Upon conversation with her, however, one sees that her face has lost much of the delicate plumpness which it probably owned in youth. She has had one child, born only to die. Her cheeks are thin, and her eyes have a tinge of sadness, which speak of physical pain or mental grief. This thinness of face makes the eyes appear larger and the brow broader than they really are. Her hands are white and painfully thin. They must have been plump and pretty once. Her lips are red with perpetual fever.

Captain Frere seems to have absorbed all his wife's vitality. In proportion as she has lost her vigour and youth, he has gained strength and heartiness. Though he is at least forty years of age, he does not look more than thirty. His face is ruddy, his eyes bright, his voice firm and ringing. He must be a man of considerable strength and—I should say—of more than ordinary animal courage and animal appetite. There is not a nerve in his body which does not twang like a piano wire. In appearance, he is tall, broad, and bluff, with red whiskers and reddish hair slightly touched with grey. His manner is loud, coarse, and imperious. What a strangely-mated pair!

March 30th.—A letter from Van Diemen's Land. "There is a row in the pantry," said Frere with his accustomed slang. It seems that the Comptroller-General of Convicts has appointed a Mr. Pounce to go down and make a report on the state of Norfolk Island. I am to go down with him, and shall receive instructions to that effect from the Comptroller-General. I have informed Frere of this, and he has written to Pounce to come and stay on his way down. There has been nothing but convict discipline talked since. Frere wearies me with his explanations of convict tricks and wickedness. He is celebrated for his knowledge of such matters. Detestable wisdom! His servants hate him, but obey him without a murmur. I have observed that habitual criminals—like all savage beasts—cower before the man who has once mastered them. I should not be surprised if the Van Diemen's Land Government selected Frere as their "disciplinarian." I hope they won't, and yet I hope they will.

April 4th.—I have found out to-night two things which surprise me. One is that the convict who attempted the life of Mrs. Frere is none other than the unhappy man whom my fatal weakness caused to be flogged at Port Arthur, and whose face reproaches me even now. The other that Mrs. Carr is an old acquaintance of Frere's. The latter piece of information I obtained in a curious way. One night, after Mrs. Frere had retired, we were talking of clever women. I broached my theory, that strong intellect in women went far to destroy their womanly nature.

"Desire in man," said I, "should be Volition in women: Reason, Intuition; Reverence, Devotion; Passion, Love. Man has vigour of reason, woman quickness of feeling. The woman who possesses masculine force of intellect is abnormal." He did not comprehend me, I could see, but he agreed with the broad view of the case. "I only knew one woman who was really 'strong-minded' as they call it," he said, "and she was a regular bad one."

"It does not follow that she should be *bad*," said I.

"This one was, though—stock, lock, and barrel. But as sharp as a needle, sir, and as immovable as a rock."

I saw by his expression that he owned ugly memories and pressed him further. "She's up country somewhere," he said. "Married her assigned servant, I was told, a fellow named Carr. I haven't seen her for years, but when I knew her she was just what you describe." (Let it be noted that I had described nothing.) "She came out in the ship with me as maid to my wife's mother."

It was on the tip of my tongue to say that I had met her, but something induced me to be silent. There are passages in the lives of men which don't bear descanting on. I expect there has been in this case, for he changed the subject abruptly, as his wife came in. Is it possible that these two creatures—the notable disciplinarian and the wife of the assigned servant—could have been more than friends in youth? Quite possible. He is the sort of man for gross amours. (A pretty way I am abusing my host!) And the supple woman with the dark eyes would have been just the creature to enthral him. Perhaps some such story as this may account in part for Mrs. Frere's sad looks. Why do I speculate on such things? I seem to do violence to myself and to insult *her* by writing such suspicions.

April 7th.—Mr. Pounce has arrived—full of the importance of his mission. I am as flippant as a school-girl concerning this fatuous official, and yet—Heaven knows—I feel deeply enough the importance of the task he has before him. One relieves one's brain by these whirlings of one's mental limbs. I remember that a prisoner at Hobart Town, twice condemned and twice reprieved, jumped and shouted with frenzied vehemence when he heard his sentence of death finally pronounced. He told me, if he had not so shouted, he believed he would have gone mad.

April 10th.—We had a state dinner last night. The conversation was about nothing in the world but convicts. I never saw Mrs. Frere to less advantage. Silent, *distraite*, and sad. She told me after dinner that she disliked the very name of "convict". "I have lived among them all my life," she said, "but that does not make it better for me. I have terrible fancies at times, Mr. North, that seem half-memories. I dread to be brought in contact with prisoners again. I am sure that some evil awaits me at their hands."

I laughed, of course, but it would not do. She holds to her opinion, and looks at me with horror in her eyes. This terror in her face is perplexing.

We sat silent for a while, and then she suddenly turned her large eyes on me, and said calmly, "Mr. North, what death shall I die?" The question was an echo of my own thoughts—I have some foolish fancies as to physiognomy —and it made me start. What death, indeed? What sort of death would one meet with widely-opened eyes, parted lips, and brows bent as though to rally fast-flying courage? Not a peaceful death surely. I brought my black coat to my aid. "My dear lady, you must not think of such things. Death is but a sleep, you know. Why anticipate a nightmare?"

She sighed, slowly awaking as though from some momentary trance. Checking herself on the verge of tears, she rallied, turned the conversation, and finding an excuse for going to the piano, dashed into a waltz. This unnatural gaiety ended I fancy, in a hysterical fit. I heard her husband afterwards recommending sal volatile. He is the sort of man who would recommend sal volatile to the Pythoness if she consulted him.

April 26th.—All has been arranged, and we start to-morrow. Mr. Pounce is in a condition of painful dignity. He seems afraid to move lest motion should thaw his official ice. Having found out that I am the "chaplain," he has refrained from familiarity. My self-love is wounded, but my patience relieved.

I have farewelled my friends, and on looking back on the pleasant hours I have spent, felt saddened. It is not likely that I shall have many such again. I feel like a vagabond who, having been allowed to sit by a cheerful fireside for a while, is turned out into the wet and windy streets, and finds them colder than ever. Now for Norfolk Island and my purgation.

The lost son of Sir Richard Devine had returned to England, and had made claim to his name and fortune. In other words, John Rex had successfully

THE LOST HEIR

carried out the scheme by which he had usurped the rights of his old convict-comrade.

Smoking his cigar in his bachelor lodgings, or pausing in a calculation concerning a race, John Rex often wondered at the ease with which he had carried out so seemingly difficult an imposture. After he was landed in Sydney by the vessel which Sarah Purfoy had sent to save him, he found himself a slave to a bondage scarcely less galling than that from which he had escaped—the bondage of enforced companionship with an unloved woman. The opportune death of one of her assigned servants enabled Sarah Purfoy to install the escaped convict in his room. In the state of society which prevailed in New South Wales at that period, it was not unusual for assigned servants to marry among the free settlers, and when it was heard that Mrs. Purfoy, the widow of a whaling captain, had married John Carr, her storekeeper, transported for embezzlement, and with two years of his sentence yet to run, no one expressed surprise. Indeed, when, the year after, John Carr blossomed as an "expiree," master of a fine wife and a fine fortune, there were many about him who would have made his existence in Australia pleasant enough. But John Rex had no notion of remaining longer than he could help, and ceaselessly sought means of escape from this second prison-house. For a long time his search was unsuccessful. Much as she loved him, Sarah Purfoy did not scruple to tell him that she regarded him as her property. He knew that if he made any attempt to escape from his marriage bonds, the woman who had risked so much to save him would not hesitate to deliver him over to the authorities, and state how the opportune death of John Carr had enabled her to give name and employment to John Rex, the absconder. He had thought once that the fact of her being his wife would prevent her from giving evidence against him, and that he could thus defy her. But she reminded him that a word to Blunt would be all sufficient. "I know you don't care for me, now, John," she said, with grim complacency; "but your life is in my hands, and if you desert me I will bring you to the gallows."

To be rid of her was not easy. Twice he tried to escape, and was twice brought back. "I have bought you, John," his partner had laughed, "and you don't get away from me. Surely you can be content with these comforts. You were content with less once. I am not so ugly and repulsive, am I?"

"I am home-sick," John Carr retorted. "Let us go to England, Sarah."

She tapped her strong white fingers sharply on the table. "Go to England?

No, no. That is what you would like to do. You would be master there. You would take my money, and leave me—I know you, Jack. We stop here, dear. Here, where I can hand you over to the first trooper if you are not kind to me."

"She-devil!"

"Oh, I don't mind your abuse. Abuse me, beat me if you will, but don't leave me, or it will be worse for you."

"You are a strange woman!" he cried, in sudden petulant admiration.

"To love such a villain? I don't know that. I love you because you are a villain. A better man would be wearisome to me."

"I wish to Heaven I'd never left Port Arthur. Better there than this dog's life."

"Go back, then. You have only to say the word!"

And so they would wrangle, she glorying in her power over him, he consoling himself with the hope that the day was not far distant which should bring him at once freedom and fortune. One day the chance came. His wife was ill, and the ungrateful scoundrel stole five hundred pounds, and taking two horses reached Sydney, and obtained passage in a vessel bound for Rio.

Having escaped thraldom, John Rex proceeded to play for the great stake of his life with the utmost caution. He went to the Continent, and lived for weeks together in the towns where Richard Devine might possibly have resided, familiarising himself with streets, making the acquaintance of old inhabitants, drawing into his own hands all loose ends of information which could help to knit the meshes of his net the closer. Such loose ends were not numerous; the prodigal had been too poor, too insignificant, to leave strong memories behind him. Yet Rex knew well by what strange accidents the deceit of an assumed identity is often penetrated. Some old comrade or companion of the lost heir might suddenly appear with keen questions as to trifles which could cut his flimsy web to shreds. He could not afford to ignore the most insignificant circumstances. With consummate skill, piece by piece he built up the story which was to deceive the poor mother, and to make him possessor of one of the largest private fortunes in England.

This was the tale he hit upon. He had been saved from the burning *Hydaspes* by a vessel bound for Rio. Ignorant of the death of Sir Richard, and prompted by pride, he had determined not to return, until fortune should have bestowed upon him wealth equal to the inheritance he had lost. In Spanish America he had striven to accumulate that wealth in vain. As *vaquero*, traveller, speculator, sailor, he had toiled for fourteen years, and had failed. Worn out and penitent he had returned home to find a corner of English earth in which to lay his weary bones.

The tale was plausible, and in the telling of it he was armed at all points. There was little fear that the navigator of the captured *Osprey*, the man who had lived in Chile, would prove lacking in knowledge of riding, seamanship, or Spanish customs. Moreover, he had determined upon a course of action which showed his knowledge of human nature.

The will under which Richard Devine inherited had been made in 1807 when the testator was in the first hopeful glow of paternity. By its terms Lady Devine was to receive a life interest of three thousand a year in her husband's property—which was placed in the hands of a trustee,—until her eldest son died or attained the age of twenty-five years. When either of these events should occur, the property was to be realised, Lady Devine receiving a sum of a hundred thousand pounds, which, invested for her benefit, would exactly compensate for her loss of interest, the remainder going absolutely to the son, if living, to his children or next of kin if dead.

Sir Richard's sister and her husband, Anthony Frere, of Bristol, were long ago dead, and, as we know, their representative, Maurice Frere, content at last in the lot that fortune had sent him, had given up all thought of meddling with his uncle's business. John Rex, therefore, in the person of the returned Richard, had but two persons to satisfy, his putative uncle, Mr. Francis Wade, Lady Devine's brother and the trustee of the will, and his putative mother, Lady Devine.

This he found to be the easiest task possible. Francis Wade was an invalid virtuoso, who detested business, and whose ambition was to be known as a man of taste. When, at his sister's urgent wish, he assumed the sole responsibility of the estate, he put all the floating capital into 3 per cents, and was content to see the interest accumulate. Lady Devine had never recovered the shock of circumstances attending Sir Richard's death and, clinging to the belief in her son's existence, regarded herself as the mere guardian of his interests, to be displaced at any moment by his sudden return. The retired pair lived thus together at North End, and spent in charity and *bric-a-brac* about a fourth of their mutual income. By both of them the return of the wanderer was hailed with delight. To Lady Devine it meant the realisation of a lifelong hope, become part of her nature. To Francis Wade it meant relief from a responsibility which his simplicity always secretly loathed, that of looking after another person's money.

"I shall not think of interfering with the arrangements which you have made, my dear uncle," said Mr. John Rex, on the first night of his reception. "It would be most ungrateful of me to do so. My wants are very few, and can easily be supplied. I will see your lawyers some day, and settle it."

"See them at once, Richard, see them at once. I am no man of business, you know, but I think you will find all right."

Richard, however, put off the visit from day to day. He desired to have as little to do with lawyers as possible. He had resolved upon his course of action. He would get money from his mother for immediate needs, and when she died he would assert his rights. "My rough life has unfitted me for drawing-rooms, dear mother," he said. "Do not let there be a display about my return. Give me a corner to smoke my pipe, and I am happy."

Lady Devine, with a loving tender pity, consented. So the returned prodigal had his own suite of rooms, his own servants, his own bank account, drank, smoked, and was merry.

For five or six months he thought himself in Paradise. Then he began to find his life insufferably weary. The burden of hypocrisy is very heavy to bear, and Rex was compelled perpetually to bear it. His mother demanded all his time. She hung upon his lips; she made him repeat fifty times the story of his wanderings. She was never tired of kissing him, of weeping over him, of thanking him for the "sacrifice" he had made for her.

"We promised never to speak of it more, Richard," the poor lady said one day, "but if my lifelong love can make atonement for the wrong I have done you——"

"Hush, dearest mother," said John Rex, who did not in the least comprehend what it was all about. "Let us say no more."

Lady Devine wept quietly for a while and then went away, leaving the man who pretended to be her son much bewildered and a little frightened. There was a secret which he had not fathomed between Lady Devine and her son. The mother did not again refer to it, and gaining courage as the days went on, Rex grew bold enough to forget his fears.

In the first stages of his deception, he had been timid and cautious. Then the soothing influence of respect and security came upon him, and almost refined him. The sensation of being ministered to by a loving woman, who kissed him night and morning, calling him "son,"—of being regarded with admiration by rustics, with envy by respectable folk—of being deferred to in all things—was novel and pleasing. They were so good to him that he felt at times inclined to confess all, and leave his case in the hands of the folk he had injured. Yet such a course would be absurd. It would result in no benefit to any one, simply in misery to himself. The true Richard Devine was buried deep in the greedy ocean of convict-discipline, chained by innumerable punishments. Richard Devine could never return to accuse him. So flattering himself, John Rex gradually became bolder, and by slow degrees suffered his true nature to appear. He was violent to the servants, cruel to dogs and horses, often wantonly coarse in speech, and brutally regardless of the feelings of others. Governed solely by her feelings, Lady Devine had at first been prodigal of her affection to the man she believed to be her injured son. But his acts of selfishness, his habits of grossness and self-indulgence, gradually disgusted her. For some time she fought against her instincts of distaste, but she was at length forced to succumb.

For the first year Mr. Richard conducted himself with propriety, but as his circle of acquaintance and his confidence increased, he now and then forgot the part he was playing. One day Mr. Richard went to pass the day with a sporting friend, one who was only too proud to see at his table so wealthy a man. Mr. Richard drank a good deal and came home in a condition of disgusting drunkenness. For John Rex to be drunk was to be himself—coarse and cruel. Francis Wade was away, and Lady Devine had retired for the night, when the dog-cart brought home "Mr. Richard." The virtuous butler-porter, who opened the door, received a blow in the chest and a demand for "Brandy!" The groom was cursed, and ordered to instant oblivion. Mr. Richard stumbled into the dining-room—veiled in dim light as a dining-room which was "sitting-up" for its master ought to be—and ordered "more candles!" The candles were brought, after some delay, and Mr. Richard, climbing with muddy boots upon the polished table, attempted to fix the wax in the silver sconces, with which the antiquarian tastes of Mr. Francis Wade had adorned the room.

"You'll break the table, sir," said the servant.

"Damn the table!" said Rex. "Have some brandy! Send for servantsh and have dance. You'll dance upon nothing one day, Tomkins!" And he began to shout and blaspheme.

"Don't you think it's time for bed, Mr. Richard?" one of the other servants ventured to suggest.

"No!" roared the ex-convict, emphatically, "I *don't!* I've gone to bed at daylight far too long. We'll have 'luminashon! I'm master here. Master everything. Richard 'Vine's my name. Isn't it, Tomkins, you villain?"

"Yes, Mr. Richard."

"'Course it is, and I'll make you know it, too! Wait till the old woman's dead, Tomkins, and you shall see! Bring up some brandy! Play up there! Where's old woman! Fetch her out and let's dance!"

"Lady Devine has gone to bed, Mr. Richard," cried Tomkins aghast, attempting to bar the passage to the upper regions.

"Then let's have her out o' bed," cried John Rex, plunging towards the door.

Tomkins, attempting to restrain him, is hurled into a cabinet of rare china, and the drunken brute essays the stairs. The other servants seize him. He curses and fights like a demon. Doors open, lights gleam, maids hover, horrified, asking if it's "fire?" The whole house is in uproar; in the midst of which Lady Devine appears, and looks down upon the scene. Rex catches sight of her, and bursts once more into blasphemy. She withdraws, terrified; and the master is at last got into his own apartments. The groom, whose face had been seriously damaged in the encounter, bestows a hearty kick on the prostrate carcass at parting.

The next morning Lady Devine declined to see her son, though he sent a special apology to her.

"I am afraid I was a little overcome by wine last night," said he to Tomkins.

"Well, you was, sir," said Tomkins.

"A very little wine makes me quite ill, Tomkins. Did I do anything very violent?"

"You *was* rather obstropolous, Mr. Richard."

"Here's a sovereign for you, Tomkins. Did I *say* anything?"

"You cussed a good deal, Mr. Richard. Most gents do when they've bin—hum—dining out, Mr. Richard."

"What a fool I am," thought John Rex, as he dressed. "I shall spoil everything if I don't take care." However, for this bout he made amends—money soothed the servants' hall, and apologies and time won Lady Devine's forgiveness.

"I cannot yet conform to English habits, dear mother," said Rex, "and feel at times out of place in your home. I think—if you can spare me a little money—I should like to travel."

Lady Devine—with a sense of relief for which she blamed herself—assented, and, supplied with letters of credit, John Rex went to Paris.

Fairly started in the world of dissipation and excess, he began to grow reckless. When a young man, he had been singularly free from the vice of drunkenness; turning his sobriety—as he did all his virtues—to vicious account, but he had learnt to drink deep in the loneliness of the bush.

Master of a large sum of money, he had intended to spend it as he would have spent it in his younger days. He had forgotten that since his death and burial the world had not grown younger. It was possible that Mr. Lionel Crofton might have discovered some of the old set of fools and knaves with whom he had once mixed. Many of them were alive and flourishing. Mr. Lemoine, for instance, was respectably married in his native island of Jersey, and had already threatened to disinherit a nephew who showed a tendency to dissipation.

But Mr. Lemoine would not care to recognise Mr. Lionel Crofton, the gambler and rake, in his proper person, and it was not expedient that his acquaintance should be made in the person of Richard Devine, lest by some unlucky chance he should recognise the cheat.

Thus poor Lionel Crofton was compelled to lie still in his grave, and Mr. Richard Devine, trusting to a big beard and more burly figure, to keep his secret, was compelled to begin all over again. In Paris and London there were plenty of people ready to become hail-fellow-well-met with any gentleman possessing money. Mr. Richard Devine's history was whispered in many a boudoir and club-room. The history, however, was not always told in the same way. It was generally known that Lady Devine had a son, who, being supposed to be dead, had suddenly returned, to the confusion of his family. But the manner of his return was told in many ways.

In the first place, Mr. Francis Wade, well known though he was, did not move in that brilliant circle which had lately received his nephew. There are in England many men of fortune as large as that left by the old ship-builder, who are positively unknown in that little world which is supposed to contain all the men worth knowing. Francis Wade was a man of mark in his own coterie. Among artists, *bric-a-brac* sellers, antiquarians and men of letters, he was known as a patron and man of taste. His bankers and his lawyers knew him to be of independent fortune, but as he neither mixed in politics, "went into society," betted, or speculated in merchandise, there were several large sections of the community who had never heard his name.

The advent of Mr. Richard Devine—a coarse person of unlimited means—had therefore chief influence upon that sinister circle of male and female rogues who form the "half-world." They began to inquire concerning his antecedents, and, failing satisfactory information, to invent lies concerning him. It was generally believed that he was a black sheep, a man whose family kept him out of the way, but who was, in a pecuniary sense, "good" for a considerable sum.

Thus taken upon trust, Mr. Richard Devine mixed in the very best of bad society, and had no lack of agreeable friends to help him spend money. So admirably did he spend it, that Francis Wade became at last alarmed at the frequent drafts, and urged his nephew to bring his affairs to a final settlement. Richard Devine—in Paris, or Hamburg, or London, or elsewhere—could never be got to attack business, and Mr. Francis Wade grew more and more anxious.

"I wish, my dear Richard, that you would let me know what to do," he wrote.

"I wish, my dear uncle, that you would do what you think best," was his nephew's reply.

Mr. Wade began to repent of his lack of determination in the beginning. Not that he was suspicious of Rex, but he remembered that Dick was always a loose fish. The even current of the *dilettante's* life became disturbed. He grew pale and hollow-eyed. His digestion was impaired. He ceased to take the interest in china which the importance of that article demanded. In a word, he grew despondent as to his fitness for his mission in life. Lady Ellinor saw a change in her brother. She went privately to the family doctor, who shrugged his shoulders. "There is no danger," said he, "if he is kept quiet. Keep him quiet, and he will live for years." Lady Ellinor, upon this, wrote to Mr. Richard, who was at Paris, and begged him to come over at once. Mr. Richard replied that some horse-racing matter of great importance occupied his attention, but that he would be at his rooms in Clarges Street (he had long ago established a town house) on the 14th, and would "go into matters." "I have lost a good deal of money lately, my dear mother," said Mr. Richard, "and the present will be a good opportunity to make a final settlement." The fact was, that John Rex, now three years in undisturbed possession, considered that the moment had arrived for the execution of the *grand coup*—the carrying off at one swoop of the whole of the fortune he had gambled for.

May 12th.—Landed to-day at Norfolk Island, and have been introduced to my new abode, situated some eleven hundred miles from Sydney. A solitary

FROM THE DIARY OF MR. JAMES NORTH

rock in the tropical ocean, the island seems a fit place of banishment. It is about seven miles long and four broad. The most remarkable natural object is the Norfolk Island pine, which rears its stately head a hundred feet above the surrounding forest. The appearance of the place is very wild and beautiful, bringing to my mind the romantic islands of the Pacific, which old geographers dwell upon so fondly. The climate just now is hot and muggy. The approach to Kingstown—as the barracks and huts are called—is difficult. A long low reef fronts the bay and obstructs the entrance of vessels. We were landed in boats through an opening in this reef, and our vessel stands on and off within signalling distance. The surf washes almost against the walls of the military roadway that leads to the barracks. The social aspect of the place fills me with horror. There seems neither discipline nor order. On our way to the Commandant's house we passed a low dilapidated building, where the men were at work, grinding maize, and at the sight of us they commenced whistling, hooting, and shouting, using the most disgusting language. Three warders were near, but no attempt was made to check this unseemly exhibition.

May 14th.—I sit down to write with as much reluctance as though I were about to relate my experience of a journey through a sewer.

First, to the prisoners' barracks, which stand on an area of about three acres, surrounded by a lofty wall. A road runs between this wall and the sea. The barracks are three storeys high, and hold seven hundred and ninety men (let me remark here that there are more than two thousand men on the island). There are twenty-two wards in this place, the largest containing a hundred men, the smallest fifteen. They sleep in hammocks, slung close to each other as on board ship, in two lines, with a passage down the centre. There is a wardsman to each ward. He is selected by the prisoners, and is generally a man of the worst character. He is supposed to keep order, but of course he never attempts to do so; indeed as he is locked up in the ward every night from six o'clock in the evening until sunrise, *without light*, it is possible that he might get maltreated did he make himself obnoxious.

The barracks look upon the Barrack Square, which is filled with lounging prisoners. The windows of the hospital-ward also look upon Barrack Square, and the prisoners are in constant communication with the patients.

The hospital is a low stone building, capable of containing about twenty men, and faces the beach. I placed my hands on the wall, and found it damp. An ulcerous prisoner said the dampness was owing to the heavy surf constantly rolling so close beneath the building. There are two gaols, the old and the new. The old gaol stands near the sea, close to the landing-place. Outside it, at the door, is the Gallows. I touched it as I passed in. This engine is the first thing which greets the eyes of a newly-arrived prisoner.

At six o'clock we saw the men mustered. I read prayers before the muster, and was surprised to find that some of the prisoners attended, while some strolled about the yard, whistling, singing, and joking. The muster is a farce. The prisoners rush into the barracks indiscriminately, and place themselves dressed or undressed in their hammocks. A convict sub-overseer then calls out the names, and somebody replies. If an answer is returned to each name, all is considered right. The lights are taken away, and save for a few minutes at eight o'clock when the good-conduct men are let in, the ruffians are left to their own devices until morning. Knowing what I know of convicts, my heart sickens when I in imagination put myself in the place of a newly-transported man, plunged from six at night until daybreak into that fetid den.

May 15th.—There is a place enclosed between high walls adjoining the convict barracks, called the Lumber Yard, where the prisoners mess. It is roofed on two sides, and contains tables and benches. Six hundred men can mess here, perhaps, but as seven hundred are always driven into it, it follows that the weakest men are compelled to sit on the ground. A more disorderly sight than this yard at meal times I never beheld. The cook-houses are adjoining it, and the men bake their meal-bread there. Outside the cook-house door the firewood is piled, and fires are made in all directions on the ground, round which sit the prisoners, frying their rations of fresh pork, baking their hominy cakes, chatting, and even smoking.

The lumber yard is a sort of Alsatia, to which the hunted prisoner retires. I don't think the boldest constable on the island would venture into that place to pick out a man from the seven hundred. I don't think he would come out again alive.

16th May.—A sub-overseer, named Hankey, has been talking to me. He says that there are some forty of the oldest and worst prisoners who form what he calls the "Ring," and that the members are bound by an oath to support each other, and to avenge the punishment of any of their number. In proof of his assertions he instanced two cases of English prisoners who had refused to join in some crime, and had informed the Commandant of the proceedings of the "Ring." They were found in the morning strangled in their hammocks. An inquiry was held, but not a man out of the ninety in the ward would speak a word.

I dread the task that is before me. How can I attempt to preach piety and morality to those men?

17th May.—Visited the wards to-day, and returned in despair. The condition of things is worse than I expected. It is not to be written. The newly-arrived English prisoners—and some of their histories are most touching—are insulted by the language and demeanour of the hardened miscreants who are the refuse of Port Arthur and Cockatoo Island. The vilest crimes are perpetrated as jests. There are men who are known to have murdered their companions, and who boast of it. With these the English farm labourer, the riotous and ignorant mechanic, the victim of perjury or mistake, are indiscriminately herded. With them are mixed Chinamen from Hong-Kong, the aborigines of New Holland, West Indian Blacks, Greeks, Caffres, and Malays, soldiers for desertion, idiots, madmen, pig-stealers, and pickpockets. The dreadful place seems set apart for all that is hideous and vile in our common nature. In its recklessness, its insubordination, its filth, and its despair, it realises to my mind the popular notion of hell.

May 21st.—Entered to-day officially upon my duties as Religious Instructor at the settlement.

An occurrence took place this morning which shows the dangerous condition of the "Ring." I accompanied Mr. Pounce to the Lumber Yard, and, on our entry, we observed a man in the crowd round the cook-house deliberately smoking. The Chief Constable of the Island—my old friend Troke, of Port Arthur—seeing that this had attracted Pounce's notice, pointed out the man to an assistant. The assistant, Jacob Gimblett, advanced and desired the prisoner to surrender the pipe. The man plunged his hands into his pockets, and, with a gesture of the most profound contempt, walked away to that part of the mess-shed where the "Ring" congregate.

"Take the scoundrel to gaol!" cried Troke.

No one moved, but the man at the gate called to us to come out, saying that the prisoners would never suffer the man to be taken. Pounce, however, with more determination than I gave him credit for, kept his ground, and insisted that so flagrant a breach of discipline should not pass unnoticed. Thus urged, Mr. Troke pushed through the crowd, and made for the spot whither the man had withdrawn himself.

The yard was buzzing like a disturbed hive, and I momentarily expected that a rush would be made upon us. In a few moments the prisoner appeared, attended by, rather than in the custody of, the Chief Constable of the Island. He advanced to the unlucky assistant constable, who was standing close to me, and asked, "What have you ordered me to gaol for?" The man made some reply, advising him to go quietly, when the convict raised his fist, and deliberately felled the man to the ground. "You had better retire, gentlemen," said Troke, "I see them getting out their knives."

We made for the gate, and the crowd closed in like a sea upon the two constables. I fully expected murder, but in a few moments Troke and Gimblett appeared, borne along by a mass of men, dusty, but unharmed, and having the convict between them. He sulkily raised a hand as he passed me, either to rectify the position of his straw hat, or to offer a tardy apology. I never before saw a man wantonly strike a constable. I fancy that the act was done out of bravado. Troke informed me that the man's name is Rufus Dawes, and that he is the leader of the Ring, and considered the worst man on the island; and that, but for the presence of an officer accredited by his Excellency, he dared not have acted as he had done.

This is the same man, then, whom I injured at Port Arthur. Seven years of "discipline" don't seem to have done him much good. His sentence is "life"—a lifetime in this place! Troke says that he was the terror of Port Arthur, and that they sent him here when a "weeding" of the prisoners was made. He has been here four years. Poor wretch!

May 24th.—After prayers, I saw Dawes. He was confined in the Old Gaol, and seven others were in the cell with him. He came out at my request, and stood leaning against the door-post. He was much changed from the man I remember. Seven years ago he was a stalwart, upright, *handsome* man. He has become a slouching ruffian. His hair is grey, though he cannot be more than forty, and his frame has lost that just proportion of parts which once made him almost graceful. His face has also grown like other convict faces, and, save for his black eyes and a peculiar trick he has of compressing his lips, I should not have recognised him. I said but little, for the other prisoners were listening, eager to witness my discomfiture. It is evident that Rufus Dawes had been accustomed to meet the ministrations of my predecessor with insolence. I spoke to him for a few minutes, only saying how foolish it was to rebel against an authority superior in strength to himself. He did not answer, and the only emotion he evinced during the interview was when I reminded him that we had met before. He shrugged one shoulder, as if in pain or anger, and seemed about to speak, but casting his eyes upon the group in the cell, relapsed into silence again. I must get speech with him alone.

I sent for Hankey, and asked him about cells. He says that the gaol is crowded to suffocation. "Solitary confinement" is a mere name. There are six men, each sentenced to solitary confinement, in a cell together. This cell is called the "nunnery." It is small, and the six men were naked to the waist when I entered, the perspiration pouring in streams off their naked bodies! It is disgusting to write of such things.

June 26th.—Pounce has departed in the *Lady Franklin* for Hobart Town, and it is rumoured that we are to have a new Commandant. The *Lady Franklin* is commanded by an old man named Blunt, a *protégé* of Frere's, and a fellow to whom I have taken one of my inexplicable and unreasoning dislikes.

Saw Rufus Dawes this morning. He continues sullen and morose. His papers are very bad. He is perpetually up for punishment. I am informed that he and a man named Eastwood, nicknamed Jacky Jacky, glory in being the leaders of the "Ring," and that they openly avow themselves weary of life. Can it be that the unmerited flogging which the poor creature got at Port Arthur has aided, with other sufferings, to bring him to this horrible state of mind? It is quite possible.

June 30th.—I took a holiday this afternoon, and walked in the direction of Mount Pitt. The island lay at my feet like—as sings Mrs. Frere's favourite poet—"a summer isle of Eden lying in dark purple sphere of sea." I followed a little brook that runs from the hills, and winds through thick under-growths until it reaches a lovely valley surrounded by lofty trees. Here stands the ruin of an old hut, formerly inhabited by the early settlers; lemons, figs, and guavas are thick; while amid the shrub and cane a large convolvulus is intertwined, and stars the green with its purple and crimson flowers.

I sat down here, and had a smoke. It seems that the former occupant of my rooms at the settlement read French; for in searching for a book to bring with me—I never walk without a book—I found and pocketed a volume of Balzac. It proved to be a portion of the *Vie Privée* series, and I stumbled upon a story called *La Fausse Maitresse*. With calm belief in the Paris of his imagination, Balzac introduces me to a Pole by name Paz, who, loving the wife of his friend, devotes himself to watch over her happiness and her husband's interest. The husband gambles and is profligate. Paz informs the wife that the leanness which hazard and debauchery have caused to the domestic exchequer is due to *his* extravagance, the husband having lent him money. She does not believe, and Paz feigns an intrigue with a circus-rider in order to lull all suspicions. She says to her adored spouse, "Get rid of this extravagant friend! Away with him! He is a profligate, a gambler! A drunkard!" Paz finally departs, and when he has gone, the lady finds out the poor Pole's worth. The story does not end satisfactorily. Balzac was too great a master of his art for that. In real life the curtain never falls on a comfortably-finished drama. The play goes on eternally.

I have been thinking of the story all the evening. A man who loves his friend's wife, and devotes his energies to increase her happiness by concealing from her her husband's follies! Surely none but Balzac would have hit upon such a notion. "A man who loves his friend's wife." I write no more!

August 24th.—There has been but one entry in my journal since the 30th June, that which records the advent of our new Commandant, who, as I expected, is Captain Maurice Frere.

FROM THE DIARY OF MR. JAMES NORTH

So great have been the changes which have taken place, that I scarcely know how to record them. Captain Frere has realised my worst anticipations. He is brutal, vindictive, and domineering. His knowledge of prisons and prisoners gives him an advantage over Burgess, otherwise he much resembles that murderous animal. He has but one thought—to keep the prisoners in subjection. "I was sent down here to keep order," said he to me, a few days after his arrival, "and by God, sir, I'll do it!"

He has done it, I must admit; but at a cost of a legacy of hatred to himself that he may some day regret. He has organised three parties of police. One patrols the fields, one is on guard at stores and public buildings, and the third is employed as a detective force. There are two hundred soldiers on the island. And the officer in charge, Captain McNab, has been induced by Frere to increase their duties in many ways. The cords of discipline are suddenly drawn tight. Any officer found giving tobacco to a prisoner is liable to removal from the island. The tobacco which grows wild has been rooted up and destroyed lest the men should obtain a leaf of it. The privilege of having a pannikin of hot water when the gangs came in from field labour in the evening, has been withdrawn. The shepherds, hut-keepers, and all other prisoners are forbidden to keep a parrot or any other bird. The plaiting of straw hats during the prisoners' leisure hours is also prohibited. At the settlement where the "old hands" are located, railed boundaries have been erected, beyond which no prisoner must pass unless to work. Two days ago Job Dodd, a negro, let his jacket fall over the boundary rails, crossed them to recover it, and was severely flogged. The floggings are hideously frequent. On flogging mornings I have seen the ground where the men stood at the triangles saturated with blood, as if a bucket of blood had been spilled on it, covering a space three feet in diameter, and running out in various directions, in little streams two or three feet long. At the same time, let me say, with that strict justice I force myself to mete out to those whom I dislike, that the island is in a condition of abject submission. There is not much chance of mutiny. The men go to their work without a murmur.

The method by which Captain Frere has brought about this desolation is characteristic of him. He sets every man as a spy upon his neighbour, awes the more daring into obedience by the display of a ruffianism more outrageous than their own, and raising the worst scoundrels to office, compels them to find "cases" for punishment. Perfidy is rewarded. It is part of a convict-policeman's duty to search a fellow-prisoner anywhere and at any time, and if resistance be offered, the man resisting can be knocked down by a blow from the searcher's bludgeon.

"It is impossible, Captain Frere," said I one day, during the initiation of this system, "to think that these villains whom you have made constables will do their duty."

He replied, "They *must* do their duty. If they are indulgent to the prisoners, they know I shall flog 'em. If they do what I tell 'em, they'll make themselves so hated that they'd have their own father up to the triangles to save themselves being sent back to the ranks."

"You treat them then like the slave-keepers of a wild beast den. They must flog the animals to avoid being flogged themselves."

"Ay," said he, with his coarse laugh, "and having once flogged 'em, they'd do anything rather than be put in the cage, don't ye see!"

Such horrible logic! I am sick unto death of the place. It makes me an unbeliever in the social charities. It takes out of penal science, anything it may possess of nobility or worth. It is cruel, debasing, inhuman.

August 26th.—Saw Rufus Dawes again to-day. His bearing is ostentatiously rough and brutal. He has sunk to a depth where he takes a delight in his degradation. This condition is one familiar to me.

He is working in the chain-gang to which Hankey was made sub-overseer. Blind Mooney, a prisoner who was removed from the gang to hospital, told me that there was a plot to murder Hankey, but that Dawes had prevented it. I saw Hankey and told him of this, asking him if he had been aware of the plot. He said "No," falling into a great tremble. "Major Pratt promised me a removal," said he. "I expected it would come to this." I asked him why Dawes defended him; and after some trouble he told me, exacting from me a promise that I would not acquaint the Commandant. It seems that one morning last week Hankey had gone up to Captain Frere's house with a return from Troke, and coming back through the garden had plucked a flower. Dawes had asked him for this flower, offering two days' rations for it. Hankey, who is not a bad-hearted man, gave him the sprig. "There were tears in his eyes as he took it," said he.

There must be some way to get at this man's heart, bad as he seems to be.

August 28th.—Hankey was murdered yesterday. He applied to be removed from the gaol-gang, but Frere refused. "I never let my men 'funk'," he said. "If they've threatened to murder you, I'll keep you there another month in spite of 'em." Some one who overheard this reported it to the gang and they set upon the unfortunate gaoler and beat his brains out with their shovels.

This occurrence has spread consternation among the overseers, and they have addressed a "round robin" to the Commandant, praying to be relieved from their positions.

The way Frere has dealt with this petition is characteristic of him and fills me at once with admiration and disgust. He came down into the yard, shut the gate, and said, "I've just got this petition from my overseers. They say they're afraid you'll murder them as you murdered Hankey. Now, if you want to murder, murder me. Here I am. Step out, one of you." All this, said in a tone of the most galling contempt, did not move them. I saw a dozen pair of eyes flash hatred, but the bull-dog courage of the man overawed them. It would have been easy to kill him then and there, and his death, I am told, is sworn among them; but no one raised a finger. The only man who moved was Rufus Dawes, and he checked himself instantly. Frere, with a recklessness of which I did not think him capable, stepped up to this terror of the prison, and ran his hands lightly down his sides, as is the custom with constables when "searching" a man. Dawes, I thought, would have struck him, but he did not. Frere—still unarmed and alone—then said, "How are you, Dawes? Do you think of bolting again, Dawes? Have you made any more boats?"

"You Devil!" said the chained man in a voice pregnant with such weight of unborn murder, that the gang winced.

"You'll find me one," said Frere, with a laugh; and, turning to me, continued, in the same jesting tone, "There's a penitent for you, Mr. North—try your hand on him."

I must have shown my disgust in my face, for he coloured slightly, and as we were leaving the yard, endeavoured to excuse himself, by saying that it was no use preaching to stones, and such doubly-dyed villains as this Dawes were past hope. "I know the ruffian of old," said he. "He came out in the ship from England with me, and tried to raise a mutiny on board. He was the man who nearly murdered my wife. He has never been out of irons—except then and when he escaped—for the last eighteen years;. and as he's three life sentences, he's like to die in 'em."

A monstrous wretch and criminal, evidently, and yet I feel a strange sympathy with this outcast.

The town house of Mr. Richard Devine was in Clarges Street. Not that this modest mansion was the only establishment of which Richard Devine was

MR. RICHARD DEVINE SURPRISED

master. Mr. John Rex had expensive tastes. His stables were the wonder of London, he owned almost a racing village near Doncaster, kept a yacht at Cowes, and, in addition to a house in Paris, paid the rent of a villa at Brompton. He belonged to several clubs of the faster sort, and might have lived like a prince at any one of them had he been so minded; but a constant fear of discovery—which three years of unbridled riot had not dispelled—led him to prefer the privacy of his own house, where he could choose his own society. The house in Clarges Street was decorated in conformity with the tastes of its owner. The pictures were of horses, the books were records of races, or novels of sporting life. Mr. Francis Wade, waiting, on the morning of the 20th April, 1846, for the coming of his nephew, sighed as he thought of the cultured quiet of Northend House.

Mr. Richard appeared in his dressing-gown. Three years of good living and hard drinking had deprived his figure of its athletic beauty. He was past forty years of age, and the sudden cessation of his active life as a convict and squatter had increased Rex's natural proneness to fat. Instead of being portly he had become gross. His cheeks were inflamed with the frequent application of hot and rebellious liquors to his blood. His eyes, bright and black as ever, lurked in a thicket of crow's feet. He had become prematurely bald. He spoke with assumed heartiness, in a tone of affected ease.

"My dear uncle, sit down. Delighted to see you. Have you breakfasted?—of course you have. I was up rather late last night. Quite sure you won't have anything? A glass of wine? No—then sit down and tell me all the news of Hampstead."

"Thank you, Richard," said the old gentleman, a little stiffly, "but I want some serious talk with you. What do you intend to do with the property? This indecision worries me. Either relieve me of my trust, or be guided by my advice."

"Well, the fact is," said Richard, with a very ugly look on his face, "the fact is—I am much pushed for money."

"Pushed for money!" cried Mr. Wade in horror. "Why, Purkiss, the trustee, said the property was worth twenty thousand a year."

"So it might have been—five years ago—but my horse-racing, and betting, and other amusements have reduced its value considerably."

Mr. Francis Wade took a pinch of snuff with a sharp motion of distaste. "I do not want to hear of your debaucheries," he said; "our name has been sufficiently disgraced in my hearing."

"What is got over the devil's back goes under his belly," replied Mr. Richard coarsely. "My old father got his money by dirtier ways than these in which I spend it. As villainous an old scoundrel and skinflint as ever poisoned a seaman, I'll go bail."

Mr. Francis rose. "You need not revile your father, Richard —he left you all."

"Ay, but by pure accident. He didn't mean it. If he hadn't died in the nick of time, that unhung murderous villain, Maurice Frere, would have come in for it. By the way," he added, with a change of tone, "do you ever hear anything of Maurice?"

"I have not heard for some years," said Mr. Wade. "He is something in the Convict Department at Sydney, I think." ·

"Is he?" said Mr. Richard, with a shiver. "Hope he'll stop there. Well, but about business. The fact is, I am thinking of selling everything."

"Selling everything!"

"Yes. The Hampstead place and all."

"Sell Northend House!" cried poor Mr. Wade, in bewilderment. "Why, the carvings by Grinling Gibbons are the finest in England."

"I can't help that," laughed Mr. Richard, ringing the bell. "I want cash, and cash I must have.—Breakfast, Smithers.—I'm going to travel."

Francis Wade was breathless with astonishment. Reared as he had been, he would as soon have thought of proposing to sell St. Paul's Cathedral, as to sell the casket which held his treasures of art.

"Surely, Richard, you are not in earnest?"

"I am, indeed."

"But—but who will buy it?"

"Plenty of people. I shall cut it up into building allotments. You are quite sure you've breakfasted? Then pardon *me*."

"Richard, you are jesting with me! You will never let them do such a thing!"

"I'm thinking of a trip to America," said Mr. Richard, cracking an egg. "I am sick of Europe. After all, what is the good of a man like me pretending to belong to 'an old family,' with 'a seat' and all that humbug? Money is the thing now, my dear uncle. Hard cash!"

"Then what do you propose doing, sir?"

"To buy my mother's life interest as provided, realise upon the property and travel," said Mr. Richard, helping himself to potted grouse.

"You amaze me, Richard. You confound me. Of course, you can do as you please. But so sudden a determination. The old house—scattered—vases—coins—pictures—I really—Well, it is your property, of course,—and—and—I wish you a very good morning!"

"I mean to do as I please," soliloquised Rex, as he resumed his breakfast. "Let him sell his rubbish by auction, and go and live abroad, in Germany or Jerusalem if he likes, the farther the better for me. I'll sell off the property and make myself scarce."

A knock at the door made him start.

"Come in! Curse it, how nervous I'm getting. What's that? Letters? Give them to me; and why the devil don't you put the brandy on the table, Smithers?" He drank some of the spirit greedily, and began to open his correspondence.

"Cussed brute," said Mr. Smithers, outside the door. "He couldn't use wuss langwidge if he was a dook, dam 'im!" Then a roar from his master recalled him.

"When did *this* come?" asked Mr. Richard, holding out a letter more than usually disfigured with stampings.

"Lars night, sir. It's bin to 'Ampstead, sir, and come down directed with the h'others." The angry glare of the black eyes induced him to add, "I 'ope there's nothing wrong, sir."

"Nothing, you infernal ass and idiot," burst out Mr. Richard, "except that I should have had this instantly. Can't you see it's marked *urgent?* Can't you read? There, that will do. No lies. Get out!"

Left to himself again, Mr. Richard walked hurriedly up and down the chamber, wiped his forehead, drank a tumbler of brandy, and finally sat down and re-read the letter. It was short, but terribly to the purpose.

> The George Hotel, Plymouth,
> *17th April,* 1846.
>
> "My Dear Jack,—
>
> "I have found you out, you see. Never mind how just at present. I know all about your proceedings, and unless Mr. Richard Devine receives his *wife* with due propriety, he'll find himself in the custody of the police. Telegraph, dear, to Mrs. Richard Devine, at above address.
>
> "Yours as ever, Jack,
> "Sarah."

The blow was unexpected and severe. It was hard, in the high tide of success, to be thus plucked back into the old bondage. Despite the affectionate tone of the letter, he knew the woman with whom he had to deal. For some minutes he sat motionless, gazing at the letter, his thoughts running furiously.

"How did she discover me! What shall I do? It is absurd to run away, for I shall be caught. Besides, I've no ready money. If I bolt at all, I must bolt at once—within twenty-four hours. Rich as I am, I don't suppose I could raise more than five thousand pounds in that time. Curse the woman! It's a bad job.—However, she's not inclined to be gratuitously disagreeable. How lucky I never married again! I had better make terms and trust to fortune. After all, she's been a good friend to me.—Poor Sally!—I might have rotted on that infernal Eaglehawk Neck, if it hadn't been for her. Handsome woman, too. I may make it up with her. I shall have to sell off and go away after all.—It might be worse.—I dare say the property's worth three hundred thousand pounds. Not bad for a start in America. And I may get rid of her yet. Damn the woman."

THE CHAPLAIN IS TAKEN ILL

Though the house of the Commandant of Norfolk Island was comfortable and well furnished, and though all that was most hideous in the "discipline" of the place was hidden, the loathing with which Sylvia had approached the last and most dreaded abiding place of the elaborate convict system had not decreased. The sight and sounds of pain and punishment surrounded her. She could not look out of her windows without a shudder. She dreaded each evening when her husband returned, lest he should blurt out some new atrocity.

"I wish, Maurice, we had never come here," said she, piteously, when he recounted to her the scene of the gaol-gang. "These unhappy men will do you some frightful injury one of these days."

"Stuff!" said her husband. "They've not the courage. I'd take the best man among them, and dare him to touch me."

"I cannot think how you like to witness so much misery and villainy. It is horrible to think of."

"Our tastes differ, my dear.—Jenkins! Confound you! Jenkins, I say." The convict-servant entered. "Where is the chargebook? I've told you always to have it ready for me. Why don't you do as you are told?"

"If you please, sir——"

"Don't answer me, sir. Give me the book." Taking it and running his finger down the leaves, he commented on the list of offences to which he would be called upon in the morning to mete out judgment.

"*John Gateby, insolence and insubordination. James Hopkins, insolence and foul language. Rufus Dawes, gross insolence, refusing to work.*—Ah! we must look after you. You are a parson's man, are you? I'll break your spirit, my man, or I'll—Sylvia!"

"Yes."

"Your friend Dawes is doing credit to his bringing up."

"What do you mean?"

"That infernal villain and reprobate, Dawes. He is fitting himself faster for——"

She interrupted him. "Maurice, I wish you would not use such language. You know I dislike it." She spoke coldly and sadly, as one who knows that remonstrance is in vain, and is yet constrained to remonstrate.

"Oh, dear! My Lady Proper! can't bear to hear her husband swear. How refined we're getting!"

"There, I did not mean to annoy you," said she, wearily. "Don't let us quarrel, for goodness' sake."

He went away noisily, and she sat looking at the carpet wearily. A noise roused her. She looked up and saw North. Her face beamed instantly. "Ah! Mr. North, I did not expect you. What brings you here? You'll stay to dinner, of course. And have you brought me the book? I have been looking for it."

"Here it is," said North, producing a volume of 'Monte Cristo'. "I envy you."

She seized the book with avidity, and, after running her eyes over the pages, turned inquiringly to the fly-leaf.

"It belongs to my predecessor," said North, as though in answer to her thought. "He seems to have been a great reader of French. I have found many French novels of his."

"I thought clergymen never read French novels," said Sylvia, with a smile.

"There are French novels and French novels," said North. "Stupid people confound the good with the bad. I remember a worthy friend of mine in Sydney who soundly abused me for reading Rabelais, and when I asked him if *he* had read it, he said that he would sooner cut his hand off than open it."

"But is this really good? Papa told me it was rubbish."

"It is a romance, but, in my opinion, a very fine one. The notion of the sailor being taught in prison by the priest, and sent back into the world, an accomplished gentleman, to work out his vengeance, is superb."

"Now, now—you are telling me," laughed she; and then, with feminine perversity, "Go on, what is the story?"

"Only that of an unjustly imprisoned man, who, escaping by a marvel, and becoming rich—as Dr. Johnson says, 'beyond the dreams of avarice'—devotes his life and fortune to revenge."

"And does he?"

"He does, upon all his enemies save one."

"And he——?"

"*She*—was the wife of his greatest enemy, and Dantès spared her because he loved her."

Sylvia turned away her head. "It seems interesting enough," said she, coldly.

There was an awkward silence for a moment, which each seemed afraid to break. North bit his lips, as though regretting what he had said. Mrs. Frere beat her foot on the floor, and at length raising her eyes, and meeting those of the clergyman fixed upon her face, rose hurriedly to meet her returning husband.

"Come to dinner, of course!" said Frere, who, though he disliked the clergyman, yet was glad of anybody who would help him to pass a cheerful evening.

"I came to bring Mrs. Frere a book."

"Ah! She reads too many books; she's always reading books. It is not a good thing to be always poring over print, is it, North? You have some influence with her; tell her so."

He spoke with that affectation of jollity with which husbands of his calibre veil their bad temper.

Sylvia had her defensive armour on in a twinkling.

"Of course, you two men will be against me. When did two men ever disagree upon the subject of wifely duties? However, I shall read in spite of you. Do you know, Mr. North, that when I married I made a special agreement with Captain Frere that I was not to be asked to sew on buttons for him?"

"Indeed!" said North, not understanding this change of humour.

"And she never has from that hour," said Frere, recovering his suavity at the sight of food. "I never have a shirt fit to put on. Upon my word, there are a dozen in the drawer now."

North perused his plate uncomfortably. A saying of omniscient Balzac occurred to him. "Le grand écueil est le ridicule," and his mind began to sound all sorts of philosophical depths, not of the most clerical character.

After dinner Maurice launched into his usual topic—convict discipline. It was pleasant for him to get a listener; for his wife, cold and unsympathetic, declined to enter into his schemes for the subduing of the refractory villains. "You insisted on coming here," she would say. "I did not wish to come. I don't like to talk of these things. Let us talk of something else." When she adopted this procedure, he had no alternative but to submit, for he was afraid of her, after a fashion.

Love had long since died out of their life. The young, impulsive, delicate girl, who had given herself to him seven years before, had been changed into a weary, suffering woman. Instead of love, he had awakened in her a distaste which at times amounted to disgust. Yet in this repulsion lay her power over him; Maurice Frere, though his wife obeyed him, knew that he was inferior to her, and was afraid of the statue he had created. Her coldness was at once her strength and her weakness. When she chilled him, she commanded him.

As Frere chatted amicably, North said little, but drank a good deal. The wine, however, rendered him silent, instead of talkative. He drank that he might forget unpleasant memories, and drank without accomplishing his object. When the pair proceeded to the room where Mrs. Frere awaited them, Frere was boisterously good-humoured, North silently misanthropic.

"Sing something, Sylvia!" said Frere, with the ease of possession, as one who should say to a living musical-box, "Play something."

"Oh, Mr. North doesn't care for music, and I'm not inclined to sing.

Singing seems out of place here."

"Nonsense," said Frere. "Why should it be more out of place here than anywhere else?"

"Mrs. Frere means that mirth is in a manner unsuited to these melancholy surroundings," said North.

"Melancholy surroundings!" cried Frere, staring in turn at the piano and the ottomans. "Well, the house isn't as good as the one in Sydney, but it's comfortable enough."

"You don't understand me, Maurice," said Sylvia. "This place is very gloomy to me. The thought of the unhappy men who are ironed and chained all about us makes me miserable."

"What stuff!" said Frere, now thoroughly roused. "The ruffians deserve all they get and more."

"Poor men! How do we know the strength of their temptation, the bitterness of their repentance?"

"Evil-doers earn their punishment," says North, in a hard voice, and taking up a book suddenly. "They must learn to bear it. No repentance can undo their sin."

"But surely there is mercy for the worst of evil-doers," urged Sylvia, gently. North seemed disinclined or unable to reply, and nodded only.

"Mercy!" cried Frere. "I am not here to be merciful; I am here to keep order, and by the Lord, I'll do it!"

"Maurice, do not talk like that. Think how slight an accident might have made any one of us like one of these men. What is the matter, Mr. North?" Mr. North had suddenly turned pale.

"Nothing," returned the clergyman, gasping—"a sudden faintness!" The windows were thrown open, and the chaplain gradually recovered. "I am liable to these attacks. A touch of heart disease, I think. I shall have to rest for a day or so."

"Ah, take a spell," said Frere; "You overwork yourself."

North, gasping and pale, smiles in a ghastly manner. "I—I will. If I do not appear for a week, Mrs. Frere, you will know the reason."

"A week! Surely it will not last so long as that," exclaims Sylvia.

The ambiguous "it" appears to annoy him, for he flushes painfully, replying, "Sometimes longer. It is, a—um—uncertain," in a confused and shame-faced manner, and is luckily relieved by the entry of Jenkins.

"A message from Mr. Troke, sir."

"Troke! What's the matter now?"

"Dawes, sir, he's assaulted Mr. Troke, Mr. Troke said you'd left orders to be told at onst of the insubordination of prisoners."

"Quite right, where is he?"

"In the cells, I think, sir. They had a hard fight to get him there, I am told, your honour."

"Had they? Give my compliments to Mr. Troke, and tell him that I shall have the pleasure of breaking Mr. Dawes's spirit to-morrow morning at nine sharp."

"Maurice," said Sylvia in alarm, "do me a favour? Do not torment this man."

"What makes you take a fancy to *him?*" asks her husband, with sudden unnecessary fierceness.

"Because his is one of the names which have been from my childhood synonymous with suffering and torture, because whatever wrong he may have done, his life-long punishment must have in some degree atoned for it."

She spoke with an eager pity in her face that transfigured it. North, devouring her with his glance, saw tears in her eyes.

"Does this look as if he had made atonement?" said Frere coarsely, slapping the letter.

"He is a bad man, I know, but——" she passed her hand over her forehead with the old troubled gesture—"he cannot have been always bad. I think I have heard some good of him somewhere."

"Nonsense," said Frere, rising decisively. "Your fancies mislead you. Let me hear no more. The man is rebellious, and must be lashed back again to his duty. Come, North, we'll have a nip before you start."

"Mr. North, will not *you* plead for me?" suddenly cried Sylvia, her self-possession overthrown. "You have a heart to pity these suffering creatures."

But North, who seemed to have suddenly recalled his soul from some place where it had been wandering, draws himself aside, and with dry lips makes shift to say, "I cannot interfere with your husband, madam," and goes out almost rudely.

"You've made old North quite ill," said Frere, when he by-and-by returns, hoping by bluff ignoring of roughness on his own part to avoid reproach from his wife. "He drank half a bottle of brandy to steady his nerves before he went home, and swung out of the house like one possessed."

But Sylvia, occupied by her own thoughts, did not reply.

The insubordination of which Rufus Dawes had been guilty was, in this instance, insignificant. It was the custom of the newly-fledged constables

BREAKING A MAN'S SPIRIT

of Captain Frere to enter the wards at night, armed with cutlasses, tramping about, and making a great noise. Mindful of the report of Pounce, they pulled the men roughly from their hammocks, examined their persons for concealed tobacco, and compelled them to open their mouths to see if any was inside. The men in Dawes's gang—to which Mr. Troke had an especial objection— were often searched more than once in a night, and in the roughest manner.

The great aim of Troke was to catch Dawes tripping, but the leader of the "Ring" was too wary. In vain had Troke burst in upon the convict at all times and seasons. He had found nothing. In vain had he laid traps for him; the experienced "old hand" was too acute. Filled with disgust and ambition, he determined upon an ingenious little trick. He was certain that Dawes possessed tobacco; the thing was to find it upon him. Now, Rufus Dawes, holding aloof, as was his custom, from the majority of his companions, had made one friend—if so mindless and battered an old wreck could be called a friend—Blind Mooney. Perhaps this odd friendship was brought about by two causes—one, that Mooney was the only man on the island who knew more of the horrors of convictism than the leader of the Ring; the other, that Mooney was blind, and, to a moody, sullen man, subject to a constant suspicion of all his fellow-creatures, a blind companion was more congenial than a sharp-eyed one.

Mooney was one of the "First Fleeters." He had arrived in Sydney fifty-seven years before, in the year 1789, when he was fourteen years old. He had been through the whole round of servitude, had worked as a bondsman, had married, and been "up country," had been again sentenced, and was a sort of dismal patriarch of Norfolk Island, having been there at its former settlement. He had no friends. His wife was long since dead, and he stated that his master having taken a fancy to her, had despatched the uncomplaisant husband to imprisonment. Such cases were not uncommon.

One of the ways in which Rufus Dawes had obtained the affection of the old blind man was the gift of such fragments of tobacco as he himself from time to time secured. Troke knew this; and on the evening in question hit upon an excellent plan. Admitting himself noiselessly into the shed where the gang slept, he crept close to the sleeping Dawes, and counterfeiting Mooney's mumbling utterance, asked for "some tobacco." Rufus Dawes was but half awake, and on repeating his request, Troke felt something put into his hand. He grasped Dawes's arm, and struck a light. He had got his man this time. Dawes had conveyed to his fancied friend a piece of tobacco almost as big as the top joint of his little finger.

One can understand the feelings of a man entrapped by such base means. Rufus Dawes no sooner saw the hated face of Warder Troke peering over his hammock than he sprang out, and knocked Mr. Troke fairly off his legs into the arms of the in-coming constables. A desperate struggle took place, at the end of which, the convict, overpowered by numbers, was borne senseless to the cells, gagged, and chained. While in this condition he was savagely beaten by five or six constables.

To this maimed and manacled rebel was the Commandant ushered by Troke the next morning.

"Ha! ha! my man," said the Commandant. "Here you are again, you see. How do you like this sort of thing?"

Dawes, glaring, makes no answer.

"You shall have fifty lashes, my man," said Frere. "We'll see how you'll feel then!"

The fifty were duly administered, and the Commandant called the next day. The rebel was still mute.

"Give him fifty more, Mr. Troke. We'll see what he's made of."

One hundred and twenty lashes were inflicted in the course of the morning, but still the convict refused to speak. He was then treated to fourteen days' solitary confinement.

On being brought out and confronted with his tormentor, he merely laughed. For this he was sent back for another fourteen days; and still remaining obdurate, was flogged again, and got fourteen days more. Had the chaplain then visited him, he might have found him open to consolation, but the chaplain—so it was stated—was sick. When brought out at the conclusion of his third confinement, he was found to be so exhausted that the doctor ordered him to hospital. As soon as he was sufficiently recovered, Frere visited him, and finding his "spirit" not yet "broken", ordered that he should be put to grind maize. Dawes declined to work. So they chained his hand to one arm of the grindstone, and placed another prisoner at the other arm. As the second prisoner turned, the hand of Dawes revolved.

"You're not such a pebble as folks seemed to think," grinned Frere, pointing to the turning wheel.

Upon which the indomitable poor devil straightened his sorely-tried muscles, and prevented the wheel from turning at all. Frere gave him fifty more lashes, and sent him the next day to grind cayenne pepper. This was a punishment more dreaded by the convicts than any other. The pungent dust filled their eyes and lungs, causing them the most excruciating torments. For a man with a raw back the work was agony. In four days, Rufus Dawes, emaciated, blistered, blinded, broke down.

"For God's sake, Captain Frere, kill me at once!" he said.

"No fear," said the other. "You've given in; that's all I wanted. Troke, take him to the hospital."

When he was in hospital, North visited him.

"I would have come to see you before," said the clergyman, "but I have been very ill."

In truth he looked so. He had had a fever, it seemed, and they had shaved his beard, and cropped his hair. Dawes could see that the haggard, wasted man had passed through some agony almost as great as his own. The next day Frere visited Dawes, complimented him on his courage, and offered to make him a constable. Dawes turned his scarred back to his torturer, and resolutely declined to answer.

"I am afraid you have made an enemy of the Commandant," said North, the next day. "Why not accept his offer?"

Dawes cast on him a glance of quiet scorn. "And betray my mates? I'm not one of that sort."

The clergyman spoke to him of hope, of release, of repentance, and redemption. The prisoner laughed. "Who's to redeem me?" he said. "It would take a Christ to die again to save such as I."

"There is another life," urged North. "Do not risk your chance of happiness in it. You have a future to live for, man."

"I hope not," said the convict. "I want to rest—to rest, and never to be disturbed again."

His "spirit" was broken enough by this time. Yet he had resolution enough to refuse Frere's repeated offers. "I'll never 'jump' it," he said to North, "if they cut me in half first."

North pityingly implored the stubborn mind to have mercy on the lacerated body, but without effect. "A noble nature ruined," said he to himself. "What is the secret of his history?"

Dawes, on his part, seeing how different from other black coats was this priest—at once so stern and so tender—began to speculate on the cause of his monitor's sunken cheeks, fiery eyes, and pre-occupied manner, to wonder what grief inspired those agonised prayers which were daily poured out over his rude bed. So between these two—the priest and the sinner—grew a sympathetic bond.

One day this bond was drawn so close as to tug at both their heart-strings. The chaplain had a flower in his coat. Dawes eyed it hungrily, and, as the clergyman was about to depart, said, "Mr. North, will you give me that rosebud?" North paused irresolutely, and finally took it carefully from his button-hole, and placed it in the prisoner's scarred hand. In another instant, Dawes, believing himself alone, pressed the gift to his lips. North returned abruptly, and the eyes of the pair met. Dawes flushed crimson, but North turned white as death. Neither spoke, but each was drawn closer to the other, since both had kissed the rosebud plucked by Sylvia's fingers.

October 21st.—I am safe for another six months if I am careful, for my last bout lasted longer than I expected. I suppose one of these days I shall have a

FROM THE DIARY OF MR. JAMES NORTH

paroxysm that will kill me. I shall not regret it. Yet how many times before the last shall this torment repeat itself? The pattern is wearisomely familiar. Penitent and shattered, I vow to lead a new life; to forswear spirits, to drink nothing but water. Indeed, the sight and smell of brandy make me ill. All goes well for some weeks, when I grow nervous, discontented, moody. I smoke, and am soothed. But moderation is not to be thought of; little by little I increase the dose of tobacco. Five pipes a day become six or seven, then mount to eleven at a leap; then lose count altogether. Much smoking excites the brain. I feel clear, bright, gay. My limbs regain their suppleness, my hands their coolness, my brain its placidity. I begin to feel that I have a will. I am confident, calm, and hopeful.

To this condition succeeds one of the most frightful melancholy. I remain plunged, for an hour together, in a stupor of despair. The earth, air, sea, all appear barren, colourless. Life is a burden. I long to sleep, and sleeping struggle to awake, because of the awful dreams which flap about me in the darkness. I loathe myself, and all around me. I know well what will restore me to life and ease—restore me, but to cast me back again into a deeper fit of despair. I drink. One glass—my blood is warmed,—my heart leaps, my hand no longer shakes. Three glasses, I rise with hope in my soul,—the evil spirit flies from me. I continue—pleasing images flock to my brain, the fields break into flower, the birds into song, the sea gleams sapphire, the warm heaven laughs. Great God! what man could withstand a temptation like this?

October 22nd.—Have spent the day with Mrs. Frere. She is evidently eager to leave the place—as eager as I am. Frere rejoices in his murderous power, and laughs at her expostulations.

I do not think she can possibly care for him. I am not a selfish sentimentalist, as are the majority of seducers. I would take no woman away from a husband for mere liking. Yet I think there are cases in which a man *who loved* would be justified in making a woman happy at the risk of his own—soul, I suppose.

Making her happy! Ay, that's the point. Would she be happy? There are few men who can endure to be "cut," slighted, pointed at, and women suffer more than men in these regards. I, a grizzled man of forty, am not such an arrant ass as to suppose that a year of guilty delirium can compensate to a gently-nurtured woman for the loss of that social dignity which constitutes her best happiness. Apart from the question of the sin of breaking the seventh commandment, I doubt if the worst husband and the most unhappy home are not better, in this social condition of ours, than the most devoted lover. A strange subject for a clergyman to speculate upon! If this diary should ever fall into the hands of a real God-fearing, honest booby, who never was tempted to sin by finding that at middle-age he loved the wife of another, how he would condemn me! And rightly, of course.

November 4th.—In one of the turnkey's rooms is to be seen a bridle, perfect in headband, throat-lash, etc., for a human being. There is attached to this bridle a round piece of cross wood, of almost four inches in length, and one and a half in diameter. This, again, is secured to a broad strap of leather to cross the mouth. In the wood there is a small hole, and, when used, the wood is inserted in the mouth, the small hole being the only breathing space. This being secured with the various straps and buckles, a more complete bridle could not be well imagined.

I was in the gaol last evening at eight o'clock. Everything was quite still. I could not help remarking to Gimblett, the turnkey, how quiet the gaol was, when he said, "There's some one speaking. I know who that is." And forthwith took from its pegs one of the bridles just described, and a pair of handcuffs.

I followed him to one of the cells, and therein was a man lying on his mat, to all appearance fast asleep. Gimblett ordered him to get up and dress himself. He did so, and came into the yard, where Gimblett inserted the iron-wood gag in his mouth. The sound produced by his breathing (which appeared to be done with great difficulty) resembled a low, indistinct whistle. Gimblett led him to the lamp-post in the yard, and I saw that the victim of his tyranny was the poor blind wretch Mooney. Gimblett placed him with his back against the lamp-post, and his arms being taken round, were secured by handcuffs round the post. I was told that the old man was to remain in this condition for three hours. I went at once to the Commandant. He invited me into his drawing-room—an invitation which I had the good sense to refuse—but refused to listen to any pleas for mercy. "The old impostor is always making his blindness an excuse for disobedience," said he.—And this is *her* husband!

Rufus Dawes, hearing of the wanton torture of his friend, uttered no threat of vengeance, but groaned only. "I am not so strong as I was," said he, as if

THE LONGEST STRAW

in apology for his lack of spirit. "They have unnerved me." And he looked sadly down at his gaunt frame and trembling hands.

"I can't stand it no longer," said Mooney, grimly. "I've spoken to Bland, and he's of my mind. You know what we resolved to do. Let's do it."

Rufus Dawes stared at the sightless orbs turned to his own. The fingers of his hand, thrust into his bosom, felt a token which lay there. A shudder thrilled him. "No, no. Not now," he said.

"You're not afeard, man?" asked Mooney, stretching out his hand in the direction of the voice. "You ain't going to back out after you swored it, Dawes? You're not that sort. Dawes, speak, man!"

"Is Bland willing?" asked Dawes, looking round, as if to seek some method of escape from the glare of those unspeculative eyes.

"Ay, and ready. They flogged him again yesterday."

"Leave it till to-morrow," said Dawes at length.

"No; let's have it over," urged the old man, with a strange eagerness. "I'm tired o' this."

Rufus Dawes cast a wistful glance towards the wall behind which lay the house of the Commandant. "Leave it till to-morrow," he repeated, with his hand still in his breast.

They had been so occupied in their conversation that neither had observed the approach of their common enemy. "What are you hiding there?" cried Frere, seizing Dawes by the wrist. "More tobacco, you dog?" The hand of the convict opened involuntarily, and a withered rose fell to the earth. Frere, astonished, picked it up. "Hallo! What the devil's this? You've not been robbing my garden for a nosegay, Jack?" The Commandant was wont to call all convicts "Jack" in his moments of facetiousness. It was a little humorous way he had.

Rufus Dawes uttered one dismal cry, and then stood trembling and cowed. His companions, hearing his exclamation, looked to see him snatch back the flower or perform some act of violence. Perhaps such was his intention, but he did not execute it. One would have thought that there was some charm about this rose so strangely cherished, for he stood gazing at it, as it twirled between Captain Frere's strong fingers, as though it fascinated him. "You're a pretty man to want a rose for your button-hole! Are you going out with your sweetheart next Sunday, Mr. Dawes?" The gang laughed. "How did you get this?" Dawes was silent. "You'd better tell me." No answer. "Troke, let us see if we can't find Mr. Dawes's tongue. Pull off your shirt, my man. I expect that's the way to your heart—eh, boys?"

At this elegant allusion to the lash, the gang laughed again, and looked at each other astonished. It seemed possible that the leader of the Ring was going to turn milksop. Such, indeed, appeared to be the case, for Dawes, trembling and pale, cried, "Don't flog me again, sir! I picked it up in the yard. It fell out of your coat one day." Frere smiled with an inward satisfaction at his spirit-breaking. The explanation was probably the correct one. He was in the habit of wearing flowers in his coat, and it was impossible that the convict should have obtained one by any other means. Had it been a fig of tobacco now, the astute Commandant knew plenty of men who would have brought it into the prison. But who would risk a flogging for so useless a thing as a flower? "You'd better not pick up any more, Jack," he said. "We don't grow flowers for your amusement." And contemptuously flinging the rose over the wall, he strode away.

The gang, left to itself, bestowed their attention upon Dawes. Large tears were silently rolling down his face, and he stood staring as one in a dream. The gang curled their lips. One fellow, more charitable than the rest, tapped his forehead and winked. "He's going cranky," said he. Dawes recovered himself, and the contemptuous glances of his companions seemed to bring back the colour to his cheeks.

"We'll do it to-night," whispered he to Mooney, and Mooney smiled with pleasure.

Since the "tobacco trick," Mooney and Dawes had been placed in the new prison, together with a man named Bland, who had already twice failed to kill himself. Bland had proposed that the three should put in practice a scheme in which two at least must succeed. The scheme was a desperate one, and attempted only in the last extremity. It was the custom of the Ring, however, to swear each of its members to carry out to the best of his ability this last invention of the convict-disciplined mind, should two other members crave his assistance.

The scheme—like all great ideas—was simplicity itself.

That evening, when the cell-door was securely locked, Bland produced a straw, and held it out to his companions. Dawes took it, and tearing it into unequal lengths, handed the fragments to Mooney.

"The longest is the one," said the blind man. "Come on, boys, and dip in the lucky-bag!"

It was evident that lots were to be drawn to determine to whom fortune would grant freedom. The men drew in silence, and then Bland and Dawes looked at each other. The prize had been left in the bag. Mooney retained the longest straw. There was a moment's pause, during which the blank eyeballs of the blind man fiercely searched the gloom, as if in that awful moment they could penetrate it.

"I hold the shortest," said Dawes to Bland. "'Tis you that must do it."

"I'm glad of that," said Mooney.

Bland, seemingly terrified at the danger which fate had decreed that he should run, tore the fatal lot into fragments with an oath, and sat gnawing his knuckles in excess of abject terror. Mooney stretched himself out upon his plank-bed. "Come on, mate," he said.

Bland caught Rufus Dawes by the sleeve.

"You have more nerve than I. You do it."

"No, no," said Dawes, almost as pale as his companion. "I've run my chance fairly. 'Twas your own proposal."

The coward who, confident in his own luck, would seem to have fallen into the pit he had dug for others, sat rocking himself to and fro, holding his head in his hands.

"By Heaven, I can't do it," he whispered, lifting a white face.

"What are you waiting for?" said fortunate Mooney. "Come on, I'm ready."

"I—I—thought you might like to—to—pray a bit," said Bland.

The notion seemed to sober the senses of the old man.

"Ay!" he said. "Pray! A good thought!" and he knelt down; and shutting his blind eyes, moved his lips silently.

The silence was broken by the footstep of the warder in the corridor. Bland hailed it as a reprieve from whatever act of daring he dreaded.

"We must wait until he goes," he whispered eagerly.

Dawes nodded, and Mooney, whose quick ear apprised him very exactly of the position of the approaching gaoler, rose from his knees radiant. The sour face of Gimblett appeared at the trap cell-door.

"All right?" he asked, somewhat—so the three thought—less sourly than usual.

"All right," was the reply, and Mooney added, "Good-night, Mr. Gimblett."

"I wonder what makes the old man so cheerful," thought Gimblett, as he got into the next corridor.

The sound of his footsteps had scarcely died away, but that the lucky man was tearing a strip from his blanket. "I think this will do," said he, pulling it between his hands to test its strength. "Here, Bland, catch hold. Where are ye?—don't be faint-hearted, man. It won't take ye long."

It was quite dark in the cell, but as Bland advanced, his face was like a white mask, so ghastly pale was it. Dawes pressed his lucky comrade's hand, and withdrew to the farthest corner. Bland and Mooney were for a few moments occupied with the rope—doubtless preparing for escape by means of it. The silence was broken only by the convulsive jangling of Bland's irons—he was shuddering violently. At last Mooney spoke again, in strangely soft and subdued tones.

"Dawes, lad, do you think there is a Heaven?"

"I know there is a Hell," said Dawes.

"Ay, and a Heaven, lad. I think I shall go there. *You* will, old chap, for you've been good to me—God bless you, you've been very good to me."

When Troke came in the morning, he saw what had occurred at a glance, and hastened to remove the corpse of the strangled Mooney.

"We drew lots," said Rufus Dawes, pointing to Bland, who crouched in the corner farthest from his victim, "and it fell upon him to do it. I'm the witness."

"They'll hang you for all that," said Troke.

"I hope so," said Rufus Dawes.

The scheme of escape hit upon by the convict intellect was simply this. Three men being together, lots were drawn to determine whom should be murdered. The drawer of the longest straw was the "lucky" man. He was killed. The drawer of the next longest straw was the murderer. He was hanged. The unlucky one was the witness. He had, of course, an excellent chance of being hung also, but his doom was not so certain, and he therefore looked upon himself as unfortunate.

John Rex found the "George" disagreeably prepared for his august arrival. Obsequious waiters took his dressing bag and overcoat, the landlord himself welcomed him at the door. Two naval gentlemen came out of the coffee-room to stare at him. "Have you any more luggage, Mr. Devine?" asked the landlord, as he flung open the door of the best drawing-room. It was awkwardly evident that his wife had no notion of suffering him to hide his borrowed light under a bushel.

A MEETING

A supper-table laid for two people gleamed bright from the cheeriest corner. A fire crackled beneath the marble mantelshelf. The latest evening paper lay upon a chair; and, brushing it carelessly with her costly dress, the woman he had so basely deserted came smiling to meet him.

"Well, Mr. Richard Devine," said she, "you did not expect to see me again, did you?"

Although, on his journey down, he had composed an elaborate speech wherewith to greet her, this unnatural civility dumbfounded him. "Sarah! I never meant to——"

"Hush, my dear Richard—it must be Richard now, I suppose—This is not the time for explanations. Besides, the waiter might hear you. Let us have some supper, you must be hungry, I am sure." He advanced to the table mechanically. "How fat you are!" she continued. "Too good living, I suppose. You were not so fat at Port Ar— Oh, I forgot, my dear! Come and sit down. That's right. I have told them all that I am your wife, for whom you have sent. They regard me with some interest and respect in consequence. Don't spoil their good opinion of me."

He was about to utter an imprecation, but she stopped him by a glance. "No bad language, John, or I shall ring for a constable. Let us understand one another, my dear. You may be a very great man to other people, but to me you are merely my runaway husband—an escaped convict. If you don't eat your supper civilly, I shall send for the police."

"Sarah!" he burst out, "I never meant to desert you. Upon my word. It is all a mistake. Let me explain."

"There is no need for explanations yet, Jack—I mean Richard. Have your supper. Ah! I know what you want."

She poured out half a tumbler of brandy, and gave it to him. He took the glass from her hand, drank the contents, and then, as though warmed by the spirit, laughed. "What a woman you are, Sarah. I have been a great brute, I confess."

"You have been an ungrateful villain," said she, with sudden passion, "a hardened, selfish villain."

"But, Sarah——"

"Don't touch me!"

" 'Pon my word, you are a fine creature, and I was a fool to leave you."

The compliment seemed to soothe her, for her tone changed somewhat. "It was a wicked, cruel act, Jack. You whom I saved from death—whom I nursed—whom I enriched. It was the act of a coward."

"I admit it. It was."

"You admit it. Have you no shame then? Have you no pity for me for what I have suffered all these years?"

"I don't suppose you cared much."

"Don't you? You never thought about me at all. I have cared this much, John Rex, that I have spent a fortune in hunting you down; and now I have found you, I will make you suffer in your turn."

He laughed again, but uneasily. "How did you discover me?"

With a readiness which showed that she had already prepared an answer to the question, she unlocked a writing case and took from it a newspaper. "By one of those accidents which are the ruin of men like you. Among the papers sent to the overseer from his English friends was this one."

She held out an illustrated journal—a Sunday organ of sporting opinion—and pointed to a portrait on the centre page. It represented a broad-shouldered, bearded man, dressed in the fashion affected by lovers of horseflesh, standing beside a pedestal on which were piled a variety of racing trophies. John Rex read underneath this work of art the name

MR. RICHARD DEVINE
THE LEVIATHAN OF THE TURF

"And you recognised me?"

"The portrait was sufficiently like you to induce me to make inquiries, and when I found that Mr. Richard Devine had suddenly returned from a mysterious absence of fourteen years, I set to work in earnest. I have spent a deal of money, Jack, but I've got you!"

"You have been clever in finding me out; I give you credit for that."

"There is not a single act of your life, John Rex, that I do not know," she continued, with heat. "I have traced you from the day you stole out of my house until now. I know your continental trips, your journeyings here and there in search of a lost clue. I pieced together the puzzle, as you have done, and I know that, by some foul fortune, you have stolen the secret of a dead man to ruin an innocent and virtuous family."

"Hullo!" said John Rex. "Since when have *you* learnt to talk of virtue?"

"It is well to taunt, but you have got to the end of your tether now, Jack. I have communicated with the woman whose son's fortune you have stolen. I expect to hear from Lady Devine in a day or so."

"And when you hear?"

"I shall give back the fortune at the price of her silence!"

"Ho! ho! Will you?"

"Yes; and if my husband does not come back and live with me quietly, I shall call in the police."

John Rex sprang up. "Who will believe you, idiot?" he cried. "I'll have you sent to gaol as an impostor."

"You forget, my dear," she returned, playing coquettishly with her rings, "that you have already acknowledged me as your wife before the landlord and the servants. Oh, my dear Jack, you think you are very clever, but I am as clever as you."

Smothering a curse, he sat down beside her. "Listen, Sarah. What is the use of fighting like children. I am rich——"

"So am I."

"Well, so much the better. We will join our riches together. I admit that I was a fool and a cur to leave you; but I played for a great stake. The name of Richard Devine was worth nearly half a million of money. It is mine. I won it. Share it with me! Sarah, you and I defied the world years ago. Don't let us quarrel now. We know by this time that we are not either of us angels. We started in life together—do you remember, Sally, when I met you first?—determined to make money. We have succeeded. Why then set to work to destroy each other? You are handsome as ever, I have not lost my wits. Kiss, and be friends, Sarah. I would have escaped you if I could, I admit. You have found me out. I accept the position. You claim me as your husband. You say you are Mrs. Richard Devine. Very well, I admit it. You have all your life wanted to be a great lady. Now is your chance!"

Much as she had cause to hate him, well as she knew his treacherous character, her strange affection for the scoundrel came upon her again with gathering strength. As she sat beside him, listening to the familiar tones of the voice she had learned to love, greedily drinking in the promise of a future fidelity which she was well aware was made but to be broken, her memory recalled the past days of happiness, and her woman's fancy once more invested the selfish villain she had reclaimed with those attributes which had enchained her wilful and wayward affections. The bitterness of despised love, the shame and anger of desertion, ingratitude, and betrayal, all vanished. She took his coward hand and kissed it, pardoning all his baseness with the sole reproach, "Oh, John, John, you might have trusted me after all?"

John Rex had conquered, and he smiled as he embraced her. "I wish I had," said he; "it would have saved me many regrets; but never mind. Sit down; *now* we will have supper."

"Your preference has one drawback, Sarah," he said, when the meal was concluded, and the two sat down to consider their immediate course of action, "it doubles the chance of detection."

"How so?"

"People have accepted me without inquiry, but I am afraid not without dislike. Mr. Francis Wade, my uncle, never liked me; and I fear I have not played my cards well with Lady Devine. When they find I have a mysterious wife their dislike will become suspicion. Is it likely that I should have been married all these years and not have informed them?"

"Very unlikely," returned Sarah calmly, "and that is just the reason why you have *not* been married all these years. Really," she added, with a laugh, "the male intellect is very dull. You have already told ten thousand lies about this affair, and yet you don't see your way to tell one more."

"What do you mean?"

"Why, my dear Richard, you cannot have forgotten that you married me last year on the Continent? It *was* last year that you were there, was it not? I am the daughter of a poor clergyman of the Church of England; name—anything you please—and you met me—where shall we say? Baden, Aix, Brussels?"

John Rex nodded. "Of course—I am stupid," said he. "I have not been well lately. Too much brandy, I suppose."

"Well, we will alter all that," she returned with a laugh. "You are going to be domestic now, Jack—I mean Dick."

"Go on," said he, impatiently. "What then?"

"Then, having settled these little preliminaries, you take me up to London and introduce me to your relatives and friends."

He started. "A bold game."

"Bold! Nonsense! The only safe one. People don't, as a rule, suspect, unless one is mysterious. The waiters here all know me as your wife. There is not the least danger—unless, indeed, you are married already?" she added, with quick and angry suspicion.

"You need not be alarmed. I was not such a fool as to marry another woman while *you* were alive—had I even seen one I would have cared to marry. But what of Lady Devine? You say you have told her."

"I have told her to communicate with Mrs. Carr, Post-office, Torquay, in order to hear something to her advantage. If you had been rebellious, John, the 'something' would have been a letter from me telling her who you really are. Now you have proved obedient, the 'something' will be a begging letter of a sort of which she has already received hundreds, and which in all probability she will not even answer. What do you think of that, Mr. Richard Devine?"

"You deserve success, Sarah," said the old schemer, in genuine admiration. "I will be guided by you. What next?"

"Next—for, as you say, my presence doubles the danger—we will contrive to withdraw quietly from England. The introduction to your mother over, and Mr. Francis disposed of, we will go to Hampstead, and live there for a while. During that time you must turn into cash as much property as you dare. We will then go abroad for the 'season'—and stop there. After a year or so on the Continent, you can write to our agent to sell more property; and, finally, when we are regarded as permanent absentees—and three or four years will bring that about—we will get rid of everything, and slip over to America. Then you can endow a charity if you like, or build a church to the memory of the man you have displaced."

John Rex burst into a laugh. "An excellent plan. I like the idea of the charity—the Devine Hospital, eh?"

"By the way, how did you find out the particulars of this man's life? He was burned in the *Hydaspes*, wasn't he?"

"No," said Rex, with an air of pride. "He was transported in the *Malabar* under the name of Rufus Dawes. You remember him. It is a long story. The particulars weren't numerous, and if the old lady had been half sharp she would have bowled me out. But the fact was she *wanted* to find the fellow alive, and was willing to take a good deal on trust. I'll tell you all about it another time. I think I'll go to bed now; I'm tired, and my head aches as though it would split."

"Then it is decided that you follow my directions?"

"Yes."

She rose and placed her hand on the bell. "What are you going to do?" he asked, uneasily.

"*I* am going to do nothing. *You* are going to telegraph to your servants to have the house in London prepared for your wife, who will return with you the day after to-morrow."

John Rex stayed her hand with a sudden angry gesture. "This is all devilish fine," he said, "but suppose it fails?"

"That is your affair, John. You need not go on with this business at all, unless you like. I had rather you didn't."

"What the deuce am I to do, then?"

"I am not as rich as you are, but with my station and so on, I am worth seven thousand a year. Come back to Australia with me, and let these poor people enjoy their own again. Ah, John, it is the best thing to do, believe me. We can afford to be honest now."

"A fine scheme!" cried he. "Give up half a million of money, and go back to Australia! You must be mad!"

"Then telegraph."

"But, my dear——"

"Hush, here's the waiter."

As he wrote, John Rex felt gloomily that, though he had succeeded in recalling her affection, that affection was as imperious as of yore.

December 7th.—I have made up my mind to leave this place, to bury myself again in the bush, and await extinction. I try to think that the

FROM THE DIARY OF MR. JAMES NORTH

reason for this determination is the frightful condition of misery existing among the prisoners; that, feeling myself powerless to save others, I wish to spare myself. But in this journal, in which I bind myself to write nothing but truth, I will write the reason plainly: "I covet my neighbour's wife." It does not look well thus written. It looks hideous. In my own breast I find numberless excuses for my passion. I said to myself, My neighbour does not love his wife, and her unloved life is misery. She is forced to live in the frightful seclusion of this accursed island, and she is dying for want of companionship. She feels that I appreciate her, that I could love her as she deserves, that I could render her happy. I feel that I have met the only woman who has power to touch my heart, to hold me back from the ruin into which I am about to plunge. Whispering these conclusions to myself, I am urged to brave public opinion, and make two lives happy.

But is she willing to risk the shame of divorce or legal offence? Perhaps. Is she fitted by temperament to bear such a burden of contumely as must needs fall upon her? Will she not feel disgust at the man who entrapped her into shame? Do not the comforts which surround her compensate for the lack of affection? And so the torturing catechism continues, until I am driven mad with doubt, love, and despair.

Of course I am wrong; of course I outrage my character as a priest; of course, I endanger—according to the creed I teach—my soul and hers. But priests, unluckily, have hearts and passions as well as other men. Thank God, as yet I have never expressed my madness in words. What a fate is mine! When I am in her presence I am in torment; when I am absent from her my imagination pictures her surrounded by a thousand graces that are not hers, but belong to all the women of my dreams—to Helen, to Juliet, to Rosalind. Fools that we are of our own senses!

God, I believe in Thee! Aid me! Pity me, sinful wretch that I am! See me on my knees before Thee! Pity me, or let me die!

December 9th.—I have been visiting the two condemned prisoners, Dawes and Bland, and praying with them. O Lord, let me save one soul that may plead with Thee for mine! Let me draw one being alive out of this pit! I weep—I weary Thee with my prayers. O Lord! Grant me a sign—one little sign, O Lord!—I will not see her. I have sworn it. Thou knowest my despair. Thou knowest why I love her. Thou knowest how I strive to make her hate me. Is that not a sacrifice? I am so lonely—a lonely man, with but one creature that he loves—yet, what is mortal love to Thee? Cruel and implacable, Thou sittest in the heavens men have built for Thee, and scornest them!

I can write no more. I will pray to Thee with my lips. I will shriek my supplications to Thee. I will call upon Thee so loud that all the world shall hear me, and wonder at Thy silence—unjust and unmerciful God!

December 14th.—What blasphemies are these which I have uttered in my despair? I have been possessed by a devil. For a week I have been unconscious of aught save tortúre. I have gone about my daily duties as one who in his dreams repeats the accustomed action of the day, and knows it not. Men have looked at me strangely. They look at me strangely now. Can it be that my disease of drunkenness has become the disease of insanity? O Lord, whom in my agonies I have confessed, leave me my intellect—let me not become a drivelling spectacle for the curious to point at or to pity! At least, in mercy, spare me a little. Let not my punishment overtake me *here*. Let *her* memories of me be clouded with a sense of my rudeness or my brutality; let me for ever seem to her the ungrateful ruffian I strive to show myself—but let her not behold me—*that!*

On or about the 8th of December, Mrs. Frere noticed a sudden and unaccountable change in the manner of the chaplain. He came to her one

THE STRANGE BEHAVIOUR OF MR. NORTH

afternoon, and, after talking for some time, in a vague and unconnected manner, began to question her abruptly concerning Rufus Dawes.

"I do not wish to think of him," said she, with a shudder. "He is a bad man. He tried to murder me when a child, and had it not been for my husband, he would have done so."

"He sometimes speaks to me of you," said North, eyeing her. "He asked me once to give him a rose plucked in your garden."

Sylvia turned pale. "And you gave it him?"

"Yes, I gave it him. Why not?"

"It was valueless, of course, but still—to a convict!"

"You are not angry?"

"Oh, no! Why should I be angry?" she laughed constrainedly. "It was a strange fancy for the man to have, that's all."

"I suppose you would not give me another rose, if I asked you."

"Why not?" said she, turning away uneasily. "You? You are a gentleman."

"Not I—you don't know me."

"What do you mean!"

"I mean that it would be better for you if you had never seen me."

"Mr. North!" Terrified at the wild gleam in his eyes, she had risen hastily. "You are talking very strangely."

"Oh, don't be alarmed, Madam, I am not *drunk!*"—he pronounced the word with a fierce energy. "I had better leave you. Indeed, I think the less we see of each other the better."

Greatly astonished at this extraordinary outburst, Sylvia allowed him to stride away without a word. She saw him pass through the garden and slam the little gate, but she did not see the agony in his face, or the passionate gesture with which—when out of eyeshot—he lamented the voluntary abasement of himself before her. She thought over his conduct with growing fear. It was not possible that he was intoxicated—such a vice was the last of which she believed him guilty. It was more probable that the fever, which had recently confined him to his house, yet lingered. So she thought; and, thinking, was alarmed to realise of how much importance the well-being of this man was to her.

The next day he met her, and, bowing, passed swiftly. This pained her. Could she have offended him by some unlucky word? She made Maurice ask

322

him to dinner, and, to her astonishment, he pleaded illness as an excuse for not coming. Her pride was hurt, and she sent him back his books and music. A curiosity that was unworthy of her compelled her to ask the servant who had carried the parcel what the clergyman had said. "He said nothing—only laughed." Laughed! In scorn of her foolishness! His conduct was ungentlemanly and intemperate. She would forget, as speedily as possible, that he had ever existed. This resolution taken, she was unusually patient with her husband.

So a week passed, and Mr. North did not return. Unluckily, the very self-sacrifice he had made brought about the precise condition which he was desirous to avoid. It is possible that had the acquaintance between them continued on the same staid footing, it would have followed the lot of most acquaintanceships of the kind—other circumstances and other scenes might have wiped out the memory of all but common civilities between them, and Sylvia might never have discovered that she had for the chaplain any other feeling but that of esteem. But the sudden wrenching away of her soul-companion showed her how barren was her solitary life. Her husband, she had long ago admitted, was utterly unsuited to her. She could find in his society no enjoyment, and for sympathy she was compelled to turn elsewhere. She understood that his love for her had burnt itself out—she confessed, with intensity of self-degradation, that his apparent affection had been born of sensuality, and had perished in the fires it had itself kindled. Many women have, unhappily, made some such discovery as this, but for most women there is some distracting occupation. Had it been Sylvia's fate to live in the midst of fashion and society, she would have found relief in the conversation of the witty, or the homage of the distinguished. Had fortune cast her lot in a city, Mrs. Frere might have become one of those charming women who collect around their supper-tables whatever of male intellect is obtainable, and who find the husband admirably useful to open his own champagne bottles. But Sylvia was not destined to this fortune. Cast back upon herself, she found no surcease of pain in her own imaginings, and meeting with a man sufficiently her elder to encourage her to talk, and sufficiently clever to induce her to seek his society and his advice, she learnt, for the first time, to forget her own griefs; for the first time she suffered her nature to expand under the sun of a congenial influence. This sun, suddenly withdrawn, her soul shivered at the gloom, and she looked about her in dismay at the barren prospect of life which lay before her. In a word, she found that the society of North had become so far necessary to her, that to be deprived of it was a grief—notwithstanding that her husband remained to console her.

After a week of such reflections, she came to Maurice and begged to be sent back to Hobart Town. "I cannot live in this horrible island," she said. "I am getting ill. Let me go to my father for a few months, Maurice." Maurice consented. His wife *was* looking ill, and Major Vickers was an old man—a rich old man—who loved his only daughter. It was not undesirable that Mrs. Frere should visit her father; indeed, so little sympathy was there between the pair, that, the first astonishment over, Maurice felt rather glad to get rid of her for a while. "You can go back in the *Lady Franklin*, if you like, my dear," he said. "I expect her every day." At this decision—much to his surprise—she kissed him with more affection than she had manifested since the death of her child.

The news of the approaching departure became known, but still North did not make his appearance. Had it not been a step beneath the dignity of a woman, Mrs. Frere would have gone herself and asked him the meaning of his unaccountable rudeness, but there was just sufficient morbidity in the sympathy she had for him to restrain her from an act which a young girl—though not more innocent—would have dared without hesitation. Calling one day upon the wife of the surgeon, however, she met the chaplain face to face, and with the consummate art of acting which most women possess, rallied him upon his absence from her house. The behaviour of the poor devil, thus stabbed to the heart, was curious. He forgot gentlemanly behaviour, flung one despairingly angry glance at her, and abruptly retired. Sylvia flushed crimson, and endeavoured to excuse North on account of his recent illness. The surgeon's wife looked askance, and turned the conversation. The next time Sylvia bowed to this lady, she got a chilling salute in return that made her blood boil. "I wonder how I have offended Mrs. Field?" she asked Maurice. "She almost cut me to-day." "Oh, the old cat!" returned Maurice. "What does it matter if she did?" However, a few days afterwards, it seemed that it did matter; for Maurice called upon Field and conversed seriously with him. The conversation being reported to Mrs. Frere, the lady wept tears of wounded pride and shame. It appeared that North had watched her out of the house, returned, and related—in a "stumbling, hesitating way," Mrs. Field said—how he disliked Mrs. Frere, and how he did not want to visit her, and how flighty and reprehensible such conduct was in a married woman of her rank and station. This act of baseness—of profound nobleness—achieved its purpose. Sylvia noticed the unhappy priest no more.

Between the Commandant and the chaplain now arose a coolness, and Frere set himself, by various petty tyrannies, to disgust North, and compel him to a resignation of his office. The convict-gaolers speedily marked the difference in the treatment of the chaplain, and their demeanour changed.

For respect was substituted insolence; for alacrity, sullenness; for prompt obedience, impertinent intrusion. The men whom North favoured were selected as special subjects for harshness, and for a prisoner to be seen talking to the clergyman, was sufficient to ensure for him a series of tyrannies. The result of this was, that North saw the souls he laboured to save slipping back into the gulf; beheld the men he had half won to love him meet him with averted faces; discovered that to show interest in a prisoner was to injure him, not to serve him. The unhappy man grew thin and paler under this ingenious torment. He had deprived himself of that love which, guilty though it might be, was, nevertheless, the only true love he had known; and he found that, having won this victory, he had gained the hatred of all living creatures with whom he came in contact. The authority of the Commandant was so supreme that to offend him was to perish, and the man whom the Commandant hated must be hated also by all those who wished to exist in peace. There was but one who was not turned from his allegiance—the convict murderer, Rufus Dawes, who awaited death. For many days he had remained mute, broken down beneath his weight of sorrow; but North, bereft of other love and sympathy, strove with that fighting soul, if haply he might win it back to peace. It seemed to the fancy of the priest that this convict was given to him as a hostage for his own salvation.

Frere, unable to comprehend the calmness with which the doomed felon met his taunts and torments, thought that he was shamming piety to gain some indulgence of meat and drink, and redoubled his severity. He ordered Dawes to be taken out to work just before the hour at which the chaplain was accustomed to visit him. He directed a gaoler to be present at all interviews, "lest the chaplain might be murdered." He issued an order that all civil officers should obey the challenges of convicts acting as watchmen; and North, coming to pray with his penitent, would be stopped ten times by grinning felons, who, putting their faces within a foot of his, would roar out, "Who goes there?" and burst out laughing at the reply. North met these impertinences with unruffled brow, and Frere could in no way account for his obstinacy, until the arrival of the Lady Franklin explained the chaplain's apparent coolness. He had sent in his resignation two months before, and the saintly Meekin had been appointed in his stead. Frere, unable to attack the clergyman, and indignant at the manner in which he had been defeated, revenged himself upon Rufus Dawes.

The manner of Frere's revenge became a subject of whispered conversation on the island. It was reported that North had been forbidden to visit the

MR. NORTH SPEAKS

convict, but that he had refused to accept the prohibition, and by a threat of what he would do when the returning vessel had landed him in Hobart Town, had compelled the Commandant to withdraw his order. The Commandant, however, speedily discovered in Rufus Dawes signs of insubordination, and set to work to reduce still further the "spirit" he had so ingeniously "broken." The unhappy convict was deprived of food, kept awake at nights, put to the hardest labour, loaded with the heaviest irons. Troke suggested that if the tortured wretch would decline to see the chaplain, some amelioration of his condition might be effected; but his suggestions were in vain. Fully believing that his death was certain, Dawes clung to North as the saviour of his agonised soul, and rejected all such insidious overtures. Enraged at this obstinacy, Frere sentenced his victim to the "spread eagle" and the "stretcher."

Now the rumour of the obduracy of this undaunted convict had reached Sylvia's ears. She had heard of the punishments inflicted on him by her husband; and her brain began to thrill with those undefined memories which had haunted her childhood. What was the link between her and this murderous villain? How came it that she felt at times so strange a sympathy for his fate, and that he—who had attempted her life—cherished so tender a remembrance of her as to beg for a flower which her hand had touched?

She questioned her husband concerning the convict's misdoings, but he harshly refused to satisfy her. This but raised her curiosity higher. She remembered how, in the garden at Port Arthur, the hunted wretch had caught her dress with words of assured confidence—she recollected the fragment of cloth he had passionately flung from him, and which her affianced lover had contemptuously tossed into the stream. The name of "Dawes," detested as it had become to her, bore yet some strange association of comfort and hope. What secret lurked behind the twilight that had fallen upon her childish memories? Deprived of the advice of North—to whom, a few weeks back, she would have confided her misgivings—she resolved upon a project that, for her was most distasteful. She would visit the gaol and judge how far the rumours of her husband's cruelty were worthy of credit.

One sultry afternoon, when the Commandant had gone on a visit of inspection, Troke, lounging at the door of the New Prison, beheld, with surprise, the figure of the Commandant's lady.

"What is it, ma'am?" he asked.

"I want to see the prisoner Dawes."

Troke's jaw fell.

"See Dawes?" he repeated.

"Yes. Where is he?"

The imperious voice, and the clear, steady gaze, confused Troke.

"He's—he's under punishment, ma'am."

"What do you mean? Are they flogging him?"

"No; but he's dangerous, ma'am. The Commandant——"

"Do you mean to open the door or not, Mr. Troke?"

Troke grew more confused. "The Commandant gave strict orders——"

"Do you wish me to *complain* to the Commandant?" cries Sylvia, with a touch of her old spirit. "Open the door at once!"

Thus commanded, Troke, with a hasty growl of its "being no affair of his, and he hoped Mrs. Frere would tell the captain how it happened," flung open the door of a cell on the right hand of the doorway. It was so dark that, at first, Sylvia could distinguish nothing but the outline of a framework, with something stretched upon it that resembled a human body. Her first thought was that the man was dead, but this was not so—he groaned. Her eyes, accustoming themselves to the gloom, began to see what the "punishment" was. Upon the floor was placed an iron frame about six feet long, and two and a half feet wide, with round iron bars, placed transversely, about twelve inches apart. The man she came to seek was bound in a horizontal position upon this frame, with his neck projecting over the end of it. If he allowed his head to hang, the blood rushed to his brain, and suffocated him, while the effort to keep it raised strained every muscle to agony pitch. His face was purple, and he foamed at the mouth. Sylvia uttered a cry. "This is no punishment; it's murder! Who ordered this?"

"The Commandant," said Troke, sullenly.

"I don't believe it. Loose him!"

"I daren't, ma'am," said Troke.

"Loose him, I say! Hailey!—you, sir, there!" The noise had brought several warders to the spot. "Do you hear me? Do you know who I am? Loose him, I say!" In her eagerness and compassion, she was on her knees by the side of the infernal machine, plucking at the ropes with her delicate fingers. "Wretches, you have cut his flesh! He is dying! You have killed him!"

The prisoner, in fact, seeing this angel of mercy stooping over him, and hearing close to him the voice that for seven years he had heard but in his dreams, had fainted. Troke and Hailey, alarmed by her vehemence, dragged the stretcher out into the light, and hastily cut the lashings. Dawes rolled off like a log, and his head fell against Mrs. Frere. Troke roughly pulled him aside, and called for water. Sylvia, trembling with sympathy, and pale with passion, turned upon the crew. "How long has he been like this?"

"An hour," said Troke.

"A lie!" said a stern voice at the door. "He has been there nine hours!"

"Wretches!" cried Sylvia, "you shall hear more of this. Oh, oh! I am sick!"—she felt for the wall—"I—I——" North watched her with agony on his face, but did not move. "I faint. I——"—she uttered a despairing cry that was not without a touch of anger. "Mr. North! do you not see? Oh! Take me home—take me home!" and she would have fallen across the body of the tortured prisoner had not North caught her in his arms.

Rufus Dawes, awakening from his stupor, saw, in the midst of a sunbeam which penetrated a window in the corridor, the woman who came to save his body supported by the priest who came to save his soul; and staggering to his knees, he stretched out his hands with a hoarse cry. Perhaps something in the action brought back to the dimmed remembrance of the Commandant's wife the image of a similar figure stretching forth its hands to a frightened child in the mysterious far-off time. She started, and pushing back her hair, bent a terrified gaze upon the face of the kneeling man, as though she would fain read there an explanation of the shadowy memory which haunted her. It is possible that she would have spoken, but North—thinking the excitement had produced one of those hysterical crises which were common to her—gently drew her, still gazing, back towards the

PERSPECTIVE OF STRETCHER ROOM BUNK

gate. The convict's arms fell, and an undefinable presentiment of evil chilled him as he beheld the priest slowly draw the fair young creature into the grim shadow of the heavy archway. For an instant the gloom swallowed them, and it seemed to Dawes that the strange wild man of God had in that instant become a man of Evil—blighting the brightness and the beauty of the innocence that clung to him. For an instant—and then they passed out of the prison archway into the free air.

"You are ill," said North. "You will faint. Why do you look so wildly?"

"What is it?" she whispered, more in answer to her own thoughts than to his question—"what is it that links me to that man? I tremble with crowding thoughts, that die ere they can whisper to me. Oh, that prison!"

"Look up; we are in the sunshine."

She passed her hand across her brow, sighing heavily, and withdrew her arm from his. North interpreted the action correctly, and the blood rushed to his face. "Pardon me, you cannot walk alone; you will fall. I will leave you at the gate."

In truth she would have fallen had he not again assisted her. She turned upon him eyes whose reproachful sorrow almost forced him to a confession, but he bowed his head and held silence. They reached the house, and he placed her tenderly in a chair. "Now you are safe, madam, I will leave you."

She burst into tears. "Why do you treat me thus, Mr. North? What have I done to make you hate me?"

"Hate you!" said North, with trembling lips. "Oh, no, I do not *hate* you. I am rude in my speech, abrupt in my manner. You must forget it, and—and *me*."

A horse's hooves crashed upon the gravel, and an instant after Maurice Frere burst into the room. Returning from the Cascades, he had met Troke, and learned the release of the prisoner. Furious at this usurpation of authority by his wife, his self-esteem wounded by the thought that she had witnessed his mean revenge upon the man he had so infamously wronged, he had made for the house at full gallop, determined to assert his authority. Blind with rage, he saw no one but his wife. "What the devil's this I hear? *You* have been meddling in my business! *You* release prisoners! *You*——"

"Captain Frere!" said North, stepping forward to assert the restraining presence of a stranger. Frere started, astonished. Here was another outrage, another insult to his supreme authority. In its passion, his gross mind leapt to the worst conclusion.

"You here, too! What do you want here—with my wife!" His eyes glanced wrathfully from one to the other; and he strode towards North.

"Maurice!" cried Sylvia, in an agony of shame and terror, striving to place a restraining hand upon his arm. He turned upon her with so fierce a curse that North, pale with rage, seemed prompted to strike the burly ruffian to the ground. For a moment, the two men faced each other, and then Frere, muttering threats of vengeance, flung the suppliant woman violently from him, and rushed from the room. She fell heavily against the wall, and as the chaplain raised her, he heard the hoof-strokes of the departing horse.

"Oh!" cried Sylvia, covering her face with trembling hands, "let me leave this place!"

North, enfolding her in his arms, strove to soothe her with incoherent words of comfort. She clung to him, sobbing. Twice he tried to tear himself away, but had he loosed his hold she would have fallen. He could not hold her—bruised, suffering, and in tears—thus against his heart, and keep silence. In a torrent of agonised eloquence the story of his love burst from his lips. "Why should you be thus tortured?" he cried. "Leave him—leave him. He has cast you off. We have both suffered. Let us leave this dreadful place—this isthmus between earth and hell! I will give you happiness."

"I am going," she said faintly. "I had already arranged it."

North trembled. "It was not of my seeking. Fate has willed it. We go together!"

They looked at each other—she felt the fever of his blood, she read his passion in his eyes, she comprehended the "hatred" he had affected for her, and, deadly pale, drew back the cold hand he held.

"Go!" she murmured. "If you love me, leave me—leave me! Do not see me or speak to me again——" her silence added the words she could not utter,——"*till then.*"

Maurice Frere's passion had spent itself in that last act of violence. He repented him of his suspicions. There was nothing strange in the presence of

GETTING READY FOR SEA

the chaplain. Sylvia had always liked the man, and an apology for his conduct had doubtless removed her anger. To make a mountain out of a molehill was the act of an idiot. It was natural that she should release Dawes—women *were* so tender-hearted. Moreover, North was to sail in the *Lady Franklin*, and might put in execution his threats of official complaint, unless he was carefully dealt with. To put Dawes again to the torture, would be to show to Troke and his friends that the "Commandant's wife" had acted without the "Commandant's authority," and that must not be shown. He would return and patch up a peace. His wife would sail in the same vessel with North, and he would in a few days be left alone on the island to pursue his "discipline" unchecked. With this intent he returned to the prison, and gravely informed poor Troke that he was astonished at his barbarity. "Mrs. Frere, who most luckily had appointed to meet me this afternoon at the prison, tells me that the poor devil Dawes had been on the stretcher since seven o'clock in the morning."

"You ordered it fust thing, yer honour," said Troke.

"Yes, you fool, but I didn't order you to keep the man there for nine hours, did I? Why, you scoundrel, you might have killed him!" Troke scratched his head in bewilderment. "Take his irons off, and put him in a separate cell in the old gaol. If a man *is* a murderer, that is no reason you should take the law into your own hands, is it? You'd better take care, Mr. Troke." On the way back he met the chaplain, who, seeing him, made for a by-path in curious haste. "Halloo!" roared Frere. "Hi! Mr. North!" North paused, and the Commandant made at him abruptly. "Look here, sir, I was rude to you just now—devilish rude. Most ungentlemanly of me. I must apologise." North bowed, without speaking, and tried to pass.

"You must excuse my violence," Frere went on. "I'm bad tempered, and I didn't like my wife interfering. Women don't understand these scoundrels." North again bowed. "Why, d——n it, how savage you look! I must have said most outrageous things. Forget and forgive, you know. Come home and have some dinner."

"I cannot enter your house again, sir," said North.

Frere shrugged his shoulders with a clumsy affectation of good humour, and held out his hand. "Well, shake hands, parson. You'll have to take care of Mrs. Frere on the voyage, and we may as well make up our differences before you start."

"Let me pass, sir!" cried North, with heightened colour; and ignoring the proffered hand, strode savagely on.

"You've a d——d fine temper for a parson," said Frere to himself. "However, if you won't, you won't. Hang me, if *I'll* ask you again." Nor, when he reached home, did he fare better in his efforts at reconciliation with his wife. Sylvia met him with the icy front of a woman whose pride has been wounded too deeply for tears.

"Say no more about it," she said. "I am going to my father. If you want to explain your conduct, explain it to him."

"Come, Sylvia," he urged; "I was a brute, I know. Forgive me."

"It is useless to ask me," she said; "I cannot. I have forgiven you so much during the last seven years."

He attempted to embrace her, but she withdrew herself from his arms. He swore a great oath at her, and too obstinate to argue further, sulked. Sylvia went to her room, and occupied herself with some minor details of clothes-packing, while North, poor fool, seeing from his window the light in hers, sat staring at it, alternately cursing and praying.

In the meantime Rufus Dawes sat in his new cell, wondering at the chance which had procured him comfort, and blessing the fair hands that had brought it to him. He doubted not but that Sylvia had interceded with his tormentor, and by her gentle pleading brought him ease. "God bless her," he murmured. "I have wronged her all these years. She did not know that I suffered." He waited anxiously for North to visit him, that he might have his belief confirmed. "I will get him to thank her for me," he thought. But North did not come for two whole days. No one came but his gaolers; and, gazing from his prison window upon the sea that almost washed its walls, he saw the schooner at anchor, mocking him with a liberty he could not achieve. On the third day, however, North came. His manner was constrained and abrupt. His eyes wandered uneasily, and he seemed burdened with thoughts which he dared not utter.

"I want you to thank her for me, Mr. North," said Dawes.

"Thank whom?"

"Mrs. Frere."

The unhappy priest shuddered at hearing the name.

"I do not think you owe any thanks to her. Your irons were removed by the Commandant's order."

"But by her persuasion. I feel sure of it. Ah, I was wrong to think she had forgotten me. Ask her for her forgiveness."

"Forgiveness!" said North, recalling the scene in the prison. "What have you done to need her forgiveness?"

"I doubted her," said Rufus Dawes. "I thought her ungrateful and treacherous. I thought she delivered me again into the bondage from whence I had escaped. I thought she had betrayed me—betrayed me to the villain whose base life I saved for her sweet sake."

"What do you mean?" asked North. "You never spoke to me of this."

"No, I had vowed to bury the knowledge of it in my own breast—it was too bitter to speak."

"Saved his life!"

"Ay, and hers! I made the boat that carried her to freedom, I held her in my arms, and took the bread from my own lips to feed her!"

"She cannot know this," said North in an undertone.

"She has forgotten it, perhaps, for she was but a child. But you will remind her, will you not? You will do me justice in her eyes before I die? You will get her forgiveness for me?"

North could not explain why such an interview as the convict desired was impossible, and so he promised.

"She is going away in the schooner," said he, concealing the fact of his own departure. "I will see her before she goes, and tell her."

"God bless you, sir," said poor Dawes. "Now pray with me;" and the wretched priest mechanically repeated one of the formulæ his Church prescribes.

The next day he told his penitent that Mrs. Frere had forgiven him. This was a lie. He had not seen her; but what should a lie be to him now? Lies were needful in the tortuous path he had undertaken to tread. Yet the deceit he was forced to practise cost him many a pang. To deaden remorse he had recourse to brandy; and though the fierce excitement of his hopes and fears steeled him against the stupefying action of the liquor, he was rendered by it incapable of calm reflection.

The days passed swiftly, and Blunt's preparations for sea were completed. There were two stern cabins in the schooner, one of which was appropriated to Mrs. Frere while the other was set apart for Mr. North. Maurice had not attempted to renew his overtures of friendship, and the chaplain had not spoken. Mindful of Sylvia's last words, he had resolved not to meet her until fairly embarked upon the voyage which he intended should link their fortunes together. On the morning of the 19th December, Blunt declared himself ready to set sail, and in the afternoon the two passengers came on board.

Rufus Dawes, gazing from his window upon the schooner that lay outside the reef, thought nothing of the fact that after the Commandant's boat had taken away the Commandant's wife, another boat should put off with the chaplain. It was quite natural that Mr. North should desire to bid his friends farewell, and through the hot still afternoon he watched for the returning boat, hoping that the chaplain would bring him some message from the woman whom he was never to see more on earth.

The hours wore on, however, and no breath of wind ruffled the surface of the sea. The day was close and sultry, heavy clouds hung on the horizon, and it seemed probable that unless a thunder-storm should clear the air before night, the calm would continue. Blunt, however, with a true sailor's obstinacy in regard to weather, swore there would be a breeze, and held to his purpose of sailing. The hot afternoon passed away in a sultry sunset, and it was not until evening had begun to fall that Rufus Dawes distinguished a boat detach itself from the sides of the schooner, and glide through the oily water to the jetty. The chaplain was returning to bring him the message of comfort for which his soul thirsted. He stretched out his unshackled limbs, and throwing himself upon his stretcher, fell to recalling the past—his boat-building, the news of his fortune, his love, and his self-sacrifice.

North, however, was not returning to bring to the prisoner a message of comfort, but he was returning on purpose to see him nevertheless. The unhappy man, torn by remorse and passion, had resolved upon a penance for his crime of deceit. He had determined to confess to Dawes that the message he brought was wholly fictitious, that he himself loved the wife of the Commandant, and that with her he was about to leave the island for ever. "I am no hypocrite," he thought, in his exaltation. "If I choose to sin, I will sin boldly; and this poor wretch, who looks up to me as an angel, shall know me for my true self."

To this end he had invented an excuse for returning to the shore at the latest possible moment. He had purposely left in his room a dressing-bag—the sort of article one is so likely to forget in the hurry of departure from one's house, and so certain to remember when the time comes to finally prepare for settling in another. He had ingeniously extracted from Blunt the fact that "he didn't expect a wind before dark, but wanted all ship-shape and aboard," and then, just as darkness fell, discovered that it was imperative for him to go ashore. Blunt cursed, but, if the chaplain insisted upon going, there was no help for it.

"There'll be a breeze in less than two hours," said he. "You've plenty of time, but if you're not back before the first puff, I'll sail without you, as sure as you're born." North assured him of his punctuality. "Don't wait for me, Captain, if I'm not here," said he, with the lightness of tone which men use to mask anxiety. "I'd take him at his word, Blunt," said the Commandant, who was affably waiting to take final farewell of his wife. "Give way there, men," he shouted to the crew, "and wait at the jetty. If Mr. North misses his ship through your laziness, you'll pay for it." So the boat set off.

Frere observed with some astonishment that the chaplain wrapped himself in a boat cloak that lay in the stern sheets. "Does the fellow want to smother himself in a night like this!" was his remark. The truth was that, though his hands and head were burning, North's teeth chattered with cold. Perhaps this was the reason why, when landed and out of eyeshot of the crew, he produced a pocket-flask of rum and eagerly drank. The spirit gave him courage for the ordeal to which he had condemned himself; and with steadied step, he reached the door of the old prison. To his surprise, Gimblett refused him admission!

"But I have come direct from the Commandant," said North.

"Got any order, sir?"

"Order! No."

"I can't let you in, your reverence," said Gimblett.

"I want to see the prisoner Dawes. I have a special message for him. I have come ashore on purpose."

"I am very sorry, sir——"

"The ship will sail in two hours, man, and I shall miss her," said North. "Let me pass."

"Upon my honour, sir, I daren't," said Gimblett, who was not without his good points. "You know what authority is, sir, as well as I do."

North was in despair, but a bright thought struck him—a thought that, in his soberer moments, would never have entered his head—he would buy admission. He produced the rum flask from beneath the sheltering cloak.

"Come, don't talk nonsense to me, Gimblett. You don't suppose I would come here *without* authority. Here, take a pull at this, and let me through." Gimblett's features relaxed into a smile. "Well, sir, I suppose it's all right, if you say so," said he. And clutching the rum bottle with one hand, he opened the door of Dawes's cell with the other.

North entered, and as the door closed behind him, the prisoner, who had been lying apparently asleep upon his bed, leapt up, and made as though to catch him by the throat.

Rufus Dawes had dreamt a dream. Alone, amid the gathering glooms, his fancy had recalled the past, and peopled it with memories. He thought that he was once more upon that barren strand where he had first met with the sweet child he loved. He lived again his life of usefulness and honour. He saw himself working at the boat, embarking, and putting out to sea. The fair head of the innocent girl was again pillowed on his breast; her young lips again murmured words of affection in his greedy ear. Frere was beside him, watching him, as he had watched before. Once again the grey sea spread around him, barren of succour. Once again, in the wild, wet morning, he beheld the American brig bearing down upon them, and saw the bearded faces of the astonished crew. He saw Frere take the child in his arms and mount upon the deck; he heard the shout of delight that went up, and pressed again the welcoming hands which greeted the rescued castaways. The deck was crowded. All the folk he had ever known were there. He saw the white hair and stern features of Sir Richard Devine, and beside him stood, wringing her thin hands, his weeping mother. Then Frere strode forward, and after him John Rex, the convict, who, roughly elbowing through the crowd of prisoners and gaolers, would have reached the spot where stood Sir Richard Devine, but that the corpse of the murdered Lord Bellasis arose and thrust him back. How the hammers clattered in the ship-builder's yard! Was it a coffin they were making? Not for Sylvia—surely not for her! The air grows heavy, lurid with flame, and black with smoke. The *Hydaspes* is on fire! Sylvia clings to her husband. Base wretch, would you shake her off! Look up; the midnight heaven is glittering with stars; above the smoke the air breathes delicately! One step—another! fix your eyes on mine—so—to my heart! Alas! she turns; he catches at her dress. What! It is a priest—a priest—who, smiling with infernal joy, would drag her to the flaming gulf that yawns for him. The dreamer leaps at the wretch's throat, and crying, "Villain, was it for *this* fate I saved her?"——awakes to find himself struggling with the monster of his dream, the idol of his waking senses—"Mr. North."

North, paralysed no less by the suddenness of the attack than by the words with which it was accompanied, let fall his cloak, and stood trembling before the prophetic accusation of the man whose curses he had come to earn.

"I was dreaming," said Rufus Dawes. "A terrible dream! The message—you have brought me a message, have you not? Why—what ails you? You are pale—you tremble."

North recovered himself with a great effort. "It is nothing. Let us talk, for my time is short. You have thought me a good man—one blessed of God, one consecrated to a holy service: a man honest, pure, and truthful. I have returned to tell you the truth. I am none of these things." Rufus Dawes sat staring, unable to comprehend. "I told you that the woman you loved—for you *do* love her—sent you a message of forgiveness. I lied."

"What!"

"I never told her of your confession. I never mentioned your name to her."

"And she will go without knowing—Oh, Mr. North, what have you done?"

"Wrecked my own soul?" cried North, wildly, stung by the reproachful agony of the tone. "Do not cling to me. My task is done. You will hate me now. That is my wish—I merit it. Let me go, I say. I shall be too late."

"Too late! For what?" He looked at the cloak—through the open window came the voices of the men in the boat—the memory of the rose, of the scene in the prison, flashed across him, and he understood it all. "Great Heaven, you go together!"

"Let me go," repeated North, in a hoarse voice.

Rufus Dawes stepped between him and the door. "No, madman, I will not let you go, to do this great wrong to this innocent young soul, who—God help her—loves you!" North confounded at this sudden reversal, crouched bewildered against the wall. "I say you shall *not* go! You shall not destroy your own soul and hers! You love her! So do I! and my love is mightier than yours, for it shall save her!"

"In God's name——" cried the unhappy priest, striving to stop his ears.

"Ay, in God's name! In the name of that God whom in my torments I had forgotten and whom you taught me to remember! That God who sent you to save me from despair, gives me strength to save you in my turn! Oh, Mr. North—my teacher—my friend—my brother—be merciful to this erring woman!"

North lifted agonised eyes. "But I love her! Love her, do you hear! What do you know of love?"

"Love!" cried Rufus Dawes, his pale face radiant. "Love! Oh, it is you who do not know it. Love is the sacrifice of self, the death of all desire that is not for another's good. Love is Godlike! *You* love?—no, no, your love is selfishness, and will end in shame! Listen, I will tell you the history of such a love as yours."

North, enthralled by the other's overmastering will, fell back trembling.

"I will tell you the secret of my life, the reason why I am here. Come closer."

The house in Clarges Street was duly placed at the disposal of Mrs. Richard Devine, who was installed in it, to the profound astonishment and disgust of

THE DISCOVERY

Mr. Smithers and his fellow-servants. Mr. Richard Devine rather hoped that—disgusted at his brutality—Lady Devine would have nothing more to do with him, and that the ordeal of presenting his wife would not be necessary. Lady Devine, however, had resolved on a different line of conduct. The intelligence concerning Mr. Richard Devine's threatened proceedings nerved her to the confession of the dislike which had been long growing in her mind; aided the formation of those doubts, the shadows of which had now and then cast themselves upon her belief in the identity of the man who called himself her son.

"His conduct is brutal," said she to her brother, "I cannot understand it."

"It is more than brutal, it is unnatural," returned Francis Wade, and stole a look at her. "Moreover, he is married."

"Married!" cried Lady Devine.

"So he says," continued the other, producing the letter sent to him by Rex at Sarah's dictation. "He writes to me stating that his wife, whom he married last year abroad, has come to England, and wishes us to receive her."

"I will *not* receive her!" cried Lady Devine, rising and pacing the room.

"But that would be a declaration of war," said poor Francis, twisting an Italian onyx which adorned his irresolute hand.

Lady Devine stopped suddenly, with the gesture of one who has finally made a difficult and long considered resolution. "Richard shall not sell this house," she said.

"But, my dear Ellinor," cried her brother, "I am afraid that you can't prevent him."

"If he is the man he says he is, I can," returned she, with effort.

Francis Wade gasped, "*If* he is the man! It is true—I have sometimes thought—— Oh, Ellinor, can it be that we have been deceived!"

She came to him and leant upon him for support, as she had leant upon her son in the garden where they now stood, nineteen years ago. "I do not know, I am afraid to think. But between Richard and myself is a secret—a shameful secret, Frank, known to no other living person. If the man who threatens me does not know that secret, he is not my son. If he does know it——"

"Well, in Heaven's name, what then?"

"He knows that he has neither part nor lot in the fortune of the man who was my husband."

"Ellinor, you terrify me. What does this mean?"

"I will tell you if there be need to do so," said the unhappy lady. "But I cannot now. I never meant to speak of it again, even to him. Consider that it is hard to break a silence of nearly twenty years. Write to this man, and tell him that before I receive his wife, I wish to see him alone. No—do not let him come here until the truth be known. I will go to him."

It was with some trepidation that Mr. Richard, sitting with his wife, awaited the arrival of his mother. He had been very nervous for some days past, and the prospect of the coming interview was, for some, inexplicable reason, weighty with fears. "What does she want to come alone for? And what can she have to say?" he asked himself. "She cannot suspect anything after all these years, surely?" He endeavoured to reason with himself, but in vain; the knock at the door which announced her made his heart jump.

"I feel deuced shaky, Sarah," he said. "Let's have a nip of something."

"You've been nipping too much for the last five years, Dick." (She had quite schooled her tongue to the new name.) "Your 'shakiness' is the result of 'nipping', I'm afraid."

"Oh, don't preach, I am not in the humour for it."

"Help yourself, then. You are ready with your story?"

The brandy revived him, and he rose with affected heartiness. "My dear mother, allow me to present to you——" He paused, for there was that in Lady Devine's face which confirmed his worst fears.

"I wish to speak to you alone," she said, ignoring with steady eyes the woman whom she had ostensibly come to see.

John Rex hesitated, but Sarah saw the danger, and hastened to confront it. "Your son married me of his own free will, madam, and even his mother can have nothing to say to him which it is not my duty and privilege to hear. I am not a girl, as you can see, and I can bear whatever news you bring."

Lady Devine bit her pale lips. She saw at once that the woman before her was not gently-born, but she felt also that she was a woman of higher mental calibre than herself. Prepared as she was for the worst, this sudden and open declaration of hostilities frightened her, as Sarah had calculated. She realised that she must not waste her strength in skirmishing. Steadily refusing to look at Richard's wife, she addressed herself to Richard. "My brother will be here in half an hour," she said. "But I begged him to allow me to come first in order that I might speak to you privately."

"Well," said John Rex, "we are in private. What have you to say?"

"I want to tell you that I forbid you to carry out the plan you have for breaking up Sir Richard's property."

"Forbid me!" cried Rex, much relieved. "Why, I only want to do what my father's will enables me to do."

"Your father's will enables you to do nothing of the sort, and you know it." She spoke, as though rehearsing a series of set-speeches, and Sarah watched her with growing alarm.

"Oh, nonsense!" cries John Rex, in sheer amazement. "I have the lawyer's opinion on it."

"Do you remember what took place at Hampstead this day nineteen years ago?"

"At Hampstead!" said Rex, grown suddenly pale. "This day nineteen years ago. No! What do you mean?"

"Do you not remember?" she continued, leaning forward eagerly, and speaking almost fiercely. "Do you not remember the reason why you left the house where you were born, and which you wish now to sell to strangers?"

John Rex stood dumbfounded, the blood suffusing his temples. He knew that among the secrets of the man whose inheritance he had stolen was one which he had never gained—the secret of that sacrifice to which Lady Devine had often referred—and he felt that this secret was to be revealed to crush him now.

Sarah, trembling also, but more with rage than terror, swept towards Lady Devine. "Speak out!" she said, "if you have anything to say! Of what do you accuse my husband?"

"Of imposture!" cried Lady Devine, all her outraged maternity nerving her to abash her enemy. "This man may be your husband, but he is not my son!"

Now that the worst was out, John Rex, choking with passion, felt all the devil within him rebelling against defeat. "You are mad," he said. "You have recognised me for three years, and now, because I want to claim that which is my own, you invent this lie. Take care how you provoke me. If I am not your son—you have recognised me as such. I stand upon the law and upon my rights."

Lady Devine turned swiftly and confronted him.

341

"You shall have your rights! You shall have what the law allows you! Oh, how blind I have been all these years. Persist in your infamous imposture. Call yourself Richard Devine still, and I will tell the world the shameful secret which my son died to hide. *Be* Richard Devine! Richard Devine was a bastard, and the law allows him—Nothing!"

There was no doubting the truth of her words. It was impossible that she would invent a lie so self-condemning. Yet John Rex forced himself to appear to doubt, and his dry lips asked, "If then your husband was not the father of your son who was?"

"My cousin, Armigell Esmè Wade, Lord Bellasis," answered Lady Devine.

John Rex gasped for breath. His hand, tugging at his neckcloth, rent away the linen that covered his choking throat. The whole horizon of his past was lit up by a lightning flash which stunned him. His brain, already enfeebled by excess, was unable to withstand this last shock. He staggered, and but for the cabinet against which he leant, would have fallen. The secret thoughts of his heart rose to his lips, and were uttered unconsciously "Lord Bellasis! He was my father also, and—I killed him!"

A dreadful silence fell, and then Lady Devine, stretching out her hands towards the self-confessed murderer, said in a whisper in which horror and supplication were strangely mingled, "What did you do with my son? Did you kill *him* also?"

But John Rex, shaking his head from side to side, like a beast in the shambles that has received a mortal stroke, made no reply. Sarah Purfoy, awed as she was by the dramatic force of the situation, nevertheless remembered that Francis Wade might arrive at any moment, and saw her last opportunity for safety. She advanced and touched the mother on the shoulder.

"Your son is alive!"

"Where?"

"Will you promise not to hinder our leaving this house if I tell you?"

"Yes, yes."

"Will you promise to keep the confession which you have heard secret, until we have left England?"

"I promise anything. In God's name, woman, if you have a woman's heart, speak! Where is my son?"

Sarah Purfoy said in level, deliberate accents, "They call him Rufus Dawes. He is a convict at Norfolk Island, transported for life for the murder which you heard my husband confess to having committed——Ah!"——

Lady Devine had fainted.

Sarah flew to Rex. "Rouse yourself, John, for heaven's sake. We have not a moment."

FIFTEEN HOURS

John Rex passed his hand over his forehead wearily.

"I cannot think. I am ill. My brain seems dead." Nervously watching the prostrate figure on the floor, she hurried on bonnet, cloak, and veil, and in a twinkling had him outside the house and into a cab.

"Thirty-nine, Lombard Street. Quick!"

"You won't give me up?" said Rex, turning dull eyes upon her.

"Give you up? No. But the police will be after us as soon as that woman can speak, and her brother summon his lawyer. I know what her promise is worth. We have got about fifteen hours."

"I can't go far, Sarah," said he; "I am sleepy and stupid."

She repressed the terrible fear that tugged at her heart, and strove to rally him.

"You've been drinking too much, John. Now sit still and be good, while I go and get some money for you."

She hurried into the bank, and her name secured her an interview with the manager at once.

"That's a rich woman," said one of the clerks to his friend.

"A widow, too! Chance for you, Tom," returned the other; and, presently, from out the sacred presence came another clerk with a request for "a draft on Sydney for three thousand, less premium," and bearing a cheque signed "Sarah Carr," for £200, which he "took" in notes, and so returned again.

From the bank she was taken to Green's Shipping Office.

"I want a cabin in the first ship for Sydney, please."

The shipping-clerk looked at a board.

"Just the thing for you, ma'am," said he. "We have got a telegram from a gentleman who has a first cabin in the *Dido*, to say that his wife has been taken ill, and he must give up his berth."

"When does the *Dido* sail?"

"To-morrow morning. She is at Plymouth, waiting for the mails. If you go down to-night by the mail-train, you will be in plenty of time, and we will telegraph."

"I will take the cabin. How much?"

"One hundred and thirty pounds, madam," said he.

She produced her notes. "Pray count it yourself. We have been delayed in the same manner ourselves. My husband is a great invalid, but I was not so fortunate as to get some one to refund *us* our passage-money."

"What name did you say?" asked the clerk counting. "Mr. and Mrs. Carr. Thank you," and he handed her the slip of paper.

"Thank *you*," said Sarah, with a bewitching smile, and swept down to her cab again.

John Rex was gnawing his nails in sullen apathy. She displayed the passage-ticket. "You are saved. By the time Mr. Francis Wade gets his wits together, we shall be past pursuit."

"To Sydney!" cried Rex, angrily, looking at the warrant. "Why there of all places in God's earth?"

Sarah surveyed him with an expression of contempt. "Because *your* scheme has failed. Now this is mine. You have deserted me once; you will do so again in any other country. You are a murderer, a villain and a coward, but you suit me. I save you, but I mean to keep you. I will bring you to Australia, where the first trooper will arrest you at my bidding as an escaped convict. If you don't like to come, stay behind. I don't care. I am rich. I have done no wrong. The law cannot touch me—Do you agree? Then tell the man to drive to Silver's in Cornhill for your outfit."

Having housed him at last in a quiet tavern near the railway station she tried to get some information as to this last revealed crime.

"How came you to kill Lord Bellasis?" she asked him quietly.

"I had found out from my mother that I was his natural son, and one day riding home from a pigeon match I told him so. He taunted me—and I struck him. I did not mean to kill him, but he was an old man, and in my passion I struck hard. As he fell, I thought I saw a horseman among the trees, and I galloped off. My ill-luck began then, for the same night I was arrested at the coiner's."

"But I thought there was robbery," said she.

"Not by me. But, for God's sake, talk no more about it. I am sick—my brain is going round. I want to sleep."

"Be careful, please! Lift him gently!" said Mrs. Carr, as the boat ranged alongside the *Dido* in the bleak May morning.

"What's the matter?" asked the officer of the watch, perceiving the bustle in the boat.

"Gentleman seems to have had a stroke," said a boatman.

It was so. There was no fear that John Rex would ever escape again from the woman he had deceived.

THE REDEMPTION

"That is my story. Let it plead with you to turn you from your purpose, and to save her. The punishment of sin falls not upon the sinner only. A deed once done lives in its consequence for ever, and this tragedy of shame and crime to which my felon's death is a fitting end, is but the outcome of a selfish sin like yours!"

It had grown dark in the prison, and as he ceased speaking, Rufus Dawes felt a trembling hand seize his own. It was that of the chaplain.

"Let me hold your hand!—Sir Richard Devine did not murder your father. He was murdered by a horseman who, riding with him, struck him and fled."

"Merciful God! How do you know this?"

"Because I saw the murder committed, because—don't let go my hand—I robbed the body."

"*You?*"

"In my youth I was a gambler. Lord Bellasis won money from me, and to pay him I forged two bills of exchange. Unscrupulous and cruel, he threatened to expose me if I did not give him double the sum. Forgery was death in those days, and I strained every nerve to buy back the proofs of my folly. I succeeded. I was to meet Lord Bellasis near his own house at Hampstead on the night of which you speak, to pay the money and receive the bills. When I saw him fall I galloped up, but instead of pursuing his murderer, I rifled his pocket-book of my forgeries. I was afraid to give evidence at the trial, or I might have saved you.—Ah! you have let go my hand!"

"God forgive you!" said Rufus Dawes, and then was silent.

"Speak!" cried North. "Speak, or you will make me mad. Reproach me! Spurn me! Spit upon me! You cannot think worse of me than I do myself."

But the other, his head buried in his hands, did not answer, and with a wild gesture, North staggered out of the cell.

Nearly an hour had passed since the chaplain had placed the rum flask in his hand, and Gimblett observed, with semi-drunken astonishment, that it was not yet empty. He had intended to take but one sup in payment of his courtesy—for Gimblett was conscious of his own weakness in the matter of strong waters—but as he waited and waited, the one sup became two, the two three, and at length more than half the contents of the bottle had moistened his gullet, and maddened him for more. Gimblett was in a quandary. If he didn't finish the flask, he would be oppressed with an everlasting regret. If he did finish it he would be drunk; and to be drunk on duty was the one unpardonable sin. He looked across the darkness of the sea to the schooner. The Commandant was a long way off! A faint breeze, which had—according to Blunt's prophecy—arisen with the night, brought up to him the voices of the boat's crew from the jetty below. His friend Jack Mannix was coxswain of her. He would give Jack a drink. Leaving the gate, he advanced to the edge of the embankment, and, putting his head over, called out to his friend. The breeze, however, which was momentarily freshening, carried his voice away; and Jack Mannix, hearing nothing, continued his conversation. Gimblett was just drunk enough to be virtuously indignant at this incivility, and seating himself on the edge of the bank, swallowed the remainder of the rum at a draught. The effect upon his enforcedly temperate stomach was very touching. He made one feeble attempt to get upon his legs, cast a reproachful glance at the rum bottle, and then, with a smile of contentment, cursed the island and all its contents and fell fast asleep.

North, coming out of the prison, did not notice the absence of the gaoler; indeed, he was not in a condition to notice anything. Bare-headed, without his cloak, he rushed through the gates into the night as one who flies headlong from some fearful vision. "This man a convict!" he cried. "He is a hero—a martyr! What a life! Love! Yes, that is love indeed! Oh, James North, how base art thou in the eyes of God beside this despised outcast!" And so muttering, he reached his own room, and saw, by the light of the new-born moon, the dressing-bag and candle standing on the table as he had left them. They brought to his mind the recollection of the task before him. He lighted the candle, and, taking the bag in his hand, cast one last look round the chamber which had witnessed his futile struggles against that baser part of himself which had at last triumphed. It was so. Fate had condemned him to sin, and he must now fulfil the doom he might once have averted. Already he fancied he could see the speck that was the schooner move slowly away from the prison shore. He must not linger; they would be waiting for him at the jetty. As he turned, the moonbeams—as yet unobscured by the rapidly gathering clouds—flung a silver streak across the sea, and across that streak North saw a boat pass. Was his distracted brain playing him false?—in the stern sat, wrapped in a cloak, the figure of a man! A fierce gust of wind drove the sea-rack over the moon, and the boat disappeared, as though swallowed up by the gathering storm. North staggered back as the truth struck him.

He remembered how he had said, "I will redeem him with my own blood!" Was it possible that a just heaven had thus decided to allow the man whom a coward had condemned, to escape, and to punish the coward who remained? Oh, this man deserved freedom; he was honest, noble, truthful! How different from himself—a hateful self-lover, an unchaste priest, a drunkard. The looking-glass, in which the saintly face of Meekin was soon to be reflected, stood upon the table, and North, peering into it, started in insane rage at the pale face he saw there. What a hateful wretch he had become! The last fatal impulse of insanity came upon him, and his fingers closed convulsively upon the object they had been seeking.

"It is better so," he muttered, addressing, with fixed eyes, his own detested image. "I have examined you long enough. I have read your heart, and written out your secrets! You are but a shell—the shell that holds a corrupted and sinful heart. *He* shall live; *you* shall die!" The rapid motion of his arm overturned the candle, and all was dark.

Rufus Dawes, overpowered by the revelation so suddenly made to him, had remained for a few moments motionless in his cell, expecting to hear the heavy clang of the outer door, which should announce to him the departure of the chaplain. But he did not hear it, and it seemed to him that the air in the cell had grown suddenly cooler. He went to the door, and looked into the narrow corridor, expecting to see the scowling countenance of Gimblett. To his astonishment the door of the prison was wide open, and not a soul in sight. His first thought was of North. Had the story he had told, coupled with the entreaties he had lavished, sufficed to turn him from his purpose?

He looked around. The night was falling sullenly; the wind was mounting. If the schooner was to sail that night, she had best get out into deep waters. Where was the chaplain? Pray heaven the delay had been sufficient, and they had sailed without him. He advanced a few steps nearer, and looked about him. Was it possible that, in his madness, the chaplain had been about to commit some violence which had drawn the trusty Gimblett from his post? "Gr-r-r-r! Ouph!" The trusty Gimblett was lying at his feet—dead drunk!

"Hi! Hoho! Hillo there!" roared somebody from the jetty below. "Be that you, Muster Noarth! We ain't too much tiam, sur!"

From the uncurtained windows of the chaplain's house on the hill beamed the newly-lighted candle. They in the boat did not see it, but it brought to the prisoner a wild hope that made his heart bound. He ran back to his cell, clapped on North's wide-awake, and flinging the cloak hastily about him, came quickly down the steps. If the moon should shine out now!

"Jump in, sir," said unsuspecting Mannix, thinking only of the flogging he had been threatened with. "It'll be a dirty night, this night! Put this over your knees, sir. Shove her off! Give way!" And they were afloat. But one glimpse of moonlight fell upon the slouched hat and cloaked figure, and the boat's crew, engaged in the dangerous task of navigating the reef in the teeth of the rising gale, paid no attention to the chaplain.

"By George, lads, we're but just in time!" cried Mannix; and they laid alongside the schooner, black in blackness. "Up ye go yer honour, quick!" The wind had shifted, and was now off the shore. Blunt, who had begun to repent of his obstinacy, but would not confess it, thought the next best thing to riding out the gale was to get out to the open sea. "Damn the parson," he had said, in all heartiness; "we can't wait all night for him. Heave ahead, Mr. Johnson!" And so the anchor was a-trip as Rufus Dawes ran up the side.

The Commandant, already pulling off in his own boat, roared a coarse farewell. "Good-bye, North! It was touch and go with ye!" adding, "Curse the fellow, he's too proud to answer!"

The chaplain indeed spoke to no one, and plunging down the hatchway, made for the stern cabins. "Close shave, your reverence!" said a respectful somebody, opening a door. It was, but the clergyman did not say so. He double-locked the door, and hardly realising the danger he had escaped, flung himself on the bunk, panting. Over his head he heard the rapid tramp of feet and the cheery

Yo hi-oh! and a rumbelow!

of the men at the capstan. He could smell the sea, and through the open window of the cabin could distinguish the light in the chaplain's house on the hill. The trampling ceased, the vessel began to move swiftly—the Commandant's boat appeared below him for an instant, making her way back—the *Lady Franklin* had set sail. With his eyes fixed on the tiny light, he strove to think what was best to be done. It was hopeless to think that he could maintain the imposture which, favoured by the darkness and confusion, he had hitherto successfully attempted. He was certain to be detected at Hobart Town, even if he could lie concealed during his long and tedious voyage. That mattered little, however. He had saved Sylvia, for North had been left behind. Poor North! As the thought of pity came to him, the light he looked at was suddenly extinguished, and Rufus Dawes, compelled thereto as by an irresistible power, fell upon his knees and prayed for the pardon and happiness of the man who had redeemed him.

"That's a gun from the shore," said Partridge the mate, "and they're burning a red light. There's a prisoner escaped. Shall we lie-to?"

"Lie-to!" cried old Blunt, with a tremendous oath. "We'll have suthin else to do. Look there!"

The sky to the northward was streaked with a belt of livid green colour, above which rose a mighty black cloud, whose shape was ever changing.

Blunt, recognising the meteoric heralds of danger, began to regret his obstinacy. He saw that a hurricane was approaching. The ominous calm of

THE
CYCLONE

the day had given place to a smart breeze from the north-east, and though the schooner had been sheltered at her anchorage under the lee of the island (the "harbour" looked nearly due south), when once out to sea Blunt saw it would be impossible to put back in the teeth of the gale. Haply, however, the full fury of the storm would not overtake them till they had gained sea room.

Rufus Dawes, exhausted with the excitement through which he had passed, had slept for two or three hours, when he was awakened by the motion of the vessel going on the other tack. He rose to his feet, and found himself in complete darkness. Overhead was the noise of trampling feet, and he could distinguish the hoarse tones of Blunt bellowing orders. Astonished at the absence of the moonlight which had so lately silvered the sea, he flung open the cabin window and looked out. As we have said, the cabin allotted to North was one of the two stern cabins, and from it the convict had a full view of the approaching storm.

The sight was one of wild grandeur. The huge, black cloud which hung in the horizon had changed its shape. Instead of a curtain it was an arch. Beneath this vast and magnificent portal, shone a dull phosphoric light. Across this livid space pale flashes of sheet-lightning passed noiselessly. Behind it was a dull and threatening murmur, made up of the grumbling of thunder, the falling of rain, and the roar of contending wind and water. The lights of the prison-island had disappeared, so rapid had been the progress of the schooner under the steady breeze, and the ocean stretched around, black and desolate. The wind increased in violence, and the arch of light was fringed with rain. Suddenly, a tremendous peal of thunder, accompanied by a terrific downfall of rain, rattled along the sky. A great wall of water rushed roaring over the level plain of the sea, and with an indescribable medley of sounds, the cyclone swooped upon them.

Rufus Dawes comprehended that the elements had come to save or destroy him. One of two events seemed inevitable—he would either be drowned where he lay, or, should the vessel weather the storm, he would be forced upon deck, and the desperate imposture he had attempted be discovered. For a moment despair overwhelmed him, and he contemplated the raging sea as though he would cast himself into it, and thus end his troubles. The tones of a woman's voice recalled him to himself. Cautiously unlocking the cabin door, he peered out. The cuddy was lighted by a swinging lamp which revealed Sylvia questioning one of the women concerning the storm. As Rufus Dawes looked, he saw her glance, with an air half of hope, half of fear, towards the door behind which he lurked, and he understood that she expected to see the chaplain. Locking the door, he proceeded hastily to dress himself in North's clothes. He would wait until his aid was absolutely required, and then rush out. In the darkness, Sylvia would mistake him for the priest. He could convey her to the boat—if recourse to the boats should be rendered necessary—and then take the hazard of his fortune. While she was in danger, his place was near her.

From the deck of the vessel the scene was appalling. All was a dull, windy blackness. Gigantic seas seemed to mount in the horizon and sweep towards and upon them. It was as though the ship lay in the vortex of a whirlpool, so high on either side of her were piled the rough pyramidical masses of sea. Mighty gusts arose—claps of wind which seemed like strokes of thunder. A sail loosened from its tackling was torn away and blown out to sea, disappearing like a shred of white paper to leeward. The mercury in the barometer dropped. Blunt, who had been at the rum bottle, swore great oaths that no soul on board would see another sun; and when Partridge rebuked him for blasphemy at such a moment, wept spirituous tears.

By five o'clock in the morning, the gale had reached its height. The ship lay over on her side, held there by the madly rushing wind, which seemed to flatten down the sea, cutting off the tops of the waves, and breaking them into fine white spray which covered the ocean like a thick cloud. Save when lighted by occasional flashes of sheet lightning, which showed to the cowed wretches their awestricken faces, this drama of the elements was performed in a darkness which was almost palpable.

Suddenly the mercury rose and, with one awful shriek, the wind dropped to a calm. The *Lady Franklin* had reached the centre of the cyclone. Partridge, glancing to where the body of drunken Blunt rolled helplessly lashed to the wheel, felt a strange selfish joy thrill him. If the ship survived, the drunken captain would be dismissed, and he, Partridge the gallant, would reign in his stead. The schooner, no longer steadied by the wind, was at the mercy of every sea. Volumes of water poured over her. Presently she heeled over, for, with a triumphant scream, the wind leapt on to her from a fresh quarter. Following its usual course, the storm returned upon its track. The hurricane was about to repeat itself from the north-west.

The sea, pouring down through the burst hatchway, tore the door of the cuddy from its hinges. Sylvia found herself surrounded by a wildly-surging torrent which threatened to overwhelm her. She shrieked aloud for aid, but her voice was inaudible even to herself. Clinging to the mast which penetrated the little cuddy, she fixed her eyes upon the door behind which she imagined North was, and whispered a last prayer for succour. The door opened, and from out the cabin came a figure clad in black. She looked up, and the light of the expiring lamp showed her a face that was not that of the man she hoped to see. Then a pair of dark eyes beaming ineffable love and pity were bent upon her, and a pair of dripping arms held her above the brine as she had once been held in the misty mysterious days that were gone.

In the terror of that moment the cloud which had so long oppressed her brain passed from it. The action of the strange man before her completed and explained the action of the convict chained to the Port Arthur coal-wagons, of the convict kneeling in the Norfolk Island torture chamber. She remembered the terrible experience of Macquarie Harbour. She recalled the evening of the boat-building, when, swung into the air by stalwart arms, she had promised the rescuing prisoner to plead for him with her kindred. Regaining her memory thus, all the agony and shame of the man's long life of misery became at once apparent to her. She understood how her husband had deceived her, and with what base injustice and falsehood he had bought her young love. No question as to how this doubly-condemned prisoner had escaped from the hideous isle of punishment she had quitted occurred to her. She asked not—even in her thoughts—how it had been given to him to supplant the chaplain in his place on board the vessel. She only considered, in her sudden awakening, the story of his wrongs, remembered only his marvellous fortitude and love, knew only, in this last instant of her pure, ill-fated life, that as he had saved her once from starvation and death, so had he come again to save her from sin and from despair. The words came to her out of the past—"Good Mr. Dawes!"

The eyes of the man and woman met in one long, wild gaze. Sylvia stretched out her white hands and smiled, and Richard Devine understood in his turn the story of the young girl's joyless life, and knew how she had been sacrificed.

In the great crisis of our life, when, brought face to face with annihilation, we are suspended gasping over the great emptiness of death, we become conscious that the Self which we think we knew so well has strange and unthought-of capacities. To describe a tempest of elements is not easy, but to describe a tempest of the soul is impossible. Amid the fury of such a tempest, a thousand memories are driven like feathers before the blast, as unsubstantial and as unregarded. The mists which shroud our self-knowledge, become transparent, and we are smitten with sudden lightning-like comprehension of our own misused power over our fate.

This much we feel and know, but who can coldly describe the hurricane which thus o'erwhelms him? As well ask the drowned mariner to tell of the marvels of mid sea when the great deeps swallowed him and the darkness of death encompassed him round about. These two human beings felt that they had done with life. Together thus, alone in the very midst and presence of death, the distinctions of the world they were about to leave disappeared. Their vision grew clear. They felt as beings whose bodies had already perished, and as they clasped hands, their freed souls, recognising each the loveliness of the other, rushed tremblingly together.

Borne before the returning whirlwind, an immense wave, which glimmered in the darkness, spouted up and towered above the wreck. The wretches who yet clung to the deck looked shuddering up into the bellying greenness, and knew that the end was come.

At day-dawn on the morning after the storm, the rays of the rising sun fell upon an object which floated on the surface of the water not far from where

EPILOGUE

the schooner had foundered. This object was a portion of the mainmast head of the *Lady Franklin*, and entangled in the rigging were two corpses—a man and a woman. The arms of the man were clasped round the body of the woman, and her head lay on his breast.

The Prison Island appeared but as a long, low line on the distant horizon. The tempest was over. As the sun rose higher the air grew balmy, the ocean placid; and, golden in the rays of the new risen morning, the wreck and its burden drifted out to sea.